# THE CRITICS RAVE
# ABOUT STOBIE PIEL!

### *RENEGADE*

"Hot, hot, hot . . . a wonderful read!"

—*Romantic Times*

### *BLUE-EYED BANDIT*

"Kudos to Ms. Piel for providing a love story with humor, passion and some whimsy. It's an all-around great read."

—*Romantic Times*

### *FREE FALLING*

"Ms. Piel has written an innovative story, blending history and romance into a sweet tale of renewed love."

—*Romantic Times*

### *THE WHITE SUN*

"The consistently entertaining voice of Stobie Piel takes us on another roller coaster ride of excitement through the stars."

—*Romantic Times*

### *THE MIDNIGHT MOON*

"This distant time and place Stobie Piel depicts will capture your imagination—and the romance and triumph of its characters will touch your heart."

—Susan Wiggs, bestselling author of
*The Lightkeeper*

"Ms. Piel keeps us on the knife-edge of curiosity as she tantalizes us with her imaginative plot."

—*Romantic Times*

# A DANGEROUS DISTRACTION

She eyed him critically for a while, then nodded. "Very well. You're not ready to confide in me. I understand, but know that I will be keeping a close watch on Mr. Bradford. It may be that my skills with photography will prove useful."

A determined woman. Melanie's words concerned Diego, for her own sake. "Senorita, it might be wisest for you to select another subject. It strikes me that Carlton Bradford stops at nothing to get what he wants."

Her eyes lit, and she stopped to face him. "Ah! So you agree with me, do you?"

He shifted his weight. "I didn't say that."

"You did, and you know it's true. You also know that your brother didn't sign that document willingly and therefore must be in danger." Diego felt cornered. Melanie leaned toward him as she spoke, and another feeling made itself known: desire. "Mr. Bradford and the people he represents are the sort who dominate others, dictate the fates of everyone—if you let them. I don't know what he wants—he was too quick to declare the supposed Spanish treasure his goal—but he is a dangerous man."

She was too bright to be dissuaded. He agreed with everything she said, so his only alternative was to distract her in some way. Melanie's lips were parted in her eagerness to gain his confidence. Soft lips, warm and pink . . . kissable.

He did not hesitate.

# STOBIE PIEL

# The Renegade's Heart

LEISURE BOOKS  NEW YORK CITY

A LEISURE BOOK®

February 2002

Published by

Dorchester Publishing Co., Inc.
276 Fifth Avenue
New York, NY 10001

ISBN 0-8439-4964-3

Visit us on the web at www.dorchesterpub.com.

# The
# Renegade's
# Heart

# Chapter One

*New Mexico Territory, 1890*

"Diego de Aguirre is pond scum." A man spoke from somewhere . . . above. Heaven, probably. The words sounded final, as if absolute judgment had been passed. Diego sighed, and hoped that since judgment had been rendered, he would at least be allowed to go back to sleep.

Another voice chimed in, raised with feeling. "He's lazy, drunken, shiftless, argumentative, and rude. Doesn't care a thing for his fellow man."

Diego opened one eye, but dim light met his sight and he winced. *Where am I?* He seemed to be encased in a small, dark space, with wood panels over his head. *A coffin?* That seemed premature. His thoughts were foggy, but he felt sure he would remember having died.

A woman joined the annoying fray. "He . . . no, I cannot speak his name . . . he's the lowest form of man." He almost recognized her voice, though he couldn't place her name. But she sounded familiar. "What he did to my sister . . ."

That should have narrowed her identity down but didn't, really. He had known many women's sisters.

A cold silence followed, broken only by disgusted huffs and bitter sighs. A man drew a long, ominous sigh. Diego knew what he would say before the words were spoken. "Diego de Aguirre will never compare to his brother."

Diego opened both eyes and ignored the pain of the light, resigned to the flurry of conversation above him. He had heard it all before. Rafael de Aguirre had been, and always would be, a hero to the people of the Tewa Pueblo, where Diego had grown up. Rafael had become a hero to all the people in the Santa Fe area, Mexican, white, Chinese, and Zuni. He had donned the mask of an ancient warrior to protect his people, and when he wasn't galloping as an avenging hero, he was a dedicated schoolmaster. He and his beautiful wife took large groups of children to Europe, to Africa, even to the Far East—which was where Diego assumed his brother was now.

"Poor Señor Rafael . . . It's a blessing, at least, that he isn't here to see how low his ne'er-do-well brother has sunk. Always had a blind spot for that boy, he did, but I could see right from the beginning that young Diego weren't nothing but trouble."

A murmur of agreement followed. Diego rolled his eyes.

No, he would never compare to Rafael. He had accepted that truth since childhood—his brother was a better man. Rafael had raised him, loved him, and cared for him, but somehow, Rafael's innate heroism had failed to rub off on Diego himself. Diego sighed and tried to shake his head, but his skull throbbed from something—too much liquor, or maybe he'd been in a fight, though he couldn't remember any such interaction from the previous night. One never knew for sure.

The worst part of it was, he was never completely free to enjoy his debasement. Rafael believed in him utterly. When he returned to Tewa, he would resume his determined encouragement of Diego's supposed better qualities, believing one day the younger brother would follow in his noble footsteps. It was merciful to remind himself that Rafael was half a world away. He wouldn't have to prove, again, that his brother's expectations would never be met.

A whistle blew in the distance, heralding the arrival of the train in Santa Fe, two miles away. Diego tried to sit up. His head banged hard against rough wood, and he flopped down again. He examined his surroundings. Somehow, he had rolled

13

from beneath the porch of Tewa Pueblo's only saloon, slid down into a pit of some sort, and ended up below the barroom floor. What had surely been a delightful evening ended ignominiously with him lying prone under the floor. Apparently, he'd had some presence of mind, because he had thought to bring a Zuni blanket with him.

Whatever he had done the night before had left a strong impression on the saloon's patrons, because they were still talking about it come morning. He folded his hands on his chest and tried to remember the previous night's course. He had ridden into the Tewa Plaza and entered the rustic pueblo saloon for a night of revelry, which must have been well spent, though the details eluded him now. He had tried to enlist his sometimes friend, Chen, and failed as usual because the cost of revelry was far too high for the more sensible Chinese man.

He had ordered a drink, winked at a barmaid . . . and everything after that was blank.

"We need Rafael now."

Diego frowned. *What now? Shoes too tight? Someone's cat stuck up a tree? Little Marietta Johnson has lost her doll?* Rafael was deemed a cure for all ills, when perhaps the people would be better off handling their own problems. No wonder he left the country. He left for peace!

"Carlton Bradford keeps coming around Tewa, asking questions. Got a bad feeling about that 'gentleman,' I do."

Diego knew Bradford, a somewhat arrogant veteran commander of the American Civil War. Diego didn't like him because the man was greedy and pretentious, but he hadn't threatened anyone. Chen admired him; but then, Chen admired money. Unlike Bradford, however, Chen had earned everything he had accumulated, and though he possessed a naturally dictatorial manner, he rarely wielded it over anyone with much success. His sole focus was his new hotel—a grand adobe structure at the center of the Tewa Plaza, which outshone anything in Santa Fe.

Though the Tewa Pueblo was small, the once-deserted Zuni Pueblo reconstructed by Diego's Argentinian father was now home to a large mixture of Mexican, Zuni, white, and Chinese settlers. A few years before, a large chest of Spanish treasure had been discovered at the site. Rumors of that treasure inspired greed, and a threat had arisen against the Tewa people. Rafael de Aguirre had donned a mask handed down to him by his father and became "The Renegade," a rider disguised as an Anasazi warrior. As the Renegade, Rafael defended his people, and earned a legacy that had become almost mythical to the people of Tewa.

Chen had made much of having ridden in "The Gang," an odd group of people who had joined with Rafael during his most heroic rescues. Even more romantic, Rafael had made off with a beautiful widow, enhancing the story. Chen's hotel was decorated with "artifacts" from The Renegade, Rafael's legendary disguise. Most of those artifacts had never been within twenty miles of Rafael or his disguise.

As far as Diego knew, Carlton Bradford had no dark designs on Tewa—no secret plans to unearth lost Spanish treasure, as Rafael's previous foe had done. He was just pompous and unlikable, and Santa Fe didn't need a hero to protect it from bad taste.

"Yes, if Rafael were here, Bradford wouldn't dare try anything . . ."

Diego had endured enough. They resented him because he wasn't Rafael, because he hadn't leapt forward and somehow restrained this perceived threat. He looked around, spied a loose panel, and then kicked it up. It broke with a satisfyingly loud splinter, and he extracted himself from beneath the saloon floor. The patrons gasped in astonishment as he rose like a dirty, disheveled ghost before them. For a moment, they appeared uniformly shocked, then broke into variations of embarrassment, anger, and concern. Their concern wasn't for Diego's reaction to their comments, but fear of Rafael's, should the story be repeated. As one of them had said, Rafael had a blind spot for his younger brother, and no word against him would be tolerated.

The bartender cleared his throat. "What . . . what were you doing under my floor, young de Aguirre?"

Diego looked down at his former resting spot below the broken panel, then shrugged. "That, gentlemen, I couldn't tell you." A smile grew on his face as a familiar surge of defiance and self-confidence blossomed in his heart. "But I slept well, I assure you."

"A quart of bourbon will do that to a man." A woman spoke, but Diego ignored her. There was the matter of the sister that he didn't want raised for further discussion.

He allowed his smile to grow, and sensed dimples emerging, always a source of infuriation to those put out with him. "It will, at that." He bowed, tipped an imaginary cap, then made for the door.

"De Aguirre . . . your brother, when he returns . . ." The bartender sounded nervous. Rafael's favor held great importance.

Diego stopped and sighed. For a moment he stared out the open door and felt the dry breeze in his face. Then he looked back over his shoulder and met the man's eyes. "I do not pretend to be a hero. I am what I have always been . . ." Diego paused and sighed, "the younger brother of a great man. He is too great a man to threaten any of you for speaking the truth."

He left them in silence and strode out into the Tewa Plaza. The morning's ignominious beginning faded to the back of his mind, to the place where reality lingered heavy and hard. Across the square stood Chen's new hotel, larger than all the other buildings, more grand and ornate than anything Diego's late father could have imagined—or desired. The Chateau Renegade seemed a strong, and embarrassing, name, but it was emblazoned with gold letters on black, complete with a black mask that was nothing like the one Rafael had actually worn. On one side of the plaque, a black horse reared as his caped rider wielded a three-pronged whip. The bola was the only accurate image, because Rafael's horse had been gray.

Chen knew how to make the most of a situation, and his establishment was constantly full. Travelers often chose to forego the hotels in Santa Fe for the more "exclusive" feel of the Chateau. Chen emerged from his lavish entrance, a frown on his face as he ignored Diego.

"What's the matter?" Diego slapped Chen's shoulder, and Chen braced in offense at the pleasant gesture.

"That inn." Diego followed his friend's gaze to a small adobe building across the plaza.

"What's bothering you? The new hotel?"

"Yes."

"I don't know what you're worried about. This place is always full."

Chen closed his eyes and drew a long breath, as if to will patience. "What you do not understand, because the concept of business and commerce utterly eludes you, is that my establishment isn't full by accident. My success is the result of concerted effort, of advertising its splendors far and wide, luring in customers . . ."

"Then sticking them for all they're worth."

18

Chen started to nod, as if this was a pleasant image, then frowned and shook his head. "My prices are fair, and well deserved."

They had engaged in this argument before, and many like it, since they were boys. They would never understand each other, but Chen entertained Diego, and Diego gave Chen a cause, someone to straighten out and set to rights, so they had stayed close despite their many differences. Rafael had raised them both, they both loved him, and their common history gave them at least some ground for communication.

"So, what worries you about this place anyway? It looks small—just a little adobe construction. It will take your overflow. What's the problem?"

"I don't like it." Chen's eyes narrowed and his expression darkened with foreboding as a tiny young woman emerged from the new inn. Like Chen, she was Chinese, and was dressed to perfection in sedate brown and black. Diego had met her a few times, and found her bright but too serious for any further pursuit.

Chen, however, might find a soul highly compatible to his own. The woman caught sight of Chen, issued a look of obvious challenge, and then marched back into her inn. Diego watched as Chen darkened still more. "She's attractive. I think her name is Victoria . . . I remember it doesn't sound Chinese. Victoria Wu, I think. Have you met her?"

"In a way." Chen's voice came low with restraint and deep anger.

"What 'way'?"

"As soon as I realized her intent, I demanded that she refrain from any sort of deliberate sabotage against my hotel."

*So much for romance.* "A nice welcome."

"She tried to steal my chef. I ordered him specially from France, and he will not be lured away by that devilish female."

"He's Italian, isn't he? Massimo or something. Doesn't sound French."

Chen glared. "He's French now."

Chen gestured toward the road from Santa Fe, then hurried back into his hotel. He motioned Diego to follow. "The train got in on time this morning; I heard the whistle promptly at nine A.M. My guests will be arriving soon. Perhaps you could make yourself useful."

"Carrying bags again?"

Chen looked impatient. "Yes. You do have a certain investment here, if you recall."

Diego turned to him, his brow raised. "I gave you my portion of the Spanish treasure to build this hotel. Not to become a porter."

"That investment makes you part owner. In a sense." Chen glowered. He didn't like sharing ownership of his beloved hotel but knew that Diego didn't really desire any responsibility for the place.

Somehow, inexplicably, when Diego gave his treasure to Chen, rather than making Chen beholden to him, he had made himself vulnerable to small jobs and insults. "Couldn't you hire some-one?"

"Will is supposed to be here, if he remembers. The influx I expect today is too much for him."

Diego arched his brow, hoping to instill some kind of shame into Chen for benefiting from their gentle, simple friend. "Will donates his help out of the goodness of his heart. You don't even pay him. What happened to the boys you hired, for money?"

Chen hesitated. "They are no longer available."

"In other words, they quit, again, and you haven't had time to get new help. Maybe if you would pay them . . ."

Chen tried to maintain an icy, dignified silence, then sputtered in agitation. "I pay them too much—and I expect them to earn their salary." He sput-tered again. "They didn't quit—I fired them."

"Ah." Diego intended to pursue this, as Chen was clearly in the wrong, but a strange cart caught his eye across the plaza and he went to the window to get a better look. The cart itself was black and shaped somewhat like a pyramid. It was pulled by a small, very fat black pony, and the girl leading it seemed to be holding an intense conversation with the beast. "What the hell is that?"

Chen studied the vehicle, then nodded. "It ap-pears to be a transportable darkroom."

"What?"

"A darkroom is used by photographers. Señor Rafael taught us all about daguerreotypes and cameras. Didn't you pay attention to anything in school?"

"I know about photography." He hadn't paid attention, because the whole process seemed tedious and long, and he was far too active a man to sit and wait for the results. "I didn't realize darkrooms were portable."

"There has been a recent surge of traveling photographers and journalists. This young woman must work for a master—it appears to be a fine setup."

Diego watched through the window as the girl stopped to adjust the pony's harness. "I don't see anyone else."

Chen eyed him in disgust. "A master does not travel with his help. She will have come ahead to set things up, and upon his arrival, his work will commence." Chen seized his ledger and looked through the names. "I wasn't alerted to the arrival of any photographic equipment."

"Maybe she's staying at the *other* hotel."

Ice preceded Chen's words. "That is impossible. A photographer of any acclaim would stay nowhere but here. I should go out and greet her." Chen glanced around, then seized a white coat from a hook. "Put this on."

Diego folded his arms over his chest. "No."

Chen issued an impatient breath. "Into the washroom. Your face is filthy, wash your hands. Where did you sleep, anyway?"

"Underneath the saloon, in the dirt."

Chen grimaced and winced, then shuddered. "I do not need to know these details."

"Then don't ask."

Chen apparently sensed a resolute mood in Diego, but obviously wasn't willing to surrender. He glanced out the window, then cast a meaningful look back. "She's pretty."

Diego shifted his weight. "How pretty?"

"Prettier than anything you've been looking at lately."

"How tall?"

"Not too tall, not small. Soft, feminine figure . . . Blue eyes."

"You can't see her eyes from this distance." Diego paused. "What color is her hair?"

Chen leaned forward and squinted. "Darker than blond, not black—somewhat . . . honey-shaded in appearance. Slight wave . . ."

Diego went to the window just as the girl turned toward the hotel and looked up. Her eyes were blue, bright and shining in the high sun. Her face was small and soft, sweetly feminine, and her lips were full and beautiful. He wanted her instantly, and yet . . . There was something about her that he immediately sensed was best avoided.

Her eyes widened as she studied Chen's sign, then narrowed in confusion. She was innocent and vulnerable, probably the daughter of a traveling photographer, and naïve young women deserved better than Diego de Aguirre.

23

Chen glared. "Go change, then come out to fetch her bags."

Diego had grown used to Chen's imperious manner, but he rarely obeyed the orders. One glance told him Chen's assessment of his appearance had been accurate, however, so he took the white coat and headed for the washroom. He studied his face in the ornate gold mirror. Despite his night of revelry, he looked well rested and handsome. He ran his fingers through his hair, which seemed clean, then dampened a towel and cleaned the smudges off his face.

The white coat covered any stains on his shirt, which would have to be good enough. Diego left the washroom and went to the entrance. Chen was talking to the girl, and sounded disappointed.

"You have no reservation?"

"No . . . Should I have made one?" Diego liked her voice. It was soft and gentle, and something in the sound was curiously . . . singular.

"I'm afraid the Chateau Renegade has no vacancies, miss. My rooms are booked months in advance."

Diego tapped his shoulder from behind. "I thought you had a room still available?" He recalled Chen's fury the day before at not having filled the hotel, despite his elaborate advertising scheme.

Chen shook his head. "Carlton Bradford booked that room last night for guests from the East, I'm afraid. They're due in today."

"Oh . . . I see." The young woman sounded tired and disappointed. "Can you perhaps suggest another inn?"

Chen froze in resistance of the obvious solution, so Diego shoved him aside and took the girl's hand. She wore brown leather gloves, and her fingers stiffened as if she hadn't expected to be touched.

"There is a very pleasant inn across the street, señorita. Let me walk you over, and I'll introduce you to the proprietress." She looked up at Diego and smiled. Her head tipped to one side as she studied his face. He felt certain she was impressed. Women usually were—until they realized that his glory didn't reach far beneath the surface.

Chen edged him away from the girl before he could tell her that he was part owner of the hotel. Chen must have noticed her innocence, too, and sensed a being worthy of protection. "My *porter* will see to your accommodations. Sadly, Miss Wu's small inn can't compare to my own standards, but I'm sure you'll find rudimentary comforts in her establishment." He paused. "I hope this won't cause you trouble with your employer."

She looked confused. "My employer?"

Chen gestured toward the cart. "I assume you work for a photographer? We couldn't help noticing the fine equipment, a portable darkroom! Most impressive, and costly."

Diego rolled his eyes. If the photographer was as wealthy as Chen was imagining, he'd probably add on another room before sunset.

"I don't work for anyone, sir. I am the photographer. Melanie Ann Muessen."

She looked proud, but also a little weary, as if she'd faced male surprise before. Something about her affected him, but he wasn't sure what it was. She seemed so alone and yet, somehow, accustomed to that state, with no desire to alter it. Oddly, Diego felt protective—a reaction made stranger because she seemed so content to be alone. He found himself squeezing her hand as if in sympathy. "You've traveled here by yourself?"

Her lovely eyes narrowed. "I am well equipped for solitary travel, sir. This is my first venture abroad, true, but after this, I intend to travel to Egypt to photograph . . ."

"The pyramids, the Sphinx . . . of course." He cut her off by mistake, and by habit. He always knew what people were going to say, but they took so long to get there. It was easier to say it for them, to get to the point.

Her soft, full lips curled to one side. "No."

"No?"

He detected a tiny satisfaction in her expression, and it had more charm than he would have guessed. She liked setting him aback. People usually did, but he liked her reaction better than most. "No. My intention in Egypt, as in New Mexico, is to photograph the people as they are now, juxtaposed against the ancient structures of their ancestors. I am interested in people, in their faces, in the essence of who they really are, set against the backdrop of the world they have made."

"Ah." He paused. "That does seem worthwhile. And after all, from here onward, people will be photographing the wonders of the world. How many ways are there to portray a pyramid?"

She eyed him doubtfully. "I hope to unveil nuances in humanity, in the souls of people."

She sounded so sincere, but a little hesitant. Perhaps his abrupt manner indicated he wasn't interested in her pursuit. He wasn't, but she interested him, and that was all that mattered.

Chen looked between them. "A worthy pursuit indeed, Miss Muessen." His tone indicated he felt the project lacking in financial prospects, but at least Chen had some respect for artists. Chen hesitated, then cast a quick look around. "We will take you to Miss Wu's inn and see that you're settled."

Diego ground his teeth together. " 'We'? Don't you have guests to greet?"

Melanie looked between them, as if wondering at the *porter's* manner toward his supposed employer, but Chen appeared unyielding as he took her arm. "It is my duty as a leading citizen of the Tewa Pueblo to see to Miss Muessen's welfare."

"Is it?" Maybe Chen had interest in the girl, too. Chen hadn't attached himself to a woman yet— unlike Diego, he sought out women seriously, with intention to court toward marriage, and no one had quite met his high standards so far.

Melanie Muessen could meet any man's standards. Diego frowned as Chen led her out into the plaza to her black cart. The pony snorted in alarm as Chen approached, and Chen eyed it like a rogue dog. Melanie offered an apologetic smile. "Porticus is a bit . . . shy."

Diego bit back a laugh. *"Porticus?"*

She looked pained. "He eats more than his small stature would seem to allow."

"I see that." Since Chen was faltering, hesitant to approach the small beast, Diego seized the opportunity. He walked toward the pony, and its eyes widened in alarm.

He heard Melanie behind him. "Wait!" She sped up beside him, placed herself between Porticus and himself, and then took the pony's lead. "The valets had a terrible time getting him on the train, and off. He's used to me."

Diego studied the pony's round belly. "You'd think a carrot would be enough to lure him anywhere."

He detected a smile on Melanie's lips, but she seemed intent on restraining emotion. He wondered if she chose this route because her feeling was slight, or so vast.

Their friend, Will, rode into the plaza, dismounted, and beamed at the sight of Melanie's fat black pony. "Whoa! That's a sturdy little fellow!" Before anyone could comment, Will strode toward the pony. Chen, Diego, and Melanie moved to stop him, but Will knelt beside the pony's shoulder, speaking softly, held out his hand, and Porticus sniffed it, then nudged Will fondly.

Melanie's eyes widened, and a sweet, appreciative smile lit her face. "You have a fine touch, sir. Porticus never takes to people this way."

The little fiend had snorted when Diego approached. Tasteless little devil. Will stroked the pony's neck, then scratched its ears, while Porticus closed his eyes peacefully. "Nice little fellow. Never seen a horse so small, stubby little legs and all."

"My father was traveling in Scotland and brought him home for me." Melanie paused. "He had forgotten that I am no longer a child."

Diego studied her face. He couldn't place her age. Her skin was flawless, but her dress was sedate. "How old are you, anyway?"

Both Chen and Will winced, followed by a series of disapproving sputters from Chen. "That is not a proper question."

Melanie sighed. "I am twenty-nine."

All three men gasped. Will shook his head. "Old, ma'am."

This was more than even Diego felt accustomed to saying. *Older than I am.* "He means that you seem so . . . young."

Her blue eyes glittered. "Is that it?"

Will looked confused. "Not really, Diego. I just figured at that age, she'd be all fat and have a bunch of kids."

Diego heard Chen groan miserably, and even he endured a surge of unfamiliar embarrassment. Still, at almost thirty, most women did have a family. "Why aren't you married?"

She gazed heavenward for a moment, and Diego endured a momentary pang of propriety for yet another rude question. "I'm not married because I don't think I'd be very good at it." She paused. "And I haven't cared much for the men who have asked."

"What was wrong with them?"

Will waited expectantly for Melanie's answer, but Chen had taken enough. He placed himself between Diego and Melanie, his face flushed with embarrassment. He pinned a hard glare on Diego. "They asked too many personal questions." Chen turned his back to Diego and bowed quickly, twice, to Melanie. "Let us escort you to Miss Wu's inn. Now." He didn't wait for agreement as he nodded to Will. "Will, go to the reservations desk and greet my guests. I am expecting a large group, as well as Mr. Bradford's party."

Will rolled his eyes—he didn't like Bradford, either. Chen started away, then stopped. "Be sure Bradford gets the master suite—he requested it specially."

Will nodded, then aimed for the Chateau. Melanie led her pony after Chen, and Diego followed the cart. Occasionally, he wished he'd thought out the aftereffects of speaking what was on his mind. But he'd never really cared that much about someone's reaction. Why he should care now whether or not he'd offended Melanie eluded him, but he found himself stifling the urge to speak with her as they crossed the plaza.

Chen stopped before the entrance of Victoria's inn, his fists clenched. Diego grinned, then went to the door and knocked. It opened, and Victoria greeted them, smiling. She never once met Chen's eyes. In turn, Chen seemed more interested in the door molding than in the tiny woman standing in the threshold.

Neither seemed willing to speak to the other, so Diego took over. "Good morning, Miss Wu. We hoped you might have accommodations for Melanie Muessen. She has traveled here from . . ." He stopped and glanced at Melanie.

"From Vermont."

Since Melanie didn't elaborate on her profession, Diego felt the need to do so on her behalf. "Señorita Muessen is a photographer. She has come to New Mexico on an impressive project." He'd already forgotten the details, so he decided to change the subject. "She also has a fat pony that requires stabling." He paused. "If you need help with it, ask Will. He gets on well with the creature."

Victoria placed her hands together, creating a welcoming vision. The effect seemed rehearsed, but also sincere. "We have the perfect space for you, Miss Muessen. Please, come in." She stepped back and motioned for them to enter. Chen hesitated, then went inside with the reluctance of a soldier entering the enemy camp.

Melanie looked up at Diego. She looked

thoughtful, as if assessing what she had seen so far of the Tewa Pueblo and its native citizens. "This isn't exactly what I expected when I came west."

"Tewa isn't a typical pueblo, and the people who make their homes here aren't typical, either."

She watched him thoughtfully. "I see that. A pueblo, I thought, was inhabited by Indian persons. When I researched accommodations, I chose Tewa for its local flair. I also liked the notion of visiting a spot known for its masked hero."

Diego sighed. "So you've seen Chen's brochure?"

"I did. It was most impressive. I'm sorry I failed to make the proper reservations. I would have liked to learn more of the Renegade."

He sighed again. "Well, that won't be difficult. Chen has made the Chateau a veritable museum of the Renegade's deeds. He won't mind if you visit. He might charge an inflated admission, but he'll let you see his 'artifacts.' "

Her eyes widened with glee. "Truly? How exciting! Where is the Renegade now?"

"In Europe. Or Japan." Diego paused. He had forgotten from where Rafael's last letter originated. "Possibly Egypt."

She looked disappointed. "I had thought, from the literature, that he rode often in defense of his people."

"He rode for about a year, and only for good cause. But fortunately, or unfortunately if you were hoping for legendary deeds performed in our midst,

32

Tewa Pueblo is quiet, safe, and very dull."

Chen stuck his head out the door, made an expression that indicated acute discomfort, and hissed. Diego nodded and led Melanie into Victoria's inn. The foyer was far more comfortable, smaller, and more informal than Chen's—Diego liked it at once. Positioned on the wall behind the reservations desk was a large mahogany-framed photograph of a Chinese family, and when Victoria took her place at the ledger, she seemed to pose beneath it.

Melanie studied the photograph, a slight confusion in her face. Victoria noticed her attention and smiled. "That is my family, the Wus."

Melanie looked puzzled, though Diego had no idea why. "Your family?"

Victoria beamed with pride. "Yes. My father and mother, myself, and my little brother."

Melanie glanced at her, then offered a gentle, almost sympathetic smile. "It is a lovely family. Very happy."

They did look happy, close and loving even in a formal portrait. Diego wondered what had separated Victoria from her adoring parents. "So what happened to them?"

Melanie winced beside him, though for once, Chen didn't react to Diego's blunt question. Instead, he stood slightly to one side, glaring at the picture. Diego understood why. Unlike Victoria, Chen had no family, nor did he know what had become of his parents when he was abandoned at nine. Rafael had acted as his father, and though he had been loved and cared for, the lack of family remained a sore point with Chen.

Victoria glanced fondly at the portrait. "My family is in San Francisco now. Although they haven't been able to visit me as yet, I receive letters often from them. They are very pleased at the success of my small, but *warm* and *friendly* inn." She cast a quick, challenging glance at Chen, who pretended to ignore her.

For a reason Diego couldn't guess, Melanie's eyes seemed moist. "I am sure they are proud of you, Miss Wu, and I am so pleased to be staying here."

Victoria fiddled with her ledger. Melanie's name was the first on her list of guests. "You're a photographer. I don't believe we've ever had a photographer at the Tewa Inn before."

Chen issued a brief snort. "You've only been open for two months. You barely had a guest before now. And what do you mean, 'we'? You're the only one here."

Somehow, Victoria managed to completely ignore Chen, and her smile never wavered. Her voice remained sweet, her attention fixed on Melanie. "Is there anything you might require to help you in your task, Miss Muessen?"

Melanie hesitated. "I would like to find a guide, to escort me to the various sights of interest in this area, and perhaps introduce me to native citizens, as well as newer arrivals. I would also like to learn more of the Renegade who made your pueblo so renowned."

Victoria considered this. "Then you'll need someone familiar with both Zuni and Mexican people." She paused. Chen and Victoria turned toward Diego. "Perhaps someone whose heritage includes both. Someone who has lived in this area all his life, and knows its history." Victoria paused again, waiting for Diego to react. He refused. "Someone whose brother was the greatest hero this land has ever seen. Miss Muessen, your perfect guide is standing right beside you."

# *Chapter Two*

The porter was the handsomest man Melanie had ever seen. He was also the most conceited. She guessed at once why he hadn't told her that his brother was the infamous Renegade—he didn't want anything overshadowing his own good looks and charm. He was accustomed to charming women—that much she had seen at first glance. He was too confident and perhaps too indolent; a man who wouldn't spend much effort on any one pursuit once it became difficult or hazardous.

Perfect guide, indeed. This sort of man immediately took over a situation, felt he knew best how all things should be handled, and wouldn't let her get a word in edgewise. If he was to be her guide, she would have to set the boundaries between them at once.

"Have you any experience as a guide?" She posed the question with deliberate skepticism, and he frowned in offense.

"I know this land, this pueblo, Santa Fe, and every other Zuni pueblo in this area, as well as I know the back of my hand, señorita." He stopped, as if he hadn't meant to defend himself, and perhaps regretted his assertion. Maybe he didn't want to be her guide. However, part of her reason for traveling to the Tewa Pueblo was to learn more about the legendary Renegade—if he was indeed in Europe, her dreams of photographing him firsthand were lost, but if the porter was his brother, she might learn something of interest, all the same.

"Won't serving as my guide interfere with your duties as porter?" She relished posing the question and watched happily as his frown deepened.

"I'm afraid Chen misled you on that count, señorita." His quick, charming voice had hardened somewhat, but the testy note still pleased her. "As it happens, he and I share ownership of the Chateau Renegade." He paused, lips quirked to one side. "Though the name was his invention."

Chen shifted from foot to foot and looked deeply annoyed. "We invested together. It is *my* establishment."

Melanie sensed that Chen's assertion was directed more at his competitor than at her, but Diego seemed to accept the admonishment. "It's his—but I am not the porter."

Melanie arched her brow. "It is a decent profession." She paused. "What was your name again?"

"Diego de Aguirre."

It was a pretty name. She couldn't deny that. And it suited him. "What is the charge for your services?"

He hesitated for a moment. "If you will donate a few pictures to Chen's hotel, and perhaps take one of Will and his family, and of my grandfather, I will be your guide for no fee."

This time, he surprised her. Chen, however, looked exasperated. "Don't you value money at all?"

Diego shrugged. "I prefer an honest trade. And I have enough money from the tiny portion left to me from the Spanish treasure."

This sounded interesting. Melanie looked between them. "What treasure?"

Diego sighed, as if reluctant to divulge the source of his treasure, but Chen's eyes gleamed. "Eight years ago, a vast treasure . . ."

Diego cut in with, "It was one small chest."

Chen ignored him. "A treasure of vast worth was discovered buried beneath one of the pueblo kivas, buried by Spaniards ages ago. A large group of pueblo people was kidnapped to work in the mine—Diego was one—and the Renegade, Señor de Aguirre, freed them. With my help, of course."

"I read that story in your brochure. It must have been very exciting, and very dangerous." She eyed Diego, who had a faraway look in his eyes. "You were there, too?"

"I was."

"A captive?"

"Yes."

Her excitement faded—something in his eyes told her that his pain ran deep on this subject. "I'm sorry."

"It happened long ago. As Chen said, my brother saved us, the treasure was secured and divided among us all—and Tewa has blossomed since."

*But you have not.* Despite herself, Melanie felt drawn to the Renegade's indolent brother. "I agree to take you as my guide, Señor de Aguirre, at the fee you stated." She paused. "You mentioned a grandfather. Is he here in this pueblo?"

"He's in Tesuque, a Zuni pueblo nearby. You'll want to go there, anyway, because it's got a fine history, 'native citizens,' and a good landscape to shoot."

Just as she'd suspected, Diego already felt himself equipped to decide what constituted a good shot. Melanie eyed his hands—his fingers were long, well formed, strong but somehow elegant. An artist's hands. Despite her instinct to disagree with whatever he suggested, her innate judgment told her to wait to see if his views had merit. "Very well. I would like to meet him."

Melanie looked around the pueblo. "Today would be best spent by you showing me around Tewa Pueblo. Then tomorrow you can escort me to your grandfather's pueblo."

Diego's eyes widened. They were deep and

brown, shadowed by the most impressive long, black eyelashes she'd ever seen. "Today? Aren't you . . . tired from your journey?"

"Not at all." Melanie dusted her gloved hands on her skirt. "There's little to do on a train but eat and sleep, and I am quite tired of that. I would like to get started."

Diego issued a muted groan. "You may be feeling fresh, but I, as it happens, endured a difficult night and could use some rest."

He looked perfectly fine. "What happened to you?"

His gaze fixed on hers, and she detected a hint of challenge, as if he dared her to think well of him when faced with so much evidence to the contrary. "I was drunk."

She wasn't surprised. "I see. You 'happened' to yourself. Well, sir, the best thing for healing a bout of drunkenness is fresh air and activity."

His dark eyes narrowed to slits. "What would you know about recovering from a night with the bottle?"

She sighed. "Too much."

Diego's lips curled up at one side. "Big drinker, are you?"

"No. My father was. Shall we proceed, or must I wait another day for you to ward off your miseries? If the past is any guide, however, I must say tonight will be much the same as the last."

Diego's expression had changed as she spoke from bright, almost teasing challenge to abject horror. "I wasn't that drunk." Chen issued a huff beside him, but Melanie studied Diego more closely. She'd been ready to write him off as a drunk, a ne'er-do-well. But she sensed something more in him. This man was no slave to the bottle, as her father had finally become. Not yet, anyway. He obviously liked to exaggerate his debauchery—but why? Whatever his reason, a man like that could be dangerous.

"I would like you to introduce me to the pueblo citizens, so that I might photograph those who particularly exemplify this land. We can start with this pueblo, and then you can escort me to the Zuni pueblos nearby."

"You have quite an itinerary, don't you?"

She nodded. "It's necessary. Shall we get started? I would like to see the area surrounding this pueblo first. I assume we have time for that today?" She didn't wait for an answer because she knew they did. "The area of the ancient kivas where the Spanish treasure was hidden should be most intriguing."

Diego uttered a miserable, drawn-out sigh. "Very well. But don't talk too loud." He turned to Chen. "Do I still have a horse, or did I lose it gambling?"

Yes, she had been right about him—he exaggerated debauchery, and he did it with diligence. "If you can't locate one, you can always ride my pony."

He cast her a dark glance, then left Victoria's porch without a word. Chen watched him go, stiffened into a straight posture, and forced a smile. "He is joking, of course. He has a horse."

Victoria nodded. "And from what I've heard, Diego never loses at gambling."

Chen's jaw clenched. "Good day, Madame Wu."

Victoria appeared equally taut in his company. "Mr. Chen."

They said no more to each other, and Chen escorted Melanie from the inn. She peeked up at him. He seemed to be glowering with unusual intensity. "I apologize if I got your name wrong, sir. I had thought *Chen* was your first name."

"It is." He paused. "I have no surname, Miss Muessen, for unlike Miss Wu, I have no family. My parents, whoever they might have been, were brought here from China to work on the railroad. I do not remember them. Nor am I sure they really knew each other in any meaningful way."

Melanie knew better than to offer sympathy. "You will make your own family one day." She paused. "Sometimes no family is better than those you are born with."

He looked at her thoughtfully, and she saw a greater depth in his eyes than she had originally supposed. Though proud and regal in nature, there was something deeper and wiser in Chen. He said nothing, but an understanding formed between them. Perhaps he sensed that her own life had isolated her and not been easy, and that she would not judge his choices because she had made so many mistakes herself.

Diego came across the plaza leading a delicate brown and white horse, and a light gray that she assumed to be his mount. For the first time, Melanie noticed that Diego walked with a slight limp, though it didn't seem to slow his pace. The gray horse had no lead and seemed to be following him like a dog. Diego stopped, and it nudged him. Diego slipped the horse something from his pocket.

He nodded toward the pinto. "I brought this mare for you. I'm assuming you don't want to ride that tiny little creature you brought."

Melanie felt stung on her pony's behalf. "Porticus is very sturdy."

"Maybe, but if you ride him, he'll demand extra feedings at night, and the pueblo doesn't have enough hay to support an appetite like that."

Chen looked between them, then caught sight of a large group gathering outside his hotel. "If you are settled, Miss Muessen, I must return to my duties as proprietor of the Chateau Renegade. Miss Wu hasn't yet secured a chef for her small establishment, so I invite you to dine with us tonight, as my guest." He seemed to add "as my guest" reluctantly, which she assumed meant she would not be expected to pay for her meal.

Diego whistled. "I hope she doesn't eat like Porticus." Chen braced, as if that thought occurred to him, too, then stole a quick glance at her figure. He seemed relieved, so apparently she didn't appear vastly overweight.

Melanie cleared her throat. "I would be happy to dine with you, Chen. Thank you."

Chen bowed respectfully, then hurried to his guests, leaving Melanie with Diego. She didn't expect to be nervous, but now that she was alone with him, she endured a sudden yet powerful urge to run.

Diego turned to her and bowed dramatically, as an echo of Chen's graceful departure. "Where would you like me to escort you, señorita?"

"First, I shall photograph a few of the Tewa citizens. Then I would like to see the area where the Spanish treasure was hidden."

Her request didn't please him. "Wouldn't you rather look around the pueblo? There's nothing to photograph out there."

"I need a shot of the place where the Renegade performed his most heroic rescue."

Diego groaned. "Oh, very well. But you won't find anything interesting there. It's nothing but rubble now."

"I would like to see it, all the same." He didn't want to go, but she had no idea why. "Is it far?"

"Outside the pueblo, not a mile."

"Very good. My darkroom and camera, and the trunks of chemicals and equipment, are all set up and ready, but I should remove my personal gear to lighten the load on Porticus."

Melanie removed the bags of her clothing and toiletries. Diego took them without asking and deposited them near Victoria's front door. "I'll put

44

these away when we return, Miss Wu."

Victoria glanced toward the Chateau. "There's no need, Diego. I've arranged for Will to assist me—once he's finished at the other hotel." She paused. "I will, of course, pay him for his services. I had thought the subject of payment would keep him on a permanent basis." She stopped and coughed, and Melanie eyed her doubtfully, but Diego grinned. It almost sounded as if Victoria was trying to lure away Chen's staff.

Diego didn't seem concerned. "If Will doesn't work out, there are several boys looking for work. They have a few days' experience after serving Chen."

Victoria nodded. "I did inquire of them, but as it happens, they were demanding in the subject of salary. For now, Will is adequate." She went back into the inn, and Diego laughed.

"In other words, she's just as tight with money as Chen."

Melanie looked around. "I would like to take a shot of your friend, Will, and perhaps of Victoria."

Diego frowned. "Will doesn't actually live in Tewa—he stays with his mother and stepfather, who incidentally is my uncle—at Tesuque. And Victoria has only been here two months."

"Still, they represent the character of this place."

His frown deepened. "I, on the other hand, have lived here all my life. I was born here." He stood a little straighter, a little more stiffly, next to his horse.

"How nice." She would take a picture of him, but not when he was posing, and certainly not when he so obviously desired the attention. "Perhaps another time."

Diego appeared offended, then caught sight of Will carrying trunks into Chen's hotel. "Will! Get over here! Miss Muessen would like to photograph you."

Will dropped the trunk on its side, and something shattered within. He hurried to Melanie, his eyes wide with enthusiasm. "What do I do, miss?"

Melanie positioned him with the two horses, in a place where his kind manner was most at home. She set up her camera and tried different angles. Will held himself perfectly still, maintaining a quiet, natural appearance. Diego waited impatiently, fiddling with his horse's saddle. Melanie focused on the perfect shot, then straightened.

"You will have to move aside, Señor de Aguirre. You're still in Will's shot."

"Am I?" Yes, he sounded decidedly disgruntled now. "Well, it is my horse."

Will cast a commiserating glance Diego's way. "I think she just wants me in her picture, Diego."

Diego stepped aside, dark eyes alight with indignation. Melanie felt a surge of satisfaction as she took the picture of Will. "Thank you, Will. That will be a fine photograph." He smiled, then returned to Chen's service.

Melanie set up her darkroom, and Diego helped, though she didn't ask for his assistance. He surprised her by recognizing much of the wet collodion process, and by handing her the right chemicals for processing the plate. "This one's for coating, that for sensitizing, and this one developing."

Melanie looked up at him. "How do you know all this?"

"My brother took a group of his students, including myself, into Santa Fe to study the work of some photographer."

"Recently?"

"When I was sixteen."

"And you remember it all?"

He huffed. "Of course. I can't say I was particularly interested, and Chen and I did get into a fight because I wasn't paying attention. . . . And we broke a plate or two in the scuffle, knocked a few weights and measuring cups off the old fellow's shelf."

Melanie held up her hand. "I don't want to know."

Diego looked proud. "Rafael had a hard time convincing the fellow to let him bring his students again the next year. He had to promise to leave me and Chen behind. That was fine with me, but it offended Chen for weeks."

"I thank you for your help, and I would appreciate your refraining from any future battles in my darkroom."

He met her eyes and smiled, and she endured a flutter of nervousness with him standing so close.

"I'll do my best. But I can't speak for Chen."

Melanie held up the image of Will, and Diego nodded, impressed. "You captured him, all right. He's got that shadow of wisdom, knowing everything, not saying too much." Diego bent closer. "You got the same expression on the horse. Except for Porticus there in the background. He's clearly chewing something."

Melanie felt satisfied. "That's generally the case with Porticus."

They emerged from her darkroom tent, and Diego helped her dismantle it, then return it to Porticus's cart. It was the first time she'd had help with her tasks, and it made the process much quicker. She felt a little tired, but she didn't want the day to end so soon, since it had already been so productive.

Diego looked around. Despite his sordid night, he looked alert and vigorous. "What next? Victoria?"

Melanie looked into the sky. "The morning is waning. I'll ask Victoria about posing later. Just now, I'd like you to escort me to the ruined kivas."

He looked as if he hoped she'd forgotten, then sighed deeply as Melanie replaced her gear in Porticus's cart. She gulped, then seized the pinto's reins and mounted. Diego had fitted the mare with a well-crafted sidesaddle, and she positioned her skirts accordingly.

He watched her adjusting her position, then mounted himself. "I take it you can ride."

"I can. My father taught me to ride so that I could help him on photographic shoots."

"He was a photographer, too?"

"He moved to America from Germany to document the Civil War. His collection of battle images is one of the most famous in existence." She paused. "It was, however, not without a price. What he saw, the suffering and pain, the death and destruction—after witnessing that, he was never the same."

Diego shook his head in disgust. "The American war sounds grim."

"I believe that is why he turned to drink. It was hard to document the horrors he saw and not be able to change anything."

Diego's expression changed. "The limitations a man finds in himself are the hardest to face." He hitched a long lead to Porticus, then tied it to his saddle. "I hope he can keep up."

"He was raised in the Scottish Highlands—he can handle anything here."

Diego leaned down and stared meaningfully at Porticus's stubby legs. "We'll see."

They started off together, with Porticus trudging along behind Diego's gray. Even before they reached the plaza gates, Melanie's nervousness soared. Maybe she should have taken a day to rest, to be alone. She had to make conversation, to set up formal, polite boundaries between them.

"This pueblo is quite lovely." She paused. "It's

hard to picture it terrorized by a renegade warrior."

He glanced over at her. "Hardly terrorized. My brother is a schoolmaster, not a warrior." He stopped and gestured at an adobe building set aside from the others. It seemed to have parts added on at different times, and had been painted in festive colors, as if children had done the decorating. It was a warm, cheerful building, but Melanie saw no children nearby.

"Who tends the school now?"

"No one. It's summer, and they're all gone."

"Gone?"

"Every summer, Rafael and his wife take the whole lot of them on a trip. I thought he was crazy the first time, but every summer, they take more. And they already have two children of their own."

"What made him decide to become a masked vigilante?"

"Our father reconstructed this pueblo, and my brother felt it was his responsibility to keep it protected. Some landowners got greedy and brought in an even worse army officer who had gotten wind of the Spanish treasure Chen told you about. Rafael dealt with them."

He made it seem simple, easy, and not the romantic tale of bravery and heroism Chen had described in his hotel brochure. "So now that he's gone, that duty falls to you?"

Diego's expressive lips formed a distinct frown. "I have no interest in heroism, señorita. But fortunately for Tewa Pueblo, they face no dire threat now."

Diego gazed up toward the hills in the west. The late morning sun fell warm on the mountains, beautiful and strangely compelling to Melanie. "If one arises while Rafael is gone, they'll have to handle it on their own."

Diego chatted ceaselessly as they rode, telling her of the pueblo inhabitants, of the antics of children, speculating as to who among them was giving his brother the most difficult time in Europe. Despite his demeanor of rakishness, he clearly loved the people in his pueblo, and found them interesting. He spoke often of Chen, delighting in his imperious manner, and in his own tendency to disobey Chen's orders. He was a friendly man, and yet Melanie sensed he kept much to himself, much that he hoped no one would ever see.

He was also a handsome man. As the morning progressed, the effect of his good looks grew stronger. He was tall, well over six feet, and his body was impressively formed, with broad shoulders and narrow hips. His facial features seemed more Spanish than anything, but also graced with something else, probably from his Zuni grandfather. His hair was black, thick and wavy, and a portion came loose often to fall over his forehead.

Diego glanced at her and smiled. Heat rose to Melanie's cheeks. He knew she had been looking at him, and he probably knew why. She cleared her throat. "You have interesting facial features, Señor de Aguirre."

"Diego. *Señor* is too formal for a guide."

"As you wish." He had to interrupt her. She fought to remember what she was going to say. "I take it you are part Indian."

"My mother was Zuni, and my father Argentinian. I am told I look like him. My brother looks more Zuni, much like my grandfather." He paused. "So you like my *features*, do you?"

The heat in her cheeks intensified. "From a photographic standpoint, they are interesting."

One dark brow rose. "From a 'photographic standpoint.' Ah, I see." He was obviously used to the admiration of women. "It would make me an interesting subject."

"No." It would. But Diego eyed her indignantly. Melanie maintained as much detached reserve as she could muster. "You don't accurately represent either the Spanish or Indian heritage, which is what I hope to photograph during my stay here."

"Is that so?" Good. He was offended, and she had removed some small element of his conceit. "Many people living here are of mixed heritage."

Which was exactly what she had hoped to record. Melanie decided to alter the conversation. "Would this be the 'winding path from the ancestors' that Chen referred to in his brochure? The path the Renegade took when sweeping down from the mountains?"

Diego sighed. Apparently, he had tired of his

brother's daring exploits. "Rafael kept his horse up here, loose. It came when he whistled. There are many paths, most secret, which lead from the pueblo into the hills, and he found it suitable to ride down this way. Also, more dramatic."

"What happened to the horse?"

"Frank? Rafael let him go, and he became stud to a small herd of mustangs up here—when he's here, he checks up on Frank. You see them occasionally. Most of them are scrawny and wild as deer, but these two we're riding are of that stock. Right now, there's a fine black fellow among them—a few people have tried to catch him, but no one gets near. He's something of a renegade himself."

"Have you tried?"

Diego cast her a doubtful glance. "No. Why should I? This one I'm riding is good enough to get me to saloons and back."

Melanie wasn't convinced. "It's just that you spoke of the black one with admiration . . . and a certain amount of longing. As if you would like him for yourself."

"It's never crossed my mind."

It had, but Melanie thought better of arguing the point. And why would he deny it, when it was so obvious? "Will we see them today, do you think?"

Diego shrugged, but he scanned the landscape eagerly. "Maybe. They're often by the old kivas. Good grazing there."

"I hope we do. I like horses, but I've never seen them wild before."

"Wild horses are probably more interesting at a distance." Diego sighed, then turned from the broader pathway and directed them up a windy, rocky trail. His expression darkened as they went on, as if this wasn't a road he enjoyed traveling. He led them onto a flat area, then toward an area of disheveled boulders. In one place, the ground had caved in.

Melanie dismounted and led her horse to investigate. "It looks like a battlefield."

Diego stayed astride and glanced around, disinterested. "At one time it was. A group of us were captured to work in the mine, digging for treasure."

"And you found it?"

"We did. Our captors found it most convenient to collapse the mine over our heads, lest we be left as witnesses."

"Your brother saved you?"

"Yes."

For once, Diego wasn't chatty. The sky had turned to gray behind his head, and the wind grew. Melanie pulled her cape closer around her body. For an instant, he looked almost ghostlike on his pale gray horse. He had left something of himself in this place, something he believed he would never get back. She wondered what it was, and why it was so dear that it had left him this bereft.

"You don't like it here."

Diego turned to her and smiled. "I was young here. I haven't been young since."

Without speaking, he dismounted and helped her set up her camera equipment. Melanie positioned herself for several angles, and settled on a shot that captured the fallen kiva against a gray sky, punctuated by boulders that seemed to represent those lives torn asunder in this lonely place. Diego stood behind her, which she didn't expect. Somehow, she thought he would want to be in every picture she took.

They set up the darkroom, and she set to work developing her shots. She had only used two plates; the wrecked kivas hadn't captured her imagination as she hoped. Diego studied the landscape shot and shook his head. "The one with Will was better."

Tact wasn't his strongest quality, but she had to agree. "Yes, this is a somewhat dismal area."

Diego went to get the horses, and stood for a moment staring down at the sunken kiva, the gray horse behind him. Melanie took the shot quietly, then darted back into her tent to develop it. Diego waited for her outside and, fortunately, didn't realize what she'd done. This image was perfect, and strangely, thanks to a miscalculation in her processing, a faint ghost outlined his shape, and the horse's. She tucked it away so that he wouldn't notice, then stepped outside the tent.

Diego was sitting on a rock staring out at nothing. "Is this sufficient, señorita, or is there something else that captures your interest in this miserable place?"

"No, I have all that I need from here. Thank you."

He helped her pack up her gear, then went to retrieve the horses.

He passed the mare's reins to Melanie and she mounted, then waited for him. "You walk with a limp."

He glanced at her as he prepared to mount. "Do I? I never noticed." He was teasing, and she squirmed with embarrassment.

"Forgive me. It was a rude comment."

Diego laughed. "I've made a few of those myself. I can hardly fault you for my own most frequent crime. Ask as you wish, señorita. Just be careful with Chen."

"What subject should I avoid with him?"

"Too many to mention. His family, or lack of it, mostly. That's a sore spot with him. His height. We used to be the same, when we were ten or so. I don't think he's ever forgiven me for outgrowing him." He paused. "Of course, I've never let him forget it."

"What about Will?"

"Not a thing with Will."

Melanie chewed her lip, but she wanted to know more about her handsome porter. "Is your injury a subject to avoid?"

"There's little to tell . . ." He didn't look at her. Instead, he looked at the sunken kiva. His eyes narrowed, and he gestured at one of the larger boulders. "But for my lame leg, I have that rock to thank."

"You were injured during your captivity?"

"During our escape."

Melanie hesitated. "Were you one of the first to break free?"

He sighed and closed his beautiful eyes. "I was the last."

His words came soft, and seemed to blend with the wind that swirled around him. Melanie wanted to know more, but a far-off neigh caught her attention, and she turned. There, standing on the high cliff overlooking the kiva ruins, stood a magnificent black horse. His strong neck arched, and his black mane flew in the wind.

Melanie grabbed Diego's arm and pointed. She practically hopped with excitement, and had to fight to keep from squealing with joy. "Is that him, the horse you told me about?"

Diego looked equally excited as he nodded. "He's a wild thing, so don't make any sudden moves." The horse lifted one foot and stomped, then tossed his head.

"He's beautiful."

A group of mares appeared on the horizon, and a large-boned dark gray came over the edge, then took position before them. The young black horse stayed apart—apparently, the older gray was still their leader. The gray surveyed Diego's group, whinnied, then trotted down toward them. Diego smiled as the horse came up to him. "This is Frank." He rubbed the horse's ears, and it closed its eyes.

Melanie eyed Frank doubtfully. "This gentle creature was the Renegade's mount?"

"He had his day. He's getting a little old, but I imagine he's got spirit left. He's held off the black fellow from taking his place for a year or more now." Frank shoved his nose against Diego's pocket, and Diego passed him a sugar block. "Rafael will return soon, old fellow. Then maybe you'll get some stable time, and some oats."

The black horse watched suspiciously but made no move toward Frank's group of devoted mares. Diego's gaze drifted from the restful Frank to the wild leader, and an expression of far-off sorrow touched his handsome face. "You'll get your chance one day, my friend. And in the end, you may wish it had never come at all."

They rode back to the pueblo in silence. The wind had picked up, and it made speech impossible, but Diego's mood had shifted since visiting the kiva ruins. Though his eyes had shone brilliantly at the sight of the wild horses, the sight of them, too, seemed to quiet him. The hint of sorrow in him touched Melanie's heart.

As they came to the pueblo gates, a loud commotion rose from the plaza. Melanie glanced at Diego, and his brow furrowed. "Is this typical for afternoon in the pueblo?"

He shook his head. "Haven't heard it in . . . years." They rode through the gates and found a large group of people filling the plaza. A man stood on a podium not far from Chen's hotel. Chen and Will stood nearby, and both looked concerned.

Melanie tapped Diego's arm. "I don't remember there being a podium here this morning."

"There wasn't."

"Who is that man?"

"Carlton Bradford. He's been living in Santa Fe, but for reasons known only to himself, has made himself a presence in Tewa. It may be that we're about to learn what's behind his visits."

Melanie assessed Bradford. He held himself straight, reflecting years spent in the military, and he had the imposing stance of an officer. Melanie recognized a light-haired young man standing near Bradford. "I've seen that blond man before. He was on the train with me. But he didn't get on in Boston—I think he boarded in Denver, and I felt sure he came from the other direction, from California."

Diego assessed the newcomers. "Most of those men with Bradford look like soldiers . . . or thugs."

As Diego spoke, Bradford turned in their direction and smiled. "Ah. Young de Aguirre. I had thought to wait for you since my announcement concerns you in some small way. But I feared you were . . . what was it? *Resting* beneath the saloon floor?"

Diego offered no reaction as he walked through

the crowd. For reasons Melanie couldn't guess, his limp seemed exaggerated, whereas before it was barely noticeable. "Señor Bradford, you appear to have stirred up the citizens of Tewa admirably. To what do we owe the honor of your oft-repeated visit this time?"

Bradford held up a document to which an official-looking ribbon had been attached. "I am here to announce, de Aguirre, that thanks in most part to your own lack of skill managing this pueblo in your brother's absence, Rafael de Aguirre has seen fit to turn ownership of this property, known as Tewa Pueblo, to a group of concerned benefactors, administered from this point forward by myself."

Melanie gaped, but still, Diego revealed no reaction. "He sold the pueblo to these 'investors'?" Diego moved forward again through the crowd. Unseen and unnoticed, Melanie followed. "Why would that be, do you think?"

"This document, transferring all administrative rights to me, was only this morning delivered to me by my attorney, Gregory Alvin." He indicated the blond man from the train—she should have known he was a lawyer.

Alvin stepped forward and handed the document to Diego. "I think you will recognize your brother's script and signature, and see that all is legal."

The crowd hushed as Diego read over the paper. Both Chen and Will stood motionless, as if waiting for Diego to save them. Diego handed the document back to the attorney. "It is Rafael's hand. I congratulate you, Señor Bradford. It seems that Tewa Pueblo belongs to you—or those you represent."

The crowd erupted as one, more people cursing Diego than Bradford. Melanie heard voices joined in outrage. "Rafael would never . . . !" "Worthless scum!" And still Diego showed no sign of reaction.

"I am sure you will manage the pueblo fairly, with the best interest of its citizens in mind." His voice was so even. Melanie felt a wild desire to fight, to fling something at the man who so brazenly claimed Tewa Pueblo. She saw the same expression on the faces of those around, on Chen and on Will, and even Victoria, who stood near her small inn, her hands clasped as if warding off a blow.

Bradford seemed pleased by Diego's acceptance. "You surprise me, de Aguirre. I had thought you might challenge my claim, since had you lived a life of less abandon, this pueblo might have been passed to you in your brother's absence. As for my management of this pueblo, I assure you, it will be fair." He paused. "Although some things will change, naturally."

"Such as what?"

"As manager of this property, I must assert what my predecessor did not, and that is that the people here are in effect tenants. My tenants. As tenants, I expect payment, and work done as I see fit. I hesitate to use the term *taxes,* but there are businesses here who pay nothing for the land they occupy."

Chen's face paled at this suggestion, but it was Victoria who unexpectedly stepped forward. "You can't mean to charge us for running our businesses!"

Bradford offered her a conciliatory smile. "Nothing extreme, Miss Wu. Just a token." He paused again—every inflection had meaning when he spoke. "As with any business dealing, we may find it profitable to offer trades. For instance, the use of your rooms without cost might amply make up for any future taxes."

Chen started to argue, but Diego held up his hand. "That sounds fair." This time, his voice sounded a little strained, as if he fought to restrain any reaction, but the crowd didn't notice his conflict. They erupted again in fury.

Why didn't he fight? Melanie's own fists were clenched. Why didn't he argue? Chen looked ready to kill, and even Will's gentle face was flushed with anger.

Diego ignored the angry crowd and kept his attention on Bradford. "You mentioned work on your behalf. What would you have us do?"

"There is no reason to make that secret. As you are all aware, the matter of Spanish treasure arose several years ago, under the leadership of several former landowners and an unscrupulous lieutenant."

62

"The treasure was found and divided among us. No more remains."

"My research has led me to believe otherwise, de Aguirre. Your brother believed, as you do, that there is nothing more to be found. Perhaps that explains his lack of interest in this pueblo—I understand he is often away, and now has found life abroad more to his liking. Call it a gamble on my part—for a healthy sum, I recommended that the investors I mentioned purchase this land from your brother, before you turn it totally to ruin. As their administrator, I will set about seeking the treasure that might still be buried beneath the earth outside the pueblo."

"Understandable."

Melanie sensed a lie. Bradford wanted something, but it wasn't treasure. Yet Diego seemed to accept that explanation without question. "I'm glad you agree, de Aguirre. With your support, I'm sure the more high-strung citizens of Tewa will also accept my leadership, and come to benefit from the new direction I will forge for us all."

He had mastered public speaking—it wouldn't be surprising to learn he had a place in politics. But the more he spoke, the more Melanie didn't trust him. Her hands felt cold, she shivered, and the wind seemed to have followed them from the kivas to the sheltered plaza.

Someone in the crowd cursed, and a round loaf of bread flew through the air, striking Bradford in the chest. It must have been stale, because it thumped like a rock. Melanie wasn't sure who threw the bread, but a man shouted at Bradford from the crowd. "You'll never take over this pueblo, you scum-sucking devil! This is our home—not a trinket to be bought and sold! It will be a bullet that flies at you next!"

Bradford's demeanor didn't change, but his eyes flashed with sudden anger. He waved his hands, and two armed men stepped forward. "There is another matter to be broached, and that is the subject of discipline. It has been, I'm afraid—that will change now. I have hired a well-trained group of guards, men who will defend both my interests and the good citizens of this pueblo. You may consider them the law from now on. Actions and threats such as this will not be tolerated."

Melanie watched in horror as Bradford's guards hauled a chubby Mexican man forward through the crowd, then led him toward the pueblo school.

Diego started after the guards, then stopped. "You're taking him to class? A good idea, señor. An hour or two of study never hurt anyone."

Bradford smiled, the expression more a sneer than anything. "Since the pueblo school is currently unoccupied, I have decided to make better use of it. It will serve as my office during the day, though I shall take up permanent residence in Mr. Chen's establishment. There is an addition in the schoolhouse that will serve admirably as a jail. I hope it will not require much use."

The first emotion she had seen flickered in Diego's dark eyes, and his wide shoulders tensed. He looked down, and she knew this time he was fighting for restraint. "Surely there is a better place to house criminals than in a school?"

"For now, this will suffice."

"A night in jail won't hurt the fellow." Diego's words came thick, but even. "I'm sure we could all benefit from a quiet evening in contemplation."

"This man's violence requires that I set a better example than that, de Aguirre. It is within my right to dictate punishment within certain, acceptable guidelines. I am a firm supporter of correction, and assault will not be tolerated."

"What more do you intend to do with this man? He is Miguel, our baker. I trust you understand the need we have for his services."

"In the morning, promptly at eight o'clock, we will stage a moderate public flogging."

"That sounds . . . medieval."

"But it is within my right, and universally accepted as effective."

The baker, Miguel, struggled against his guards, but it was Diego he turned on. "You . . . It is you I should have struck, you cowardly, useless rogue. Oh, to the day your brother left, leaving only you in his stead!"

Diego said nothing as they dragged the baker into the schoolhouse. He turned his attention back to Bradford. "You have shocked us with your news, Señor Bradford. Perhaps you will grant lenience as we absorb this sudden change in our pueblo."

"My temperament has always been lenient, de Aguirre, but do not try my patience. I have produced documents of ownership, and much will change in Tewa Pueblo, beginning now. Give me no trouble and it will go easy for you. From what I have heard of you, that is all you require. But should any of you defy me, you will find me a stern leader."

Rigid and unyielding seemed more accurate to Melanie. His announcement had the quality of a bad dream, and the thought of flogging—it felt as if she had been drawn back in time. Apparently, her face gave away her feelings, because Bradford caught sight of her. He stepped down from the podium and approached her. Diego moved to stand beside her, but he did nothing to dissuade Bradford's approach.

"Who are you, young woman? I've never seen you in Tewa before."

She met his eyes, unwavering. "I am Melanie Ann Muessen. I am a photographer. I intend to document the people of this area."

"You have honored us with your presence in Tewa. I hope you will stay on, despite my inadvertent interruption, as my guest. It would be of great service to have you photograph the changes in this pueblo, so that the good I do here will be recorded."

"It is my intention to photograph the native citizens of this area. I am, however, not for hire."

"You will, of course, keep me informed of your progress?" In other words, he wanted to know everything she photographed.

"Should I decide to photograph you, Mr. Bradford, I will be certain to request your permission."

His eyes flashed, as if he recognized a subtly defiant heart. "You will dine with my party tonight, then." It wasn't a question.

"I am Chen's guest tonight, but I am residing at Miss Wu's inn."

"Surely you would be better off at the Chateau Renegade? I will see to it that a room is provided."

He wanted her close, to keep an eye on her activities. Melanie held his gaze evenly. "I am satisfied with Miss Wu's inn. I will stay there."

He looked as if he wanted to argue, but a quick glance at Victoria's inn seemed to assure him that the proximity was enough. "I'm sure we will see much of each other, Miss Muessen." He turned to Diego. "And you, young de Aguirre, since you've so graciously accepted my ascent to power here, you will join us for dinner as well."

"It would be an honor, Señor Bradford."

Diego's polite reaction astonished Melanie. Perhaps he had seemed somewhat careless, but she never dreamed he could be this weak of will. Surely his brother's legacy meant something to him. Well, it meant something to her, even if she hadn't seen it happen firsthand. If Diego wasn't going to fight this man, Melanie would find a way on her own.

She would watch him, and turn her camera on anything that might be evidence against him. She offered a cool smile and stepped aside.

Bradford returned to the podium and stood before the crowd like an officer addressing troops.

"This pueblo is now under my direction. I assure you, the new owners of Tewa have your best interests at heart, and their confidence in me will soon be shared by all of you. Rafael de Aguirre understood that our offer was best for all. Some few may prove hostile to this change, but let me be completely clear. There is nothing any of you can do to alter the situation."

# Chapter Three

"Well, what are you going to do?"

Diego stood by the window of Chen's office, while Chen spun back and forth in agitation and Will sat tensely on the edge of Chen's desk. "What would you have me do? It was Rafael's handwriting, his signature. The paper appeared legal."

"Rafael would never have sold this pueblo. You know that, Diego."

"I know."

Chen made another pass around the room, his polished shoes making a marching tap as he spun by. "He would certainly never decide to live abroad 'indefinitely,' and no more would he issue a vague promise to have the pueblo children sent home to their parents on a ship 'soon.'"

"I know."

"If it is his signature, it was forced, and you know what that means."

Will nodded. "It might mean Señor de Aguirre and his family are in some kind of trouble."

Chen eyed him impatiently. "Obviously they're in danger! If they're alive at all."

Diego turned from the window. "Rafael is alive. I would feel it if my brother died."

Chen thumped his fist onto his desk, startling Will. "We have to find him."

Diego studied his friend. Chen was more excitable than he seemed. "Where do we start, Chen? Egypt, Spain, Japan? We don't even know where he is. And what about the pueblo children? Already their parents are justifiably concerned. If we act rashly, we may be putting them all at risk."

Will rubbed his chin thoughtfully. "Figure the thing is, we have to find out what Bradford is up to, beat him at it fair and square, get the pueblo back, and then we'll get Señor de Aguirre and his family back, and the pueblo children, too. That promise of Bradford's, to send the children back, that won't be happening, you know."

Chen resumed pacing around the room. "It seems all too likely."

Will watched Diego. "The thing is, to save Rafael, we need the Renegade."

Diego glared. "We don't have the Renegade. Rafael left a mask behind, not a man to wear it."

Chen stopped and frowned. "He expected *you* to wear it."

"No."

"The people in this pueblo need protection, and your brother needs someone who can take charge and set Bradford in his place, papers or no papers."

"No."

Chen went to his safe, speedily dialed numbers, and it opened. He shoved aside a box overflowing with jewels, a gold bar, and several packages of money, then withdrew an object wrapped in black cloth. Without a word, he presented it to Diego, but Diego refused to accept the gift.

"I know what this is, Chen, and you're giving it to the wrong man."

"I'm giving it to its owner. Rafael gave this mask to you. You need it now. He needs it."

"No."

"Damn, you're stubborn!"

Will whistled in agreement. "And that's a fact."

Chen adjusted the cloth around the mask, revealing the outline of an ancient and proud face, the face of a god. "I have composed a lengthy letter detailing our situation and sent it to the governor of the territory, but I have my doubts as to the possibility of its success."

"Given that Bradford has close ties to the governor, you're probably right." Chen would try all the legal avenues, but Diego knew, because he knew human nature, that Bradford had covered all the angles before he made his move.

Diego bowed his head into his hands, silent for a long while. Then he sighed, so deeply that it

71

seemed torn from his core, and stood up. Will looked at him eagerly. Chen stopped pacing and held his breath.

"So . . . have you decided? What are you going to do?"

Diego pulled on his coat and aimed for the door. "I am going to clean up. And then, gentlemen, I am going to dine with the new owner of Tewa Pueblo."

Carlton Bradford had seized the largest, most central table in Chen's lavish dining room, and his guests' conversation filled the room as Diego entered. No other table was occupied. Bradford noticed him and waved him over. "Come, de Aguirre, join us. Tonight we toast the new direction of your father's pueblo. You should be with us for that honor."

Diego's muscles tensed, and for a moment he offered no response. He had learned something of his own instincts this day. When the urge to fight, to defy arose, another sense claimed him—smothered the impulse. He was the brother of a warrior, and he had the same fiery blood in his veins. But what did that mean for himself or the people of his pueblo?

He forced himself to smile. "You are a gracious host, Señor Bradford. I am honored." He paused and glanced at the well-stocked wine cart. "I trust that since we're celebrating, there is wine enough to spare?"

Bradford cast a quick, knowing glance at his associates, who uniformly smirked. "More than enough, de Aguirre." He waved at Chen. "Perhaps our proprietor will pour."

Chen tensed. He considered it beneath him to serve in any capacity at his hotel, but he uncorked a bottle. His fists clenched around it, so Will took over and began sloshing it randomly into glasses. Bradford snarled when a red droplet splattered against his frock coat. "Watch what you're doing, idiot!"

Will continued splashing wine into goblets as if Bradford hadn't spoken. Diego glanced at Chen, and both suppressed smiles. Diego help up his goblet for Will. "Will is somewhat hard of hearing, sir. You'll have to overlook his little errors." Will had always been simple, but in no way was he an idiot. He was, and always had been, one of the wisest people Diego knew. A tiny smile formed on Will's lips as he allowed a small stream of wine to pool on the table near Bradford's fork.

Annoyed, Bradford looked around for someone else to pour. Chen backed away, then darted toward the kitchen. Bradford seized the wine bottle and passed it to Diego. "You pour, de Aguirre. You must be good at it by now."

Diego smiled, poured a large portion of wine into his own goblet, then set the bottle aside. Dismayed, Bradford took the bottle, and each guest served himself.

"Well, de Aguirre. What do you think of Tewa's new ownership?"

"I haven't met the new owners, have I? Only you, their representative, so I can't truly say what I think of them." Diego took an exaggerated drink of wine, then set the goblet aside. "But if the wine flows as freely as it does tonight, I can think no ill of the change, señor."

It was what Bradford expected from him, and Diego watched as the man's opinion of him solidified. He wasn't a threat—any fear Bradford might have harbored that Rafael's ne'er-do-well brother would turn rebellious dissipated. Bradford leaned forward in his seat, an eager light in his eyes. "I have great plans for Tewa, de Aguirre. You may not be held in the highest estimation by the people here, but you can help me win their cooperation."

"I will surely do that." Diego managed to slur his words, only slightly, as an indication of impending drunkenness. Foolish, because it took far more than one small goblet of red wine to affect him, but Bradford needn't learn his high tolerance for alcohol. Diego had realized years ago that if he exaggerated the effects of drink, he could learn much from people that they wouldn't ordinarily confide. It might work with Bradford—perhaps not this night, while he was on his guard, but in time.

How much time did they have? Rafael wasn't dead. Diego would have felt his brother's loss. Instead, he felt helplessness, frustration, and anger from his brother. He pretended to focus on his wine, and learned that Bradford's attorney, Alvin, was the one who supposedly contacted Rafael in France—odd, because Rafael had mentioned once that one trip to France was enough. Bradford's other associates spoke less, and seemed to be waiting, relying on Bradford to dictate the next move in whatever scheme they were involved in.

As much as he disliked Bradford, Diego found Gregory Alvin even more grating. He said little, but he had a mocking quality that implied that the only person who mattered was himself. He treated Bradford with respect, but even that seemed shallow. Diego had no doubt that Alvin viewed Bradford, like everyone in his life, as a means to an end.

Alvin's smug expression altered to surprise, even amazement, catching Diego's attention. The attorney's eyes widened, and the men at the table turned toward the door.

Diego, turned, too, and his own breath caught. Melanie Muessen entered the dining room, her long hair done up behind her head, with soft tendrils framing her lovely face. Unlike her attire during the day, tonight she wore a dark blue gown that hugged her waist and accentuated breasts that were fuller and more enticing than Diego had remembered from their first meeting. Earlier, she had hidden her beauty with drab colors and cumbersome fabric—tonight, it shone. Her light brown hair glittered with traces of gold, and her soft skin seemed radiant in the lamplight.

More than her startling beauty, the attitude obvious in her blue eyes captured Diego's attention. She looked proud, and ready to fight. As he watched her standing there, Diego forgot where he was, why he was there. He half expected ballroom music to commence, so that he could sweep her into his arms and dance, enchanted, through a starry night.

As one, the men at the table rose, but Diego stayed seated. He realized his mouth was open, so he snapped it shut, but it drifted open again. She met his eyes and her brow furrowed—his reaction confused her. It was possible she didn't know how beautiful she was, how much feminine perfection she embodied.

He should be standing—there was something about propriety that said a man stood when a lady entered a room. He jumped up, knocked over his wine goblet, and the bottle teetered on the edge. He caught it, grimaced, and set it aside. At least he was giving a good impression of drunkenness. But somehow, with Melanie standing before him like an angel, his desire to present a facade of debauchery faded.

Bradford strode forward and held out his arm. "My dear Miss Muessen! I am so pleased you could join us."

Her chin rose, but she didn't take his arm. "I came to the Chateau Renegade tonight, Mr. Bradford, because Chen had previously invited me to do so. I do not intend to be your guest. The fact that you have sentenced a man to flogging makes you a person to avoid."

Diego's mouth dropped again. For an instant, Bradford's eyes flashed. But then he smiled. "Miss Muessen, I hope to change your opinion of me, and I can assure you that I will do everything in my power to benefit the citizens of Tewa. But you must understand, though I know your feminine nature abhors any suggestion of violence, that discipline must be established and maintained. Flogging may sound violent to a woman's ears, but it is common practice among the military, and has always been most effective."

"That man threw a piece of stale bread at you, not a bomb, sir."

"Ah, but what comes next, Miss Muessen? Clearly, the ignorant citizens of Tewa aren't ready to accept the changes I offer. In anticipation of their rebellion, I have already taken steps to confiscate all weaponry. In fact, all guns in the pueblo have been seized by my guards."

Melanie's lips curled to one side. "Isn't that against the American Constitution?"

Bradford glanced at his attorney, who came forward. "The New Mexico Territory isn't subject in full to American law, Miss Muessen. As well, a pueblo that is inherently Indian has its own laws."

"If this pueblo is 'inherently Indian,' then perhaps its affairs should be governed by the Zuni who live here."

Bradford chuckled. "Women, women. They will

never understand the ways of man. But that is their charm, is it not, gentlemen? Beauty is enough to make us tolerant."

It was probably a good thing Bradford had confiscated the pueblo's guns, or Melanie Muessen would surely have found a way to shoot him. Her eyes cast lights like daggers, and her small fingers clenched into fists. Bradford took Melanie's arm and directed her to their table. "Come, my dear. We could not allow you to sit alone tonight."

She glanced at Diego as if seeking support, and he gave her a steady gaze. She seemed to take comfort in his presence as Bradford seated her to his left, opposite Diego. Bradford poured a small portion of wine into her goblet, as if pouring milk for a child. Melanie eyed it with misgivings. "What do you say, de Aguirre? Miss Muessen's loveliness outshines all our troubles, does it not?"

Diego looked into her eyes. "She has stolen my breath and my heart."

She frowned, probably annoyed at his lighthearted tone, but Diego had surprised himself with the comment. He was generally lavish in praise of women, and rarely meant the words he said, but this praise felt more honest. There were words he never said, feelings he never expressed, because though he had never really been in love before, he had seen its depth in his brother and knew its power.

Melanie adjusted her napkin and eyed him doubtfully. "You flatter me, Señor de Aguirre. I hope I have not stolen your appetite as well."

Diego fingered his goblet. He wanted her to take him seriously. And yet, tonight, it was the last thing he could hope for. "My appetite for wine remains, at least. And if Chen is preparing roast quail again, wine may be all I can take."

Chen came then from the kitchen, followed by his faux French chef and Will, who had donned a white jacket, presumably to act as waiter. Chen stood back formally as the chef directed Will in halting English. Again, smoked oysters were served, enough to drive Diego to indeed live on wine. Will managed to place the least appetizing portions of the dinner before Bradford, and spared both Diego and Melanie the oysters.

The chef sputtered with anger when Will mixed up the courses, but Will paid no attention. He placed his hand on Melanie's shoulder, fondly. "I fed your fat little pony first, miss. Got a fine meal, he did. Oats and barley and a whole lot of hay. Had it half finished before I left his stall."

Melanie smiled and seemed comforted in Will's presence. "Thank you, Will. Porticus will be grateful. And I will pay you for your troubles, of course."

"There's no need for that, miss. I like horses, and your fat little fellow is more like a pet."

"I will pay you nonetheless."

Chen nodded in agreement. "It's a fair transaction."

Bradford listened to their interchange, then

leaned forward, resting his elbows on the table. "The matter of taxes will have to be addressed soon. In order to develop Tewa as I have planned, a small element of everyone's income will need to be exchanged."

Melanie's eyes narrowed. "On second thought, Will, I will perhaps donate a photograph of your choice for your labors. I do not want my money falling into the wrong hands."

She certainly had spirit, and she was quick. She had seemed shy at first, not a woman to assert herself, but there was more to Melanie than Diego had first imagined. He held up his goblet and drained it in her honor. "I have always felt trade was a more agreeable system than the exchange of paper money—or gold. But with your interest in Spanish gold, Señor Bradford, you may not agree."

Bradford's expression held taut for a moment; maybe he guessed Diego was testing him. But a smile replaced his wariness. "Gold interests us all, doesn't it, de Aguirre? Think of how a second find could benefit this pueblo!"

"It won't be easy, señor. The kiva mine collapsed many years ago."

"I'll have my guards start excavating one of the remaining kivas, then. The gold could be hidden anywhere."

Diego still wondered if the gold was Bradford's real goal. He refilled his goblet, then addressed the strangers. "There is the matter of Miguel, the baker. Wouldn't it benefit you also to reduce his punishment, perhaps to a public apology?"

Bradford's face was set, the lines hard and unyielding. "I understand your concern, de Aguirre, much like the refinement of Miss Muessen's gentle nature. But I have found from the positions of authority I have held previously that one must deal with miscreants firmly. When handled in this way, those intent on greater rebellious acts will most often refrain."

Diego affected a casual, disinterested expression. "You've held such positions before, then?"

Bradford refilled his own goblet. "I served the Union Army as an officer during the Civil War. I promise you, there is no better training than war."

Melanie's eyes narrowed. "My father's experience proved otherwise."

Bradford smiled, a reaction that must have grated on Melanie. It certainly annoyed Diego. "Unfortunately, not all men withstand the rigors of battle equally. Some bloom—others fade and die."

Melanie frowned. "I cannot imagine a man who would 'bloom' in war."

Bradford offered a short, contrived laugh. "Women will never understand this characteristic of men. But I assure you, my reputation during the war was untarnished. As I'm sure Chen will report, when his query to the governor is answered."

Faint color tinged Chen's cheeks, but he made no response. Diego held up his goblet and swirled the wine to capture the lamplight. "I, for one, am quite satisfied with your claim, Señor Bradford. Af-

81

ter all, you couldn't have gotten this far with a scandalous background."

"I'm pleased you see reason, de Aguirre. I trust you will convince your fellow citizens of Tewa that the pueblo is in the safest hands."

Diego took a sip of wine and arched his brows. "I will do my best, señor, but as you know, I am not held in the highest esteem in Tewa. It is a shame my brother didn't bother to return with this news himself; they would have taken it so much better from Rafael."

"I'm sure he will return, in time, although as he told you in his letter, it has been his intention to remain abroad for some time to come."

Melanie looked back and forth between them, as if trying to gauge the meaning behind their words. He knew she hoped he would offer defiance, and for her sake, he wished he could overtly challenge Bradford. But now was not the time. Bradford saw no threat in Diego—it was important that illusion stay strong.

They finished their dinner with safer conversation, and Diego was unable to lure more information from Bradford. If he'd been less distracted . . . But Melanie sat opposite him, her blue eyes glittering, and he found his attention wavering from his dissection of Bradford to a more pleasing study of her face. He liked the way she ate. Not a picky female who dabbed self-consciously at her meal, she possessed a determined appetite. She considered her plate, chose what she liked, and ate it all.

Like him, she ignored the smoked oysters and con-
centrated on the crispy parts of the quail. When
Chen brought raspberry-filled pastries to the table,
Melanie selected the largest portion and ate every
bit.

Diego was charmed. Too often, women took
small bites—at least, when dining with men—always aware that they might be watched. In her
quiet, singular way, Melanie was more certain of
herself than anyone he'd ever met before. But he
couldn't lose himself in contemplation. Something
bothered him, something he didn't want to face,
but he knew the time was coming. He felt as if all
he had never been and could never hope to be was
now looming before him. Bradford was a threat—
even Rafael would have found him a formidable
opponent, and perhaps had already.

The dinner concluded, and Bradford requested
brandy, which Chen dutifully produced. Diego
hated brandy, but it wouldn't do to let Bradford
know he had any limits where alcohol was concerned. He drained his goblet of wine, rose from
the table, and took a dramatic bow. "Gentlemen . . ." He paused to adjust his eyebrows, as if
drunk. "And of course, Miss Muessen. Please excuse me from the finalities of your festivities." He
stopped and shook his head, as if those words had
tangled upon themselves.

Bradford looked up at him, still smirking. "I
hope you're not leaving us so early, de Aguirre."

"As it happens, I am. The bartender would be

hurt if I failed to pay him a visit. Perhaps I'll take a walk first." He eyed the bottle of brandy, then seized it and lifted it above his head. "But not alone."

From the corner of his eye, he saw Melanie watching him, and he couldn't fail to see her disappointment. He wanted to take her aside, to explain, but it would do neither of them any good. He couldn't start trying to win her approval, not when any connection to him would cause her pain. He bowed again. "Señors, señorita, *buenos noches,* good night."

Diego started away, but Melanie stood up, too. "If you're leaving, you can walk me to Miss Wu's inn."

Gregory Alvin rose and came around the table to her side. "I believe you could select a more . . . reliable escort, Miss Muessen. I would be pleased to see you to your room."

Diego tensed. Under no circumstances would he leave her alone with Alvin. He had the look of a womanizer, a man who expected more than a kiss from a woman. For an instant, Diego wondered if he shared those qualities. Alvin's gaze lowered to Melanie's bosom, and Diego dismissed any similarity between himself and the lawyer. As much as he admired her beauty, it was her gentle but defiant spirit that enchanted him.

Melanie cast Alvin a dark, forbidding look. She turned to Diego, took his arm before he had a chance to offer it, and edged him toward the door.

"That will not be necessary, Mr. Alvin. Señor de Aguirre has established himself as my guide, and there are matters of our itinerary that must be discussed."

She took a taut breath, then glanced back at Bradford. "I thank you for your hospitality, Mr. Bradford. I hope your good nature will extend to your unfortunate prisoner tomorrow. Good night."

Without waiting for a response, Melanie pulled Diego out the door and into the plaza outside. She stopped and released his arm as soon as the door closed behind them. She turned to face him, but Diego avoided her gaze and fiddled with his brandy bottle instead. "Well, what are you going to do?"

That seemed an oft-repeated question this night. Diego pretended not to know what she meant and offered a bewildered expression that apparently wasn't effective.

"Do not for a moment tell me that you trust that man, or believe his story about your brother." Her bright eyes dared him to lie to her, and he found he couldn't do it, not outright.

"Much remains to be seen, señorita."

"A deliberately vague response."

He hesitated. Melanie wouldn't be an easy woman to dissuade. Maybe he could distract her. He fished in his coat pocket and withdrew his napkin. She eyed it suspiciously. "You stole one of Chen's napkins?"

"I am part owner of the place. In which case, I cannot be said to have *stolen* anything." He

85

paused, exasperated. "Since you appear so fond of treats, I thought you might enjoy a second helping." He unfolded the napkin, revealing the second-largest raspberry pastry.

To Diego's surprise, Melanie's cheeks flushed pink in the lamplight, and she bit her lip hard. "I hadn't eaten all day."

"Do not apologize, señorita. Your appetite does you proud."

"My father used to say I ate like a shark in what is known by biologists as a 'feeding frenzy.' "

Diego pressed his lips together hard to keep from laughing. "A woman who enjoys the delights of life to their fullest capacity is far more appealing to a man than one who denies herself."

Melanie cringed and his heart warmed with affection. "The chef is very skilled."

"Take the pastry."

She hesitated, then did. Their fingers met, and he found himself prolonging the touch. "Thank you."

"You are beautiful, Melanie Ann Muessen. In more ways than just the sweetness of your face and the pleasant curves of your body."

He expected her blush to deepen, but instead her eyes narrowed. "I've noticed an odd thing, Señor de Aguirre. While we were dining, you seemed rather . . . tipsy. But now your words are clear, your manner precise. Somewhat presumptuous, but precise. Why is that, do you think?"

"My head clears quickly. The fresh air."

"There's more to it than that, and don't try to convince me otherwise."

"Your pastry awaits, señorita."

She eyed him critically for a while, then nodded. "Very well. You're not ready to confide in me. I understand, but know that I will be keeping a close watch on Mr. Bradford. It may be that my skills with photography will prove useful."

They started across the plaza toward Victoria's inn, but it seemed wisest to keep abreast of Melanie's schemes. "In what way could your profession help?"

She pondered this as they walked. "I'm not sure yet. Although you may not be aware of this, the field of journalism has made great use of photographs recently. If we can prove that Bradford is mistreating these people, this supposed sale might be overturned by the American government."

A determined woman. Melanie's words concerned him, for her own sake. "Señorita, it might be wisest for you to select another subject. It strikes me that Carlton Bradford stops at nothing to get what he wants."

Her eyes lit, and she stopped to face him. "Ah! So you agree with me, do you?"

He shifted his weight. "I didn't say that."

"You did, and you know it's true. You also know that your brother didn't sign that document willingly and therefore must be in danger." Diego felt cornered. Melanie leaned toward him as she spoke, and another feeling made itself known: desire. "Mr. Bradford and the people he represents are the sorts of people who dominate others, dictate the fates of everyone—if you let them. I don't know what he wants—he was too quick to declare the supposed Spanish treasure his goal—but he is a dangerous man."

She was too bright to be dissuaded. He agreed with everything she said, so his only alternative was to distract her in some way. Melanie's lips were parted in her eagerness to gain his confidence. Soft lips, warm and pink . . . kissable.

He didn't hesitate. As she waited expectantly, he stopped, set the brandy bottle on a post, and placed his hands on her shoulders. Before she could speak, he drew her close and kissed her. A sharp breath escaped her, and he brushed his lips over hers to quiet her. She trembled in his arms, shocked . . . And yet . . . With a suddenness that shocked him, too, Melanie kissed him back. Her lips parted, and she tasted his kiss, molding gently into his arms. Fire swept through Diego's veins at her unexpected passion. She kissed the way she ate, with innate sensual delight.

She popped out of his arms like a cork. "I . . . I've had too much wine!"

Diego just stared. "Too much wine? You took two sips." He had been watching her intently—both sips were accompanied by small, subtle shudders.

She shook her head to clear her senses. Her senses, he thought, could not be any more ravaged than his own. She lifted her hand and pointed her small finger at him. "You, sir, have too much . . . you are too . . ."

She was flustered, and charming. Diego smiled. "Hard to resist?"

She closed her eyes and turned her face toward the sky. "You have great conceit."

Diego stood back and bowed, his smile widening because she hadn't disagreed. "I see our mutual ardor has shaken your delicate sensibilities. I will bid you good night, for now. Enjoy your pastry, señorita. May it bring to your mind other memories, just as sweet. A soft breeze in your hair, a touch . . . a kiss . . ."

She frowned and held herself straight, as if she was trying to accentuate her height in comparison to his. "Good night, Señor de Aguirre." She paused. "Despite this event, I trust you will resume duties as my guide tomorrow."

Diego eyed his bottle of brandy. "Not too early, I hope."

"No. I will be on hand to photograph whatever Mr. Bradford attempts with that poor baker. It may be that my presence will dissuade him from actually beating the man."

"Or he'll confiscate your camera."

She pondered this. "I could hide myself."

"It probably won't be necessary. Bradford seems too sure of himself to try to stop you. He may even request that the event be photographed."

Melanie's eyes glittered as if issued a challenge,

and a welcome one. "He will be sorry he ever invited me to stay."

Diego gazed into her face, his pulse still quick from their kiss. "No man could ever be sorry for your presence."

Melanie's brow arched—she didn't seem to believe his compliments were genuine. Instead, she cast a dubious glance at his brandy. "You aren't going to drink that, are you?"

"I can think of no better use for it."

"I was under the impression you didn't like brandy."

She was certainly perceptive. Diego seized an impatient breath. "I preferred to enjoy it without Bradford's company." He didn't wait for her to poke holes in that statement. He backed away, bottle in hand, then bowed again, dramatically, then blew her a kiss. When she frowned, he winked, and she frowned still more. "*Buenos noches,* señorita. Until tomorrow."

She offered a quick, formal nod, then scurried onto the porch of Victoria's inn. She stopped and turned back slowly, her head tilted to one side as she surveyed him from the greater distance. "Good night, Señor de Aguirre. Sleep well."

Diego held up the bottle of brandy and offered a rueful smile. "With brandy as my companion, I'm sure I will."

"Give me the damned mask, and I'll need a horse—one no one will recognize."

Chen stood back and motioned Diego into his bedroom. He was still in yesterday's clothing, hadn't slept, and didn't seem surprised by Diego's request. He was already holding the mask when he answered the door. "Will has gone to fetch you a horse now. He said to meet him before dawn outside the gates, just to the north."

Diego eyed the mask as if it held all the darkest hours of his fate to come. It had been forged by ancient hands, by Anasazi craftsmen, meant to don the power of the gods on the shell of a mortal man. With their grace, that man would summon their power inside himself. He left it in Chen's hands. "How did you know I would come?"

"For the same reason Will is out finding you a horse—we know you. No matter how loathsome your life has become, how far into putridity and foulness you might sink, how disgusting your descent into debauchery, or how disreputable . . ."

"Never mind that."

"No matter *what,* we know you. Rafael knows you. You're the person to wear this mask."

"Why?"

"Because you're the least likely to be suspected."

"And how am I supposed to fight? I walk with a limp, if you remember. I haven't touched a sword in years, and I never did learn to use Rafael's *bola* with any skill. Bradford has confiscated all the guns here, and even if he hadn't, I'd be hard-pressed to come up with enough ammunition to do any damage."

"You don't have to fight an army—you just have to show Bradford that he doesn't have free rein over this pueblo. Your best bet is the sword, so use it." Chen went to a tall mahogany cabinet and pulled out Diego's old fencing sword. "Like the mask, this sword once belonged to your father. You enjoyed fencing; I know, because I still have a scar on my right shoulder from your practice sessions. You missed and struck me, but Rafael excused your poor aim."

Diego frowned. "I didn't miss."

Chen's eyes flashed. "I have always suspected that you meant to strike me!"

Diego took the sword. The hilt felt cold in his palm, but when he gripped it, it seemed to warm to him like an old friend. "I can use this from a horse, I suppose, and if I have to be on foot, I can leap around and run—maybe no one will notice the limp."

"I can tell you this, Diego, which I have never bothered to say before: When you're drunk, your lameness disappears."

Diego looked at Chen, blank. "That's not possible."

"As is much in you, your affliction resides mostly in your head."

"My thigh was shattered—do you attribute that to my imagination, too?"

"No. I simply say that when you're drunk, no trace of it remains."

"Are you suggesting I get drunk to perform as the Renegade?"

Chen grimaced. "Not at all! I'm just telling you that, for a short space of time at least, you should be able to walk without a limp. Accept that it's a product of your twisted, unreasonable thinking and you will be able to defeat it, and throw off anyone who suspects your identity."

"If you're right, we're in luck."

"The rest of the time, you will need to keep up the guise of drunkenness." Chen paused. "That may be difficult, considering your new interest."

"What 'new interest'?"

Chen slanted one eyebrow. "It has not escaped me that the estimation of Miss Melanie Muessen warrants your attention."

"She's a beautiful woman, with a good heart, and she's interesting. Nothing more than that."

"You couldn't take your eyes off her at dinner."

"She did look good tonight."

"You looked like a helpless fawn."

"A buck." Diego paused. "I don't think she's pleased with me."

"And for now, that serves you well. I'll help you. Will, too. But you can't allow anyone else to suspect—not until we know what Bradford is up to."

"I know that, and I would do nothing to place her in danger." He stopped to consider the best course for Melanie. "It would seem wisest for her to move on, to head off to Egypt."

"It might be, but I doubt she will go."

93

"Why not?"

"Because she was looking at you like a fawn, too."

The hour before dawn in Tewa was cold, especially when the wind blew, summer or not. Chen stood huddled in a long coat, while Diego fiddled with the cumbersome black cape Rafael had once worn on his rides. "This damned thing doesn't provide much warmth. Where in hell is Will? Did he travel to Spain to find an Andulasian?"

"He'll be here. He said he knew the perfect horse."

"I hope he doesn't get Frank. That fellow is old, and everyone will recognize him as Rafael's."

"I advised him that Frank was a poor choice, but Will said he had something better in mind."

They waited a while longer in silence. As the first light of dawn pierced the eastern horizon, the sound of hoof falls rose, and Will appeared out of the last shadows of night. He was riding his old stout pinto, and leading behind it . . . the renegade black mustang.

Diego's mouth dropped as they approached. Will dismounted, patted the horse's powerful neck, and smiled pleasantly, as if he'd bought a gentle gelding at auction. "What do you think of him?"

Diego couldn't move. "How did you catch him? He's wild as an elk, and twice as fast."

Will shrugged. "I've made friends with him before tonight, Diego." He spoke as if Diego were an idiot not to have guessed this fact. "I've been be-friending him, giving him carrots—he likes apples and any kind of sweets you can give him, by the way—for maybe a year now. I've been on his back a few times—didn't like the saddle much at first, so I used an Indian blanket instead. You and Señor de Aguirre used to ride Indian-style—it shouldn't be a problem. I just used a rope bit, too, but it works fine. Use a gentle hand—he doesn't need much of a touch."

"You've *trained* him already? Why haven't you claimed him yourself?"

Will seemed surprised. "I knew what I was do-ing, Diego. I knew he needed training, and nobody ought to be finding out."

Diego looked at Chen, who appeared equally mystified. "Did you know about this?" How long had his two friends been planning to corner him into becoming the Renegade, anyway? Maybe Bradford's ascension to power was a ruse to force him into a role he didn't want, to save him from debauchery.

Chen shook his head. "This one Will did on his own. I'm impressed, though."

Will smiled. "I knew you'd be needing him, Di-ego. He's a lot like you. Stubborn, wild, reckless—he'll take any jump before him, but he won't chal-lenge Frank. And I'm thinking Frank's just about ready to head back to the stable, retire from it all. Mares, they're a hard lot to keep in line, from what I've seen."

Diego smiled, too. "That much is certain."

"When Bradford showed up, I knew he meant trouble. He was patient about it, sure, and so I figured I had time. Worked out real good, didn't it?"

Despite himself, Diego was moved. Will, who knew people because he carried no illusions or pretense, saw things as they were. For reasons Diego couldn't guess, Will had faith in him. Diego went to the horse and held out his hand. He softened his naturally abrupt motion, then reached into his pocket and offered the horse a sugar block. Considering how many of the precious treats he'd slipped to Porticus when Melanie wasn't looking, it was lucky he had any left.

The horse sniffed it, assessed Diego, and then took the offering. Will patted his neck again, then stepped back. "He can be a little skittish, but he's fast and strong. Jumps like a deer, too. Take him out, get used to him, and then get back here before poor Miguel gets whipped."

"I don't know what to say."

Will looked confused. " 'Thank you' is good."

Chen grinned. "You asked."

Diego smiled and touched Will's shoulder. "Thank you, my friend. I don't know that I deserve such friendship as you both have given me, but I will try to honor your faith, for my brother's sake."

Chen stepped forward and held out the mask. Diego knew he should take it—he had no choice— but his blood moved like ice. Chen didn't speak, nor try again to pressure him, and Will waited quietly.

Diego closed his eyes and remembered helping his brother, years ago, as he prepared for his heroic rides. He had never once imagined himself in this role. Always, it was be Rafael riding to save others, to defend their father's land. Diego was nothing more than the Renegade's younger brother.

He took the mask from Chen, placed it over his face, and tied it around his head. For a moment, he stood still as stone, and Chen stood with Will, silent like ghosts in the night. Neither spoke. They both knew what this moment meant to him.

He hadn't known, not fully, what it would do to him to wear this mask. In it, he felt himself changing, as if who and what he was and had been for all his life faded, leaving room for some other man, an ancient man, to fill his being. Through the mask's eyes, he looked out at the first traces of morning and knew he would ride into a day he didn't want, disguised as a man he could never be.

His heart quailed at the thought; *I can't do this.* He closed his eyes, intending only to blot out the task before him. Instead, a small face emerged in his mind, her eyes bright as she challenged Carlton Bradford. Melanie had no reason to defend Tewa Pueblo, no reason to care for its people, and certainly would have been safer not involving herself in its disputes. She cared, because she grasped the deeper meaning of the pueblo's existence, the community Diego's father had begun and Rafael had built.

It mattered to him, too. He would never have chosen to be the pueblo's defender; he wasn't particularly well equipped to do so. But if one delicate, solitary woman cared enough to put herself in danger, he could ride this day.

He looked into the western mountains, and a cool wind blew in his face. The same wind had swirled around his ancestors, and it would carry him now. He took the black horse's reins and mounted. The horse stomped and reared to be away, but Diego held him in check. He didn't expect the wildfire of a hero's heart in his veins—he was facing the reality that he wasn't the right man for the disguise. But he knew what he had to do.

"I will ride in your shadow, my brother, but I will ride. And with your shadow behind me, may I do half the good you have done, and save this land for your return."

The night waned, and morning dawned in the east. Locked inside the schoolhouse turned into a jail, an angry, fat baker waited for a sentence he didn't deserve, just so that Bradford might exert control by fear over those who dared remain in Tewa. Miguel had been one of the loudest to issue disgust over Diego's long fall from grace—he had doubled his prices for any purchase Diego made, and once had tried to convince Rafael to force Diego into the Mexican army.

# The Renegade's Heart

For Miguel, Diego would do the thing he dreaded most, the thing he had for so long vowed he would never attempt. He would become the Renegade.

# Chapter Four

Melanie set up her camera in the northeast corner of the plaza, not far from Victoria's inn. At times, she regretted not having acquired one of the newer models, a smaller box camera with the flexible film that had recently become available, but she had progressed enough to use dry plates rather than the old-fashioned wet plates that required far more equipment. Still, preparation for the perfect shot was time-consuming, especially since she wasn't sure where Bradford intended to position the baker.

The pueblo's citizens already filled the plaza, but though she expected outrage, they remained silent, stoic in the cool morning light. Bradford's guards, already unwelcome to the local inhabitants, stood around the former schoolhouse, waiting for their leader's instructions. A cross-rail had been set up not far from Bradford's podium, presumably to serve as the site of Miguel's flogging.

Melanie hadn't seen Bradford, and Diego hadn't appeared yet, either. She found herself hoping that Diego had somehow managed to talk Bradford out of his violent show of power.

Chen came out to stand by the front door of his inn, but Will was nowhere in sight. Victoria joined Melanie, quietly assessed her camera and equipment, then shook her head when the guards turned an old woman aside. "That was Miguel's wife. They haven't let her visit him. You would think he had committed a great crime by the way they are acting."

Melanie nodded. "It is a show of power and nothing more. I cannot believe Bradford will go through with it."

Victoria drew a long breath. "I came here because Tewa Pueblo offered a freedom I hadn't found anywhere else. Here, a person's past didn't matter. Not where you came from, or anything but what dreams you held. Rafael de Aguirre was the first person to welcome me, and his wife arranged for my purchase of the inn. I saw people of all kinds living here, children of all races playing. But now . . . It seems that a place that offers freedom and acceptance will always draw the attention of men who consider those things threats."

Victoria sounded wistful, as if though she had held high hopes, freedom's demise was nothing she didn't expect. Melanie patted her arm. "I don't believe such a thing can truly be destroyed. It is only tested."

"I hope you are right." The guards brought out Miguel, and Victoria shuddered. "I can't be a witness to this." She moved to return to her inn but noticed Chen. Melanie watched as Victoria braced herself. "Then again, as a citizen of this pueblo, I must remain a presence."

Victoria's words strengthened Melanie's own resolve. She adjusted the camera's angle to work better with the morning sun, then waited. Carlton Bradford appeared at the door of the schoolhouse and stretched, a gesture clearly performed for its effect on his audience. Melanie frowned. "He appears nonchalant in the extreme. I wonder how long he rehearsed that effect in front of his mirror before presenting the act to us."

Victoria huffed. "Mr. Bradford began visiting this pueblo shortly before Rafael left. From the first, I believed he had some ulterior motive for his visits. His manner toward Rafael was . . . watchful."

"I'm sure he has been plotting his method of seizing this pueblo for a long while. He seems an orderly, thorough man."

Victoria tapped her lip with her finger. "In general, I approve of methodical people, those who plan ahead, know what they want, and take action to get it."

Melanie cleared her throat. "Like Chen?"

Victoria's eyes narrowed. "The man of whom you speak does, of course, have some of those qualities, which in general are somewhat admirable: foresight, dedication, a higher purpose. However, my rival in innkeeping has proven himself difficult and stubborn in many other capacities."

Melanie suppressed a smile. "But I do feel Chen has a spiritual depth that Mr. Bradford lacks, and also that beneath his quest for success is a genuine desire to help others."

Victoria's lip curled to one side, as if she resisted agreeing with Melanie's assessment. "Though Mr. Bradford expressed a desire to serve this pueblo, I do not believe it enters at all into his motivation."

"No." Melanie paused. "I wonder what the people who hired him want."

Victoria sighed. "Perhaps he invented these benefactors to cover his own interest."

"It's possible, but Mr. Bradford doesn't seem that imaginative to me, not the sort to think this up on his own."

Bradford stepped away from the door, and four guards led Miguel from the schoolhouse jail. Melanie frowned. "Does it really take four large men to drag that poor baker to his fate?"

Victoria shook her head. "Miguel is stubborn as well as fat, and his opinions are strong."

"I thought he was harsh where Señor de Aguirre was concerned."

Victoria eyed her doubtfully. "Do you mean Diego?"

"Yes."

Victoria smiled. "I don't believe I've ever heard him called that before. 'Señor de Aguirre' always seems to refer to Rafael. Diego is more often called by . . . less fortunate titles."

Melanie's brow furrowed. "I do not understand why the people of this pueblo resent him so. Perhaps he has a few less than admirable qualities, and perhaps he hasn't taken after his heroic brother, but he seems a good person, agreeable in nature. He's certainly intelligent and witty."

"And incredibly handsome."

Melanie found herself blushing, so she bent to fiddle with her camera. "I suppose he is good-looking."

"I've often thought that contributed to people's opinion of him. He is too pleasant, too easy to like, too handsome. His dalliances with numerous young women also contribute to their anger." Victoria's voice trailed while Melanie pretended not to care. Had it? Though she had tried to keep the matter in perspective, Diego's teasing, passionate kiss had stirred her senses, and kept him in her thoughts constantly since the previous night. She was a woman, who kept most often to herself. She never attempted to garner male attention—flirting was beyond her. But Diego made her feel feminine and attractive. Apparently, he shared that gift with many women.

Melanie adjusted the camera's angle again, losing the good shot she had found before. She sputtered in agitation, more at herself for her wayward imagination than for her mistake. "I suppose he is not to be taken seriously."

She felt Victoria watching her and suspected the innkeeper guessed her foolish attraction for a man who clearly had terrorized the hearts of pueblo women for years. "I would not say that, exactly. I would advise a woman—any woman—who finds his attention on her to keep herself wary, to wait until he comes forward in a genuine way."

Melanie straightened. "Don't you think he's genuine?"

Victoria pondered this while Melanie waited. Like Chen, Victoria seemed to possess powerful insight and depth. "He is genuine to a certain degree. He presents himself as he believes himself to be—that is true. The heart he offers is light, and he pretends nothing else. Though he has disappointed several women, he never offered them anything but a dalliance with a handsome young rogue. Wait until he offers you the real man."

"He won't be offering me anything."

Victoria's brow angled. "Hasn't he already?" Melanie's blush spread down her neck and up to her hairline. Victoria smiled and touched her shoulder. "Forgive me. I was concerned that you return to the inn safely last night, and I looked out the window a few times." She paused, allowing the obvious and horrific meaning to dawn on Melanie. Victoria had seen their kiss.

Melanie uttered a small, shuddering groan and

turned her face to the sky. "I am not normally so foolish."

"We all have a foolish side, don't we?"

"Do you?"

Victoria looked idly around the plaza, but her gaze skipped over Chen. "Oh, I have toyed with foolish impulses, foolish dreams. It is wiser to keep fixed on one's duty, and those tangible things in life one desires."

Good advice. Next time Diego de Aguirre smiled at her, she would keep it in mind and ignore him. "My father was a photographer—he did great work during the war, and I have always aspired to follow in his footsteps."

Bradford made his way to the new podium and took his place, but he waited to speak until the crowd hushed. "As you are all aware, I have reserved this time today for the punishment of a miscreant who yesterday attempted assault and issued a serious threat against my life. This behavior will not be tolerated, and it is to be hoped that after his punishment is awarded, no one will care to repeat his act."

Bradford nodded at the guards, and they hauled Miguel to the cross rails. The fat baker struggled, and several women began weeping. Melanie focused her camera and prepared for her shot. Her heart beat in strange, hard jerks, and suddenly she realized she must be sharing her kindhearted German father's reaction when he first set up his equipment on a bloody field of battle.

*I can do this.* Melanie loved her art—she knew what she was doing, and she felt confident. After the war, her father had given up any meaningful work, but his love of photography had been infectious, and she had always dreamed of carrying on where he left off. Now was her chance to do something meaningful, something to benefit others through her craft.

Where was Diego? He might be lighthearted, but she couldn't believe he would stand by and let the baker suffer this way. When he was near, she felt stronger. Maybe together . . . She remembered Victoria's words and stopped herself.

The guards bound Miguel to the cross rails, and one produced a long riding crop. Bradford faced Miguel. "This is your chance to recant your defiant and impulsive attack, baker. Do so and your punishment will go easier."

The baker scrunched his round face and spat. "Curse you, Bradford! May you rot in hell!"

It seemed to Melanie that Bradford both expected and welcomed the baker's response. He motioned to a guard, who took position to begin flogging the prisoner.

The wind seemed to rise in the west and swirl through the plaza. Dust rose, and the sound of a horse galloping echoed between the pueblo walls. The crowd stirred as if a ghost had come down from the mountains. Though Melanie wasn't sure what it was, her own heart stirred with hope.

As if by the wind's own force, the pueblo gates

swung open. Melanie watched in amazement as a great black horse galloped into the plaza. His rider wore a black, hooded cape...and an Indian mask. Her breath caught as the horse stopped and reared, replicating the figure on Chen's hotel sign.

The crowd erupted in wild cries of joy. Melanie heard Rafael's name, and the title, *Renegade*. The pueblo citizens parted for their mythic leader, making a path that led to the bound baker. The guards rushed for their guns, but they were unprepared for his approach. Bradford looked shocked. Apparently, the Renegade was an unexpected foe.

The Renegade urged his horse into the crowd—the animal seemed nervous, as if unused to the task. Melanie's eyes widened as she got a clearer view and recognized the wild black mustang she had seen with Diego. Her heart raced in excitement. Victoria tapped her shoulder fiercely, but Melanie couldn't take her eyes from the Renegade. "What?"

"Take his picture!"

Melanie responded to Victoria's hissed command, but her hands were shaking as she adjusted the camera to focus on the man in black. He noticed her, and for a brief instant slowed his horse. Despite his mask, she knew he was smiling. He twitched his horse's reins, and it reared slightly off the ground, then held the position. She took the photograph, then reloaded the plate.

As if satisfied that she had gotten the shot, the Renegade moved forward through the crowd. He had no weapon that Melanie could see—no three-pronged whip as Rafael had used and as Chen had on display in his hotel. Bradford held up his hand, but his guards aimed their weapons. "Hold your fire until we learn what this prankster has in mind."

The Renegade halted his horse and faced Bradford's podium. "The west wind blows unexpected, does it not?" His voice was strangely accented—it sounded Spanish, but with an Indian inflection Melanie hadn't heard before. She didn't recognize the sound—it was deep and quiet, but whoever he was, the man would surely have altered his voice lest he be recognized.

It didn't matter. She had known him from the moment he rode through the gates. Diego de Aguirre had followed his brother's path and become the hero she had guessed he could be.

Bradford sneered. "So the legendary Renegade makes an appearance? It should do well for Chen's hotel, but it is soon yet to add another chapter to his brochure. What brings you here?"

"I come for this, Señor Bradford. You say this pueblo belongs to you. It does not, nor to anyone here. It belongs to me, and I am its spirit come to life. When you challenge me, I will be here. When you threaten one of mine, I will be here. When you fight me, I will defeat you." As he spoke, he drew a sword. It looked old, as if crafted from another time. "I come from the ancestors of the Zuni, and from the Spaniards, too. I am Chinese and white,

109

Mexican and Indian. Let this man go free and I will give you peace."

Bradford laughed. "An interesting claim. This man is my prisoner, and by threatening me, you will become the next. You think to obscure your identity—you have failed. We all know you . . ." Bradford paused, and Melanie's heart held. Was it as obvious to everyone as it was to her? "Diego de Aguirre, in a sorry attempt to recapture your brother's dramatic glory. I hadn't thought you capable, but apparently a night with a bottle gives you more courage, and less sense, than I had imagined possible."

Now the Renegade laughed. "As for my identity, I am insulted." He twirled the sword, and it caught the morning light. For an instant, he hesitated, and Melanie knew as if she saw into his mind that he was afraid—not of Bradford, but of some other challenge. He doubted. The Renegade leapt from his horse and bounded up the podium, taking Bradford off guard. With the skilled hands of a master, he split the buttons on Bradford's jacket, then pinned the sword tip to his throat. "Order your men to release the baker. Now."

The voice was cold and hard, heavily accented. This time, Melanie couldn't imagine Diego's voice in the Renegade's. Bradford's face reddened with anger and fear. A trickle of blood emerged as the sword pierced his flesh. Melanie forced herself to man her camera and take the shot. "Release the baker or die."

Bradford's eyes darted to the side, his fear palpable. His voice came as a croak. "Do it!"

The guards untied Miguel, who stepped aside, his face aglow, as if an angel had appeared. "Bless you. *Rafael.*"

It was like the baker to thank Rafael when it was Diego who had saved him. Melanie frowned. But the Renegade didn't move or release Bradford. "I will not tolerate this kind of action against my people, señor. Know that if you try again, my reaction will be swifter than today, and more deadly. Whatever you do against one of my people, I will return upon you, but double."

The Renegade backed away from Bradford, who jumped down from the podium, waving frantically at his guards. "Shoot him! You fools! Arm yourselves!"

The guards scrambled to retrieve the guns they hadn't expected to need against the baker, but the Renegade was quicker. Before one rifle was aimed, he had knocked it aside, then spun to fight another. He disarmed and injured several guards, then bounded back to his horse, leapt astride, and spun away.

A deafening cheer arose around the plaza, hats were thrown, people wept in joy at the Renegade's return. Melanie's own eyes filled with tears when he stopped at the gate to wave to them. He saw her again, and he placed his hand to his mask, then bowed slightly. He couldn't imagine that she didn't know who he was, so she smiled.

A guard fired his gun, but the shot went wild. The Renegade's black horse reared, and the Renegade called to his people. "I am never far. I am within you. And I will return like the wind when you need me."

With that, he galloped away, thundering into the west with the wind circling him, dust coiling in his wake. The horse disappeared along the winding path Melanie had ridden with Diego, and though the guards raced for their horses in an attempt to pursue him, she knew they would never catch him now.

The plaza erupted in wild excitement. Bradford shouted for calm and again seized control of the podium. When it was quiet enough for him to be heard, he spoke. "Diego de Aguirre will be shot on sight if he dares return here."

Someone laughed, and to everyone's surprise, it was Chen. Victoria clasped her hand over her eyes. "He has lost his mind. And he will be considered an accomplice because he is Diego's friend."

Chen walked to the podium, unconcerned. Melanie hoped they had thought out this plan better than it seemed. Bradford glared as the Chinese man climbed the steps and joined him on the podium. "Chen, you are too well acquainted with de Aguirre to be assumed innocent."

Chen was still smiling. "That is true, Mr. Bradford, but if you consider the rider we have just seen to be Diego, you are woefully mistaken."

"I am no fool, Chen. It is no hardship for de

Aguirre to mimic his brother—to wear his mask, his cape."

"Maybe, but it would seem another man has taken that task upon himself and not Diego."

"His voice may have been altered, but that is nothing de Aguirre couldn't do."

"Then consider this, Mr. Bradford." Chen sounded confident, though Melanie had no idea why—she certainly wasn't convinced. "As everyone in this pueblo knows, Diego de Aguirre walks with a decided limp. He was lamed as a boy when the mine collapsed. Many here remember that day and will attest to the fact that Diego's leg was crushed by a rock. The Renegade we saw here today moved with no lameness at all."

Miguel clapped his pudgy hands. "I knew it! Rafael has returned to us!"

Bradford's eyes remained narrowed—he must have known Rafael couldn't have returned, but Chen's claim apparently resonated with him. "I have seen de Aguirre limp, but that might be a ruse."

"One practiced for ten years? That seems foresighted for a man who has spent more time practicing with a bottle than a sword."

Diego did limp—Melanie had noticed it herself. But she felt it was Diego—the way he posed, however briefly, for her camera and nodded to her when he left. If he hadn't worn a mask, she would have sworn he had winked.

Bradford seemed less certain. "Whoever it was,

he will be captured and brought to justice." He paused. "It may be that I was . . . hasty in arranging the baker's punishment, however, and as a sign of my goodwill, I will reduce the sentence and let him go free, this time only."

So Diego's scheme had worked. The Renegade had frightened Bradford enough to keep him from beating an innocent man. But how long would that last? For now, Melanie was content. She had several dramatic shots, more than she had dreamed when she came to Tewa. How Diego would explain his absence from the pueblo she wasn't sure, but he would undoubtedly have some kind of alibi. Perhaps he would claim to have been in Santa Fe.

A loud groan and a thump distracted everyone. Melanie turned. It came from beneath the saloon, which was situated behind the podium. Melanie stared in astonishment as a dirty, disheveled figure crawled from beneath the porch, rolled a few feet, and then stood up. A collective gasp, followed by several disgusted sighs, arose as Diego brushed back a lock of black hair and blinked.

Bradford seized a pistol from one of his guards and strode toward Diego, but he paid no attention. He cleared his throat and winced at the morning sun, then held up an empty bottle of brandy. He eyed the crowd and grimaced. "Could you all keep it down a bit? I have a damned powerful headache this morning."

Bradford stopped, uncertain, and assessed his assumed foe. "What in hell were you doing under the tavern, de Aguirre?"

Diego leaned his head back, his eyes closed. "I was enjoying the peace and quiet of the earth's embrace—it being the only thing second to a woman's."

A few people laughed, but more issued disgusted comments. Melanie just stood, astonished beyond words. *It can't be.* Her eyes narrowed. Diego de Aguirre was smarter—and quicker—than she'd imagined.

Diego looked around, confused. "What's going on around here? Gunshots, shouting. What next? A cannon blast?"

Bradford's jaw formed an unyielding square. "As it happens, your local legend paid us a visit—following in your brother's esteemed footsteps. Some among us considered that it might be you in the disguise."

Diego scratched his head and yawned. "Another time, perhaps. This morning . . . I could use some coffee. Chen, if you please."

He started away, but Bradford grabbed his shoulder. Diego turned back, bemused. "It would not be wise to threaten me, de Aguirre."

"I wouldn't think of it, Señor Bradford. Would you care to join us for coffee? It appears you've had a difficult morning yourself."

Diego's light tone had the desired effect on Bradford; Melanie could see him relax as he turned his attention elsewhere. "I have more important matters to handle, de Aguirre. Someone has decided to resurrect the Tewa Renegade—it is my job to see that his next ride is his last."

"Well, good luck to you, señor. The whole thing was disruptive, and a good night's sleep was lost. Chen . . ."

Melanie stared as Diego went into the Chateau Renegade with Chen. The Tewa people returned to their daily tasks, bustling with conversation about the Renegade's return. Victoria stood quietly beside her, then touched her arm. "You thought it was him, didn't you?"

Melanie didn't answer at once. "I still do." She glanced at Victoria and saw compassion. "Don't you think it's possible?"

"Not really. Oh, I would imagine Diego had some hand in it, and Chen, too. But I would guess our new Renegade is someone else entirely, perhaps someone from Tesuque Pueblo—Rafael has many friends, all of whom would want to help him, and who are more likely than Diego to assume his disguise." Victoria paused. "As well, I noticed right away that the Renegade wasn't lame."

Melanie pinned her gaze on the Chateau's closed door. "Perhaps I am foolish to think him capable of such heroism. One day I will see the man behind the mask. But if it's Diego de Aguirre's face I find, I, for one, will not be surprised."

Melanie gathered up her photographic equipment, then realized it was still morning. The Renegade's arrival had thrown off her planned schedule. As exciting as it had been, her enthusiasm turned to her own craft once again. Whether or not he was the new Renegade, Diego was an adept guide. His charm, quick wit, and good looks had to be considered as points in his favor, but Melanie found herself wishing she had selected a less disturbing guide, such as Will. Chen, she supposed, would have charged too much for the favor.

Melanie eyed the Chateau Renegade. *He might as well make himself useful.* She gathered her gear, then marched over to Chen's hotel, ignored Bradford's attorney as he held the door for her, and went inside. She found Diego seated with Chen while Will moved around the restaurant, pouring coffee and drinking it. Despite his demand for the drink, Diego's mug sat steaming—and untouched.

They seemed to be in conversation, but it stopped immediately when they noticed Melanie. She frowned. "Don't let me disturb you."

Chen rose and bowed, but Diego groaned and rubbed his forehead. "Must you talk so loud, señorita? My head . . ."

Her sympathy proved nonexistent. "Your head would clear faster if you drank a large quantity of water—and removed yourself to the open air."

His lips twitched at her abrupt manner. "Would it?"

"Such would be the case—and you have promised to escort me to various spots of interest so that I might photograph them."

117

"Now?"

"That was your promise."

Diego sighed miserably, groaned, then stood up. "You have no understanding of my condition this morning."

"I have too much."

His dark eyes looked bright, although he was undeniably dirty from his second night beneath the saloon floor and he did look tired. "My memory of last night is somewhat foggy, but I could have sworn you took part in the events. I can almost recall walking you back to Victoria's inn. Almost, I recall . . ."

Melanie's cheeks flushed hot and pink, and she took a fierce step toward him. Before she realized it, her fists clenched. "Don't you dare!"

He smiled, satisfied. "Perhaps it was a dream."

"It was." She wanted to hit him. Strange, because in all her life, she'd never considered violence before.

He managed to look as if he was winking without actually doing so. "A sweet dream."

She closed her eyes to refrain from hurting him. "Are you going to serve as my guide or not?"

He folded his arms over his chest, which she couldn't help noticing was broad and strong. "Where would you like to go today? Perhaps a quick jaunt into Santa Fe? Or maybe a bit farther—a ride to California?"

"I would like to visit your grandfather's pueblo. You said it was close."

"Two miles."

"Can your head tolerate that agony?"

"I suppose so." Diego seemed to be considering something, and he stole a quick glance at Chen, who nodded. "I haven't seen the old fellow in a few weeks—it would be good to pay him a visit, have a chat." He paused. "Very well, I'll take you. But I warn you, señorita, my grandfather is considered by most to be a cantankerous old devil, and he generally resents white people. He probably won't like you much."

Melanie pulled on her gloves and adjusted her hair, which she had bound with a ribbon behind her head. She felt professional and distant, the exact manner she hoped to maintain with Diego. "I don't expect to like him either. I just want to take his picture."

"Come to think of it, you'll get on just fine. You're two of a kind."

Diego took a dutiful sip of coffee, which Melanie felt he had done to delay them and to irritate her, then headed for the door. She hesitated. "Don't you feel the need to wash before visiting your grandfather?"

He eyed her doubtfully. "Why?"

She paused. "Don't you care what he thinks of you?"

He gave a faint smile. "Not much, no."

*Or what anyone thinks.* Melanie couldn't muster any form of condemnation. She admired his independent nature, his lack of care for winning over the opinions of others. "I suppose he's used to you this way."

"By now, señorita, most people around here are."

"I've seen that." They knew what to expect of him, what he would give—and what he wouldn't. She should accept it now and ask nothing, and then she might enjoy him for what and who he was.

Diego studied Melanie's face for a while in silence, perhaps wondering what she was thinking. He gazed up at the elaborately carved ceiling, thoughtful. "On the other hand, it might be pleasant to . . . 'freshen up,' as they say, before a long day of labor. Half a moment, señorita."

He left the dining room, catching Melanie off guard. "Where is he going?"

Chen looked at her and smiled. "It seems my friend cares what someone thinks, anyway."

When Diego returned, his face was clean, his hair had been brushed carefully, and he had put on a new shirt. He carried a deliberate air of nonchalance, but Melanie suspected he was waiting for her reaction.

She almost wished he'd stayed dirty. Diego de Aguirre "freshened up" well. Too well. His wavy black hair gleamed, and he had left his shirt open enough for her to see his firm flesh beneath it. He hadn't shaved, but the slight growth of beard served to make him seem devastatingly masculine. "You look . . . much better." His brown eyes glittered with satisfaction. He wormed compliments out of her, then would undoubtedly reference her words for the rest of the day. "At least I won't have to ride downwind of you now."

Will chuckled, but Diego's mood wasn't altered by her slight. "You can ride beside me to your heart's content. How fortunate . . . for us both." He smiled, charming, and with deliberate attention to dimples. Melanie adjusted her sleeve idly, then headed for the door. It would be best to ignore his attempts to rattle her, but it wouldn't be easy.

Diego followed her from the inn, and Will brought their horses, and Porticus as well. Diego seemed preoccupied as they mounted and started off. They rode past Miguel the baker as he held an enthusiastic conversation with three women, all of whom bore especially large loaves of bread. They ignored Diego, but Miguel noticed Melanie and waved.

"Did you photograph the Renegade's return, Miss Muessen?"

Melanie brought her mare to a halt, surprised that the people of Tewa already knew her by name. "I did, yes. I believe it will be a good picture."

A tall, thin woman nodded, excited. "I hope you caught the moment when his horse reared. As glorious as Señor de Aguirre always was, our new hero has the more impressive mount. Black! And so powerful. Many have speculated that he has truly taken possession of the wind—Rafael de Aguirre is well known to have had special gifts, as you may have heard. We believe our new hero has tamed the renegade mustang."

"It looked like the same horse to me, too." Melanie cast a quick glance at Diego, who looked bored, disinterested, and very cynical. "Who do you think he was?"

The woman placed her hand over her heart. "Oh, miss—I wouldn't dare say, but you must understand this: When a mortal man puts on the mask of the ancestors, he shares the souls of the gods."

Diego rolled his eyes. "Can we move on, señorita? The day is waning, and I have plans for this evening."

The tall woman frowned in disgust. "A date with the bottle, no doubt. If nothing else, it is a blessing your brother wasn't here to see another man ride in his shadow, when it is you he dreamed would follow his path."

Melanie felt stung on Diego's behalf, but he appeared unaffected, or maybe he was accustomed to their disparaging remarks. Diego didn't respond to the woman, but Melanie couldn't help herself. "Every man has a different path to follow. This new renegade has his own challenges, and he must face them in his own way."

The woman snorted, then turned back to the baker's table. "One thing is certain—the Renegade didn't spend his night beneath the saloon."

Melanie urged her horse forward. Diego whistled an uneven tune as they rode through the pueblo gates. Diego glanced at her as they rode. "So, what did you think of him?"

She knew exactly who he meant, and why he was asking, but she affected an innocent expression. "Miguel?"

"The new Renegade. I take it you photographed his daring rescue of our fat baker? Since I was . . . indisposed at the time, I wouldn't mind seeing the image you recorded."

*Naturally.* "It wouldn't bother you?"

His brow furrowed. "No. Why should it?"

"I would think it a sensitive subject."

"Why?

"This new Renegade has taken your brother's disguise—which some might say was rightfully yours."

Diego didn't flinch or even blink. "Actually, it was our father's costume first."

"Truly? He was a vigilante, too?"

"An actor. He staged theatrical productions even before he'd completed restoring Tewa—he liked costumes, and clothing himself as the various gods. My grandfather was offended, of course. But Rafael says the old fellow never missed a performance. He criticized my father's interpretation of Zuni myths, but it sounds more like teaching than he'd ever let on."

"Your father must have been a very interesting man."

"Some said crazy."

Melanie nodded. "Dramatic. A true artist." She

paused. "The new Renegade had a dramatic bent, too."

"Did he?"

"He stopped to pose."

Diego didn't comment.

"He appeared tall, and strong of build."

Diego's expression remained unreadable, like a mask. "You noticed him as a man, then?"

"Not at all." Melanie's cheeks felt hot. "As an artist myself."

"Ah. What else caught your *artistic* interest?"

"His hair was covered, he wore black gloves—he was careful to hide his identity."

"That makes sense, given that his life would be forfeit if Bradford learned who he was."

"Yes. His voice was also disguised. I detected several accents, none of which seemed entirely authentic."

"Of course, you aren't familiar with the various dialects here."

"I know his voice was faked."

"You are a clever woman."

She waited until he looked at her again. He looked so innocent and so handsome, playfulness mixed with something else, something she had never encountered before. His gaze flicked to her mouth—a dangerous sensuality lay beneath his light manner, a reason to believe there was more hidden in Diego de Aguirre than even he knew.

"I thought he was you, you know."

He didn't seem surprised, though she had hoped

to take him off guard. "Did you? Why?"

The noon sun touched his warm brown skin as if seeking out its unwilling heir. "Because he was dangerous, too."

Diego laughed. "Ah, señorita, where would you ever get the idea I'm dangerous?"

"Señor de Aguirre, where would I ever get the idea you weren't?"

# Chapter Five

He would have to be on his guard around Miss Melanie Muessen. As they rode toward the Tesuque Zuni Pueblo, Diego decided she was definitely prying—though she claimed to have accepted the evidence proving he couldn't have been the Renegade, he saw doubt in her eyes. More than that, she wanted to believe him capable of heroism.

He was tired, and he was confused himself. He wasn't at his best in concealing himself from Melanie. Despite himself, he had enjoyed the adulation, and he had loved the thrill of it, challenging Bradford, seeing the fear in his enemy's eyes and knowing he had caused it. Then he had ridden out through the pueblo gates, from the place he had lived all his life, and wondered who he was.

He knew Melanie, and he knew why she wanted to see more in him than actually existed. He had seen enough women swooning over his good looks and charm to recognize infatuations. Worse still, Melanie wasn't a woman given to easy infatuation. He knew, because he had known her from the moment they met, that her heart was true and deep, and once given, its keeper would hold its treasure for all time.

He had to stop her before it was too late. Melanie deserved better. She deserved a hero, a man like . . . the Renegade. When he wore the mask, he could imagine being a hero—when he had ridden into the plaza, he had seen her, standing there looking feminine and small, vulnerable, and he had imagined whisking her onto his horse's back, carrying her away. . . .

It was he who had been carried away. The whole thing had felt unreal, as if some force had taken over his body. He had remembered to alter his voice—maybe not well enough, according to Melanie, but no one would recognize him. But when he confronted Bradford, it had been as if another man spoke through his voice, a stronger man, a noble man. Passion had burned in his veins—no wonder he imagined carrying Melanie Muessen away.

"I've been thinking . . ." Melanie interrupted him. Diego breathed a muted sigh of relief. He had been losing control of his thought.

"Yes, señorita? What occupies your thoughts?

Dangerous heroes, or exotic settings to charm your camera? Or . . . perhaps both?"

She frowned, but her aggravation lacked real feeling or depth. She liked him, and she was getting used to his teasing. "As a matter of fact, I was thinking of your brother's predicament. I assume you believe he's still alive?"

*Rafael* . . . "I know that he is."

"I would tend to agree with you. The question is, where is he and what does Bradford intend to do with him?"

"I have no idea."

Melanie tapped her lip with her index finger, but Diego noticed that the smallest finger held itself slightly out and apart from the others. He smiled. "That's a curious little finger."

She glanced down. "My pinky?"

"It pops out and curves—very delicate, and a little odd. Singular. And strangely charming. Like yourself."

She peered at him cautiously, as if wondering whether he meant to tease her. "As I was saying . . ." Her blue eyes cast a warning. "I believe Mr. Bradford must be holding something over your brother . . ."

"That much is obvious."

"But he can't hope to maintain that control for long. By all accounts, your brother is a clever and resourceful man."

"Yes. I would guess Bradford is in some way using the schoolchildren and Rafael's family—if he has threatened them, Rafael would have no choice."

"He claimed they're abroad, wasn't that it?"

"Yes."

"I don't believe it."

Diego looked at her in surprise. Her small face appeared thoughtful, serious. "Rafael and his wife have taken schoolchildren abroad every summer for ten years. Why would you doubt his claim?"

"Because Mr. Alvin came from the west, probably California, and not the east as he claimed. I don't believe there was time for him to track down your brother in Europe, somehow gain control over him, and then return with these legal documents."

Diego pondered this but wasn't sure what it meant. He hated seeing slow-witted, but nothing leapt to mind. "So?"

"It means . . ." She sounded as if she struggled with patience. "It means that Bradford must have intercepted your brother before he boarded a ship, not after."

"It seems a reasonable guess." Diego paused. "In that case . . ."

She nodded, her eyes bright. "In that case, the Renegade's return is a danger to your brother's life—as well as his only hope."

This time, he understood her point before she made it. "If pressured, Bradford may act hastily with Rafael and his family."

They looked at each other, and unspoken understanding passed between them. "Then I hope, señorita, that the Renegade remembers to be careful."

Melanie offered a penetrating gaze. "I hope so, too."

Diego wanted to tell her everything, to share his fears. It was a mad impulse, but he quelled it only with effort. He understood the situation. If he made a mistake, if he chose the wrong path, his brother's life might be forfeit. Melanie watched him, sweet and sincere. If she involved herself with the Renegade, she, too, would be in danger. If she involved herself with him, he couldn't protect her from the greatest danger he knew—himself.

Already he had to fight the desire to seduce her. He had never dallied with a woman whose heart could be hurt deeply. He'd disappointed women who wanted a conquest, to win him to please their own conceit. He'd never hurt one who looked at him with such innocent eyes. As guarded as Melanie was, she was also trusting. She deserved the attention of a better man—a man who put others before himself, a man with courage, resourcefulness, and daring.

She deserved the Renegade. Even as the thought arose, Diego fought it. The mask he'd worn hid the real man, a man who had failed when his people needed him. He would wear the mask because he had no choice, but he couldn't allow it to mislead himself, or Melanie, again.

*   *   *

"Keep quiet, don't ask questions, and stay behind me."

Melanie absorbed his instructions with a blank expression. Her blue eyes didn't blink, but very slowly, her full, soft lips curled at one corner. Even more slowly, her eyes narrowed. Diego waited, resigned to the indignation of a feminine outburst. Her lips formed around the words before she spoke. "I don't think so."

He took an impatient breath. "Look, I don't say this for my own sake. That's just the way it is here. My grandfather is old-fashioned. The role of Zuni women is different."

"I'm not a Zuni woman."

"There's no mistaking that." Melanie looked so soft and gentle. It was hard to accept that she could be so fractious. "But you're visiting his pueblo . . ."

"As a photographer interested in accurately replicating images of his culture—those that aren't too private or sacred—to share with the world with the hope of encouraging a better understanding between people." She paused, as if proud of her words. "Tell him that."

"He won't like it."

"Tell him anyway."

They waited outside Tesuque, but Diego wasn't eager to proceed. His grandfather wasn't an easy man to deal with, and he could be harsh and unkind at times. Diego had never personally angered the old man, but he'd seen Rafael on his wrong side often enough. Though he had more or less accepted Rafael's wife, there was still much grumbling over his eldest grandson's "frivolous" taste in women. Of course, Diego wouldn't be presenting Melanie as his woman, but he didn't like to think of her insulted or hurt, either.

Melanie's lips had curled into a ball as she waited for him to lead her into the pueblo. "I have decided to do as you suggest, since it's important for me to learn how to introduce myself to native persons of any culture. If I offend them, I won't be able to gain entrance and pursue my craft."

"That's what I was trying to tell you." Diego still didn't feel comfortable escorting her to his grandfather. "Don't take anything he says personally. There's no reason to let your feelings get hurt."

Her brow arched. "I guard my feelings well."

He looked into her eyes and saw that she believed her claim. He also saw that she was wrong. "What you can't protect, I will guard for you."

She eyed him quizzically and her lips softened into a gentle smile. "Thank you."

Leading Porticus, they rode into Tesuque together. As soon as they passed through the gates, Melanie edged her mare behind Diego's horse. It was like her to take his instructions literally. He glanced back at her. Her face was knit in a serious, determined expression, and for reasons he didn't understand, his heart felt squeezed in his chest. She was so deeply sincere, so earnest. Somehow he had to protect her from his grandfather's gruff manner and scathing words.

A group of Tesuque children raced around in a game, then spotted Porticus. They squealed and charged in delight. The pony quivered and backed away, but Melanie dismounted and went to hold him. She spoke to him in a quiet and serious voice, and he calmed himself. The children circled him like wolves around a wounded deer, and Diego closed his eyes. Melanie scratched the pony's ears, and the oldest boy, Anaba, followed her example.

Most of the children spoke no English, but she seemed to communicate well enough. Usually, it was Diego the children circled when he came to visit—he was a favorite with children no matter where he went, even in those places where he'd offended every adult in residence. Porticus had taken his place.

Anaba looked up at Diego with wide eyes and spoke in Zuni. "Where did you get this funny little animal? He looks like the renegade black mustang, only small."

Diego hesitated. "He is the same." He issued an elaborate sigh and shook his head. The children stared, wide eyed and astounded.

"How did you make him so small?"

Diego smiled. "I put him in hot water and left him too long in the sun."

The children began to realize Diego was joking. A small boy struck his leg and laughed. "Can we play with him?"

Melanie looked back and forth expectantly. "What did you tell them?"

133

"That I shrunk the renegade mustang by putting him in hot water and baking him."

Melanie grimaced, but he detected a small smile. "Do they want to play with him? He seems to have accepted their attention."

"That is exactly what they want, señorita. Perceptive of you."

"I was a child once, too."

Diego watched as Melanie retrieved her camera equipment from Porticus's pack. As she worked, she showed the children her gear and let them investigate it. She didn't seem concerned that they would damage something valuable—she allowed them to finger dials and buttons, and to look through the small window.

They glanced at Diego for explanation. "The señorita is going to make pictures of you, like drawings only more real, and then your children's children will know what you looked like."

His promise thrilled them, and they began jostling for position to be first in line. Diego held up his hand. "Later, when the sun is setting. First, we have to get my grandfather's permission."

The children looked at each other and sighed. Anaba shook his head. "It will be a long while, then. We will play with the pony instead."

"Offer him food—anything should do—and he'll follow you anywhere."

They led Porticus away, baiting him with pieces of corn. Melanie watched them go, pleased. "We'll never get him to leave after this day."

"We could always roll him."

She laughed, and Diego felt a warm glow of satisfaction. He liked making her smile—he liked making her indignant, too, but laughing was better. He had always enjoyed affecting women, holding their attention—but this was different. It wasn't about him, but about her. Melanie was different.

Generally, he felt a woman could face the world without his assistance. But now, today, he would stand between Melanie and his cantankerous grandfather because something special inside her deserved better than to be slighted for the color of her skin.

Melanie looked around. "What now? I should get permission to set up my equipment, shouldn't I?"

He repressed a groan. "There's no way around it—we have to speak with my grandfather. Just remember what I told you. Don't talk too much. Keep it to 'yes' and 'no,' and don't forget the 'sir.' " He paused. "Try not to meet his eyes; it's challenging to look a leader straight in the eye. Maybe you should keep your head down."

"Maybe you'd like me to put a bucket over my head?"

He winced. "No . . . just . . . let me do the talking."

"That's always been so successful in the past."

"It will be here. Trust me. Tewa isn't a real pueblo; the people aren't truly Zuni, or anything else. They're people who don't fit anywhere else."

Melanie's eyes widened. "A man is coming over here." She looked nervous, then shuffled dutifully behind Diego. She kept her head down but peeked up as if cheating at cards.

Diego turned and his uncle waved. He elbowed Melanie. "You can relax. It's my uncle, Patukala."

She bit her lip. "He won't find me offensive?"

Her tentative question wrapped an unfamiliar ache around his heart. "Of course not! And you're not 'offensive,' just white. My uncle married a white woman—a truly difficult, cantankerous woman if ever there was one. Will's mother, actually."

Melanie looked curious, but when Patukala approached, she kept her eyes averted. Patukala looked between them, and one brow arched. Diego felt uncomfortable. "Hello, Uncle. I've brought this woman, Melanie Muessen, to Tesuque to photograph its people, the buildings."

Patukala assessed Melanie. His expression remained inscrutable, but he nodded, then turned his attention back to Diego, and he spoke in the Zuni tongue. "We hear that the Renegade has returned."

There was no point in deception, not among people who knew him better than he knew himself. "Yes."

Patukala glanced at Melanie again. "She wants to photograph the Tesuque?"

"My grandfather."

Patukala arched his brow and appeared dubious.

"He will not allow it, but I want to be there when you ask him."

Patukala motioned them forward, and Diego followed with Melanie close behind. She tapped his shoulder when no one was looking and he looked back. "What is it? If you've changed your mind, I'm sure I can get us into another pueblo—Pojoaque, maybe."

"Why would I want that? This one is beautiful. Where is your uncle taking us?"

"To my grandfather." Maybe he shouldn't have let himself sound so ominous, but Melanie had to be forewarned. He stopped while Patukala went into the old man's hut. "Don't forget . . ."

"I know . . . keep my head down, my eyes on my feet, my hands folded, and don't open my mouth, ever."

"Good, you're ready."

Patukala held the door open, and Diego went in. He felt Melanie standing behind him. A quick glance told him that she had obeyed his instructions and looked sufficiently servile, modest, and unassuming. His grandfather sat cross-legged at the rear of his hut, surrounded by red and black rugs and large Zuni pottery. He wore a wide-brimmed hat, which seemed to be a new addition to his generally traditional attire.

Diego spoke in Zuni, relieved that Melanie couldn't understand their language. "Good day, Grandfather. I like your hat."

The old man touched the brim and looked

proud. "I traded a dog I didn't like for it."

"A good trade, sir."

His grandfather patted the small rug beside him. "Sit, Grandson. It's been too long since your last visit."

He hadn't noticed Melanie. Maybe she'd done too well at seeming invisible. Diego fought to seem casual. "We've had an unusual visitor at Tewa. I've brought with me a woman named Melanie Muessen. She is a photographer . . ." The old man looked up and spotted Melanie. Diego held his breath as his grandfather's eyes narrowed. "A photographer is a person who makes images using . . ."

"I know what it is, Grandson. Help me up!"

Diego gulped, but his grandfather struggled to stand. Diego rose and helped the old man to his feet, then cringed as he went to inspect Melanie. The old man circled her once one way, then the other. Melanie never looked up. His grandfather stopped and looked at Diego. "Why is she staring at her feet?"

Diego hesitated, but his grandfather tapped Melanie's shoulder, then spoke in English. "What's the matter with you, young woman?"

She peered at Diego, a sliver of accusation in her eyes, then back at his grandfather. Diego stepped forward and placed himself between them. "Melanie was being respectful, sir . . . as I instructed her to do."

"That's why you're looking at your feet, young woman?"

Melanie pressed her lips together, then nodded. "Yes. Sir."

"Well, stop it. Now! You shouldn't be looking at your feet, girl. You should be looking at me!"

Melanie glared at Diego. "He told me not to!"

"My grandson is right, of course, and knows the way of the Zuni. And his advice was sound, too— for any woman beside yourself."

Melanie looked confused, but no more than Diego felt himself. "Why is that, Grandfather?"

"She is a photographer, isn't she? Well, then! She should be making images of me for my descendants, which I am counting on you to produce, since your brother . . ." He began to sputter, and spoke again in his own language. "Your brother whose name I will not utter since he again dragged four Tesuque children to those pointless lands across the sea—since he again left his ancestral home, deserting his rightful place . . ."

Melanie moved around Diego and studied his grandfather's face. "You have impressive bone structure, sir. You will look good in a photograph."

The old man beamed and appeared excited. Diego couldn't believe his eyes. "You don't mind, Grandfather?"

"Mind? It is important that the greatness of the Zuni be remembered for all time to come." His grandfather again lapsed into the Zuni tongue. "Your woman is wise, and has seen that. We will make arrangements to have her adopted by our clan—it will be necessary that you marry her first, or the whole thing gets too confusing, what with lineage passing through the mother."

Diego's mouth dropped, and he issued a silent prayer of thanks that his grandfather hadn't spoken in English. "Miss Muessen has only recently arrived in Tewa, Grandfather. She has come to take pictures—not to be my woman." The old man didn't look convinced. "I don't think she's interested in taking a husband."

His grandfather patted his shoulder fondly. "You will change that easily, my grandson." He turned to Melanie, reverting to English again. "Now, for my image, young woman. I should be seen in a proper setting, with the mountains behind me in the distance, with the pueblo wall to one side."

Remembering how Melanie objected to his own suggestions, Diego fully expected her to correct his grandfather, but instead, she considered his advice, then nodded. "That sounds good, sir. With the afternoon sun slanting across the pueblo, it should look particularly impressive."

Patukala looked at Diego, shrugged, then left. Diego watched in amazement as his grandfather seized Melanie's arm and directed her out of his hut, chatting amiably as if to a daughter. They understood each other, just as he'd jokingly predicted that morning. His fears that Melanie needed protection proved groundless—using that strange inner strength she possessed, she didn't seem to need anyone. He couldn't help a tug of disappointment.

His grandfather stopped in the doorway of his hut and looked back at Diego, speaking in Zuni. "Patukala says the Renegade has returned."

"Yes."

"Because his brother is in danger?"

"Yes."

A slow, ageless smile spread across the old man's face. "*I knew he would.*"

"It wasn't *his* choice."

"Don't you know, Grandson? It never is." He turned back to Melanie. "Come, young woman! I have in my mind an image of myself, facing the mountains—a slight wind will be necessary for the desired effect . . ."

They went out into the pueblo, and Diego followed as his grandfather took Melanie on an elaborate and detailed tour of all the rooms, buildings, stables, and crops. He listened in amazement as his grandfather told her of the seasonal rituals, the dances, and the structure of Zuni culture. Melanie asked questions, which the old fellow answered in excruciating detail and with boundless enthusiasm for her instruction. Melanie then set about posing him in various spots. The old man took to the task as if he'd found his life's calling. He donned six different costumes, some that Diego felt sure no outsider had ever seen before, and allowed Melanie to adjust his vest, headpiece, and even his hair for her shots.

As the sun set over the mountains, Diego began

to wonder if he'd been dreaming all along. He'd probably wake soon and find himself beneath a tavern floor. His grandfather demanded a special meal in Melanie's honor, orders fortunately spoken in Zuni, because he had begun referring to her as his granddaughter.

Melanie looked happier than Diego had yet seen her. She obviously felt accepted and appreciated—her face glowed. She packed up her camera gear, then came to him with her hands clasped in excitement. "What a wonderful day! I have so many good pictures—I can't wait to develop them! Thank you, Diego, for bringing me here. Your grandfather is such a warm, considerate man."

"No one, ever, has called him that before."

"I can't imagine how anyone could think anything else."

Diego opened his mouth to argue, then shook his head. "This has been among the oddest days of my life."

"Stranger than waking up under a saloon?"

"Much stranger. I thought he'd hate you, but he took to you like . . ." He stopped himself from saying *family*. "He certainly took to you."

"I liked him, too. He posed better than anyone I've ever met."

"He enjoyed it, that much is certain."

Melanie looked content and happy. "Today, I captured images no other photographer ever has before. Your grandfather possesses the most interesting expressions. It's what I've always wanted—

to find the light of humanity in someone's eyes."

Irrationally, Diego felt jealous. She had, after all, avoided taking *his* picture even once. Well, she'd taken a few of him as the Renegade, but he had been wearing a mask.

"Is something wrong?"

"Why do you ask?"

"You're frowning."

If he wasn't on guard, Melanie might guess what bothered him. "It seemed to me you took an inordinate number of pictures of my grandfather. You might want a more . . . varied collection."

"Such as images of yourself?"

He had seen it coming, tried to avoid it, and instead, walked right into it. Diego refused to meet her eyes. He didn't have to—he knew what her expression would say, that her right eyebrow would be slightly elevated, her lip curled to one side, and that she would look particularly pert and knowing.

"There are many interesting faces for your study, señorita, besides my grandfather."

"Name one."

No one leapt to mind, but he couldn't let her catch him in a fit of vanity. "Patukala's wife, Sally—she's got a crusty, sailor's-wife appearance, and her disposition is at best testy. You'll meet her at dinner."

"She sounds promising. Although I'm not sure about the 'sailor's wife' part."

"She's weathered but interesting. Patukala seems

143

to think she's the most beautiful woman around."

Melanie looked thoughtful. "Do you think so?"

"She's too grumpy to be beautiful. She used to hit me if I annoyed her. Not that it hurt, but it was irritating. The only thing that made it endurable was that she smacked Chen more often."

"What about Will?"

"I don't recall him ever needing to be hit."

Melanie sighed and shook her head. "She sounds difficult. What did you and Chen do to annoy her?"

"Nothing that we don't do now . . ." Diego stopped himself and frowned. "You must be hungry, señorita. I'll take you to wash, and you can interrogate Sally tonight."

Sally liked her, too. He shouldn't have been surprised, but as he watched Melanie seated beside Sally, chatting and smiling, Diego couldn't help feeling left out and alone.

"Your woman accepts our ways well." Fortunately, the old man spoke in Zuni, or Melanie might have overheard another embarrassing conversation between them.

Diego eyed his grandfather, feeling as testy as he'd accused Sally of being. "I told you, Grandfather, she's not my woman. She came here to take pictures, and that's all. She has no interest in me."

"She came here because your spirit summoned her, my grandson. When a man is ready, truly ready, his woman will arrive."

"I've had many women, sir."

"I didn't say 'any woman.' I said 'your woman.' There's a difference. And there is only one."

"I didn't realize you were such a romantic, Grandfather."

The old man darkened. "I am not romantic. It is the way of things. There are two halves to a whole, whole in themselves, but not complete."

"Ah."

"You don't understand, because you have not been complete. A man can take many mates, many wives, and some may last a lifetime. But there is only one with whom he is complete."

Diego had lost the train of his grandfather's logic. His gaze returned to Melanie. She sat a distance away from him, conversing with Sally. The light of the campfires reflected on her pale, warm skin. Her blue eyes glittered. She had tied her heavy, long hair in a thick ribbon, left to form a river of honey waves down her back. She was beautiful, and he could almost imagine being "complete" in her arms, holding her and loving her. Generally, after the seduction was past and the body's delight faded, he found himself bored in a woman's embrace. But he wouldn't be bored with Melanie.

It was just the desire to bed a lovely woman, to unravel her mysteries and to prove that she wanted him, too. If he held her and kissed her again, the spell she had unwittingly woven over him would

145

fade. If he sated himself, his mind would again wander to other pursuits.

What he didn't understand was why he hadn't fully pursued her so far. He'd had ample opportunity, but for the most part he'd withheld his charm and kept his naturally sensual nature bound like a beast too dangerous to approach. He'd seen Melanie's sensual side—he had no doubt that she would respond, and respond well.

She spotted him staring at her and smiled, a friend to a friend. She liked him, and she trusted him. But one more kiss couldn't hurt.

His grandfather had stopped talking. Since childhood, Diego had formed a habit of pretending to listen and letting his mind drift elsewhere. Rafael had listened dutifully to the old fellow's lectures; Diego never caught the point, and yet it was Diego the old man adored, Diego who could do no wrong. Why this should be, Diego had never known. No matter how much trouble he was, Rafael loved him. Chen remained his friend after countless battles, and Will never said an ill word about him. His friends had risked their lives to save him, and not one of them seemed to realize he wasn't worth it.

He hadn't meant, ever, to deceive them about his worth, but somehow, they had been deceived anyway.

He didn't mean to deceive Melanie, but still, she seemed infatuated despite her "guarded heart."

"The spirit, Grandson, has a purpose of its own,

not always shared with the mind. It follows its path like a river—there's nothing you can do to alter the river. It's what you do with its twists and its rocks and its beauty that matters."

Diego sensed the end of a long lecture, which had been mostly unheard. "Good advice, sir."

"The Renegade is the river."

"Uh-huh." Diego closed his eyes and tried not to sigh. Apparently, the lecture had more twists and rocks than the river. "Is that so?"

"Your brother would not sell the pueblo."

Diego hesitated, confused by the change in subject. "I know that, Grandfather."

"Only if the Renegade defeats the invader will your brother return."

"The 'Renegade' doesn't know how. He put fear into Bradford—he didn't stop him."

"He will."

# Chapter Six

"I was right about you, Miss Muessen."

Diego had left his grandfather's side and seemed intent on pestering Melanie once again. She took a small sip of yucca tea and tried to pretend she didn't enjoy his teasing. "Oh? How is that?"

"You and my grandfather are two of a kind."

"Thank you."

His eyes flashed at her response, but he sat down beside her and took a drink from her cup. "You've certainly endeared yourself to the grumpiest people I know—my grandfather and Sally."

"I don't know how you could ever have called her testy. She's a lovely woman, gentle and intelligent, very thoughtful." She stopped, shook her head, and clucked her tongue. "I'd hate to think what you did to goad her into striking you." She paused. "Although, now that I think of it, I've been tempted to strike you a few times, too."

"Have you, indeed? As I said, you have much in common with both my grandfather and Sally."

Melanie felt proud. "Your grandfather and Sally seem independent, strong, sure of themselves. I do share those qualities. Thank you."

"You are small, delicate, fragile, vulnerable, and extremely sensitive." His voice grew deeper with each accusatory word, and he leaned toward her as he spoke.

Offended, she stood up to glare down at him. "I am not."

He noticed her expression and rose, too, towering over her. "I'm afraid I must stand by my claim, Miss Muessen. You are the most vulnerable woman I have ever met."

To her horror, tears stung her eyes, though she wasn't sure why she should react so emotionally to his ridiculous claim. "You're wrong about me. I've managed very well on my own for quite some time." She paused. "And I'm not 'small.' I'm an average height for a woman. It's just that you're so tall in comparison." She paused again. "And I'm *not* vulnerable."

"You are."

"I'm not." This wasn't working. She needed proof. "You're simply used to women swooning at your feet, foolish women, women who require no more than big brown eyes and long lashes, or perhaps a strong body and a smile that is both boyish and too knowing. It's your vanity, an element of conceit that seems to run particularly strong in you that makes you think I must in some way resemble the multitudes of women you have swayed, when in fact I barely notice you."

He caught her shoulders in his strong hands, pulled her close, and kissed her. She should have seen it coming, but she'd been too busy denying his power over her. She should have hit him, but instead she wanted more.

His whole body molded to hers, protecting her and hurtling her into the worst danger of her life. Wild, male power wrapped around her, drawing her in and igniting a fire somewhere deep inside her. She tried to resist, but he bent to kiss her neck, her throat, then the corner of her mouth. His tongue played against her lips, and Melanie went weak.

He tasted like heaven, and she felt as if he was what she had missed all her life. She wanted to push him away but instead pulled him closer. If she could have pulled him inside herself, she would have found a way.

He kissed her until she felt breathless, until she didn't think she could stand without holding on to him. She was doing the worst thing she could imagine.

She was swooning.

Melanie propelled herself off his chest with a firm jab. She fought to hurtle a retort or accusation at him, but when she forced herself to meet his eyes, she saw that he was as shocked and shaken as she was. Worse still, he hadn't bothered to take her aside for his madman's kiss—they were standing no more than ten feet from his grandfather. In one horrific, sick glance, she saw Sally, Patukala, and Diego's revered grandfather all staring.

Sally and her husband turned away and pretended to chat. Diego's grandfather looked proud and nodded sagely at Diego. Melanie clasped her hand to her forehead and groaned. "I think I'm . . . overtired. To the point of delirium." She peeked up at him. He just stared and said nothing. "It's time for you to take me home. Back to Tewa."

Melanie watched Diego's face as it changed from shock to the look of a man wearing a mask. His whole body changed from its strong, straight stature to a languid posture. Even his eyelids took on a lazy, unconcerned quality.

"As it happens, señorita, I have decided to stay on a few days here. I've . . . worn out my welcome in Tewa. It happens often, you know. I drink too much, trouble someone's sister . . . and I come here to recuperate. As you may have noticed, they treat me like a king in Tesuque."

Even his voice had changed. Melanie's throat felt tight. " 'Trouble' someone's sister?" She almost growled the words, and he didn't meet her eyes.

"It happens."

"Not with me, it won't!"

For an instant she saw the Diego she thought she knew in his quick glance. For an instant, he chal-

151

lenged her, as if to say, "We'll see." Instead, he shrugged without concern. "Don't take a kiss too seriously, señorita. Beauty like yours is hard to resist."

She felt as if he'd slapped her. She had believed, like a fool, that his attraction to her was founded on more than whatever he considered beautiful. She had believed he cared, that he felt that strange, special fluttering in his heart for her that she felt for him. Like a crack of lightning over her head, he'd destroyed that illusion.

"I see." Her voice sounded thick and, more horribly, her eyes stung as if she might cry. She would not cry. She wouldn't think about it, she wouldn't think about him. "May I ask how I shall get back to Tewa? I don't recall the route you took very well, let alone in darkness."

"I'll see that you get a good guide." His voice sounded strange, too. Diego turned away, and Melanie watched as he spoke with his uncle. Patukala looked confused, but he nodded, then returned with Diego. "My uncle will ride with you. It's early yet, and the moon is full." He paused. "I assume you'll be in Tewa for a few days yet?"

Her heart ached. He didn't care if he ever saw her again. "That was my intention."

"I'll be here for a day or so, until things cool off in Tewa. Will should be able to help you until I get back. I'll check then to see if you need anything."

She didn't know what to say. "If I'm still in Tewa, fine."

He really didn't care. He looked idle; he glanced around as if to see what—or who—in his grandfather's pueblo might entertain him now. His gaze drifted over her and settled somewhere to her left. She didn't dare look to see whom he was watching now. Melanie turned her back to him and a child brought Porticus and her mare. She mounted without looking at Diego, then waited for Patukala.

Diego stood back. He chatted with a group of children, laughing at something one said about Porticus. Patukala rode toward her and moved her mare forward. She heard Diego, but she wouldn't look back. "Take care when you return, señorita. Don't anger Bradford, and stick close to Chen."

Melanie didn't respond. She urged her mare forward, pulling Porticus behind her. The pony seemed reluctant to leave. She passed through the gates of Tesuque, and she didn't look back.

Melanie sat on the edge of her bed at Victoria's inn, staring out the window on the Tewa Plaza. She hadn't done well in keeping her mind off Diego de Aguirre. He hadn't pretended to be anything but a careless, fun-loving man, a man who enjoyed women. From the moment she met him, she'd known that, but somehow, she hadn't really understood. She knew it now, but it was too late to stop her heart from the low ache she'd endured since she left his grandfather's pueblo.

Diego's uncle hadn't been much comfort on the ride back to Tewa. He had asked about her career, about her future plans, but he seemed to feel any other inquiry to be impolite. Melanie suspected he knew that her heart ached, and that she felt foolish for setting it so easily and so soon on Diego. Maybe the uncle had seen many such women pining for his handsome, rakish nephew.

Someone knocked on her door, and Melanie jumped. Her heart sped. Before she could stop herself, she acknowledged the hope that it was Diego. She hesitated, then went to open the door, but it was Chen who stood looking tense on the other side.

"Miss Muessen . . . Forgive me, please, for disturbing you at this late hour."

Melanie felt tired and foolish, but she stood back to admit him. He appeared even more awkward before he stepped inside. "Is something wrong, Chen?"

"I'm not sure." He paused, as if hesitant to broach a delicate subject. "You returned from Tesuque without Diego. I had expected him."

Melanie fiddled with the hem of her sleeve. "It was a last-minute decision on his part. He felt he had worn out his welcome here and should spend a few days with his grandfather until things cooled off."

Chen didn't respond at once, seeming to be absorbing what that might mean. "He gave you no warning?"

"None." Her voice came a bit stronger than she meant it to, and Chen looked at her quickly but didn't question the reason for her mood.

"It's unlike him to spend more time than necessary with his grandfather."

"I can't imagine why. Diego's grandfather adores him."

Chen offered a rueful smile. "Perhaps that's why. But no matter. Did anything precipitate this decision?"

"Nothing that I know of." She spoke too quickly, and Chen looked embarrassed. Too easily, he must have guessed what had transpired between them in Tesuque. It had probably happened often before. She had to change the subject; she didn't want to hear how foolish she'd been, or how many other women had sat alone with aching hearts because of Diego de Aguirre's restless attentions.

Chen seated himself in a rough-hewn wooden chair, paused to admire its rustic handiwork, then stole a furtive glance at Victoria's furnishings. Melanie sat in the matching chair and crossed her legs at the ankles. Chen's presence calmed Melanie, and her heart lightened. There was something about his assuredness, his caution and broad imagination that made her feel safe. He thought the way she did, only with far greater attention to reality than she had ever been able to maintain.

Chen placed his thumb and forefinger against his chin. "So Diego decided to stay in Tesuque . . ." She would have expected Chen to be annoyed, but instead he seemed to understand. "Is there anything else to report?"

Melanie hesitated. Report? "Not that I know of." She paused. "One thing on the ride home struck me as odd, though."

Chen leaned forward expectantly. She half-expected him to take out a pen and begin jotting notes. "What was it?"

"When we reached the outskirts of the pueblo, we spotted Bradford's guards at work clearing one of the ancient kivas. Diego's uncle told me they weren't working on the site of the old treasure."

Chen's brow furrowed as he contemplated this. "I didn't believe Bradford's claim of a renewed treasure hunt, but perhaps I was wrong."

"They're working hard, but not eagerly, if you understand the difference."

Chen eyed her with a new sense of admiration. "I do understand. Those men are working as if they have to, not with the expectation of finding treasure. When a man digs for treasure, a certain madness overcomes him. He digs with fury, his heart burns, because he knows that which will fuel his future, his power, is at last within his grasp."

As Chen spoke, his dark eyes gleamed and his hands clenched, as if he, too, were digging. Melanie sat back and stared at him, then glanced uncertainly to the side. "You speak as one who knows."

Chen caught her confused tone, then shook himself, as if to be free of a blissful trance. He cleared his throat and his expression. "As a matter of fact, I have. Briefly . . ."

"The Spanish treasure Diego told me about?"

"Yes, that." He paused and sighed. "There was so much in that glittering chest! Every Tewa citizen benefited from that treasure, which is why Bradford can profit from taxing even Miguel the baker. The treasure we found was worth so much that Rafael can take his family and a whole tribe of schoolchildren to Europe year after year. Diego shared his portion with me by investing in my hotel, and yet he remains one of the wealthiest men in this territory."

Melanie's eyes widened. "Is he? He doesn't act like a rich man." She paused. Maybe this explained his carelessness. "Has a life of ease made Diego . . . well . . ." She wasn't sure how to ask the question without revealing her personal interest in the man, but Chen seemed to understand.

"A ne'er-do-well rogue with interest only in loose women and a bottle?" Before Melanie could respond, because this description was what she feared, Chen laughed and shook his head. "I can't deny that my friend has lived his life with a certain abandon. But money—neither the gain nor lack of it—could never change Diego de Aguirre. He is what he has always been—a man whose intelligence and kind heart conflict with an inherently rebellious nature, a man who understands too much of the world to play its games."

That sounded better than "ne'er-do-well rogue," but it wasn't exactly comforting. "He seems bothered by the past, and especially by any implication that he might follow in his brother's footsteps."

Chen appeared uncomfortable and took time with his answer, confirming Melanie's suspicions that he feared revealing too much. "Years ago, during the time Rafael first rode as the Renegade, Diego was taken captive with many other Tewa people. Diego's captivity was used to trap Rafael. For a brief while, Rafael's wife Evelyn and I were also taken captive and placed in the kiva mine." He paused and looked momentarily wistful. "That is where I first encountered the Spanish treasure. I was there for the historic moment of its discovery. Oh, how it gleamed, even by dim torchlight!"

"Chen . . . back to Diego, if you please. Why does that experience bother him so much, even years later?"

"As I was saying . . . Diego proved himself a leader even then. He marshaled the other captives into a clever plan of delay, keeping them alive while the rest of us struggled to defeat our devious enemy. He had a chance to escape, but he didn't take it, not when it would have meant leaving the others. He stayed even when our enemies collapsed the mine. He stayed and got everyone out, though he was badly injured in the process."

Melanie's heart moved at Diego's heroism. This was the man she knew him to be. The man she couldn't help loving. "He should be proud."

"Perhaps, if that had been the end of it, he would be proud. Maybe it would even have gone to his head and he'd have become unbearable. I don't know. But the captives were freed from the mine only to face certain slaughter before enemy guns. Diego was already injured. He lay there helpless, unable to protect anyone, cursing himself for what he considered his own failure."

"But those people didn't die."

"No, most survived. I had escaped and sought help from Diego's grandfather, whom you have recently met. The Zuni warriors came and rescued the stricken captives, but Diego has never forgiven himself for being unable to help. I believe he considered himself invincible before that day. It forced him to realize that even he had limits. Beyond that, maybe the pressure of following in Rafael's path inspired his innate rebelliousness. He wanted to be his own man, even if it meant being the scorned younger brother of a great one."

"He tries to prove that he isn't heroic, that he isn't worthy of love and trust. Maybe I am wrong to think otherwise." Melanie stopped, embarrassed, but Chen touched her hand in awkward comfort.

"Diego's heart is bigger than he knows. Give him time."

"He seems to be taking his brother's disappearance lightly."

Chen glanced at her. "He cares, but none of us feel entirely sure how to handle the matter."

"The Renegade knows."

"I hope so, Miss Muessen."

Melanie sat forward. Chen had shared his confidences with her. Maybe he would tell her the

159

truth. "Victoria thinks you know who he is."

Chen's eyes widened in surprise and agitation. "Does she? And how would she, a woman who has been here a scant few months and has occupied herself with luring in business that should rightfully have been mine, know anything about the people here, let alone myself?"

Melanie repressed a smile. "Perhaps she has studied you more intensely than you realized . . . as competition."

He nodded, serious. "That is likely. A woman such as herself would leave no stone unturned. I have noticed that at the bakery she inspects each loaf before making her selection. Her attention to the detail of corn, beans, and especially meat products is particularly keen."

Melanie coughed. "I take it you have studied her, too." Chen cast a suspicious glance her way. "As competition."

"It is important to know what one's opposition is doing."

Another knock interrupted them, and Melanie went to the door. Victoria appeared, looking thoroughly innocent, carrying a tray of food. As Chen had said, the loaf indeed looked well chosen. "I thought you might enjoy a small meal before bed, Miss Muessen." As always, Victoria gave no sign of noticing Chen at all. She managed to place the tray on a table while keeping her back to Chen. "You must have had a tiring day."

"Thank you, Victoria." Melanie dutifully tried

the bread, which was good, but she wasn't hungry. Chen rose to inspect the offerings. He seized a green vegetable and looked as if he'd been robbed.

"This yucca was meant for my chef! He informed me it was required for a special dish he intended to create, but that all the plants had been purchased. By you!"

Victoria kept her attention on Melanie. "They are delicious, aren't they? Do have one, Miss Muessen. I have several prepared for my guests."

Chen glared. "*Guest.*"

Victoria dusted her hands on her white apron. "As a matter of fact, I have several guests now; my inn is almost full. Apparently, the presence of Mr. Bradford and his party has disturbed some of your other guests, and they decided my inn might be more peaceful."

Chen seemed lit from a fire within as he took in this information. "*You . . .*" He backed toward the door, fury stiffening his limbs. "This will not stand, madam! It is unscrupulous, devious, and black of deed!"

He left without delay, and Victoria seated herself in the chair he had occupied. She looked supremely satisfied. "He's a high-strung little fellow, isn't he? Given to surprising outbursts at odd times."

"Were you surprised, Victoria?"

Victoria met Melanie's gaze and allowed for a tiny smile. "No."

They fell silent for a while, but Victoria's presence comforted Melanie, perhaps because she sensed they both felt alone. Life had to be confronted alone—Melanie knew that—but it was good to have another woman who knew what it meant to hope and to dream, to get up in the morning knowing those dreams would most likely remain always in the distant future.

Small satisfactions were best, and more easily counted on than far-off dreams of true love and romantic intimacy. Melanie considered herself a capable, independent woman, and she couldn't let Diego change that quality. She admired Tewa Pueblo and its odd mix of cultures, its inherent freedom. Already she cared for the people who considered it home.

"I would like to know who Mr. Bradford is working for . . ." She spoke aloud, not meaning to share her thoughts with Victoria. But the Chinese woman sat forward with interest.

"He's been very careful about concealing their names. He simply refers to them as 'investors.' Clearly, he doesn't want anyone to know who they are."

Melanie's eyes narrowed. "I wonder why." She paused. "I assume Mr. Bradford has left his office and is at Chen's hotel now?"

Victoria nodded. "He is. As I informed my competitor, Mr. Bradford has taken to entertaining his guests in lavish style—well into the night. Apparently, he enjoys his liquor as much as Diego is reputed to do."

" 'Reputed?' " Melanie frowned, annoyed with

the reminder of Diego. "Señor de Aguirre must have enjoyed it adequately to have ended up beneath a saloon."

Victoria shrugged. "Oh, he drank often enough, but never quite as much as he made it seem. I think he gets away with more . . . mischief if perceived to be drunk."

"Mischief." Melanie knew what Victoria meant. With women. "The man has no scruples."

"I wouldn't say that, exactly. He has a reputation, and not undeserved, but from what I've seen, those women he has 'dishonored' pursued him, and not the other way around. Perhaps he liked the flattery, or maybe that's all he thought he could have from a woman."

Melanie didn't want to hear anything more about Diego. "I'm sorry, Victoria. I'm so tired—as you said, it's been a long day. But thank you for bringing my meal."

"You didn't eat much of it."

"I will, I promise."

Victoria rose to leave. She went to the door, then turned back. "It isn't always easy to be strong, I know. Life doesn't always give us what we need or desire, so it is important, I think, to make ourselves a force to be reckoned with. It's important to know what we want, because no one will give it to us unless we fight for it ourselves." She paused, wistful yet sure. "Don't you agree, Miss Muessen?"

Melanie sighed. "I would like to be a force." Victoria wanted power, not unlike Chen, to make her mark on the world, to matter, to leave the world better than when she came. But was that what Melanie wanted, truly? Victoria left, but Melanie sat a long while staring at the door. Her career mattered, because it interested her, because she recorded more than just images. Her father had said she had a gift for capturing emotion even in a simple landscape.

She saw emotion everywhere because she felt it so deeply, but it always seemed to come from an odd angle. Sometimes it was easier to photograph its nuances than to feel it. Diego had proven that beyond question. But what did she want? Maybe he had proven that, too. She wanted true intimacy, depth of feeling. She wanted love, to share it to the depths of her soul with another person.

Diego had been clear about one thing—she wouldn't find what she was looking for with him. But Victoria was right: It was important to know what you wanted, and not to let anything steal it.

Love was somewhere in the future. It might remain forever in her dreams. But here in Tewa, she might be able to be a force. Melanie felt weary to her bones, but another emotion was stronger. She eyed her camera, then stood up and looked out her window toward Chen's hotel. Two guards stumbled down Chen's front steps, laughing, and obviously drunk. Bright lights gleamed inside from the restaurant windows. Bradford would be up late entertaining his guests.

His room would be empty.
But not for long.

Getting in to Carlton Bradford's room wasn't the hard part. As Melanie looked around the lavish surroundings of the Chateau Renegade's Master Suite, she realized it would be getting out that might prove difficult. She had slipped into the hotel through the kitchen entrance unnoticed, waited for an opportunity, and then sped up the stairs to the guest rooms. The Master Suite was located at the end of the hall, so she'd had no trouble finding it. It wasn't locked. In a hotel filled with his own minions, Bradford must have felt there was no one to fear.

But every time Melanie started to look around, another guest passed by the door, and her heart stopped. The window looking over the plaza was open, but it was too far a jump, and she didn't see a way to climb down. If she was caught coming down the stairs . . . She'd have to chance it—after she found what she'd come for.

A stack of papers lay on a wide desk, but nothing looked interesting. She found a map detailing the ancient kivas, with a mark in red ink over what she guessed was the site they now dug. However, from what she remembered, the kiva they worked on was simply the least ruined and so the easiest spot to dig. She assumed Bradford selected it for that reason and, because it was only a ruse, needed no greater search. She stuffed the map into her bag to study it later.

Melanie opened drawers but found nothing that could be connected to the pueblo deed. She took note of addresses she saw—they seemed to be from California, rather than the east, where Bradford was supposedly from. The handwriting appeared feminine, with curls and attention to perfect penmanship, but nothing appeared condemning. Perhaps Bradford was courting a woman in California. A quick scan of a letter told her the target of his affections was playing the courtship very coolly.

Melanie felt foolish. Rather than uncovering evidence of Bradford's mysterious benefactors, she'd discovered a polite courtship and nothing more. It was like peeping into someone's tame diary. Disappointment crashed over her and she stood at the center of the room, miserable.

What had made her sneak into Carlton Bradford's room, anyway? She knew the answer before she finished posing it. She wanted to find evidence, something that would help Diego. She wanted to prove to him that she was more than an object of idle seduction, that she was worth the trouble of caring.

*I am overtired.* Melanie blinked back tears. *And pathetic.* He should be proving to her that he was worth her time and interest, and yet here she was . . . And how would she explain her presence if caught in the Master Suite? As if to highlight the dark tide her evening had taken, the door opened. Before she turned to see who was there, the lamp went out, leaving her in complete darkness.

Melanie froze. Whoever had entered the room had certainly seen her. "Sleepwalking! I was sleepwalking!" She turned around, eyes still blinded by the sudden loss of light. She held out her arms to ward off any attack, or at least to halt it before it happened. There was no response to her outburst, but she knew someone was in the room. "Hello?"

Terror crept up on her, seeped into her limbs, and left her unable to move. "Hello? Mr. Bradford?" Her voice had grown so small that she could barely hear it herself.

The door opened again, letting in a bright flash of light from the hall. Before she knew what was happening, a dark figure leapt toward her, caught her in his arms, and bounded toward the window. Melanie was too shocked to scream, too stunned to be afraid.

Someone shouted—it sounded like Mr. Bradford—and another voice came from the hall. But all Melanie saw was the ancient, carved mask of her captor as he pulled her through the window.

She had been taken by the Renegade.

Events happened too quickly for Melanie to follow. Somehow, he had her on a ledge on the second story of Chen's hotel. Before she knew it, he had grabbed hold of a thick rope, and they were swinging across the plaza. Men shouted from below. As the Renegade landed on the roof of the schoolhouse, still holding her tightly against his strong body, Melanie saw a guard take aim to shoot. Will tripped the guard casually, and the shot went wild.

The Renegade cursed—at least she assumed it was a curse. It sounded more Zuni than Spanish, but Melanie was too shaken to be sure of his inflection. He picked her up like a doll and carried her, then ran along the adobe roof. It must have been a path he knew well; he jumped over wooden boards without hesitation, missing places where the adobe jutted upward.

A woman screamed—Melanie recognized Victoria. "He has Miss Muessen! Stop shooting, you idiots!"

Another shot fired on top of Victoria's command—someone didn't care if Melanie was killed or not. The shot had a different sound, not of a rifle but of a pistol instead. How she knew this, Melanie wasn't sure, but it stuck in her mind as important.

The Renegade found what he was looking for and jumped down on the other side of the schoolhouse. He didn't wait to explain, nor did he put Melanie down. He ran along the outer wall as if carrying her was nothing, then darted behind the stables. In the darkness Melanie saw the outline of a horse—the Renegade's black mustang. He leapt astride, taking Melanie with him. He didn't use a saddle, only a thick wool blanket bound on the horse's back. Just as the guards raced from the pueblo gates and charged around the corner of the wall, the Renegade urged the horse into a sudden gallop.

Within the space of a fleeting few minutes, Melanie had been swept from Carlton Bradford's suite into a race across darkness into the hills.

She hadn't been able to utter a single word.

Her senses rallied and her shock faded, but they were riding too fast for her to talk or question him. It would have been easier if he hadn't worn a mask—something about that carved face made him seem magical, ancient, and perhaps dangerous. An image flashed in her mind of Aztecs sacrificing their victims on golden altars.

He wasn't dangerous. She knew that—because she knew him. He must have had a good reason for sweeping her out of Bradford's suite, and out of Tewa. Why he felt the need to drag her into the mountains she wasn't sure, but there had to be some logic behind it.

When they reached the shelter of trees, the Renegade slowed his horse to a canter. He seemed to be concentrating on the paths ahead. At two junctures, he stopped before choosing which way to go. After awhile, apparently satisfied that no pursuit could find him, he allowed his horse to walk. Its sides heaved from the exertion, yet it seemed filled with boundless energy, ready to burst ahead again at the lightest touch.

Melanie tried to look at her captor, but she saw nothing but the fading moonlight reflecting on his carved mask. He turned from the path unexpect-

169

edly, as if he'd almost missed it, then swung his leg forward over the horse's neck, bringing Melanie to the ground with him. Before she could speak, he came toward her. Something in his stance conveyed to her that he wasn't happy.

"What . . . ?" He stopped and cleared his throat, as if to adjust his voice. "What in hell were you doing in Carlton Bradford's room?"

She wrapped her arms around her waist but refused to back away. "I was looking for something."

"What?"

"That's none of your concern."

"It is if you want me to return you to Tewa. Ever."

Despite the circumstances, she didn't believe his threat. "Come morning, I'm sure I can find my own way back."

"If you live to morning . . ."

Melanie placed her hands on her hips. "You're going to kill me? Then do it and be done. I've had a long day."

He didn't react. Melanie waited. "Señorita, it would be wise for you to answer me."

"Would it? Very well. I will tell you—if you tell me first why you abducted me."

She couldn't see his face, but she felt sure he rolled his eyes. "*Abducted you?* I caught you snooping in Bradford's room and saved you before he caught you himself."

"How did you know I was . . . investigating?"

"I didn't."

"Ah! So you were there to do the same thing."

"I am mildly curious about the identity of Bradford's Californian benefactors, yes. Which is, I assume, the source of your interest." He paused, but Melanie refused to comment. She hoped he might think she had some other investigation in mind. "But I doubt you'll find anything incriminating in Bradford's unlocked bedroom."

"Then what were you doing there?"

He hesitated. "I was in the lawyer's room next door."

"Did you find anything?"

He hesitated. "No more than you found in Bradford's."

"As it happens, my investigation wasn't without results." It wasn't much, but more than he had found, apparently. "I learned that Bradford has a lady friend in San Francisco."

She *knew* he rolled his eyes this time. She felt it. "Well, that is an exciting find, Miss Muessen. A man is courting a woman. How unusual!"

"It might prove significant . . . later."

His head tilted at a doubtful angle. "Really?"

"Anything we learn about him must be considered helpful." Even disguised as the Renegade, he was annoying. "Isn't it time you told me your true identity?" *As if I don't know . . .*

"It would be unwise for me to tell you that, señorita. For your sake as well as my own."

"I would not betray you."

171

He reached out and touched her arm gently. When Diego had touched her, it had been quick and impulsive. He generally moved away, as if he hadn't meant it—but the Renegade didn't back away. "Nor I, you, señorita."

Melanie's body awoke with a strange tingling, one she barely recognized. It had to be Diego, but she needed to test the matter to be positive. But how? "I would like to see your face."

She felt certain he smiled. "You wear no mask tonight, yet I can't see your face in the darkness. When the moon drops behind the mountains, neither one of us will see the other at all."

It sounded like a promise. Melanie swallowed hard. "What do you intend to do with me?"

He moved a little closer. "What would you like me to do?"

She was trembling and she didn't know why. It wasn't fear. "I don't know."

He reached out and touched her face, so softly that she barely felt his fingers on her skin. "You are beautiful, señorita. More beautiful than anything I've ever seen."

Her breath caught in her throat. "I have heard such idle flattery before."

"Señorita, don't you know? It depends on the man speaking those words. But I wouldn't lie to you. You are beautiful, so lovely that you steal my breath. And you're brave—you've only been in Tewa a short while and yet you care enough to risk yourself pursuing its justice."

172

"You're risking yourself."

"Perhaps I am not worth as much as you."

She hadn't expected him to be so tender—she expected more conceit, as befit his dramatic rides. Maybe the Renegade was Diego's real self, and debauchery his mask. "You're the one wearing the mask."

The Renegade adjusted the mask and sighed. "Unfortunately. It's not comfortable." He pondered this a moment, then tore off a section from the lining of his black cape. He drew his sword and worked on the cloth while Melanie waited.

"What are you doing?"

"You'll see." He turned his back to her and removed the Indian mask, then set it carefully aside. He tied the black cloth around his face, then turned back to Melanie.

She moved closer to inspect him, but in the darkness the cloth revealed no more than the Indian mask. It covered his eyes and forehead but revealed his lips and chin perfectly. And they were very familiar. "Well, you look more . . . familiar."

He stiffened, and Melanie smiled to herself. "Like the figure on Chen's sign, I mean."

"That's what made me think of this."

"What's wrong with the Anasazi one?"

"I learned during my first ride that the wooden mask chafes the nose. Apparently, my ancestors weren't interested in comfort."

He was standing close to her—she could almost feel the warmth of his body. "What are you going to do with me, now that you've captured me?"

"I didn't 'capture' you, señorita. I rescued you."

"Whichever description suits you ... but that doesn't answer my question."

He considered a moment, then pulled the Indian blanket from his horse's back and removed the bridle. He stroked the horse's neck, then set him free.

Melanie's nervousness returned. "Why did you let him go?"

The Renegade turned back to her. "I can't bring you back there tonight—it would be too dangerous with Bradford's guards stalking around the place. In the morning, I'll see that you're returned safely."

This sounded vague, but Melanie was too tired to argue or press the matter. "So ... we sleep here?" She paused as the prospect became clear. *"Together?"*

He laid the Indian blanket on the ground, then removed his cape. "You have nothing to fear, señorita. But I can't very well leave you out here alone just to protect your virtue in the eyes of the world."

"My virtue? And protect me from what? Wild animals?"

"Well ... yes."

She knew how to test his identity beyond doubt. But it might be more dangerous than wild animals. She had to test the Renegade himself.

# Chapter Seven

This was exactly what Diego didn't want to happen. Lying alone, completely alone, with Melanie Muessen beside him; everything was conspiring to disarm him, to make him weak—and to make him care for her. He'd kissed her like an animal lunging at prey—in front of his grandfather and the whole tribe. How could a woman so singular and so peculiarly vulnerable send him into such a primitive lust?

He hurt her, because to protect her, he had to distance himself from her. He hurt her, because she terrified him, because when she was near, he saw nothing else, because he could find himself kissing her before he knew what he was doing. The hurt in her eyes haunted him—she'd looked so confused, and then so brave when she rode away from

Tesuque without questioning him, without making demands. He'd hurt the pride of other women; he'd listened to their demands and outrage when he refused to do what they wanted. It wasn't Melanie's pride he'd hurt—it was her trust and her heart.

He told himself it was for the best, but he was here with her now, close to her, all in the name of protecting her. But something had changed.

He wasn't the same man when he wore the mask, or even the cloth substitute. The words he spoke to her seemed unfamiliar, yet they came without forethought, out of the core of him. Worse still, nothing he did could dull his attraction to her. His skin felt hot, and beneath the mask, it became hard to breathe. He adjusted it as quietly as he could, but Melanie watched intently. Her expression indicated that she was planning something.

She propped herself up on one elbow and gazed down into his eyes. "If your mask is uncomfortable, Sir Renegade, perhaps you wouldn't mind removing it."

"It's fine now." What if she took it upon herself to remove his mask while he slept? He wouldn't put it past a woman who'd been caught investigating Carlton Bradford's bedroom. He needed to distract her. But how?

Melanie reached out to touch his lips, and Diego froze. She ran her small, soft finger over his top lip, then the bottom, feeling its contours. He held his breath, stunned by her unexpected sensuality. "Señorita, you are treading in dangerous waters."

# Join the Historical Romance Book Club — and GET 4 FREE* BOOKS NOW!

A $23.96 Value!

## Yes! I want to subscribe to the Historical Romance Book Club.

Please send me my **4 FREE\* BOOKS.** I have enclosed $2.00 for shipping/handling. Each month I'll receive the four newest Historical Romance selections to preview for 10 days. If I decide to keep them, I will pay the Special Members Only discounted price of just $4.24 each, a total of $16.96, plus $2.00 shipping/handling ($19.50 US in Canada). This is a **SAVINGS OF AT LEAST $5.00** off the bookstore price. There is no minimum number of books I must buy, and I may cancel the program at any time. In any case, the **4 FREE\* BOOKS** are mine to keep.

*In Canada, add $5.00 shipping/handling per order for the first shipment. For all future shipments to Canada, the cost of membership is $19.50 US, which includes shipping and handling. (All payments must be made in US dollars.)

**NAME:** _____

**ADDRESS:** _____

**CITY:** _____  **STATE:** _____

**COUNTRY:** _____  **ZIP:** _____

**TELEPHONE:** _____

**E-MAIL:** _____

**SIGNATURE:** _____

If under 18, Parent or Guardian must sign. Terms, prices, and conditions subject to change. Subscription subject to acceptance. Dorchester Publishing reserves the right to reject any order or cancel any subscription.

He wasn't having any trouble disguising his voice—the effect she had on him altered everything, and his voice came low and husky with repressed desire. He didn't dare look at her, but he felt sure she smiled.

"You are an interesting man, whatever face you wear. Interesting, and strangely compelling." Melanie's voice had changed, too; now it was lower, and far more seductive.

She studied what she could see of his face with a direct, analytical expression. Then, with ponderous attention to detail, she kissed him. He couldn't believe it. She wasn't the same woman—he'd confused her with another. He'd kissed her before, but it had been on his initiative.

This was different, and excruciating. The tip of her tongue slipped between his lips and his whole body clenched in restraint. He hadn't thought Melanie capable of such a blatant seduction, let alone with a man she didn't know, a man in a mask, a man who had abducted her. . . .

His hands shook as he gripped her shoulders. "Señorita . . . Do you have any idea what you're doing?"

She peeked up. "I'm testing . . ." She coughed, then continued. "Kissing you. Do you like it?"

He groaned. "I'm beyond liking it." He paused. "Is this some kind of dark, feminine design to get me to reveal my identity?"

She hesitated, surprised. "Would it work?"

"I don't want to find out." He felt an irrational

177

surge of jealousy. Melanie was responding to a stranger, creating feelings and a passion he didn't know he possessed. But she had let Diego—himself—kiss her, too. Maybe she was too innocent to realize what she was doing. "You know you're arousing me, don't you?"

Her fingers played with the sash of his mask, toying with the skin below his ear, then down his throat toward his chest. "That is a pleasing thought."

So much for innocence. "I had no idea you were such a temptress."

"I find you attractive. I see no reason not to touch you."

His throat clenched with both desire and jealousy. "Isn't there anyone . . . else in your life?"

She laughed. "Of course not. Who would interest me here?"

He frowned, and hoped she couldn't see his expression in the darkness. "Then you have formed no attachment at all to any man in this area?"

Melanie offered a casual sigh. "Oh, perhaps . . . Other men . . . hmmm." A long pause followed. "No, not really."

He knew she was lying. She had to be. He'd seen the way she looked at him—at Diego. "I find that hard to believe."

"Do you?" He didn't have to see her face to know she looked both wide-eyed and innocent. "And who, here in this remote pueblo, do you think might capture my fancy? Chen, perhaps? But no, he is too occupied with his hotel to pay much attention to a woman—except Victoria, of course, and she's his competition. Will?"

He huffed, annoyed. "You're too high-strung to interest Will. He's calm and peaceful—you'd drive him crazy."

"Surely you don't think I'd find Bradford attractive."

Diego's voice came strained with irritation. "I was not thinking of our enemy."

"Then who . . . ?" She giggled, a tinkling and pert sound. "You couldn't be thinking of Diego de Aguirre—he who spends his nights beneath taverns, when he's not troubling someone's sister. Not him?"

He couldn't speak, so he didn't respond. Melanie laughed again. "Ah, Señor Renegade, how silly you are to be jealous of him. And it is jealousy I hear in your voice, is it not?"

Again he refused to answer. It was.

"No, no . . . Diego was amusing, yes. I'll admit he was an adequate kisser. But I realized quickly that his interest in me was shallow. He says there is nothing more to his character, nothing deeper, nothing heroic. And I, of course, believe him."

"Then you're not attracted to him at all?" He felt suddenly, and painfully, vulnerable. Diego looked up into Melanie's face. He couldn't see the details, but he saw her eyes glimmer, and the outline of her heavy hair falling around her face. He reached to free it from its ribbon, and it fell forward over her shoulder.

"I am attracted to you."

She wanted him, the Renegade, but not Diego, because Diego had hurt her, because his interest was *shallow*.

"How do you know my interest is any deeper than his?"

"You risked a lot to save me." She moved a little closer, so that he felt her soft hair touching his face. "And I am a woman, Señor Renegade. I know you want me."

Diego gulped. He couldn't let her know that he cared because he knew he had nothing a man should give a woman. He knew he wasn't worthy of her. But as the Renegade, he was something more. "I have a duty here, señorita. I cannot take off this mask to win you. I cannot promise you a lifetime together, and that is what you deserve from a man."

"I don't ask it." She sounded earnest, and he believed her, but he also knew she deserved more. "But I only wanted a kiss."

"Is that so? I think, señorita, that you want much more than a kiss."

He ran his hands down her back, feeling her waist taper inward, the soft swell of her bottom. She gasped in surprise, but she didn't stop him. He couldn't take her virtue or her virginity, but he could make love to her otherwise.

"Maybe . . . maybe I do." She bent and kissed

180

his throat, and he felt her quick fingers unbuttoning his shirt. Her lips grazed his skin and his heart throbbed. He couldn't lose control of himself, not with her. He had to protect her, even from herself.

Her hand splayed over his chest and she moved to kiss his mouth. He locked his arms around her and returned her kiss. His tongue played against hers and her breath quickened. She sucked gently, tentatively—natural ability had been an understatement. She was gifted at love; he should have known.

Diego rolled her onto her back and she reached for him. He couldn't stop kissing her—his mind worked in a wild blur of desire. He touched her shoulder, then the swell of her breast. He couldn't remember what she had been wearing when he caught her in Bradford's room—something dark gray and nondescript—but whatever it was held her breasts tight and snug. They were fuller than he'd expected, taut with her arousal. He found the tiny pearl button of her high lace collar and unfastened it, and realized there were several more to be loosen. His knuckles touched her throat and he felt her racing pulse, felt her quick breaths as he unbuttoned her blouse and then the bodice.

He wanted her, flesh against flesh, to touch her soft skin, to know her. She didn't try to stop him, though her limbs tensed when he pulled her bodice apart and finished unbuttoning the long line of small buttons. She was neatly corseted beneath, with a petticoat and chemise, designed long ago as armor, he felt certain—but Diego knew his way with feminine undergarments, and nothing would fend him off for long.

She needed him—he tried to tell himself it wasn't because he'd hurt her already. But she needed him, as a woman needs a man, to hold her, to love her, to join with the deepest part of herself. Sex was power, a person's deepest power, and she had held it at bay too long.

Diego paused before unlacing her corset. He wanted to touch her more than he'd ever wanted anything. Her skin was soft, pure. He rested his cheek against her breast, then turned his face to kiss her skin. Her breath caught, as if she hadn't expected his touch, as if she hadn't realized how thoroughly he'd undressed her. She squirmed and tried to adjust her corset, but he caught her hands and moved to look down into her face. He couldn't see her well, and he knew she couldn't see him, especially masked. He wondered if he looked frightening; her eyes did seem particularly wide, reflecting the starry sky.

"I would not hurt you for the world, señorita. I wouldn't frighten you, or cause you any pain. But you are beautiful this way, so soft to the touch and so dear. If I touch you here, know it is because I worship you. If I kiss you, know you are my treasure. I will not take you, not tonight, but I will make you wish I had."

She gasped as if challenged, and thrilled to accept. She reached for him, and his decision was made. A wild, uncontrolled part of Diego seized him. He spread her corset apart, then cupped her breast in his hand. Her thin chemise gave no hindrance as he kissed her and sucked her nipple into his mouth.

Melanie's breath caught then released in a shuddering moan as he laved the hard peak with his tongue, then grazed his teeth over its tip. He teased her until her body writhed, until she clutched his shoulders, until he knew she was his for the taking. He sucked and licked, distracting her as he slid his hand up her thigh, over the rim of her stockings and between her legs. He slipped his fingers beneath her cotton drawers and found her dewy and warm. Desire stabbed through him—images of filling her with himself tore through his mind. She wanted him, and she needed him.

She needed him to be stronger, this night, and he would hold to that if it killed him. His groin felt tight as a drawn bow, he ached so for release, but he kept his touch light, and at first she didn't seem to notice what he was doing. He brushed the tip of his fingers over her moist cleft, and her whole body tensed. His thumb circled her feminine bud, and she squealed, then shot upright, dislodging him.

"You can't touch me . . . there!" She shook herself as if she'd been dreaming, then snatched her bodice together. He couldn't see her well in the darkness, but he knew she was trembling. "You can't touch me *here,* either."

Diego gathered himself together. His erection

pressed hard against his snug black trousers, and he thanked the night for concealing his lust from a woman so innocent. "Señorita, I just did."

She clamped her hand to her forehead. "What am I doing?"

It was like her to get carried away without realizing what she was doing. Diego fought to restrain himself, then reached to touch her loose hair. He wanted to explain that a union between a man and a woman was nothing for shame, he wanted to tell her he would never have carried them to their rightful fulfillment. At least, not tonight, not this way. He had to say something to calm her. "Did you like it?"

He froze as soon as the words escaped. He never seemed to say the right thing. Rafael had been sensitive with the woman he loved, with everyone. Diego blurted out the wrong thing at the wrong time daily.

"Yes."

She surprised him with her matter-of-fact reply. Diego scratched his head, then readjusted his mask. "What?"

"I liked it. Very much."

He didn't know what to say, exactly. "Then why did you stop me?"

"You touched me . . . in a spot that no one but myself has touched, in a way that . . . while pleasurable, has a certain effect of . . ."

Diego grinned. "Making you crazy?"

She nodded vigorously. "Yes."

184

Melanie possessed a certain lack of inhibition that took him entirely off guard. She was intuitive, sensing what he wanted and needed, and she was creative, which might have been the best combination he'd ever encountered. Better still, she was honest and open. It didn't make sense—she was quiet and restrained, with an obvious tendency to lose herself in thought and solitude. But here, when the air itself seemed heavy with sex, she came alive, and all the mystic power inside her came to the fore.

He played with her hair and she relaxed. "It is too fast for you."

"I felt . . . as if I had no control over myself. I was scared."

"Are you frightened still?"

She considered this, and he could imagine her expression perfectly—serious, sincere as she pondered the most truthful answer. "No . . ."

He moved his touch from her hair to her shoulder, then moved closer beside her. "I should have warned you. Would that have helped?"

"Possibly." She looked up at him, studying him in the darkness. "What were you doing?"

Diego hesitated. Melanie was honest—he might as well be, too. "I was going to play with you and tease you until your small, delectable, beautiful body writhed, until your very soul erupted and shattered into the sweetest ecstasy you've ever known."

She puffed a quick breath, and his own pulse soared. "But not . . . ?"

"I would not take that joy myself, not tonight. I would not steal your virture, nor leave you with my child. I just want to give you . . . rapture."

"Why?"

*Because I will treasure the image for the rest of my life.* "It would please me."

She flopped back on his makeshift bed and her hair spread out around her shoulders, catching starlight like waves on the sea. "Very well."

" 'Very well?' "

"You may do so."

His body clenched with conflicting impulses. "Señorita, please don't think I'm denying you, but there's something I have to know."

She peeked at him, impatient. "What?"

"Are you sure you have you no feelings . . . for any other man, besides myself?"

She looked at him, strong and sure and confident. "I know my heart, Señor Renegade, and I know the man who holds it."

Maybe he deserved this. As Diego, he had toyed with her, held himself at bay, preferring to tease her, to make her want him when he intended nothing but flirtation. The more he cared for her, the more he backed away.

He was jealous of himself. What had happened to the man who would take a woman, believing she could fend for her own emotions when it was over? Melanie reached up and tapped his thigh.

"Have you changed your mind, Señor Renegade? You promised me rapture."

The Renegade and Diego combined with sudden force into one. "Rapture it will be, my beautiful señorita." He lowered himself beside her. He kissed her slowly. He ran his hand down her body, over the swell of her breasts, then pulled up her skirt and her petticoat. Melanie held her breath, but she didn't resist as he pushed aside her loose drawers.

Her heart pounded and her pulse raced—he felt its speed against his lips as he kissed her neck. He delayed the touch she waited for, circling her woman's core, grazing the soft hairs at the apex of her thighs. He deepened their kiss and engaged her tongue in a gentle, teasing dance.

He felt as if he'd never touched a woman this way before, and maybe it was true. He'd never cared this way, never felt the almost painful ache when she moaned or gasped, when her arms tightened around his shoulders. She squirmed beneath him, and he could feel the ache inside her, too. She longed for his touch, she longed for him. He dragged his fingers lightly over her tiny, hidden bud, then dipped into the damp, feminine warmth of her.

She gave herself like an angel, with soft, shuddering sighs and sweet whispers. Her breath caught and exhaled with surprised delight, then with a lower, husky moan as he increased the pressure. He played with her, he toyed with her femininity and her passion, he reveled in her reactions, and he held his own need at bay.

Melanie's head tipped back as her rapture approached. He saw her white teeth biting into the soft flesh of her lower lip as she fought against her last, primitive surrender. His whole body throbbed with the demand to join her, to drive himself deep inside the inviting warmth of her. He circled the small peak and slipped his finger inside her just as her voice broke with a sharp, surprised cry of pleasure. The cry dissolved into a husky, gravelly moan, caught with waves of bliss. Her body writhed around his finger, her hips arched, an instinctive call to draw him inside.

He had never been a man to resist provocation, but somehow he held himself back, though his arousal strained, his groin throbbed and ached. His own release seemed imminent even as hers gradually abated and stilled. Melanie lay flat on her back before him, eyes wide with shock, her lips parted for swift breaths.

When at last she spoke, it was with the voice both of perfect satiation and doom. "I have done it."

Diego caught his breath, fighting to calm his own unfulfilled need. "What is that, love?"

Only her eyes shifted as she looked at him. "I have followed him down the dark path of debauchery. I have become just like Diego de Aguirre."

\* \* \*

"I have not *debauched* you."

They had argued for hours. The sun already threatened in the sky. Melanie didn't seem upset by their sexual encounter. She seemed dead-set certain that she was altered in some way, and that she had become . . . Diego. It was he who couldn't let the matter rest.

"It's ridiculous. You gave in to a little temptation. You deserve it."

She nodded, misunderstanding him. "I must, or it wouldn't have happened. It's because I've allowed myself overly enticing dreams and imaginings."

"Dreams? Such as what . . . ?" He stopped himself and shook his head. "Listen to me—what we did was beautiful. It's not as if I pillaged your body."

"I feel pillaged. But I do not blame you. I requested that you do exactly what you did." She paused, her small face knit in thought. "It's obvious that I have a dark side to my character, one that lusts and craves and is without restraint."

"Well, yes . . ." He caught himself and stopped. "But those are good things."

Melanie yawned. "It doesn't matter if they're good or bad. They must be inherent to myself, and I must accept them." Her eyelids drifted shut, but then she peeked at him through just one eye. "You must accept it, too. I never said you had debauched me, only that I had started down that path. It was my choice."

This wasn't at all the way he wanted her to look at their lovemaking. "We shared a . . . passionate embrace."

"It felt like more."

"Only because you respond so well, so thoroughly, with such vigor." Damn! He was getting hard again—his erection refused to thoroughly abate, anyway, but it was wearing on his patience.

"I suppose you're right, in a way. I gave myself to you, but it wasn't reciprocated. You didn't give yourself to me in turn."

He rolled his eyes and groaned. "I was protecting you."

She yawned again and curled up on her side. "That was good of you. I would like to know, however, more about your body. Is it much like mine?"

He eyed her doubtfully. "Your body is small, soft, and extremely feminine. My body is tall, hard, and strong. So hard I can barely move, in fact."

"That's not what I meant. I meant, is the male body capable of that wonderful . . . ecstasy you gave to me?"

"Yes!" He sat up and bowed his head into his hands. "Yes . . . Yes, something similar. More . . . productive, in a way. But I think the feelings are much the same." She was tormenting him. "Go to sleep, señorita, or I will soon break every vow I've made on your behalf, and you *will* be debauched, and debauched constantly for days to come."

Melanie yawned for the third time and looked

peaceful. "That time will come, I know. Maybe it's a more interesting world when you're viewing it through the eyes of debauchery. I don't know. Diego seemed to think so."

Her voice faded as she drifted finally toward sleep, but Diego just lay staring down at her. Somehow she had shifted from infatuation to *becoming* him, to finding that part of him in herself. She was a strange woman, no question. She seemed willing to find the vilest harlot inside herself, and then to understand and accept it.

She was absolutely nothing like the girl who'd first led a fat black pony into Tewa. She was something he'd never encountered before, or dared dream of, or ever imagined he deserved. She was the woman of his dreams, and of his heart. And for her sake he had to wear a mask and never take it off, lest her own dreams be destroyed.

Melanie slept peacefully, but Diego couldn't make himself comfortable. As the sun rose, he knew better than to lay there waiting for her to wake. In the full light of day, this close, she would certainly recognize him. He pressed a gentle kiss on her forehead, then got up and quietly left her sleeping. The cool morning air failed to freshen him much, but fortunately his black horse was grazing nearby and didn't seem adverse to a morning ride. Diego caught him, but he left the saddle blanket with Melanie. He leapt astride but found the act more uncomfortable than usual thanks to his night of unfulfilled passion.

He rode down from the hills until he came within sight of Tewa, then dismounted and released his horse. Bradford's guards were up early working on their kiva dig; it appeared to be almost cleared of debris. Why Bradford bothered Diego couldn't guess, but each day the guards returned to their task.

Diego evaded their attention, then followed paths he'd known since boyhood. He crept through the windows of three pueblo bedrooms, including Miguel's, a route that extended his journey but had become habit, and made his secret way to the Chateau Renegade.

Bradford had posted guards at the gate—Tewa Pueblo was beginning to look more like a fort than a village—but Diego knew how to avoid the sight of overtired watchers. He slipped into the Chateau through the kitchen and went to Chen's bedroom. He knocked softly, twice, and waited impatiently for Chen to open the door.

The door opened a crack, and a bleary Chen looked out, frowning. Chen stuck his head out to look down the hall, then yanked Diego inside. "You miserable, villainous rogue, free of scruples and any kind of shame . . . What did you do with her?"

Nothing he hadn't expected. "I *saved* her."

Chen's frown deepened until his lips formed a downward *v*. "Is that what you call it? It is one thing to don your mask and cape for the sake of good, as your brother did. Quite another to use it for the purpose of abducting and seducing innocent young females."

"I donned my mask and cape to explore Bradford's quarters. Unfortunately, Melanie got there first."

"*Melanie.* I see. You're calling her by her first name."

"You're jealous. And what I did to her is none of your concern."

Chen's brow angled. "I am not jealous. When I consider marriage, it will be for the most practical of reasons. My future wife will bring much to our union."

"What? Love, tenderness, the evocations of sweet feminine intuition?"

Chen looked bewildered. "No. Why would I want that? She'll be rich."

Diego groaned and flopped into Chen's favorite and most expensive chair. "You're a romantic to the core."

"No less than you!" Chen stood before him, annoyed. "Where is she?"

"She's in the hills—I caught her snooping around in Bradford's room. Before I could get her out of there, he caught us, so I hauled her off. I couldn't think of anything else to do with her."

"Then you treated her with the utmost sensitivity and care during the night, and left her unscathed?"

Diego hesitated. "She's unscathed . . . for the most part."

Chen fell back on his bed, defeated. "Does she know who you are?"

"No."

"That's something." It seemed enough, because Chen sat up and brought himself back to the matter at hand. "How are you going to distance your identity from the Renegade this time?"

"You'll go find Melanie; I'll go back to Tesuque and stay there another day. See that Bradford knows I'm there, will you?"

"And what about Miss Muessen?"

"I'll deal with her . . . in my own way. Privately."

"I was afraid of that. Well, I can think of nothing better."

A sharp rap on Chen's door startled them both, followed by Carlton Bradford's voice. Chen shoved Diego toward the window, but Diego stopped. "I can't hide—there's no time. Open the door."

"*What?*"

Diego pulled off his black cape and hid it under Chen's mattress, and Chen hid the Anasazi mask in his wardrobe closet. "Do it. I know what I'm doing."

Chen obeyed, but he looked pale. He opened the door while Diego lounged in his chair. Bradford stepped in and glared at Diego. "De Aguirre—what in hell are you doing here? I understood you were with the Indians at Tesuque."

Diego yawned and feigned an obvious headache. "My grandfather has an aversion to the . . . more delicate pleasures. I . . . made advances, shall we say, to one of his favorite nieces, and the old fellow kicked me out. They're remarkably short of drink there, too."

Bradford looked suspicious. "My guards have been posted at the gates. No one has entered since the Renegade left last night, taking Miss Muessen with him."

Diego rubbed his shoulders—they were stiff, so there was no real effort at subterfuge. "And indeed, no one has, Señor Bradford. I arrived early in the evening yesterday. I don't recall any guards posted at particular alert then. But I'm afraid I missed your daring Renegade again. I was . . . indisposed, as it were, with another young woman who captured my fancy—adequately enough for a night's amusement, anyway."

"What woman?"

"I couldn't bring myself to say her name."

Bradford's eyes narrowed in disbelief. "I had no idea you were so concerned with a woman's virtue, de Aguirre."

"Not her virtue, señor. Her father bears a remarkably hefty fighting arm." Diego watched as Bradford's familiar sneer returned. "But I guess this further settles the matter of my identity. I couldn't be the Renegade, sadly."

"How is that, de Aguirre?"

"Well, as you say, the Renegade left, and your guards have been posted ever since. I'm hardly in a state to avoid armed guards, I assure you."

Apparently he looked as disheveled as he pretended to be. A night of repressed desire did that to a man. Bradford pressed no further. He turned to Chen. "The matter of Miss Muessen needs to be investigated, and I would like your help, Chen, in doing so."

Chen glanced at Diego. "Investigated? As I saw it, the Renegade needed a hostage, and Miss Muessen happened to be available."

"Maybe . . . but there may be more to it than that."

Diego endured a stab of apprehension. "What more?"

"What neither of you may know is that Miss Muessen was apparently already in my room."

Chen issued a quick, scoffing noise. "That hardly seems likely. I'm sure he brought her there . . ."

"Why? I think not. Is it a coincidence that Miss Muessen, the daughter of a well-known photographer, skilled at propaganda, has arrived at the same time as the Renegade returns?"

Diego fought to keep himself casual. "You can't think that quiet, gentle, soft-spoken woman capable of aiding the Renegade, señor. Or perhaps you think she *is* our daring legend? I didn't see him firsthand, but I would guess the man in black is somewhat taller than our petite señorita."

"Nonetheless, it bears investigation. I have guards out looking for her now, but when she returns, I will keep a close eye on Miss Muessen's activities. It may be that her 'gentle, soft-spoken' manner is the real disguise."

# *Chapter Eight*

"Thank you, Will, but I could have found my own way home." Melanie sat astride the mare Diego had given her, the Renegade's saddle blanket draped over her own saddle. For reasons she couldn't guess, Will had brought Porticus along in his search. Maybe he intended to use the pony like a dog to sniff out Melanie's trail, but Porticus seemed more interested in nearby shrubs than in Melanie.

Will mounted his stout pinto, smiling. "Figured with Porticus along I'd find you first, before them guards."

"There were guards looking for me? Mr. Bradford must have been concerned."

"Chen says he's more suspicious than concerned, miss. Told me to tell you to be careful."

"Mr. Bradford is suspicious of me? Why?"

"Thinks you're in with the Renegade, even though we know it ain't true."

"How do you know that?"

"He ain't the sort to be in league with anyone."

"You know him."

Will said nothing. Melanie felt strange in the morning light. A changed woman who, on the surface, looked exactly the same as she had the day before. Will whistled an uneven tune and pretended to follow the flight of a bird overhead.

She knew her lover's identity. One kiss had been enough to tell her that, and to assuage any doubts she might have had otherwise. That kiss had been a test—and it had turned into an unexpected seduction. A seduction that left her confused, and more at the Renegade's mercy than she had been when he swept her from Bradford's office. Stranger still, she felt as if she knew him less after their encounter than before. He had too many facets to his character to comprehend.

"Tell me about the Renegade, Will. What is he like, as a person? You can tell me that, at least."

He looked uncomfortable, but she was more likely to get information from Will than from the more careful Chen. "Oh, he's one of a kind, and that's a fact, miss."

"I take it he has Zuni blood."

Will coughed. "Did he tell you that?"

"He made reference to his ancestors, yes."

"Well, then. Did he? Well, well."

"Is it true?"

"Yes, miss. Figure it is."

"Has he always been so . . . complicated?"

Will huffed and nodded vigorously. "Yes."

"Why?"

Will extended his neck and scratched his shoulder. "Oh, well, it might be how his life's gone. Or maybe he was just born that way."

That certainly helped . . . Melanie sighed. "Why would a man pretend to be one way when he is quite the opposite inside?"

Will turned to her, his eyes glittering. "Because he's scared of what he really is, miss. It ain't the bad people get scared of in themselves. They're used to that. It's the good—that terrifies most folks to death."

"It didn't terrify the former Renegade, Rafael."

"Oh, it did in a way, miss. He was scared when he fell in love, that's for sure. And love, that's good."

"Is this new Renegade . . . like Rafael?"

Will smiled, soft and mysterious. "I'd say he's a lot more like Señor Rafael than he knows."

"Do you consider him an honest man, Will?"

"More honest than he means to be, miss."

"A good man?"

"Better than he knows."

Melanie bit her lip. "Do you think I can trust him?" That was what she really wanted to know.

Will looked at her and smiled. "Miss, when you don't have to ask me these questions, then you can trust him. Trust takes time—it don't come in a day."

They rode on in silence, but by the time they reached the Tewa gates, she knew how to handle this new turn of events. She would give him time. As much as she needed to trust him, he had to learn to trust her, too.

The gate swung open unexpectedly, and Carlton Bradford greeted them. He stepped forward and took her mare's reins. "Ah, Miss Muessen . . . You have returned, I see, unscathed from your encounter with the Renegade. How good of Will to retrieve you! None of my guards were able to locate you—I was about to commence a search myself."

"I had already started back to the pueblo when Will found me. There was no need to send out guards." Bradford was watching her strangely, and Melanie's discomfort in his presence grew. "If you don't mind, Mr. Bradford, I'm very tired. I'd like to go to Victoria's inn and sleep."

"I'm afraid that will have to wait, my dear."

"Wait for what?"

"I have a few questions, just a simple inquiry. You have, after all, spent time with the Renegade."

"I know nothing of him. He left me in the hills, alone, and I waited for morning to find my way back. Will met me, and I'm here. I can tell you nothing more."

"Ah. I see. Then perhaps we could discuss what you were doing in my room last night." He waited for her shock to subside, then nodded. "I will escort you to my headquarters. Now."

Bradford's office was the front room of Rafael's schoolhouse. The oak desk looked better suited for a schoolmaster's use than a commander's, but somehow Bradford had made the thoughtfully crafted room look like a military headquarters.

"Who is he?" Bradford's voice came surprisingly stern, and Melanie began to feel nervous.

"I don't know."

He settled back into his chair, a smile that more resembled a smirk on his face. "Come, my dear, surely you can't expect me to believe that. I understand a woman's little whims. He's a daring figure, brash, exciting . . ."

"I don't know him well enough to say."

"Don't you? Generally, when a woman spends an entire night with a man, she knows something of him."

Bradford had no way of knowing what she had done in the night, and she felt even more certain that it was none of his business, but Melanie couldn't restrain a surge of guilt. She hated to feel powerless, as if her fate might rest in another's hands. But Bradford's life was based on how completely he could control others. If his goal was money, then his desire for control lay at the bottom of it all.

"I told you, Mr. Bradford, the Renegade left me last night to fend for myself. I waited until dawn's light to make my way back here. I have nothing to answer for, least of all to you. You have some say, perhaps, over this pueblo. But you have no authority over me. This isn't a military establishment—as much as you have made it resemble one."

Her defiance took him off guard, and angered him. "You are in error, Miss Muessen. I do, in fact, have considerable power. My authority permits me to handle defiance in this pueblo as I see fit."

"I have not defied you."

Bradford nodded slowly. Every gesture he made seemed designed to intimidate her. Melanie drew a slow breath to quiet her nerves. "Haven't you, Miss Muessen? Then perhaps you would explain what you were doing in my suite last night."

"I was lost."

His smirk deepened. "That seems unlikely. Tell me, what in my room did you deem worthy of interest, and your camera's attention?"

"Nothing at all, Mr. Bradford." Her mind worked quickly, fueled by his arrogance and certainty that all things revolved around himself. "It was the Renegade I hoped to photograph." Her words surprised herself almost as much as him.

"What?"

"Yes. I saw him sneak into the pueblo, you see, and I decided to catch him in action, so to speak. And I would have, too, if you hadn't interrupted us."

"I had not realized your equipment works in darkness."

He had her there. "It would have been . . . shadowy, true, but interesting nonetheless. Your room was well lit, at first."

Fortunately, Bradford didn't know enough about photography to counter her unlikely assertion. "Your interest in the Renegade may not be for the best, my dear. He is undoubtedly a dangerous, reckless man."

"He did me no harm last night. But perhaps a free-spirited, bold man such as that is more a threat to you than to me."

Her words angered Bradford more than she'd expected. "Your defense of the Renegade betrays you, Miss Muessen. Take care, or you will find yourself in a position similar to his, opposing the rightful law of this pueblo."

"Mr. Bradford, I can leave Tewa whenever I choose. I doubt your authority reaches far enough to stop me."

"You may leave, of course. For now. Your camera, however, will stay behind until I determine what unauthorized use you have made of it."

"I won't permit theft." Somehow she managed to restrain her anger, but it wasn't easy. Melanie rose from her chair and braced her fingers on Bradford's desk. Once, Rafael de Aguirre had sat behind this desk, grading his students' papers, helping children learn to read, perhaps explaining to Miguel the baker that Diego didn't mean any real harm by his latest prank. Now it had been commandeered by a man with no imagination, no caring, and no purpose other than his own.

Bradford's smirk never left his face. "Theft? Photography—many consider it a dangerous invention."

"Why? Because it records truth?"

His smirk faded. "Because it distorts reality, confusing weak minds."

Melanie went to the door. "If there's nothing else—and I assume you can't imprison me for being abducted—then I shall leave now."

She left before he could respond, but his set jaw indicated he had nothing to say, anyway. She went out into the open air, feeling as if she'd been in battle. Her hands were shaking, and her skin flushed hot, then cold. She had been threatened; her instincts were keen enough to understand that.

Melanie walked past Chen's hotel, lost in thought, then past the saloon, on her way to Victoria's inn. Someone bounded down the saloon steps, bumping into her, and a bottle cracked on the dry pueblo clay.

Melanie squealed, then looked up into the dark Spanish eyes of Diego de Aguirre. She couldn't help her reaction to him. He blinked, and his long black lashes cast shadows on his high cheekbones. He looked almost as nervous as she felt. "Señorita, pardon me. But you should watch where you're going."

He was teasing her as if nothing had happened between them. Still tense from her encounter with

Bradford, she pointed her finger at Diego. Her fingers did indeed look small, and the pinky was still curved and out to the side. She tried to align it with the others and failed. "You . . . you are a menace!"

He fought back a smile, which grated on her nerves further. "It is I who suffered a loss from our collision." He gestured at the broken bottle as its pungent liquid oozed over the clay.

Melanie glared. "If you don't mind, I am very tired. Excuse me." She tried to squeeze past him, but he bent to pick up the shards of glass, sighing as if at a treasure lost, and effectively blocked her departure.

He glanced at her sidelong as he made a neat pile of the shards. "I understand you had an . . . eventful night."

How like him to remind her! And how embarrassing! "That is none of your concern."

"You look happy. I am pleased."

"Are you? Then at last I can sleep in peace."

Diego nodded toward the schoolhouse. "What did Bradford want with you?"

Melanie shook her head. "He thinks I'm in league with the Renegade."

"You told him you're not, I trust."

"Yes, but I don't think he believed me. He thinks I know who he is. I would, of course, never reveal that."

He eyed her suspiciously, but she said no more. "Bradford didn't threaten you, did he?"

"He did, subtly. But he has no authority over

me, so far, though he would like me to believe differently." She glanced toward the schoolhouse jail and frowned. "He is more dangerous than I first imagined, and I like him even less than I thought. But I trust he found me formidable, too." She paused. "As will you."

"Then you mistake my opinion of you, señorita. I have realized you were formidable since I met you."

"Good." She stepped over Diego's broken bottle and kept her eyes averted from his, partly because she felt embarrassed and partly because she feared to reveal too much. *Trust takes time . . .* She intended to give it time.

Diego stood up and moved to let her pass, but his soft voice stopped her. "Señorita, you know you can always leave this place."

She glanced back. "I have no intention of leaving. I believe I can do good here, and that my profession may be of some use. I'm not sure how, exactly, but Mr. Bradford seemed wary of my skills with photography. Even he must believe it can be used against him."

"It might be wiser not to cross him, Melanie, especially if he feels he has reason to distrust you already."

"I have no intention of crossing him. I simply intend to go about my business here without taking direction from him."

Diego assessed her thoughtfully. "You remind me of someone."

Her eyes narrowed. "Who?"

Diego looked pained and issued a long groan before responding. "Me." He didn't wait for her reaction. He bowed in his careless, offhand way, picked up the broken bottle, and then headed for Chen's hotel alone.

Melanie slept through the daylight hours, waking only when Victoria came to bring her a tray of food for supper. She sat groggily on her bed while Victoria set out plates and filled a small goblet with white wine. Melanie barely heard what she said.

"This wine, you might be interested to know, was requested by Chen's Italian-masquerading-as-French chef, Massimo. Unfortunately, I arrived first to purchase it."

Melanie smiled. "The chef must be furious."

"Curiously, that does not appear to be the case. Each time I have intercepted something integral to his planned course, he has taken the defeat well." Victoria stood back to assess the table layout. "My efforts even seem to amuse him, though I am not certain why." She paused and shrugged. "Probably because he's Italian. I understand they find much humor in life's oddities."

Melanie restrained herself from pointing out that daughters of German photographers found an element of humor in Victoria's well-timed interceptions, too. "I hope he doesn't tell Chen what happened to this bottle."

Victoria's brow arched. "He will, of course, because it was Chen who demanded this particular vintage."

*And that was the point.* Melanie kept her expression straight and tried the wine. "It's very good." She wondered if she would follow Diego down the path of drunkenness, too, and wake beneath a tavern herself. She tried another sip and decided it wasn't worth the effort.

Victoria seated herself while Melanie dined. She leaned forward with girlish excitement. "What was he like? Was it very frightening to be carried off?"

Melanie looked up from her meal. "It was more . . . interesting than frightening. The part where he swung across the pueblo and landed on the schoolhouse roof was unnerving; I wasn't sure what he was doing, and I was afraid we would crash into something."

"I was impressed that you didn't scream. I find the shrill cries and shrieks females occasionally make both contrived and extremely foolish."

Melanie swallowed the last of the bread and nodded. "I agree. Even if one is captured, one can at least maintain one's pride."

"And dignity. You were dignified. Even when he tossed you over his shoulder and carried you off into the night."

"That was uncomfortable, but I'm afraid I was too confused to fight much."

Victoria fidgeted. "And later? Was he . . . gentlemanly?"

Melanie remembered his touch, his sweet seduction, and the wild creature she had become beneath his skill. "I am not violated, if that's what you mean."

"But something happened. He kissed you. Did he take off the mask?"

"He has two masks: the Indian one, and a simple black one that covers his eyes and forehead."

"I think he is too rebellious and impertinent for my tastes. One feels that he would often disobey authority and take unusual paths in life."

Melanie smiled. "He has already, that is certain."

"Did you learn anything about him?"

"He is kinder and more romantic than I expected. I sensed a great capacity for warmth and tenderness in his heart."

Victoria's brow puckered. "You're falling for him."

"Perhaps I am . . . but for now, I know he has something more important than me to consider."

Victoria rose and laid her hand gently on Melanie's shoulder. "Unless he's a fool, Miss Muessen, he will know there is nothing more important than you."

Victoria left, and Melanie lay back on her bed, staring at the ceiling. She wasn't tired, having slept all day, but it was too late to do anything else. Someone shouted outside, so she got up to look out the window in time to see Diego stumble drunkenly from the saloon. A woman shouted at him and called him a rogue, and Diego laughed. He walked uncertainly toward the Chateau, and Melanie returned to bed.

Trust . . . How much time would it take for it to take hold? One moment she felt herself believing everything. But doubt remained. Diego was a light-hearted man. It might amuse him to toy with her in two guises. She wasn't sure what to expect from him next. She wasn't even sure if the brandy he had carried in his hand was real.

The curtain of her open window ruffled in a dry breeze, but Melanie was too sleepy to close it. The full moon shone through the curtains, a beautiful and eerie light, with the pueblo walls in silhouette beyond. A shadow passed across the moon, and Melanie froze. A black cape swung from the shoulders of a silent, broad-shouldered man . . . But maybe she had been dreaming.

She waited but saw nothing. *My imagination* . . . She closed her eyes again and let herself relax. A dog barked, and a woman laughed, the usual sounds of night in Tewa. A night bird called and was answered from the woods outside the pueblo. Melanie rested her cheek on her hand and felt peaceful. The pueblo lamplights filtered through her window and played on her wall. She watched them move like lovers dancing, like an Indian ritual.

A gloved hand clamped over her mouth and her heart skipped a beat. If Bradford had come to kill her . . . Panic swelled like a sudden tide, and she fought. Her attacker wrapped his leg over her and held her pinned by his weight. With all her might, she sank her teeth into his hand. He swore, but he didn't release her.

"Señorita, this is not the greeting I hoped for."

Melanie froze, then gasped when she realized who it was. He spoke quietly, close to her ear. "Can I trust you not to cry out, love?"

*Trust me . . .* She nodded, and her heart sped again, but no longer in fear. He released her, then pulled off his glove and ministered to his hand, an effect she thought exaggerated. "I'm sorry about biting you."

He nodded, then sucked the perceived wound. "I had no idea you were so violent."

"I wouldn't have been if you had thought to announce yourself in some other way."

He replaced his glove. "Who else would I be?"

"I thought Mr. Bradford had sent one of his guards to kill me."

He was still wearing his black mask, tied over and behind his head. "That seems extreme. Why would he want to do that?"

"I don't know, exactly. I fear a man who intimidates with words would resort to greater violence if a threat arose. It's foolish to think I might be considered a threat, I know."

"Perhaps not, señorita. He doesn't want you documenting anything in this pueblo, that is certain. You may not have noticed, but when I was rescuing you from his room, someone shot at us after Victoria had warned them that I was carrying you. That person shot with a pistol, not a rifle. The only person here who has a pistol now is Bradford himself."

Melanie sat up, excited. "I did notice that, but I'd forgotten to mention it last night."

"You had more important things on your mind, perhaps?"

"I was distracted."

He reached to touch her cheek, though he still wore gloves. "Would you like to be . . . distracted . . . again?"

"Yes." She shouldn't seem so eager. Another woman would think to play with him, to leave him uncertain of her feelings, to be coy with her desire. But she was so glad he had come to her. His manner had been so confusing. She hadn't been sure if he toyed with her or if he really cared. His presence indicated that he cared.

She placed her hand over his. "I need you. I hope that you need me."

He cupped her face in his hands and moved closer until their noses touched. "I'm here, love."

Gently, she kissed him, and he gathered her into his arms. Something more than desire possessed her. She needed him; she felt desperate to hold him, to know him. They kissed wildly, and she almost believed he felt the same. She didn't know what she was doing, not fully, but she peeled his black shirt apart and pressed her lips against his hard chest. "I was afraid you wouldn't come, you know."

He rested his cheek on the top of her head. "I

couldn't stay away, though I know it would be safer and wiser for both of us." He gripped her shoulders and eased her back to look into her face. "I have to know you're safe. Bradford is suspicious of you, and it's because of me. You must swear to me that you won't risk yourself again."

"Would you make that same vow for me?" He didn't answer, and she nodded. "I thought not. Then you can't ask it of me."

"Nothing is worth your life." He turned away and seemed to be fighting something inwardly. He looked back at her, resigned. "I've come to tell you to leave."

"Leave? No! I will not." Her heart thudded with the cold ice of rejection. He wanted her gone, too. Her confidence swung full to the other side, back to doubt, and trust faded. "Please, I can't."

"Melanie, I'm a danger to you. You deserve a better life, to travel around the world photographing its wonders and its children. I can't let you risk yourself because of me. I'm not asking you because I don't care, I promise you. I care for you more than I ever thought I could care for anyone. But I can't let you stay here, not when the danger seems suddenly pointed at you."

"Bradford is suspicious of anyone who defies him." Melanie stopped. He said he cared for her, and she heard it in his voice. He might have come to send her away, but he was also there because he wanted her. Melanie ran her finger along his jaw. "You want me gone? So soon?"

He gulped and seemed tense. "It would be for the best."

"The best, I think, remains to be seen." She trailed her finger over his mouth, down his throat, then his chest as she unbuttoned the rest of his shirt. He held himself tight, and she felt a wild surge of power. "You did such wonderful things to me last night. I still tingle at the memory. My body aches to feel that way again. But you, I think, were left unsatisfied. I wonder, my sweet Renegade, what satisfaction I might bring to you."

His hands clenched on her shoulders. "Too much, señorita, too much."

"You touched me. If I touched you that way . . ." Before he could stop her, she let her finger drop lower until she met a hard bulge beneath his snug trousers. She knew what it was, but the size and power of his erection took her off guard. She hesitated, but white heat filled her veins. It was she who brought him to this impressive state, she who filled him with fire, even when he was unwilling and tried to resist.

She ran her fingers in outline of his length and he caught his breath. She increased the pressure of her palm against him and he groaned, then quickly seized her hand. "Señorita, you don't know what you're doing."

"I'm doing what you did to me."

"I find it difficult to restrain myself with you."

"Then don't." She freed her hand from his grasp and returned to that part of him that fascinated her. She rested her cheek against his chest and examined his arousal more thoroughly. Even through the fabric of his trousers, it felt hot, and hard. His heart pounded like a drum, and she relished the sound. She kissed his neck while she played with him, and his whole body went tight.

"You deny yourself, Señor Renegade. Why, when you didn't deny me? I want to touch you as you touched me. I want to kiss you and feel you in ecstasy."

He swallowed hard. "I can't take you, Melanie, not that way. There's too much at stake. You don't even know me."

"I know you. I know that you are strong and good, and that you care for me. How much more do I need to know?"

He uttered a small moan of defeat. "You need to know . . . a lot more. You need to be able to trust me."

"I trust you now."

"Maybe you shouldn't!" He moved back from her, then hopped up from the bed. He backed against the wall as if he feared her. He did—it was her power he feared. The strongest, most exciting, wonderful man she knew—he was weak at her touch. He wanted her love so much that he'd come to her against his will. He'd begged her to leave while his body screamed for her to stay.

She felt like a lion stalking prey, knowing it was hers already as she left her bed and went to him. He tipped his head back, his lips parted for harsh breaths. She placed her palm over his heart and felt it pound beneath her fingers. She kissed his hard chest, then slid down his body until she knelt before him.

He leaned back against the door, seeming too weak to fight. Melanie felt more powerful than she'd ever imagined possible. A primal force rose within her, making her strong, honing her feminine instincts to a wild and creative perfection. With her gaze locked on his, she cupped his arousal in her hands, then moved her palm slowly up and down its length. He exhaled with a hoarse, shuddering breath, then touched her head. He might think to stop her, but she was too strong now. She pressed her mouth against him and his breath became a moan.

She knew women of ill repute made love to men with their mouths—she had heard it while photographing the city streets of New York and been shocked beyond words. Now the thought appealed to her in a way that seemed impossible. She unfastened his trousers as he watched in amazement— he wouldn't think her capable of such an act, and so much the better. The value of surprise did much to increase passion, and she would use it now.

She freed his arousal and he gasped, pleasing her. He was beyond surprise—he was stunned, and she knew she had won. She clasped him in her hand, her other placed on his hip to steady herself. His size surprised her, as well as the slick heat of him, the hardness, and the pulse of fire she sensed inside him. She caressed him, and now he leaned against the door to keep himself from falling. Melanie's success intoxicated her, and she moved to kiss the blunt tip of him.

He made some utterance, some semblance of a word, but she took him in her mouth and his words died. She licked and sucked, teasing him and loving him until his every breath was a groan, until his hips moved of their own accord. His reactions taught her what gave him pleasure, what he couldn't resist, so she increased her efforts there. He reached the same precipice to which he had taken her, and the wild thrill of conquest shook her almost to her core. Her own body ached and involved itself in making love to him.

He seized her and lifted her from the floor before she knew what he intended. She struggled, dismayed at the interruption, but the Renegade carried her to her bed, then tore off her nightdress as he lay her on her back. She saw his gloves fly as he threw them aside, and then he lowered himself above her. He would take her now, as she had nearly begged him to do, but a shred of fear claimed her. It was no more than she wanted— she'd said she needed him, and she had approached him as a woman with no virtue at all, as a harlot. He had every reason to take her fully, to satisfy himself with her, no matter what he had promised.

She waited, fighting the fear that his entrance might hurt, but she didn't resist as he bent to kiss her. She felt his arousal between her thighs, she felt

217

him move against her as they kissed. The hard, hot length of him rubbed against her woman's core, but still he didn't enter her body. He buried his head in her neck and moved faster, pressing harder against her. She ached now for his entry—she didn't care if it hurt. She clamped her legs around him and moved with him—the pressure of him met the small, feminine peak that he had attended so well the night before, and fierce waves crashed through her again.

He groaned, a cry torn from his deepest core, and the warmth of him spread across her thigh. She knew what it was—he had reached his own ecstasy and, as he had told her, it was indeed "more productive." He stilled in her arms, his face buried in her hair, his breath swift and shaky as his body cooled. He kissed her cheek, then moved to lie beside her. She checked what she could see of his expression in the darkness.

"You don't make it easy to protect you, señorita."

She felt shy, and worse, like a woman who has lost her mind and committed an act she can't conceal. "It wasn't my intention that you should."

He drew a long, pleased breath. "You are far more skilled than I ever dreamed." He looked over at her. "But you have never done this before."

"How do you know?" Maybe she'd done it wrong somehow, though he seemed pleased with her efforts. "Did I do something wrong?"

He laughed. "How much more 'right' can a

218

woman be? No, but I know you. It was the first time you'd ever considered the act, let alone done it."

At least he didn't think her a harlot. "When I was studying in New York City, I set up my equipment on a street where the ladies of the night . . . plied their wares."

"What were you doing in such a place? It sounds dangerous."

"It was, I suppose. My teacher had told me a street bearing the same number, but I went in the wrong direction. I did end up with some very interesting photographs, though. The ladies of the night were most cooperative, though their customers avoided the area until I left."

He laughed again. "I'll bet."

"Their conversation was interesting, and though I found most of it repellent at the time, just now . . . it didn't seem so terrible."

He kissed her forehead. "Just now . . . it was the best thing that ever happened in my life." He drew her into his arms and they lay close, contented. "Did the ladies tell you the act might be reciprocated?"

"Reciprocated? No . . . how?"

"That I might do the same to you."

Melanie pondered this, wondering how it might transpire, but her blood heated at the thought. "They didn't mention that."

"Then there is more left to your instruction." He kissed her again and hugged her, warm and full, then rose reluctantly from her bed. "I must leave you, love, lest I place you in further danger. But when next we meet, I will show you all your harlot friends didn't mention."

She gestured at the foot of her bed. "I took your saddle blanket—you may need it."

He smiled and bowed, then replaced his scattered clothing. "Thank you—riding without it lacks comfort."

As the Renegade, he slung the blanket over his shoulder. She watched as he checked the window, then slipped out. It was like him not to use the door, even if he could. It almost seemed like habit to find the more secretive way, as if it pleased him to take paths others ignored or avoided.

As she considered what she had just done, she, the virgin daughter of a famed photographer, knew she followed those same paths, too.

# Chapter Nine

"Something's up. Bradford asked three times this morning about the train's arrival time and has already sent a coach—two coaches—into Santa Fe." Chen stopped. "Diego? Are you listening?"

Diego gazed out the window of Chen's hotel and sighed. "More or less."

Chen seated himself and took a sip of tea. "What do you think it means?"

"She loves me."

Chen groaned, then reached across the table and struck him. "About Bradford!" He paused. "Who loves you? Not Miss Muessen?" He clapped his hand to his head. "Is that where you were last night, after your able mimicry of falling down drunk in front of Bradford?"

221

"That was well performed, wasn't it? I'm glad I didn't have to go so far as vomiting."

"We all appreciate that." Chen struck him again. "Snap out of it! Bradford's up to something, and we need to be one step ahead of him."

"Oh, all right. You want to anticipate Bradford's action? Why don't we just wait to see who he's fetching in the coach, then take it from there?"

Chen offered no argument, but he didn't look pleased. "I suppose there's nothing else to be done. I'd feel better if you were less preoccupied, though. The Renegade may have to appear at a moment's notice. And he can't be mooning over Miss Muessen while there's a job to be done—for her sake, as well as his own."

"I know that, Chen." He knew it, but he hadn't been able to stick to it at all. Of course, he'd never imagined Melanie could turn into such a seductress either. The image of her coming across her bedroom, kneeling before him, her eyes shining like a goddess . . . It haunted him and filled him with a mad desire to repeat the encounter again and again.

Chen drummed his fingers on the table. "There's another problem."

*Of course.* "What's that?"

"We need to come up with something that proves conclusively to Bradford that you couldn't be the Renegade."

"I've done that well enough already. He doesn't seem suspicious."

"He holds on to the possibility, Diego. I have a

plan that I think might work, once and for all . . .
if Will . . ."

A coach's arrival interrupted Chen's thought,
and they went to the door to see Bradford's new
guests. Another coach stopped just behind the first.
A child shouted in glee, then leapt from the coach.
Five other children tumbled after the first, bounding and jumping around the plaza. Six children
leapt out of the second coach, then raced into the
open arms of their parents. A young woman who
seemed to be their guardian followed, took off her
lacy bonnet, and looked around the pueblo as if at
a sight of great wonder.

Chen turned to Diego in amazement. "The
pueblo children have returned."

Diego nodded. "I see that. But where is my
brother? And who is that woman?" A knot formed
in his stomach, though he wasn't sure why. The
children were safe. At least in this regard Bradford
had held to his word.

Chen touched Diego's arm. "Bradford is greeting
their parents now. Let us join him."

They went out into the plaza just as Melanie and
Victoria came out of her inn. Miguel the baker
lifted his small son into the air, laughing. The boy
seemed to have lost weight since he left his father's
care, but other than that, he and the other children
looked healthy and well.

Bradford greeted the young woman chaperoning
the children. "Allow me to introduce Miss Harriet
Richardson, from San Francisco. She has escorted

your children from the ship, and on the train, so they have been in the best of hands."

Harriet smiled and adjusted a small girl's bonnet. "I've done nothing else but tend these darling little children. Oh, they were such a mess! But Mr. Bradford was so generous and wanted only the best for our journey."

She seemed pleasant, a woman who exuded sweetness and femininity. When she spoke to Bradford, her tone was almost flirtatious. Though she was young and pretty enough, Diego knew enough of woman to recognize one who practiced the art of manipulating male vanity. He noticed Melanie watching her suspiciously, and he smiled. On the surface, there was a similarity between the two women, but even when Melanie had blatantly and perfectly seduced him, she hadn't been cunning.

Bradford spotted Melanie. "Miss Muessen, I would think this occasion suitable for your photography skills. Come, a tender shot of the reunion of parent and child. Surely you don't want to miss this?"

Melanie cocked her head to one side. "While it is touching, and I am pleased to see the children returned, I find that type of photograph both contrived and occasionally misleading."

Bradford's smile tensed, but he held it in place. "I believe their return has surprised the Tewa inhabitants, who don't seem willing to trust me. But you don't seem surprised."

"I've expected it from the first. What would surprise me would be if Rafael himself returned."

Harriet turned to Melanie. "I have a great interest in photography. Perhaps Miss Muessen will teach me something of her craft. Not that I have the skill to hope to emulate her professional status, but my instructor said my work held great promise."

Diego frowned. *Probably flattered his pride, too.* He felt offended on Melanie's behalf, but she seemed more confused than annoyed. "If you wish, Miss Richardson, I would be happy to show you my camera."

Bradford turned to Diego and Chen. "Chen, de Aguirre. I am pleased you were here to see the triumphant return of the pueblo's children. I trust that, lacking Miss Muessen's intuitive skills, you were both surprised by their arrival?"

Diego glanced at Miguel, who glared. "I never doubted you, Señor Bradford."

Miguel huffed. "Didn't you? You young fool. The return of our young is thanks to the Renegade and not to this devil. But where is your brother? His fate may not be so pleasant." Miguel carried his son into their apartment, disappearing before Bradford could order punishment again.

But Bradford didn't seem concerned. "Ah, there are those who simply cannot bear change. He'll come around eventually."

"No doubt. But the matter of my brother and his family, Señor Bradford—am I to believe they have chosen to extend their stay in Europe, or will they, too, be rejoining us soon? Perhaps to explain Rafael's decision to relinquish control here?"

Bradford met Diego's gaze, and though his smile—perhaps it would be better termed a smirk—remained, his eyes flashed a dark challenge. "I'm sure you'll hear from your brother again soon."

"It would be unlike him not to write. In fact, he's never gone this long before."

"Soon, de Aguirre. You'll hear soon, I'm sure."

Diego didn't like Bradford's tone, but pressing now would be a mistake. "I hope he doesn't question me on my visits to the saloon again. I grow tired of defending myself to my honorable brother."

Four of the children were Zuni from Tesuque, and stood alone near the coaches. Diego eyed Bradford. "The coach can't travel the road to Tesuque. Will and I can bring them to their parents."

Bradford held up his hand. "There's no need for you to go, de Aguirre. I'll send Will with a cart to take them home. I want you and Miss Muessen to join me for dinner. There is cause for celebration tonight. You especially might find the news interesting."

What next? Diego forced himself to remain idle and disinterested, but it wasn't easy. Victoria stepped forward. "While they wait to rejoin their parents, they can come to my inn, and I will make them lunch."

Diego wanted a chance to speak to those children who spoke Zuni, so he followed. To his surprise, Chen came, too, though he couldn't have felt welcome in Victoria's small dining room.

Bradford looked displeased as they left, but his attorney spoke to him, and he nodded. "Miss Richardson must be famished, too. Join them, Harriet."

Victoria frowned but agreed. "I have plenty for all."

Chen's eyes narrowed to slits. "That, madam, is certainly a truism. You purchased each luncheon item that I had instructed Massimo to gather."

Victoria didn't look at him, but a faint smile graced her lips. "My guests must be treated with special care at all times."

"If they eat all you bought, you'll need a wheelbarrow to get them out of their rooms."

Harriet glanced between them, then laughed. "I knew I would like it here. My parents visited Tewa Pueblo a few years ago. Being among the most prominent families in California, they, of course, travel often, but even so, they said this place was special. The people seem so prosperous, although naturally it wasn't the wealth of Tewa that interested my parents. They told me how warm and friendly everyone is, more like a family than a village. I knew I would feel right at home."

Diego frowned. It wasn't warmth that interested Harriet. Most likely it had been the mention of its prosperous citizens that captured her attention. "So you're intending to stay, are you?"

Harriet's sweet smile never wavered. "Mr. Bradford did ask that I stay on. If the villagers permit me, I hope to take over the school now that the former schoolmaster has moved on."

This was too much. Diego glared. "That position may be temporary, once Rafael returns."

Harriet appeared sympathetic. "You haven't accepted fully that he has moved on, have you? I know you all must be very upset by his decision to leave, and I'm sure Mr. Bradford does things differently."

"You might say that, yes. My brother certainly never thought to flog a person for an outburst of temper, that much is sure."

Chen and Melanie looked at him in surprise. He had repressed his anger in front of Bradford, but somehow Harriet irritated him more. Her plan of taking over Rafael's beloved school was more than he could stand.

Harriet seemed to miss his mood. She reached across the table and placed her hand on his arm. "Mr. de Aguirre is your brother? I understand completely. It must have been hardest on you to have him leave this way."

He wanted to smack her hand off his arm, but instead moved to place a white napkin on his lap, which Chen commented on with a raised brow. Harriet studied his face. "You're not at all what I expected. I had, forgive me, heard that Mr. de Aguirre's younger brother was something of a rakehell."

Diego glanced at Chen. "Rakehell?"

Chen shrugged. "A drunken, reckless rogue. It's an accurate term applied to you."

Harriet laughed. There was something contrived about her outbursts that lacked sincerity. "I can't believe that! You're much too young ... and far too handsome to have spent your life in drunken revelry. I had no idea the men of Tewa were so exotic and masculine." She certainly valued male attention, that much was certain, but her flattery fell short of Melanie's small words of approval. "Don't you agree, Miss Muessen?"

Melanie picked up her sandwich and took a large bite. Diego loved to watch her eat. Nothing stood in her way when she fixed her attention on food. It was amazing she wasn't as fat as the baker's wife, but perhaps she wore it off in nervous energy—or only ate once a day. "He's not entirely repugnant." She spoke thickly, around her sandwich, but somehow the words rang like music compared to Harriet's lavish praise.

Harriet seemed surprised by Melanie's comment but kept her attention on Diego. "No matter what you say, I can fully believe you're a danger to any woman you meet."

"I've managed to leave Miguel's wife alone." Diego stole a quick glance at Melanie. As he hoped, her small face was knit with disapproval. "But as it happens, only last night I again committed the ultimate sin of drunkenness, as Chen can attest."

Chen nodded, but seemed more interested in inspecting Victoria's china—he stole a quick glance at the underside of the saucer, probably assessing its maker and subsequent value. It must have been good, because Chen huffed a breath of disgust.

Harriet didn't seem put off by his claim. "They say that reformed rakes make the best husbands."

"I hope never to learn the truth of that myth, Miss Richardson. Now, if you'll excuse me, I want to have a word with my young . . . cousins."

"Oh? Are you related to these dear children?"

*In a sense . . .* "Cousins." He repeated his claim with deliberate sarcasm, but Harriet didn't take notice.

Diego swung his chair around, and the four children looked up at him. They all seemed guarded, but with Harriet breathing down their necks, he doubted he would learn the reason why, even though he spoke in Zuni. "You have been away a long time, but you will see your parents soon."

The little girl glanced at Harriet and looked nervous. Diego touched her arm. "It's all right, Lusita. She doesn't speak our language."

The child didn't seem to accept this logic, so Diego tried another angle. "Did Rafael take you to many interesting places in other countries?"

She shook her head. "No, no, Diego. He didn't."

"He didn't?"

"No, he left us, and this woman came to watch us. We didn't go on a ship or anything. We were in a city. I do not ever want to go to a city again."

Diego's heart chilled. "Where did Rafael go?"

"I don't know, Diego. He left us."

"What about Evelyn and their daughter?"

"They left us, too. That woman says they went on to the other countries without us because we were too expensive."

"Did Rafael tell you why he was leaving without you?"

"No, we didn't see him after that. This woman told us."

As he'd guessed, Harriet wasn't as innocent of Bradford's schemes as she pretended. If the child was right, it was unlikely that Rafael ever left American shores himself. But where was he?

"One more thing, Lusita. Have you seen the man called Bradford before?"

"No." The child placed her small finger against her chin and looked thoughtful. His heart warmed. If he married, he would have children. He'd never thought of it before, never imagined himself as a father. Rafael seemed designed for the task, but Diego hadn't been responsible enough, nor could he have imagined putting another's needs first. Something had changed. He glanced up and saw Melanie watching him, and his heart melted with affection.

Lusita tapped his knee, and he returned his attention to her. "I have seen that other man, though. The pale one who met us when we got off the coach."

"The attorney? Mr. Alvin."

"I don't know his name, but he came to see Miss Harriet one or two times, and he was there when she told us that Señor Rafael had left."

"That's good to know, Lusita. Thank you for telling me."

Diego started to move, but the child took his hand. "Miss Harriet told us that a bad man has come to Tewa, and that Mr. Bradford was going to protect us from him. But she said the bad man wore a cape and a mask, and she called him 'The Renegade.' I do not remember when Señor Rafael was the Renegade, but I know he wasn't bad. My parents said he saved the pueblo, and many people."

"That's true, Lusita. He saved me, too."

"Will the new Renegade save us?"

Diego hesitated. "What makes you think you need to be saved?"

Lusita's brow arched and she looked much wiser than her small age. "Señor Rafael wouldn't leave us, Diego. We all know that. We didn't dare say so because we were afraid, but we knew. No one steals something to be good—they do it to be bad, so the man who stole Señor Rafael's school must be bad."

"Reasonable. You may be right. But don't worry. It's true, a new Renegade has returned, and he won't give up until the pueblo is back in its rightful hands."

Lusita smiled and patted his hand fondly. "Good. I hope you don't take too long though, Diego. I want to go back to school."

Will entered the room and called to the children,

and Lusita stood up, leaving Diego with his mouth open in astonishment. She knew. The child knew, without question or doubt, that he was the new Renegade. He had established himself all his life as the person least likely to save anyone. Yet people still believed in him. It didn't make sense.

Will took the children in a small cart, but Diego stayed seated. Harriet didn't seem interested in the children's departure, though she'd said an emotional good-bye to them when they left the inn. Melanie stood with Victoria, quieter than usual, more uncertain. Harriet had a way of commanding attention while seeming modest and interested in others. She wanted attention on herself and no one else, but with Melanie in the room, it wouldn't be an easy victory.

Diego planted himself beside Melanie, but she refused to look at him. He wondered if she was distracted by memories of their night together, but she looked more troubled than anything. "Are you well, señorita? You seem . . . preoccupied."

She puffed an impatient breath, one he had grown accustomed to when he, as Diego, had irritated her. He wasn't sure what he'd done now, but she seemed tense. "I'm perfectly fine. There's something that concerns me, though. Mr. Bradford looks like a cat with a mouse, and I don't like it."

Harriet turned to her, her eyes wide with surprise. "Don't you trust Mr. Bradford? He has always seemed so strong and confident to me. He

233

takes everything he does step by step, in the most methodical fashion. I'm always so scattered, so I admire a man with such steadfast purpose."

Melanie didn't respond, but Diego eyed her with irritation. "You've known him long, then?"

"He's acquainted with my family, and so I have seen him several times. He has always been fond of me."

*In other words, she was playing him like a fish on a hook.*

Diego wasn't impressed, but Melanie looked concerned. "I hope you are careful, Miss Richardson. Mr. Bradford isn't the sort of man I would trust as a suitor."

"Oh, no! I'm sure he's not interested in me in that way. He's just kind, and enjoys my conversation."

Diego resisted the urge to groan and cough, but Melanie didn't seem aware of Harriet's deceptive qualities. "I hope you're right, but if I were you, I'd stay here at Victoria's inn rather than at the Chateau."

"I couldn't do that, Miss Muessen, not when Mr. Bradford has already arranged my accommodations at the other hotel."

Chen stepped forward and cast a dark glance Melanie's way. "And he has paid for those accommodations in advance, so a refund is not in order."

Victoria didn't seem concerned with the loss of a prospective guest. "All my rooms are taken anyway, I'm afraid."

Melanie's brow puckered. "Are they?"

Victoria issued a meaningful look Melanie's way, then nodded pleasantly. "As of this morning, yes." She glanced at Chen. "I must say, however, that my policy on refunds is much more generous than that across the street. I find a full refund beneficial to future visits."

Chen glared, offended. "Indeed? That would seem unwise, madam, in the extreme. A full refund must constitute a loss."

"A loss today, but greater gain tomorrow."

Chen pondered her claim. "As an investment, do you mean?"

Victoria nodded. "In a sense."

Harriet replaced her white lace gloves and moved to exit the dining room. "I should return to my host now that the children are on their way. It's been a long and tiring journey."

Diego followed her. "From where? San Francisco, was it?"

Like Bradford, Harriet's pleasant smile never lapsed. "That is where the ship came in, yes."

"I find that odd, since Rafael has always chosen to depart from the eastern cities, to give the children a chance to visit New York, Boston, Charleston . . . as history lessons. He lectures them about the greed of the American government while his wife tells them grand tales of the Civil War."

"Perhaps he believed San Francisco a more interesting sight this time."

"Not likely. His wife's family is in Boston. They

always visit her old home on their trips. Always."

Harriet tapped her lip. "Well, it is a mystery, then. But I'm sure it's an innocent change of plans and will be cleared up in no time."

She wasn't easy to fluster. But maybe the Renegade would get more out of her than Diego could. As Victoria led her out into the reception area, Diego lingered behind, plotting. Melanie eyed him doubtfully. "Why do you look so grumpy? And why were you so rude to that girl? She seems pleasant enough."

He huffed. "I've got a bad feeling about that one."

"I didn't realize you had a bad feeling about any woman. What is it about Harriet that bothers you?"

"I don't know, exactly. She's a manipulative woman who wants everything her own way, and I'll bet she usually gets it."

"I can't believe Miss Richardson is that bad. She's pretty." Melanie paused. "Didn't you notice?"

"Not as pretty as you. Beyond that smile, she's hard, even though she plies the emotional act."

"I'm older than she is."

Diego reached out to touch her cheek, then snapped his hand back, but he couldn't keep himself from sighing. "You'll always look young, señorita, even when you're an old woman. It's your eyes. They sparkle, you know, with a purity like that of a child, but deeper, with the wisdom of an ageless woman."

Melanie's mouth dropped open, and Chen elbowed him hard. Her cheeks flushed pink and she looked at her feet. "Thank you." He wanted to touch her, to tell her that no woman compared to her.

Chen elbowed him again and Diego coughed. "Just a little flattery."

Melanie looked up at him, her expression strange, but she didn't speak. Chen motioned Melanie into the reception area, and Diego followed. Harriet looked around the front room, pausing to inspect each wall hanging. "What a lovely room, Victoria! I admire your skills at decoration. I'm not half so talented, I'm afraid." Her gaze stopped on the portrait above Victoria's front desk. "What a beautiful print!"

For a reason Diego couldn't guess, Melanie tensed and stepped forward as Harriet went to examine the picture. "Yes, I thought I recognized this photograph. It's a print of the prestigious Zhang family of San Francisco. They are well-known hoteliers. Yes, that's their daughter, Ting. I was their governess for several months. It was so much work. Their children are dears, but so spoiled! Wherever did you get a copy of their picture? Oh, of course. They must have been guests here."

Victoria blanched, and the truth dawned on Diego. No wonder Melanie had worn an expression of sympathy when she first saw the picture of Victoria's supposed family. Somehow, she had known it couldn't be true. Victoria's voice came small and in a monotone when she answered. "Yes, they were guests . . . at a hotel where I worked in San Francisco, years ago."

Harriet went to the door, oblivious to Victoria's discomfort. "I already feel so at home in Tewa Pueblo. Thank you for lunch, Victoria. It was wonderful. We must visit again later."

Harriet left, and the silence that followed was deafening. Melanie seemed to be struggling for something to say, and for once, Diego felt certain the less he said the better. Chen stepped forward and stared at the picture. If nothing else, Chen was a tactful man. He would know better than to . . .

"You *lied?* This isn't your family?"

Diego bounded forward and seized Chen's arm to pull him away, but Victoria lifted her chin and met her nemesis's eyes. "That is correct. The Zhang family had two prints made because the first was slightly blurry. They threw it away, and I retrieved it from the garbage. Is that what you wanted to know? Well, I have told you."

Diego tried to remove Chen from the inn, but he stood firm. "Where is your real family?"

Victoria shrugged, and her face wore a resigned expression of false carelessness. "Who knows? In San Francisco, I imagine. I hear nothing of them, and I don't want to."

"Why not?" Diego wished he could disappear and take Chen with him.

"Because, Mr. Chen, my parents could hardly be termed 'family.' My mother was a harlot cursed with opium, my father a Chinese pickpocket cursed with greed. I was raised by his aged mother, who sent me to do her work until I was old enough to work on my own. Ten, was it? Or nine? I don't remember. I worked as a maid in a crumbling hotel where only thieves and drunkards dared stay. But it didn't defeat me, not completely."

Pride glimmered through Victoria's bitterness and pain. "I worked harder and better than anyone, and earned myself a job at the most exclusive hotel in the city, cleaning the rooms of people rich enough to buy castles when I could barely afford food. I learned to cook, and I vowed I would one day own such an establishment, and then I would treat people as they deserved to be treated. I promised myself that I would be the owner of my own inn, and it would be the finest of its kind." She paused. "And it is."

To his astonishment, Diego's vision blurred and he blinked away tears, but Victoria's attention stayed on Chen. "You may be amused, Mr. Chen, to learn that it was your brochure that first brought me to Tewa. The story of the Renegade was mildly amusing, though I recognized at once that you had greatly embellished the details for effect, and to draw in more customers. A good tactic, I thought. I also realized yours was the only hotel in the pueblo, and that with your prices, there would certainly be an overflow from which I might benefit."

Diego touched Victoria's arm, fighting emotion lest he embarrass her with his sympathy. "You came here because of the community my brother created, Victoria, where all people are treated as equals, where no child is too poor to be given the dreams of a lifetime. You came because you belong here."

Melanie looked at him in surprise, then back at Victoria. "That portrait, Victoria—it's nothing compared to what you've made yourself. One day . . ."

Victoria sniffed and shoved tears from her cheeks. "No. I've been a fool, and humiliated myself by my raw and stupid fantasy. I have deluded myself long enough." She whirled around and tore the portrait from the wall, then sped through her kitchen to the back of the inn. They heard a loud crash, and the shattering of glass. Melanie started after her, but Chen caught her arm.

"No, Miss Muessen. Let me. It seems Victoria and I have more in common than I realized. I will go."

Diego and Melanie stood together, stunned, as Chen went after Victoria. Diego took Melanie's arm. "I think we should leave. Mr. Bradford has invited us to dine with him tonight. We may learn more there. And Victoria needs to be alone." He paused, baffled. "Or with Chen, as the case may be."

They walked outside, but Melanie stopped and looked up at him. "You were crying."

Diego frowned and scoffed. "I was not. It's dusty in there."

"You were crying."

A humiliating observation, if ever there was one. "You knew. About Victoria, I mean. How?"

"I recognized the plate used in that picture and knew it had to be fairly recent. Certainly not old enough to be of Victoria as a child."

"You knew she was lying?"

"Dreaming, Señor de Aguirre. Dreaming of her family as she wished they had been. That's not so wrong, is it?"

"No. It's not wrong to dream of a greater life."

"Do you? Dream of being something great?"

"I'm not much of a dreamer, señorita."

"I saw the tears in your eyes today. Señor de Aguirre, you are nothing if not a dreamer."

It wasn't easy to concentrate on Carlton Bradford's guarded conversation with Melanie sitting beside him. Chen had returned from Victoria's inn, quiet and contemplative, almost as distracted as Diego had been after his tryst with Melanie. Harriet sat between Bradford and his attorney, who seemed trapped between his admiration of the disinterested Melanie and the more accessible Harriet. If Bradford truly had something important to reveal, he hadn't broached it yet.

Diego wasn't in the mood for wine. For one thing, he intended to go to Melanie's room again, and he wanted his senses at their most acute. But more than that, somehow he'd lost his taste for his once-favored drink. He pretended to drink, then set the goblet aside untouched. "Come, Señor Bradford, you promised us news, didn't you? I have plans for the evening that don't include the quiet sipping of weak wine."

Melanie peered up at him suspiciously. "It doesn't taste weak to me."

Diego patted her hand. "You're not an expert like myself."

Melanie rolled her eyes and sighed. "An honor, to be sure."

Bradford waved his hand at Chen. "You, Chen . . . This news should interest you, too."

Chen had again enlisted Will as a waiter, but though Bradford ignored him, Will stopped fiddling with plates to listen. Chen stood by the table, then refilled Diego's already full goblet. "Your news, sir?"

Bradford stood at the head of the table and banged a spoon on his glass. "I have waited until tonight to reveal to you all news of great interest, news you have long waited to hear." He paused for effect, and until everyone was silent. "Rafael de Aguirre will soon return to Tewa."

Diego couldn't speak, but Chen stepped forward, astonished. "Señor de Aguirre is returning? What about his wife and their daughter?"

Bradford seemed unconcerned, casual, but the effect was more that of a predator who felt too confident for nervousness. "As I understand it, Rafael intends only a short stay at Tewa and so has left his wife and daughter in Europe. He plans to settle there, having enjoyed his travels so much in the past."

An outright lie. As much as Rafael loved venturing abroad, his heart was in Tewa, and he would never leave for long. Diego might find life in other lands pleasant, but Rafael's roots were much deeper. Diego knew better than to argue. "I hope he thinks to invite his younger brother on his return journey. I understand the wine in France is particularly well concocted."

Bradford's eyes narrowed. "France?"

Diego shrugged. "Or is it Germany? The beer, then. Either way, I shall enjoy the diversion."

Harriet appeared excited by Bradford's announcement. "I can't wait to meet him. The stories of his daring escapades are legendary. My parents found those stories so thrilling that they visited to this very hotel for a whole month!"

Diego had no memory of the hotel guests, but Chen nodded. "Richardson, yes, I remember. They were among my first guests, after I had sent my brochure to a Western Travelers Association in San Francisco. They stayed for three weeks and occupied the Master Suite. They even took rooms, though inferior ones, for their two servants, a married couple. They requested an unusual vintage of wine, but I, of course, was able to locate it."

Diego smiled. "You were fortunate Victoria

hadn't set up shop at that time or she would have 'located' it first."

Chen nodded, serious. "She is an able woman."

*Quite a shift from "demonic she-devil."* Diego arched his brow, but Chen pretended to ignore him.

Harriet sipped her wine with more enthusiasm than she'd eaten her meal, though, as always, Melanie had made short work of her dinner. Harriet liked being the center of attention, but Melanie seemed to drift from the conversation, as if her mind fixed itself on something more interesting. He hoped it involved him, and suspected it did.

Harriet turned to Bradford. "I wonder how the new Renegade will react to Mr. de Aguirre's return?"

Diego grit his teeth. "If it happens, I'm sure the new Renegade's job is done."

Harriet met his gaze. "Have you seen him, Diego?"

"So far, I've missed his rides."

She laughed, but again, it sounded contrived and began to annoy him. "Is that so? One might suspect you have followed in your brother's footsteps and are the Renegade yourself."

She might be annoying, but she was certainly perceptive. Melanie looked at him sharply, and he knew she held her breath. "I'm afraid I've been eliminated as a suspect, Miss Richardson."

Bradford looked between them, and he laughed, too, with no more sincerity than Harriet. "Yes,

Harriet, my dear. Young de Aguirre fancies the ladies and his drink far more than riding on behalf of 'justice.' "

Harriet didn't look convinced. "But they've never been seen in the same place at the same time, isn't that true?"

Bradford's eyes shifted to Diego. "Yes."

Diego leaned back in his chair. "I'm flattered, Miss Richardson, that I might be considered so bold and so daring. But I'm afraid I've never been the type for heroism."

She offered a shy smile. "You sell yourself short, I think. You're certainly a strong man, and capable of the acrobatics I've heard the Renegade displays."

Just when he thought he'd made headway at concealing his disguise, Harriet had to show up. Diego forced himself to laugh, fearing he sounded as grating as Bradford and Harriet. "My 'acrobatics,' I'm afraid, have tended to end up with me beneath a saloon floor. But you flatter me." He stood up and bowed. "I thank you." He glanced at Chen, then at Melanie. There would be no tryst tonight. The Renegade had a new enemy, an enemy far less easy to fool than Carlton Bradford.

# Chapter Ten

Melanie busied herself in her portable darkroom. Once she became more successful as a photographer, she planned to modernize her equipment, move from her father's antiquated camera, and perhaps try the new roll film, which could be stored and developed later. She knew she had an emotional attachment to the equipment her father had used during the Civil War. Before he died, he had passed it on to her, and it would be hard to change the process now.

The equipment Porticus carried in his cart weighed at least a hundred pounds, the work cumbersome for Melanie alone. Sometimes she wished she had someone to travel with her, to help her set up. Her instructor in New York had taught her to prepare the plate in advance by chemical methods, and that had made the process easier, but it would still be pleasant to have help. With help, she might have moved from the more usual ten-by-twelve plate to something grander—even twenty by sixteen, which would be perfect for her expected trek to Egypt. But she would need a man to help her, and she couldn't yet afford a porter.

Diego made an able porter. Melanie fiddled with the plate and tried not to imagine him in Egypt, pointing out the best scenes, nabbing unsuspecting peasants to pose for shots before the Sphinx. She attributed it to lack of sleep—she had expected a visit from her lover, but he never came. She wasn't worried; she knew he would come when the chance presented itself.

When she had at last fallen asleep, she dreamt that she sat with Diego in the saloon, drinking some kind of liquor that in her dream tasted more like lemonade. They had been playing cards and she won, exasperating him. It had been a pleasant dream, and she woke happy that morning. Today, she felt confident enough to handle anything.

"Miss Muessen! Are you in there?" It was Harriet, sounding cheerful. "I hoped I might see your portraits."

Melanie hid a groan, though she could think of no reason to dislike Harriet. "One moment, please." She set up the images she had taken of the Renegade and those from Tesuque, as well as the ones of Will, but she hid the image she had taken unawares of Diego by the old kivas. It was her most beautiful shot, capturing his longing, his loneliness. She loved it, though she hadn't the courage to show it to him.

Melanie opened her tent flap to admit Harriet. She was again perfectly dressed, her hair arranged carefully, and she was, as always, smiling. Her mouth seemed formed to smile, and as she bent to pass through the door flap, Melanie realized that some people had their mask built in. In a way, the Renegade's mask was the least deceptive of all the people she had met in Tewa.

Harriet ignored the pictures from Tesuque and the one of Will and focused her attention on the Renegade. "This is a dramatic shot. He's so handsome!"

Melanie eyed her doubtfully. "He's wearing a mask. How can you tell what he looks like?"

Harriet pointed to the outline of his body. "See how broad his shoulders are, and how tall he must be! He's certainly not an old man, nor very young, with a physique like that. He must be very similar in build to Diego."

Melanie studied the picture. "I suppose they're not entirely dissimilar."

Harriet took a quick glance at Melanie's equipment, but she didn't seem interested in the gear. "I would love for you to do a photograph of me, Miss Muessen. Do you charge a large fee for portraits?"

"Well . . ." Melanie found herself thinking like Chen, wondering how much she could rightfully charge for a portrait. "I would be happy to photograph you, Harriet. My fee isn't terribly large for portraits. No more than, say, a night at Chen's hotel . . . in the Master Suite."

Harriet looked pleased. "Why, that's so reasonable! My parents commissioned a photograph of me last year to hang in my bedroom. That photographer charged at least triple your fee. We must do it at once."

Melanie sighed. Financial gain wasn't her forte. She had to start taking lessons from Chen, because apparently she could have charged more. Melanie followed Harriet from the darkroom tent and waited while Harriet looked around. "I would like to be seated on that bench, I think. Next to the flowers, with Chen's hotel in the background."

Maybe Diego was right; Harriet did seem pushy, despite her feminine demeanor. Melanie set up her tripod and box camera, then settled on the best angle. Harriet positioned herself on the bench and seemed to be trying different expressions. Everything looked contrived—Harriet was strangely stiff, and somehow Melanie felt she wasn't centering in on the essence of Harriet's true self. She'd never had trouble before, but maybe Harriet wasn't willing to show what lay beneath her pleasant surface.

A light wind swirled around the plaza, and a portion of Melanie's hair came loose from its binding to dance around her face. Melanie tried to tuck it back in, but it remained stubbornly free. Miguel the baker came out of his shop to inspect her task.

As unpleasant as he had been to Diego, he beamed with warmth when he saw Melanie. "Miss Muessen! You're looking particularly graceful today, like a little fairy or a butterfly." Melanie eyed him doubtfully, but the baker grinned. "It's no wonder the Renegade has taken such a fancy to you."

Melanie bent to snap the shot of Harriet, and in a flash caught an expression that seemed both genuine and disturbing. A hard light of envy, covered by a thick smile—this was the image captured in an instant of truth. Melanie gulped. It wasn't a shot Harriet was likely to appreciate. "One moment, Harriet. I'd best try again. I believe I caught you . . . blinking."

"Oh, dear! I'll try to hold myself still. Maybe if I fixed my hair." Harriet tugged a portion loose and it swirled across her chin. It looked better, softer . . . and somehow familiar. Melanie took the picture, and though she had captured less of Harriet's inner demons, it was a shot more likely to earn the price of Chen's Master Suite.

Harriet waited outside the darkroom while Melanie worked. As she'd predicted, this shot was much more flattering. She held it up, then presented it to Harriet. Harriet gasped in genuine pleasure. "It's beautiful! You've portrayed me exactly as I am."

Melanie fought an urge to groan, but Mr. Alvin came by and stopped to admire the portrait. Again, shades of Chen flared in Melanie, and she wondered if the lawyer might be persuaded to offer up a ransom for his own portrait. "What do you think, Mr. Alvin?"

He inspected the portrait, but he turned to Harriet with his praise. "It's lovely, Miss Richardson, like yourself. It's even better than the one your parents commissioned, and that was exquisite."

Harriet looked nervous, though Melanie had no idea why. Mr. Alvin appeared flirtatious, but he had been overly friendly with Melanie, too. He was a young man without much depth of feeling, so why his interest should concern Harriet, who seemed to thrive on male attention, eluded Melanie.

Melanie sighed. "I'm pleased you like it, Harriet."

A shout from the jailhouse school stopped their conversation. Chen came from his hotel and Victoria from hers, and soon everyone in the pueblo mustered in the plaza. Harriet gripped Melanie's arm. "What's going on?"

"I have no idea." Melanie's heart skipped a beat, because somehow she *did* know. The Renegade had returned . . .

The tall man in his black cape, wearing the Anasazi mask, shoved Carlton Bradford through the door of the schoolhouse and out into the plaza. The guards seized their weapons, but the Renegade held a sword to Bradford's throat, and no one dared act. Bradford's face was white, his eyes wide with both fear and fury.

251

Harriet clasped her hand over her heart. "Is that him, the Renegade?"

Melanie nodded, but her heart was in her throat. If he failed, if he made one mistake . . . She held her breath, but the Renegade seemed confident as he pushed Bradford forward, the sword still positioned to kill. "Señor Bradford has an announcement to make, and a benefit to share with all of you."

Bradford's face flushed, but he didn't struggle. "You won't get away with this."

The sword pressed harder against his neck, and Bradford coughed. "All right!"

"Tell the inhabitants of Tewa your good news, Señor Bradford. Now."

The Renegade eased the sword slightly away from his neck, and Bradford struggled to speak. "The taxes I've acquired for the benefit of Tewa . . ."

The Renegade gripped him tighter. "Taxes stolen from Tewa citizens . . . Go on, señor. Let us hear what benefits Tewa can expect."

Bradford grimaced, his face tight with fury. "I will restore the money . . ." The words came torn from his throat.

The blade pressed against his throat, and the Renegade prodded him. "Now?"

Bradford nodded once. "Now."

The Renegade spotted a guard moving toward him, and he tucked the sword under Bradford's chin. "Another step and you gentlemen will be out of work."

Bradford glared at the guard, and the man lowered his rifle. The Renegade nodded, and Melanie knew he was enjoying the moment. "This morning during my impromptu visit to your office, I found your 'earnings' wrapped and ready to mail, though no address was supplied. Instead, you will return it to these people, and in their hands it will stay. Should you attempt to retrieve it, know I will return, while you sleep perhaps, and see that you never wake again. Do you understand?"

Bradford nodded, furious. "You won't get away with this."

"A redundant phrase, señor. I've 'gotten away' with much so far." With his free hand, the Renegade pulled a large envelope from his cape. He tossed it to Chen, who caught it in midair and immediately proceeded to count the bills. Chen's eyes grew wider and wider as the sum increased.

"Amazing! This is more than I'd realized we'd paid." With a certain reluctance, Chen proceeded to distribute the cash to Tewa's eager inhabitants. Only Victoria bothered to count her portion.

The Renegade edged Bradford back toward the schoolhouse. "You told us, señor, when you arrived, that you hoped to hunt for Spanish treasure. Though that treasure long ago proved nonexistent, it seems you've found a suitable replacement for gold in our citizens' funds."

Bradford twisted his head from the sword's edge.

"They are my tenants, and they must pay for the right to live here! This pueblo is under my control, and there's nothing you can do about it."

"When I hear those words from Rafael de Aguirre himself, I will have no choice but to accept you. Until then, know that I will haunt your every step. There will never be a night when you can sleep without fear that I will return."

The Renegade shoved Bradford forward onto his knees, then bounded back into the school. Bradford scrambled up, shouting orders. "Follow him! Shoot him! Don't let him leave this pueblo alive!"

Melanie watched in terror as the guards raced around the plaza, bursting into the apartments and shops of the pueblo. The Renegade darted past a window, then leapt onto the wall amid a hail of gunfire, but he remained unscathed. He jumped down into the rear stables and disappeared again. Men ran everywhere, and the Tewa inhabitants gathered together near Chen's hotel.

Miguel's wife shouted orders that no one listened to. "We have to stop them, to protect the Renegade." Her husband took her hand.

"He knows what he's doing, my dear. Just watch."

The stable gate splintered, and the Renegade appeared astride his black horse. It seemed calm despite the shouts and gunfire, and in the chaos, its rider stroked its arched neck. Melanie shaded her eyes against the high sun. He looked different somehow, smaller, but she couldn't be certain because he was leaning forward over the horse's neck. He aimed for the gate, but the guards raced to close his exit.

Just as they moved to bar the gate, it swung open from the other side, and Diego de Aguirre limped in carrying a half-empty bottle, his black hair disheveled. Melanie's mouth slid open. Diego looked around and then rolled his eyes, but he didn't move out of the Renegade's way. The Renegade saw his opening and urged his horse to a gallop.

Diego didn't move. Instead he rubbed his head as if it pained him. "Now hold there, you. This has gone far enough."

The Renegade charged toward him, and still Diego didn't move. Melanie's heart slammed with fear. "Diego! Get out of there!"

As her words met the air, the black mustang careened into Diego and knocked him aside. Diego rolled, his body contorted, then lay still. The Renegade didn't slow—he galloped from the pueblo with the guards following in what Melanie knew was a vain pursuit.

Chen ran to Diego's side, but Diego didn't move. Melanie stumbled through the crowd. Diego was too quick and too brave, and far too reckless for his own good. She was no fool. She knew what he did, and she could guess fairly well how he did it. But this time he might have gone too far. This time the Renegade might have destroyed himself.

\* \* \*

255

Chen enlisted two other men, and all three carried Diego to his room in the Chateau. Melanie followed, fighting emotion. He was breathing, but he didn't open his eyes. Once, when Chen bumped his head on the railing, Diego seemed to frown, but other than that, he gave no sign of waking. His arms hung to his sides—Melanie had to keep propping them back over his chest.

Will came bounding up the stairs after them, breathless. "Is he all right?" He poked his head in the door, and Chen nodded.

"He's doing fine."

"The Renegade didn't hurt him too bad, did he?" Will sounded sincerely concerned, but Chen didn't seem as worried as Melanie felt he should. She couldn't recall seeing Will in the plaza, but everything had happened so fast, she might have missed him.

"The Renegade's horse trampled him, Will. His ribs may be broken." Melanie pulled back the covers. They lay him on his bed, and Melanie adjusted the coverlet over him. "He must be kept warm until a doctor can be summoned."

Chen looked at Will. "Doctor?"

Will cleared his throat. "I'll go fetch Patukala."

Melanie eyed him doubtfully. "Diego's uncle? Is he a doctor?"

Will shrugged. "They call him a medicine man. He'll do."

Melanie turned to Chen, fully expecting him to object, but Chen just nodded. "Yes, Will. Get Patukala, and be sure to let Mr. Bradford know we have medical help on the way."

Will hurried away, but Melanie wasn't ready to accept this kind of treatment. "I don't think a medicine man is adequate to tend Diego. He needs a real doctor. If he doesn't regain consciousness soon . . ."

"I'm sure he will. *Any moment now.*"

As if in response to Chen's command, Diego opened one eye, then the other. He winced, as if grasped by sudden pain, then turned his head to the side. He held up one hand, grimacing, as if the slightest motion pained him. "I'm all right. Don't worry about me, señorita. It's bad . . . but I'll pull through . . ."

He had enough energy for speech, anyway. Melanie seated herself at his bedside. She hesitated, then clasped his hand in hers. It felt warm rather than cold, which she hoped was a good sign. "Lie still, and try not to talk. Will has sent for . . . your uncle. I think we should find a more conventional doctor."

Diego glanced at Chen, then back at Melanie. "There's no need, señorita. Patukala knows what he's doing. And I don't trust modern medicine, anyway."

Melanie squeezed his hand tight, fighting back tears. "What have you done this time? I'm so sorry this happened, Diego."

"Hmm?" He peeked up at her, then smiled. "I knew it was you."

"What?"

"I've suspected you all along, Miss Muessen. You're the Renegade, aren't you? You ran me down."

"I never did!" He was teasing. She wanted to hit him.

"Then what have you to be sorry for? And did you get a shot of him with Bradford?"

"No . . . I didn't think to use my camera. I guess I won't make a career out of journalistic photography. I'm not quick enough."

He shook his head. "No, you're better suited to landscapes and portraits, blending people with their environment. As you told me the day we met . . ." He smiled, and his eyes closed.

"Are you sure you're all right, Diego? The Renegade . . . needs to be more careful."

"I just got in his way, that's all." Diego patted her hand. "Don't worry yourself, señorita. I'll be all right. In a few days . . ."

Chen coughed. "You'll be bedridden more than a few days."

Diego eyed Chen, but he didn't seem disturbed. "You'll bring my meals here, I trust? Serve me in bed?"

Chen glared. "I suppose I must."

"I tire of roast quail, incidentally. I'd like something more interesting. And dessert . . . No puff pastries, Chen. Tell Massimo."

Melanie stared at him. "I don't think you should eat until your uncle has examined you."

Diego looked disappointed, but Chen nodded vigorously. "And you'll need a long rest before I would *think* to risk your health with food."

They heard footsteps from the hall, and Chen nodded toward the door. "Someone's coming."

Diego frowned. "The Renegade didn't trample my head, Chen. I can hear."

Chen went to the door, but Melanie stayed with Diego. "It's Bradford and that woman."

Diego groaned. "Not Harriet?"

"Yes."

Chen opened the door before Bradford could knock, but his expression turned from mild annoyance to one of great concern. "Quietly, please. He's in a great deal of pain."

Melanie raised her brow, but she said nothing. Diego seemed much better than she'd dared hope given the fall she'd witnessed, but maybe it was the thought of conversing with Bradford that anguished him.

Harriet entered the room, followed by Bradford. She hurried to Diego's other side and placed her hand on his forehead. "He feels so warm! It's possible he has a fever."

Melanie felt her lips twitch. "I don't think a fever could have built this soon after his accident. A fever comes when a wound has turned septic, or an illness has grown inside. Persons who are injured badly in an accident feel cold."

Harriet kept her attention on Diego. "Still, he

looks so pale. Are you all right, Diego? Can you hear me?"

Diego opened one eye, looking more forlorn than only a few moments previously. "I won't be moving any time soon, that's for sure."

"We couldn't help but worry." Harriet shuddered. "The Renegade is obviously a violent and dangerous man. All the while he held a sword at Mr. Bradford's throat, I could feel his eyes on me."

Diego looked up, with both eyes this time. "On *you*?"

Harriet nodded vigorously. "I felt his attention pinned on me. It was terrifying. I hoped he would look away, at Miss Muessen perhaps, but he didn't. He just kept staring."

Diego's eyes flashed with an incredulous light. "I don't think you have much to worry about, Harriet. The previous Renegade, my brother, was notoriously nearsighted. He couldn't see much past his nose without his spectacles, let alone a woman standing across the plaza. Maybe this one is, too."

Harriet wasn't convinced. "No, I feel sure of it. He was watching me. He is the type of man to pursue young women. After all, he abducted Miss Muessen already."

Bradford listened to the conversation with interest. "You may be right, Harriet. Such a man, without scruples, is a danger to a beautiful woman like you. We must keep you protected."

Harriet moved to stand near Bradford. "Thank

you, Mr. Bradford. I don't know how I will sleep at night, knowing he's out there."

Melanie decided she didn't like Harriet, and that Diego had been right about her. "He treated me well enough."

Chen slapped a wet cloth on Diego's forehead, then glanced at Harriet. "And by all accounts, the Renegade is smitten with Miss Muessen."

Bradford placed his arm over Harriet's shoulders. "A man like that isn't beholden to one woman. Wherever she goes, men are captivated by Harriet because she embodies all the feminine virtues—grace, good manners, and sensitivity."

Bradford's words implied that Melanie lacked these qualities—he must have taken note of her aggressive appetite at dinner, or maybe it was her tendency to speak her mind and challenge him, even *threaten* him. If she was sensitive, she wouldn't let anyone know, whereas Harriet was the type to wear her heart on her sleeve. Or at least, what she wanted people to think was her heart.

Diego grimaced, then motioned toward Bradford. "If I am at last off your list of suspects, Señor Bradford, I would like to sleep. My uncle is on his way to prod and poke at my various injuries. Since he's treated me in the past, I want to be well rested for the assault to come."

Bradford nodded. "He had me fooled, that is certain. I almost thought your drunkenness was a ruse, de Aguirre. But you're as shiftless as they say." He smiled, as if this had been a compliment, and Melanie felt stung on Diego's behalf. Diego, however, just smiled in return.

"Glad to hear it. I'd hate for people to get the wrong idea, and then have to disappoint them." Melanie said nothing, but she wondered if Diego's words were meant for her. Maybe it was time to straighten him out about what she knew—and what she didn't know. But what she didn't know loomed too large for her to address now. What *did* he want with her? Why was he toying with her this way, as two men, two lovers? Was it love, or something far more basic?

But now wasn't the time to ask. By the way Diego's gaze kept returning to her, shifting from her lips to her breast, she guessed she would have time alone with him soon. His eyes darkened, and she knew he wanted her. Her pulse quickened, but at the same time something about his attitude annoyed her. He knew they would make love again. He expected it. Yet he kept this secret from her, assuming she didn't know. Assuming that, like a fool, she believed herself in love with a stranger.

Bradford left, and Harriet followed. Harriet stopped at the door and looked back. "I'll be back to check on you, Diego. You won't be lonely!"

They left, and Diego groaned. "Chen, lock that door, will you? And if she tries to bust in here again, tell her I'm sleeping. *Looking at her*, indeed. I don't think so." He squeezed Melanie's hand, and she recognized the eagerness of his desire in his touch. "I hope you will visit often, señorita. But you look tired yourself, and I see it's already dark outside my window. Perhaps you should return to Victoria's inn and get some rest yourself."

*Of course. He'll be in my room within an hour.* "I'll go. You should rest."

Diego leaned back, a smile on his lips. "I am weary to the bone. I need rest more than I can say." A veiled reference to what he really needed, and that was their passion. He looked so pleased with himself. Melanie's annoyance grew. It almost felt as if she was a game to him. Well, if that was the case, Diego de Aguirre had another thing coming.

Chen went to the door and held it open for Melanie. "I must leave you, too, Diego. My duties require my attention."

Diego elevated his finger and pointed. "And there is the matter of my dinner, Chen."

Chen frowned. "You're much too sick."

"I can handle it. And I'm hungry. Bring a glass of wine, but nothing too strong. I don't want to overdo it." He glanced at Melanie and grinned. "Might as well make the most of it. I don't get him at my mercy often."

Melanie didn't smile, though Diego didn't notice her reaction. But his words fanned her own fear. Chen wasn't the only one at Diego's mercy.

"I've come, love." The Renegade slid her hair forward over one shoulder, then bent to kiss her neck. Though still troubled by doubts, his touch didn't fail to stir Melanie's senses. She battled her reaction to the desire he provoked, then turned to face him.

"I knew you would." He moved to hold her, but she placed her hand on his chest to stop him and looked him straight in the eye. "There's something I have to discuss with you, and I need to do it here, where there's no danger of being overheard."

He clasped her shoulders and moved to kiss her again. He was wearing the black mask again, which apparently concealed his entry into Tewa better than the more colorful Indian mask. "It can wait, love. I've missed you, you know. I'm sorry I couldn't come to you last night, but as you may have heard, I had other business to attend to. Nothing as pleasurable as this, however."

"This is too important."

He fiddled with her hair. "You're not worried about Diego de Aguirre, are you? He's not dead, after all. I'm told he'll recover. Don't worry about him."

He was taking this too lightly. Melanie frowned. "Don't you ever think about my feelings, or how this all will end up?"

He backed away, more serious as he finally noticed her dark mood. "I think about it often, Melanie. I want to protect you. I'm afraid I haven't done as well as I'd hoped."

"Protect me? From what? Danger? What about my heart?" He started to speak, but she held up her hand to stop him. "There is something you should know."

"What is it?"

She straightened, her gaze penetrating his. "I am in love with Diego de Aguirre."

He appeared shocked even through his mask. "*You are?* Him? Why?" He paused. "Of course he is handsome . . ."

Melanie rolled her eyes. "I am in love with you . . . too." He looked uncomfortable. "Have you ever wondered what that might do to me?"

He stammered a moment, then shrugged. "The heart's voice speaks in mysterious ways." He stammered again. "It's like a river . . ." He clamped his hand over his forehead, pained. "I'm starting to talk like my grand . . ." He stopped himself and coughed. "Like a crazy old man."

So he had no intention of revealing his identity . . . Melanie turned her back to him. "I see. For all you know, I am suffering intolerable pain, my heart torn between two lovers."

Diego reached behind his head, untied the mask, then pulled it off. He was grinning, expectant as he waited for her reaction. For a long, timeless while, she stared into his twinkling Spanish eyes. Then, so slowly that she barely knew what she was doing, Melanie clenched her fist into a tight, firm ball and slammed it into his taut, unsuspecting stomach.

# *Chapter Eleven*

She hit him. Worse, the blow knocked the wind out of him, and he doubled forward in both surprise and considerable pain. "Miss Muessen . . ." He paused to catch his breath. "I would thank you to remember that I have only just today been through an accident of surpassing difficulty as well as substantial bruises."

Melanie's bright eyes were lit as if by fire. "How dare you?" She made a fist again, and he backed away. "How dare you think I didn't know?"

Diego's face knit in both confusion and pain. "*What?*"

"I have known you were the Renegade all along. I knew it before you did! I knew you would put on that mask. I even knew you'd pick that black mustang."

His mouth dropped in surprise. "You did?"

"Yes. I knew it because you're vain, and you wanted that horse. How could you think I wouldn't know you, especially after you kissed me?"

Diego stared in astonishment. She had known all along. "Why didn't you say something?"

"Why didn't *I* say something! What about trust, about love? I kissed you, after you abducted me from Bradford's room, to test my theory, to be sure it was you."

"So . . . my kiss is that distinctive, is it? I should have known."

She looked like she might hit him again. "I am a woman. Women are sensitive and know these things. But you took it a lot further . . ."

"*I* took it further? Who seduced who?"

A satisfying blush flooded her cheeks. "You knew I didn't have your level of experience in this area."

"Well, you learn quickly, señorita!" A mistake. She made a fist and swung again, but he dodged it. "You are a violent woman."

She didn't seem offended. She seemed rather proud instead. "I wanted to learn your intentions toward me. And it appears those intentions involve my bed and little else! I wanted to know you trusted me, as I have trusted you."

"I was trying to protect you." He reached out to touch her shoulder, but she smacked his hand away. "We went to great lengths to conceal my identity. Today, further than I would have cared to go."

"I guessed that. Somehow, you switched places with Will, and he pretended to run you down."

"It was impressive, wasn't it? Not easy, though. We had my horse hidden in the stables. I had to give Will the mask and cape, then run around the pueblo to the gate before the guards could close it. Close thing, it was, too. But it was Will who trained . . ."

"I don't need to hear you boasting about your subterfuge! I have waited for you here tonight, knowing you would come, because it is time for us to be honest with each other."

"Melanie, you don't seem to understand. I was acting on behalf of your best interest."

"How noble! It didn't stop you from ruining me, did it?"

"You're hardly ruined."

"I have been nothing but an amusement to you."

He touched her whether she wanted him to or not. "Melanie, if it only amused me, I wouldn't have told you the truth tonight."

"You were just afraid I'd back out and you wouldn't have any *fun* tonight!"

How could she think that? Had he really been so good at making himself a . . . rakehell? "That's not true. I love you, Melanie."

She eyed him with a dark sneer, disgusted. "You can't expect me to believe that."

"It's true. It took me by surprise, that's certain.

But you wormed your way into my heart, and I can't think of anything but you, I want nothing but you."

"*Wormed my way?* How romantic!"

"I didn't inherit my father's poetic skills, but I mean it. You are my woman." This didn't go over any better than "wormed my way." Melanie swung her small fist again, and Diego ducked just in time to avoid a blow clearly aimed at his face. "Stop that! How am I supposed to explain a black eye?"

She stopped, considering. "I will refrain from striking you again because I know you must maintain your ruse for the sake of your brother, his family, and the pueblo itself."

"I thought you would be pleased, Melanie. You seemed to be savaging yourself for loving two men. I couldn't think of any other way to calm you."

"*Calm me?*"

"I see it didn't exactly work."

"No, it didn't. How can I ever trust you, or believe in what you say you feel for me? Everything to you is a momentary amusement. Maybe it amuses you to say you love me today, but tomorrow I could be forgotten."

"I've never said those words to another woman."

"And why would I believe that? No . . ." She stopped, sputtered, then shoved him toward the window. "Get out."

"You want me to leave?"

"Yes!"

He wanted to argue, but instead endured a growing sense of doom. She had known what he was doing all along. She had been waiting for him to reveal his true self, and his true heart. He had—but it wasn't the man or the heart Melanie Muessen wanted or deserved.

Diego bowed, then went to her window. "I never meant to hurt you, señorita. I am not a great man. I have never been. But when I say I love you, those words come from my heart. I will leave because you ask it, but if you never trust anything again, please trust my love."

He didn't let her answer. Those words were torn from deep inside him, and for the moment, he couldn't face her reaction. Diego slipped through her window and went out into the night alone.

"Ah, Chen, have I always been such a fool?"

"Yes."

Diego sighed heavily. "What have I done?"

"You've been callous, thoughtless, selfish, and blind."

Diego frowned at Chen, who poured a cup of morning tea and sat down to drink. Diego had returned to his supposed sickbed, but he hadn't slept. He needed time for contemplation, but Chen wasn't helping much. "You might consider words of encouragement rather than condemnation for a change."

"You asked. I answered."

Diego sighed, then folded his arms behind his

head. "I'm not arguing with you. But she was so angry . . ."

"How hard did she hit you?"

Diego glanced at Chen. "Hard. Didn't I tell you that already?"

Chen smiled and looked satisfied. "You did, but I enjoyed hearing it so much the first time." He gestured at the untouched tray of food. "You haven't eaten anything. And after all the work I put Massimo to."

"I'm not hungry."

"Just wanted to order me about."

"For all the good that does. You just turn around and order someone else."

"True, but that in itself takes effort."

Diego closed his eyes. "Fortunately, my fall in the plaza left me with considerable bruises. I'd hate to think what Melanie's blow added to that. But if Bradford checks, there'll be plenty to see."

"He seems convinced already. We have nothing to worry about there. It's Rafael's fate that concerns me. And what about his wife and his children? What could have happened to them? Bradford must have them somewhere—but where? They talk of his return. What do you think it means?"

"I don't know. I can't believe they'll bring him back, but I don't see any other way for Bradford to solidify his claim. I'll have my grandfather put a watch out for him, but I don't know what good it will do. The next move is Bradford's."

Someone knocked on the door. Chen set his cup aside to answer the door, and Diego shuffled himself into a position indicating ill health. He wasn't wearing a shirt, so he left the blanket draped to show the worst of his bruises. Chen checked to see if he was ready, and Diego nodded.

Chen affected a serious expression, far more like a physician than Patukala had been, then opened the door. Diego expected Bradford, or worse, Harriet, but it was Melanie who entered.

His heart took a quick bounce, and he found himself holding his breath. He moved to adjust his blanket, but she noticed his bruises, and her eyes widened. She glanced at Chen. "I need to speak to him alone."

Chen nodded, then scurried away, as if relieved to have no part in the conversation to come. Melanie closed the door, then came to Diego's bedside. She said nothing, and his nervousness grew.

"Would you like some tea or a scone, señorita? Chen brought me breakfast, but it's not my drink of choice."

"No, thank you."

She took a quick breath, then seated herself on the chair by his bedside. She gestured at his bruised side, then looked a little pale. "Did I do that?"

Diego coughed to keep himself from laughing. "No. This is the result of my fall. Apparently, I'm not as good at acrobatics as I thought." He paused and looked into her face. When had she become so dear that he no longer simply admired her as a beautiful woman, but saw in her face all her sweetness, all her vulnerability, and a heart so close to his own that he almost felt it beating? "It is inside that your blow cut most deeply, señorita."

He wasn't teasing and she knew it. "I'm sorry I hit you. Violence should never be a solution to anger."

"But it often precedes thought." He paused. "Have you . . . spent much time in thought?"

She chewed her lip, then shrugged. "Some."

Diego sat up to face her. "I didn't sleep at all."

Her bright gaze flashed to him. "I didn't either."

They smiled together, and Melanie bowed her head. Diego wanted to touch her, but he restrained himself. "I am not a great man, Melanie, and I don't deserve you. But I can't imagine my life without you. I picture myself standing by the train when you leave, and I know that when you're gone, that part of me that came alive in you, that will be gone, too. I would follow the train, I would follow you across the sea, wherever you go, just to be near you, even if you don't want me there."

Tears glistened in her eyes, and in his, and fell to her cheeks. She looked at him, then placed her hand over her heart. "You are here, in my heart. I could leave, but there's no place in the world I could go and not feel you."

Diego clasped her small hands in his. Her pinkies both propelled themselves outward, curved to the side in their unique way. He kissed each finger, then held her hands against his cheek. "From the

273

moment I first saw you out the window of the Chateau, I knew you were something so precious, something far above me."

Melanie shook her head. "But I felt the same. I saw you, and I looked in your beautiful eyes, and something about you touched my heart." She paused and looked embarrassed. "It's in the picture I took of you."

"What picture? As I remember, you've never found me quite adequate to be your subject, except as the Renegade."

She blushed. "I have taken several pictures of you when you weren't looking."

Diego's heart filled with happiness. She had cared all along, and wanted to immortalize his image because he had been important to her. "When?"

"I took one the day I met you. Then two at Tesuque, one with your grandfather when he was lecturing you and you were pretending to listen but weren't. Another with the children. You were kneeling and laughing, and you looked so beautiful, and their faces are filled with such love." Her tears started again, but he wasn't sure why, until he realized he was crying, too. It was relief, and joy, and knowing something he'd thought forever elusive, impossible, was now his.

"I would like to see them."

Melanie looked proud. "When this is over, when your brother and his family are safe and Tewa back to what it should be, then I will set up my pictures in the plaza, and everyone can see."

"Hold that image, my dear love, and treasure it, because I am so afraid that's all it will ever be. A dream."

Melanie left her chair and sat on the bed beside him. "You're afraid the moment will come and you will fail."

He closed his eyes, but pain filled his chest and seeped through his limbs. "I have failed before."

Melanie wrapped her arms around him and hugged him, and he rested his cheek on her head. "You're talking about when the kiva mine collapsed, aren't you?"

"You don't understand, Melanie. I tried so hard. I gave all I had. But I learned my limits that day. No matter how hard I tried, I couldn't save those people alone."

"Diego . . . your leg was broken. No one of you, even your brother, worked alone."

He had heard this reasoning before. Rafael had said these same words, over and over, but Diego had never quite believed them. But Melanie had seen good in him when he wasn't trying, when he was trying to be anything but good. She had fallen in love with him despite every fault and vice he'd worked on over the past ten years. "Why did you allow me to make love to you as the Renegade?"

Melanie kissed his cheek. "That wasn't my intention—at first. I just wanted to test your identity by kissing you. But then I realized there was something more. When you wear that mask something happens, but it's not a disguise. It's more of an unveiling. You become in the Renegade what you really are, what you have been all along."

Diego shook his head. "It is a disguise, Melly. Rafael's disguise. I've just borrowed it."

"You think that, but I know better. The Renegade is all the things you try to hide, all the things you think you can never be, but are. He is noble and brave, he cares for others, and when they are in danger, he puts them before himself. He hides himself in a mask, but it is the mask of selflessness, and a heart that can't be moved. But your heart can be moved, Diego. It was moved at Victoria's story of her childhood, it was moved because Miguel the baker didn't deserve a whipping, however mean he's been to you. It's moved because you know your brother is helpless and needs you. And it's moved by me, because you know I love you."

"I thought you were impulsive, Melanie, flinging yourself into life and into love because you didn't realize how little I deserve you. I thought Rafael believed in me because he loved me, because he couldn't see my failures. I thought that of Chen and Will, too. I have never understood why they stuck by me, or why they foisted the mask on me when I seemed the person least likely to wear it."

The door opened and Chen walked in, followed by Will. "Then you never understood us." Chen placed his hands on his hips and looked satisfied, like a king who has arranged a great display of power and glory that proves his own reign is supreme.

Diego frowned. "You were eavesdropping."

Chen started to shake his head, indignant, but Will nodded cheerfully. "We were, Diego. Well, Chen was when I came up the stairs, and he hushed me, so I ended up listening, too."

Chen cast a dark glance at Will, took the seat Melanie had vacated, and resumed his tea. "So you've known the Renegade's identity all along, Miss Muessen?" He didn't sound surprised. "Very clever."

Melanie nodded, proud. "I am not a fool."

Diego felt proud, too. "I have a distinctive kiss."

Chen grimaced and held up his hand. "I do not need to know these details."

Diego folded his hands behind his head, pleased. "Then don't pry into matters that are none of your concern."

Melanie idly adjusted his pillow, dislodging him. "You are certainly worthy of friendship, anyway."

Diego eyed her with overt skepticism. "If that's what you call it."

Chen set his tea aside. "What else would have sent me crawling under a saloon at night, in the cold, in the filthy, bug-infested, and utterly loathsome space into which you'd rolled?"

Diego's eyes widened. "Was it you who put the Zuni blanket over me? I remember thinking it odd that someone had bothered to cover me."

Chen looked surprised, but Will smiled, content.

277

"That was me, Diego. I heard Chen lecturing you, even though I knew you weren't listening. He went on . . . and on and on. After he left, I put a blanket on you."

Diego smiled. Even in his darkest hours, had he ever been truly alone? "Thank you, Will. It was thoughtful."

Will patted his knee fondly, then ate one of Chen's scones. "Been looking after you. That's all."

Diego stared at him. "Why?"

Chen adjusted his position, edging Will aside. "Because we know you, Diego. As callous, rebellious, and disobedient, as irritatingly unwilling to conform to even the barest semblance of social protocol, as willing to attempt debauchery in any form . . ."

Diego frowned. "Get to the point."

Chen looked pleased with himself. "As bad as all that, when the time came, there was only one man to wear the Renegade's mask, and that was you. You've been beating yourself up for years because you weren't able to save everyone. But you did what you had to do, and gave your all, even when things looked hopeless. Just as you've done now. You said that first night that you would try to honor our faith in you. And you've done that."

Diego sighed. "Have I? All I've really done is take Bradford unawares and hold a sword at his throat."

Chen shook his head. "You kept him from stealing money from the people here, Diego. That must count for something."

"I haven't learned the identity of Bradford's investors in California."

Melanie broke off a piece of the second scone and ate, then spoke with her mouth still full. "I don't think they're exactly strangers." She paused to swallow. "I think those letters I saw in Bradford's room were from Harriet. Maybe the investors are her parents. Remember she mentioned that her parents visited Tewa once?"

"It's possible. But I don't think Harriet has been honest about her heritage. Still, she's certainly involved with Bradford, though I'm not sure how it helps us."

Diego gazed out his window as the morning light glanced off the pueblo wall. He heard Miguel call to his wife across the plaza, and the woman laughed in response. This was his home, now threatened by people motivated only by greed and self-interest. "In the end, Bradford will destroy this place, and leave it more barren than before my father restored it."

Melanie clenched her fist into a tight ball. "We will stand up to him, Diego. I am not afraid of Bradford."

Diego squeezed her fist, relaxing her tight fingers. "You do stand up to him well. It has always surprised me, because you seem so vulnerable, so sensitive."

"I told you I wasn't."

Chen looked unusually thoughtful. "You are right, and wise, Miss Muessen. I, too, have looked to establish myself with power and influence, using devices and methods outside myself. I thought, for a long while, that it would be necessary to marry a woman of heritage . . ."

Diego nodded at Melanie. "He means rich. I take it you've changed your mind?"

Chen smiled slightly, but Diego knew Chen's sense of privacy would never really be penetrated. "I have realized there are treasures greater than money and power."

Will stared at him, then shook his head. "I think he means he's fallen in love with Miss Wu, and though she doesn't have much money, he's figuring to marry her."

Chen blushed furiously. "That, Will, is a private matter not to be discussed."

"Well, we talked about Diego falling for Miss Muessen enough—figured it was fine enough to talk about you."

Chen braced in offense. "That is different. Diego has no sense of decorum or privacy. Everyone knew he was falling for Miss Muessen. My life, on the other hand, is not to be discussed, ever, by anyone."

Diego winked at Will. "While he's in the room, at least."

Will smiled. "Good enough, then."

Chen looked suspicious, but apparently had no argument, nor could he come up with a way to control conversations held in his absence. "If we might return to the subject at hand ... What do we do to save Rafael and his family?"

Melanie smiled. "We use the one thing Tewa has always had, one thing that has never failed. The Renegade."

# Chapter Twelve

"How did you manage not to limp? Or is your lameness itself an act?"

Melanie sat alone with Diego, finally left in peace by Will and Chen. Diego fiddled with her hair idly as the warm, mid-morning sun filtered through the open window. "I have no idea. If I'm running, leaping, bounding, then it isn't noticeable, and I've stayed on horseback as much as possible. Chen observed that I don't, apparently, limp when drunk."

"Why should that be?" Melanie grimaced. "You don't drink before donning that mask, do you?"

He looked offended. "Of course not! I have to ride without a saddle. Liquor would make that far more difficult than it is already. Beyond that, I seem to have lost my taste for the stuff." He paused, then lowered his voice. "Which was, I'm sorry to say, never quite as strong as legend had it."

"I knew that. You don't have the defeated look of a true drinker. You looked as if you wanted to be defeated, because you were afraid of the next challenge, but nothing owned you, nothing controlled you."

He sifted her hair over her shoulder, then examined her garnet and pearl drop earbobs. "Except you."

"I don't own you, Diego. I am part of you. We are part of each other. You met me, and at the same time saw inside yourself. It was the same for me. You became the Renegade. I became . . . a harlot." Melanie frowned. "I cannot help noticing that yours was the more honorable progression."

"That, my dear, depends on your point of view. But I will say that I'll welcome setting aside my mask the next time we make love."

They both fell silent, then looked at each other. Melanie felt nervous. He was already her lover. But now she could look into his brown eyes and see his shyness, see the expressions on his face as thoughts crossed his mind. She had made love to the Renegade at night, but now the sunlight poured through his window, and nothing was hidden, not his face, not hers.

He touched her face to ease a strand of hair back over her shoulder, then kissed her forehead. His kisses had always been loving, even when impulsive in nature. Yet she had so deeply feared they were meaningless, that he had touched too many other women for her to be any different.

Melanie peered up at him. "Why am I special to you?"

He smiled. "Would you like me to list the reasons?"

She chewed her lip. "Many women are special. And you've . . . well, you've known quite a few, as I understand it." She almost hoped he would tell her that rakishness, like rumors of his drunkenness, had been exaggerated, but Diego just nodded casually.

"I have learned from my considerable experience in this area that women and men hold the notion of intimacy quite differently."

"That much I have seen without experience." She paused, disappointed. "How?"

"For women, even the most jaded harlot, a sexual encounter is emotional, and they expect a connection with the man afterward."

Melanie frowned. "You mean, she expects him to remember her name?"

Diego nodded, as if that had indeed been, at times, a hardship. "Exactly. Some women want the man to care for no better reason than to prove to themselves they're important, or that their sexuality gives them power. Some are just deluded. Either way, the need is inherently emotional. But for men, there are levels of intimacy. Sometimes it's just an act of pleasure, sought out because the man is . . .

284

in the mood, or because she wants him, so she's enticed him. Or he's drunk, maybe." He was trying his best to be delicate, to protect her sensitive and romantic nature. It couldn't have been easy, given Diego's blunt and honest nature, so Melanie appreciated the effort.

"This isn't the most reassuring speech I've ever heard, Diego. How am I different? Why did you remember my name?"

"I've wondered that myself."

Melanie restrained a desire to strike him, but it wasn't easy. "I have struggled to remember yours, too."

"I had thought that once I had you, you would no longer enchant me."

Melanie placed her hands over her face. "I am so deeply glad that I didn't know what you were thinking."

Diego nodded. "I am, too."

Melanie groaned. "I'm not sure I want to hear the rest, but go on."

"I'm not sure I know myself. I thought I did, that I wasn't in the habit of deluding myself. I didn't think I was cut out for love, any more than for heroism."

"But you were wrong."

Diego's brow furrowed. "I'm not sure I was wrong. But I learned something about heroism, too. You don't have to be cut out for it, or born to it, as I always believed Rafael had been. There has to be a need, and you either choose to accept its challenge or you don't. You do your part. I cannot say it was mine alone. Chen planned it, like a pharaoh envisioning the Sphinx. Will prepared for it like a Roman soldier. And I rode out to battle disguised as an Anasazi warrior."

Melanie pondered this a while, thinking he must have paid more attention in school than he had implied. "What part do I play?"

"You're the reward, of course, given to the warrior if he succeeds. Like Helen of Troy."

"I want to be more than *that!*"

He looked surprised, as if he had no idea what offended her. "What do you want to be?"

"I want to be a hero, too."

He seemed genuinely surprised by her reaction. "Do you?"

"Most women do. They may settle for being the reward, or manipulating the king from their position behind the throne, but *everyone* wants to matter, to play their part, to effect the outcome of the situations in their lives. Look at Harriet. Maybe she's going about it in a strange way, but she's certainly active in her fate, though she pretends to be passive."

"Hers is a more manipulative route than yours, I think."

Melanie gazed up at the ceiling. "And look at Mr. Bradford. He could be a worthwhile person. He certainly has an orderly mind. But he is infected with greed and a lust for power, so he can't be useful to anyone. I understand, in a way, because

I have spent most of my life hiding from the world because I was afraid it would dominate and control me as it had my father."

"You may be right, Melanie, but I doubt explaining this theory to Bradford would change his mind."

"No, probably not. But we've got the upper hand because we have accepted ourselves. You've faced the hero inside you, and even though I'm afraid, I haven't let fear dominate me. Chen is doing what he does best, bossing people like a king, and yet his heart has opened just when it seemed most unlikely. We're ready—I think that's why we're here in the first place."

"And if we fail instead?"

Melanie smiled, then kissed his cheek. "We've already won, Señor Renegade."

"How is that?"

"Because you said 'we.' "

Melanie sat beside Diego on the edge of his bed, her hands folded on her lap. She felt nervous again. She wasn't sure why. The last time they had been together, she had lost her mind, lost control of herself and been anything but shy. Melanie shuddered, then cleared her throat to hide her discomfort.

Diego noticed. "Is something troubling you, señorita?"

"No . . . no, no. Not exactly troubling."

"What, then?"

"A lot has happened . . ."

"Yes."

287

"Many things I didn't expect."

"Nor I, señorita."

She glanced at him and saw that he repressed a smile. Her nervousness soared. "Those things that happened between us, in particular, surprised me."

Diego's brow arched. "Surprised *you?* You cornered me against a wall—I barely remember what happened after that, only as a sensual blur of perfection, a treasure of the senses. If anyone has a claim to surprise, it's me, not you."

He wasn't the type of man to leave such subjects delicately unmentioned. Melanie cringed. "I don't know what came over me."

"Blind, uninhibited lust—that's my explanation for it." As excruciating as this was, Diego didn't seem willing to stop there. "You're a deeply sensual woman, passionate, with a remarkable imagination. Better still, you're willing to explore my body, and give me yours."

"Those sound like the qualities of a harlot."

"Not at all! A harlot, in fact, lacks all those characteristics. They're cold, hard, devoid of imagination. They offer no treasure of themselves, probably because they don't believe they're worth it to begin with. Sad, but true."

"You've made a study of this, I see."

He nodded, devoid of guilt or shame. And maybe he was right to carry none. A man like Chen would have earned no such experience because guilt was something that could easily haunt him. Not Diego. "I've learned about people along the way. But only recently, with you, have I learned much about myself."

Melanie bit her lip. "What did I teach you?"

Diego smiled, and his bright eyes twinkled. "That I have much to learn." His smile deepened. "Have I taught you anything, love?"

She tried not to blush and failed. "More than I ever thought existed. But not just that. I thought that it was most important to make things right, to be strong. But now I think that what matters is love. The wrong Bradford and those like him do is to destroy freedom, and love thrives in freedom."

"My brother said something like that during one of his frequent lectures. *'Love is all.'* He told me that when the woman of my dreams appeared, I would move heaven and earth to have her, and that nothing would stand in my way."

Melanie smiled. "I like that very much."

They looked at each other. For an instant, Diego looked as shy as she felt. But then a subtle change came over his expression. His eyes darkened to a rich, sensual brown and his full lips curled into an almost imperceptible smile. She felt more than saw the change in his mood, and her own nerves tingled in response. "Perhaps I should let you sleep?"

Her voice came high and she felt foolish. Diego's brow arched. "Have you forgotten, señorita, that my incapacity is feigned? I am, I assure you, in the fittest and most vigorous of health."

She swallowed and tried to remain calm. "You're quite bruised."

"I barely feel it."

Melanie looked around the room, casually assessing the furnishings. "Did you select these cabinets or did Chen? The mirror is particularly nice."

"The cabinets are Chen's, the mirror mine." He knew she was making conversation, and he probably guessed why. It would have been easier if he teased her, but instead, he watched her face and let her ramble on.

"Very nice. So this is where you live?"

"More or less. My brother built a hacienda outside the pueblo when he decided to make his school bigger, and he likes me to stay there when he's gone."

"But instead, you stay here, in the smallest room in Chen's hotel."

Diego shrugged. "The hacienda is lonely without Rafael and his family, so I spend my time here instead. And it's a lot closer to the saloon."

Melanie knew differently. "Patukala pointed out your brother's hacienda when he brought me from Tesuque. He also told me that you let a widow and her three children stay there, and that you've been paying her to look after it—while doing all the work yourself."

Diego looked uncomfortable. "She needed a little help, and it was convenient. A shopkeeper from Santa Fe is courting her, so she'll be moving soon."

"A shopkeeper you introduced to her."

"Is there nothing my uncle didn't tell you?"

"He didn't tell me why you keep these things to

yourself. You saw a need in a person, as you always do, and you took care of it. I think . . . I think you saw a need in me, too."

"I saw a beautiful, sensual woman who thought she wanted to be alone, and who thought the best thing she could do was to guard her heart. But your heart is a treasure, Melanie. Your need is a treasure, too."

He touched her cheek, then ran his finger over her lips. He moved to kiss her, so slowly that she heard every heartbeat, so that every breath seemed an eternity. His lips brushed over hers, and he cupped her face in his hands, then kissed her forehead and her cheek. Their noses touched and he smiled. "Like Eskimos . . ." He kissed her again, more sweetly, and with more tenderness than she thought possible.

She expected him to deepen the kiss, but instead he drew back to look into her face. His eyes glittered with the intense, bright passion she had sensed in him from the moment they met. "I love you, Melanie. I have loved you before, hidden as some other man, a better man. I would love you now as myself."

*I love you, too.* Melanie glanced at the window, then back at Diego. "It's sunny. Daylight."

"It's a beautiful day, yes." He looked confused. "What of it?" He paused, and his brow knit in concern. "Do you need time? If you've not quite forgiven me, if you need to think . . ."

"Diego, there's no need for forgiveness. I needed

to know you, and to understand you. Now that I do, there's nothing to forgive." She touched his face. "I love you, and all that you are, I welcome. It's not that." She hesitated, not certain how to voice what bothered her.

"What, then?"

"It's *day*."

"I locked the door when Chen left. No one will bother us."

"But it's *day!*"

He began to understand, but rather than having been brought to his senses, her concern seemed to amuse him. "The Renegade loves at night. I, on the other hand, would prefer to see the sun on your little body, playing in your hair. I want to see everything I do to you reflected on your face."

A small squeak emerged unexpectedly from her lips. "But you will see everything! Those places where I'm not quite so slender, perhaps, or which may in general be private and . . . not to be seen!"

"A man likes to watch his woman when he makes love to her, especially in daylight." He called her his woman deliberately, but she was growing accustomed to the term. "Your body is beautiful, your skin is soft and warm, and I love the feel of you. Do you know, your skin has an appealing pale gold coloring? You would be perfect naked in sunlight."

Melanie began to wonder what he would look like in sunlight, too. If she could examine him without unveiling herself, an encounter in daylight might prove interesting. He must have noticed her intrigued expression because he was smiling when she glanced at him.

"Nighttime, señorita, is a long way off. And think, during the day Chen's guests are out and about. Bradford is escorting Harriet around the pueblo as if he owns it. Chen is visiting Victoria, when he thinks no one knows. Will is off feeding the horses. Porticus alone should keep him busy late into the afternoon. We're alone, my angel."

Diego played with her hair, then trailed his fingers down the side of her neck. He moved her hair aside, then kissed her throat. "If you would prefer to wait for the cover of darkness . . . for the hours and hours until the sun sets . . ." He tasted her skin, then barely nibbled over her racing pulse. His hand moved lower, over her breast, and Melanie caught her breath.

"That does seem a long while away."

"An eternity." He circled her breast as he kissed her neck, and her nipple hardened in response. He touched her chin, then took her mouth in a long, leisurely kiss. He tasted her lips, and she tasted him. Diego moved back from her. With his gaze on hers, he unfastened the silver clasps of her snug bodice, then peeled it apart. His gaze flicked from her eyes to her mouth, then back, and he slid the bodice down over her arms. He didn't remove the bodice. Instead, he left it half undone, which effectively restrained her motion and kept her arms pinned at her sides. More embarrassing still, this posture had the effect of squeezing her breasts together above her corset and chemise. His gaze lowered, then darkened at the image of her round, full breasts.

Her heart throbbed, sending merciless pulses to her sensitive woman's core. He slipped his finger between her breasts, then lowered her chemise. He unlaced the ribbon, then unfastened the top hook of her corset. He slid his hands beneath the corset and freed her breasts. She caught her breath and held it as he bent to kiss her.

His touch was the sweetest torment, agonizingly slow as he circled each nipple with his tongue. He sucked and laved the taut peaks until she writhed with need, still trapped in her own bodice. She had feared vulnerability. She was vulnerable now, and yet safe with him. She closed her eyes, half fighting, half desperate for him to continue.

Diego edged her back on his bed, then pulled off her stockings and petticoat. Her skirt remained tangled around her thighs, strewn across his sheets. He didn't kiss her or touch her. Instead, he pulled off his white shirt and tossed it aside. Melanie's eyes widened at the sight of his broad, strong chest. He was right; it was better to view a body in sunlight. His smooth dark skin gleamed, and his black hair hung loose to his shoulders. He left the bed to remove his trousers, then stood before her, naked. Desire filled her; she longed to touch him. She struggled to free herself from the restrictive bodice, but Diego laughed, then knelt beside her.

He positioned himself between her legs, and Melanie gazed up at him like a wild animal, desperate with need. His male arousal was poised hard and thick from his body, a potent reminder of his own need. She dampened her lips with a swift dart of her tongue. He smiled, then bent near to her most personal area, and she couldn't stop him because her bodice still clamped her arms at her sides. She couldn't move to stop him, though her fingers curled as she tried to reach his hair.

He pushed her skirt up past her thighs to her waist, and it bunched around her middle. The dampness of his kiss on her breast tingled in the dry breeze.

Diego adjusted her skirt, then found its clasp. "This is a hindrance to my sight." He pulled it aside so that her bottom half was bare.

Melanie seized a quick breath. "Then maybe you would remove my bodice, too, as it's a hindrance to me."

Those dark eyes glittered. "Not a chance, señorita. The sight of you this way does more to me than I can tell you."

He didn't have to tell her anything. She saw desire burning in his eyes. He leaned forward and kissed her squeezed breasts, then trailed a slow line of kisses from below her bodice to her stomach, lower. She knew what he was doing—he would reciprocate what she had done to him.

He gave her no time to ponder what this might mean. He slid off the foot of the bed, adjusted her hips to face him, then knelt on the floor. He wrapped her legs over his shoulders, grazed his fingertips over her soft triangle of hair, then lower to the heated moisture of her desire.

Melanie gasped at his touch, then again when his mouth replaced his fingers. Pure pulses of fiery need sped through her, dancing and twirling inside her body. She felt the tip of his tongue graze her most sensitive spot, then lave it with more and more intensity. He circled the small bud while his finger dipped into her core. He teased her until she cried out with delirious pleasure. Her pinnacle approached, and he slowed, over and over until she thought she would go mad with desire. He brought her to the same edge so many times that her body seemed wound to its tightest capacity, easing her back to return again and again.

Her fingers clenched; every muscle in her body drew taut. Her head tipped back and she heard herself whimpering for release. His warm mouth caressed her, and then he sucked with just enough pressure to send her into cascading waves of pleasure. Her legs locked around his neck and her hips writhed, but before the waves slowed, he moved away. His hands shook as he pulled off her bodice.

Melanie lay before him, shocked, her body alive and tingling. She wanted more. Her gaze locked with his as she took his length in her hand. It throbbed with the hot power of his own desire and his eyes closed as he shuddered. "I want more."

Her voice sounded husky, like another woman's, but Diego nodded.

"All that you want, my love."

He positioned his thick shaft against the moistened entrance to her body, and she felt its pulse against her heated, slippery flesh. They looked at each other, and she saw an equal measure of vulnerability in his eyes. His expression changed as he watched her, and she knew this moment was as new for him as it was for her. Until Melanie, he had never made love to a woman he adored before—he had never looked down into her trusting eyes. And he was scared, because he was afraid he'd do something wrong. She knew him well enough to know that.

His innate sensuality thrilled her, just as she admired his boldness, the rebel inside him, but his vulnerability touched her more than anything else. She slid her legs over his, then placed her hands on his hips. She gazed up at him, then began to move so that her soft cleft caressed his length and circled his tip as a sweet promise of what she offered him.

His doubt disappeared. He endured her ministrations a moment longer, then groaned with the effort at restraint. "I want you inside me, so deep inside me that neither one of us will know where I begin and you end. I want us to be one thing, Diego."

As she spoke, she arched her hips. He hesitated until his blunt tip edged between her damp, silken folds. A shuddering moan tore from him, and he entered her.

The pressure within startled her, but the brief shock of his entry gave way to the most intense pleasure Melanie had ever known. He filled her completely. Her whole body wrapped around him— to hold him, to know him, and to make herself part of him.

He withdrew, then entered her again, and again, each time with more force until the blindness of desire consumed her. Their bodies writhed and arched to meet each other, riding each pulse of ecstasy higher. She gripped his shoulders to steady herself, and he drove himself harder inside her. They were one thing, locked in a passionate embrace. She felt more alive than she'd ever imagined possible. The connection spiraled and grew tighter, then burst into one intermingling crescendo, together. Her body quivered and accepted all of him, and his poured itself into her. Their cries mingled and joined, until at last he lowered himself into her arms.

She held him close, so far beyond words that she thought she would never speak again. Diego turned his face to kiss her, and they moved together again. The sunlight moved through the bedroom, then dwindled behind the pueblo walls outside, but passion abated only to rise again.

Nothing ended—it went on and on, and the hours themselves blended while they loved.

# *Chapter Thirteen*

"What time is it?" Diego opened one eye and looked around his dark bedroom. Melanie lay tucked close beside him, her hand on his chest, but she didn't answer. He checked her face. She slept with a small smile curving her lips, content.

Nothing in his life had prepared him for what they'd shared this day. He'd never known desire that flared and never slacked, he'd never experienced his bliss so many times, yet wanted it again so desperately. Melanie had felt the same, wanted him as much as he wanted her.

He'd exhausted her. She'd exhausted him. It was pure ecstasy. Melanie stirred beside him, stretched and yawned, then wrapped her arm over his chest. Now he understood his brother's happiness, and why he shared it so easily. When love came, it overflowed from an infinite well.

"We should consider dining, my dear." He wasn't hungry—his satisfaction permeated his whole body and left no need in its wake, but Melanie sat up and looked eager.

"Do you think Chen will bring a meal here? I hope he thinks to include me!"

"I'd forgotten the extent of your appetite. Don't fear, my angel. If he brings one plate, we'll order another . . . and you may indulge in the first."

She didn't argue. It was all he could do to restrain comment. Too much teasing might dampen her enthusiasm for a resumed encounter. "Only if you're not terribly hungry . . ." She paused, and added as an afterthought, "We could share the first tray."

Diego shook his head. "A generous offer."

Her eyes narrowed, as if she suspected he found humor in her robust appetite. He kept his expression straight and innocent, but she didn't appear convinced. Someone charged up the stairs, then banged on Diego's door before either he or Melanie could react.

Melanie yanked the sheets from Diego and wrapped herself to her neck. Diego rose, then tugged on his trousers. He offered a feeble, weary cough. "Who is it?"

"It's Chen! Who else? Open this door!"

Diego went to the door, but Melanie squealed

and dove beneath the blanket. "What do you want? We . . . I'd like to dress first."

"This can't wait. Let me in!"

Diego tossed Melanie's cast-off articles of dress to the bed. She seized them in a tangled pile, fled to his upright wardrobe cabinet, shoved herself inside, and then closed the door behind her. She caught part of her blue skirt in the door. He fixed it for her. She nodded in thanks, then closed herself in again.

Diego opened the door for Chen, who stumbled forward in surprise. In her efforts to dress in a small space, Melanie thumped inside the cabinet. Chen's eyes widened. He looked at Diego, then held up his hand. "I don't want to know."

"Probably for the best. What do you want? Why did you come barging in here? And where's dinner?"

"No time for that. Diego . . ." Chen seemed breathless. So much for a night of bliss to equal the day's joy. "Will was outside the pueblo with the horses—he has your black mustang hidden in the woods near the hacienda. Where's your cape and the mask?"

Chen darted around the room, opening drawers and cabinets. He stopped before the wardrobe closet, and Diego seized his arm. "The cape and mask are in there." He offered a meaningful pause. "They are not alone."

The door opened a crack. An arm extended, holding the mask and Diego's cape, which Chen took. The arm quickly withdrew again, closing the door with small, curved fingers. Chen met Diego's eyes, then looked back at the closet. His mouth opened, but Diego shook his head. "You don't want to know. Remember?"

Chen nodded. "For the best . . ."

"Now, what do you want the Renegade for, and why can't it wait until tomorrow?"

"There's a coach on its way from Santa Fe now."

"So?"

Chen puffed an impatient breath of pure exasperation. "This isn't the coach's usual run. You've got to ride out and stop it, find out what's going on before it arrives. The coach will be a while longer; the road is winding, and Will came through the woods. Bradford has been waiting all day. He's downstairs dining with Harriet now, but he's expecting something. Something big."

"What?"

"I don't know. Whatever it is, you'd be better off intercepting it now than waiting until it's here in the pueblo."

"You're right. I'll go now. Can we trust that Bradford won't check on me tonight?"

"We'll put Will in here—he can mimic your voice if need be, but I don't expect trouble there."

The cabinet door burst open and Melanie extracted herself from Diego's clothing. "Holding up a coach sounds dangerous. What if it's nothing?" Her hair hung in long, tangled waves. She caught sight of herself in the mirror, then quickly adjusted it. She glanced at Chen. "Good evening, Chen."

"Miss Muessen . . ." Chen didn't seem surprised by her guilty presence in Diego's room, just embarrassed to have witnessed it. "You two need to be more careful."

"Diego is no threat to me, Chen."

Chen's brow arched dramatically. "That, I'm sorry to say, is already disproved utterly. However, you can't choose who moves your heart, as I have only recently discovered myself. There's nothing to be done about it. No, the danger I perceive is from Bradford. If he learns about your relationship, he can use it against the Renegade. If events transpire with Rafael as I fear, that is indeed a grave threat."

Diego turned to Melanie, then kissed her forehead. "I have to go, love. Go back to Victoria's inn, and promise me you'll stay out of the way, stay safe."

Tears welled in her eyes, but she didn't cry. "What about you?"

"I'll be all right." Diego placed the cape over his shoulders, and Chen passed him the mask.

"Holding up a coach should come naturally to you."

Diego frowned. "Thank you. But I'm not the one who should be afraid. It's the coach's passenger."

The coach moved slowly along the dark road, drawing ever closer to where the road forked between Tewa and the smaller path to Rafael's hacienda. The horses' hoofbeats sounded in time with

Diego's heart as he held his black mustang in check. He felt like a masked bandito about to hold up a train, but he had to intercept the coach; he had to stay a step ahead of Bradford if he was to save the pueblo, and his brother.

Diego waited until the coach moved beneath the jutting rocks, then urged his horse forward. The mustang leapt over the rocks and bounded down onto the road. The harness horses stopped in confusion, neighing as they reared, and the coachman shouted in alarm, then drew a gun. Diego moved quickly, and the coachman's hastily aimed shot went wild. He leapt from his horse's back onto the driver's seat, then shoved the man off.

He turned the team from the onward path and took the road toward Rafael's hacienda. He drove them fast, with his black horse racing beside the coach, obedient, until there was no chance the coachman could catch up. Diego drew the team to a halt, then jumped down. He knew whatever treasure lurked inside would be guarded, but the man who appeared at the coach door was Bradford's attorney.

Diego slapped his sword against the man's neck, pinning him against the door. "Mr. Alvin, I believe. Good evening to you, sir." Diego gestured at the ground beside the coach. "Down. Now!"

The lawyer's eyes were already wide with terror, his face pale in the lamplight as he stumbled down from the coach. "You! You devil, there's nothing you can do. Face your real enemy, Renegade." He jerked his head, indicating another passenger.

A tall man emerged from the coach, and Diego's heart quailed. Rafael stepped down from the coach and stood beside the lawyer. Diego's hesitation revealed his shock, and the lawyer laughed. "Didn't expect this one, did you? Here's your enemy, Renegade. Do you think the ignorant pueblo people will cheer you now that their real hero has returned?"

Alvin's words rang with mockery, but Rafael faced the Renegade. He looked tired, maybe older than when he'd left only two months earlier. Strain wrote itself across his proud face, but Diego couldn't let his own fear show. He hesitated before speaking. Would his brother know him as the Renegade? Diego couldn't let that happen, not until he knew what they were holding over Rafael. He cleared his throat, altering his voice beyond recognition. "A hero, Señor Alvin, is defined by his actions, and not his reputation."

Rafael didn't speak. He seemed tense, afraid. But not of the Renegade. Of something else, something far more dangerous. Alvin glanced at his captive, and Diego realized that whatever held Rafael now was more powerful than any chains. "Tell him, Señor de Aguirre. You've returned—there's no need for his dramatics now."

Rafael hesitated, then shrugged. "What do you want, Señor Renegade, that I could provide you? I am only recently returned from France. What treasure I have is yours, if that is what you seek."

*France.* Rafael had only traveled to France once, and he hadn't enjoyed the trip. He much preferred Spain and Portugal, and had intended to take the children into the Alps. He'd said France deliberately.

"The treasure I seek is you, Señor de Aguirre. Your return, as you may have guessed, is much awaited in Tewa. I expected another packet of gold secreted in Carlton Bradford's protective care, but I see his treasure this time is of another kind."

Despite the sword Diego held at his neck, Alvin seemed certain of his position and safety. "You defend Tewa from nothing, Renegade. As you can see, the pueblo's beloved son has returned, and now you are truly revealed as a criminal."

Diego's irritation soared. He edged the sword point against the lawyer's thin neck, then yanked a rope free from the harness. He bound the lawyer's hands behind his back, then tied him to the carriage. "I suggest you maintain silence and try nothing. Startled horses care very little who is dragged behind them."

An effective threat. Alvin blanched and held himself motionless. An idea presented itself. Diego had successfully held up the coach—Rafael was now his prisoner and could hardly be blamed for his abduction, not when it happened right before Bradford's righthand man. With Alvin secure, Diego directed his sword at Rafael.

"You, señor, will come with me."

Rafael tensed. "I must return to Tewa—tonight."

"I have a better plan."

Rafael shook his head. "You don't understand. I must return."

His brother could be stubborn. "It is you who misunderstands, señor. And I hold the sword."

He should have known. It wasn't wise to threaten Rafael. "Then run me through now, because otherwise I'm going to Tewa tonight."

Diego grit his teeth. *I need to talk to you, you fool!* Maybe Rafael realized that too easy acquiescence would incite suspicion. "I'm not offering you a choice." He positioned his sword, but Rafael moved faster. He dropped to his knee, rolled, and retrieved the attorney's cast-off pistol. Diego stood frozen as Rafael aimed the weapon at Diego's head.

"Ride on, Señor Renegade, back into the hills. I am doing what I have to do, and I can't allow you to stop me."

"What? Turn Tewa over to a man with the scruples of a snake? You don't know what he's done since you left."

"I don't care." Rafael sounded sincere, and he sounded desperate.

"Don't you? Then you won't be bothered to learn that your successor decided that Miguel's quick temper was equal to rebellion, and that he deserved flogging for the crime? Maybe you don't mind that he's sold the soul of Tewa, and that every person living there is now beholden to him?

307

Or that Chen is paying taxes high enough to send him back to the rails?"

Pain flickered in Rafael's eyes. "My life is no longer here. The people must solve their problems on their own." The words came forced—he didn't mean it, but somehow, Rafael was trapped. He didn't lower the gun.

Anger and pain flared in Diego's heart. "Then you'll have to shoot me, because I'm not letting you ride back into Tewa and destroy it or the people who trust you."

His brother's dark eyes glimmered with unshed tears, matched by the hot sting of his own. "Stand aside, Renegade, and let us pass. I have returned, and there is nothing you can do to stop what must, *must* be done."

Diego had known he was quicker than Bradford, that the surprised guards would never be quick enough to catch him. But Rafael . . . How could he challenge his own brother, no matter what madness afflicted him? As if he guessed Diego's thoughts, Rafael altered his aim away from Diego's head. He wouldn't shoot to kill . . . but he would shoot.

For the first time since donning the Renegade's mask, Diego truly took his life in his hands. He bowed his head as if in acquiescence, then leapt forward. Rafael dropped the gun, but he fought like a lion. They had never fought before. Rafael had never laid a hand on Diego, not in anger, not in punishment. When Diego was a small boy, how often had he flung himself into his older brother's arms for comfort and received all the love of a parent?

They fought for life, in fury and desperation. They were the same height, the same build. Neither man was stronger. But Diego was still armed. He jerked back, then to the side. He caught Rafael by the neck and pinned him back with the sword. He had won, but tears fell to Rafael's high cheekbones. His voice came hoarse, broken, and filled with anguish. "My wife . . . they have my wife and my children."

Diego's heart labored, and in the stillness of night he heard his brother's heart pounding, too. "Do you know where they are?"

Rafael's breath came in tortured gasps. "No. But they will kill her if I don't do as they've asked. She's pregnant and sick. Please . . . There is no other way. I've tried. Don't try to stop me."

"There has to be another way." Diego lowered his sword and released Rafael. "And I will find it. Do what you have to do, señor. Know that we will find your wife."

Rafael shook his head. "They took her from me on the train from San Francisco. I don't know where she is."

"She can't be far, Rafael, not if they mean to use her against you. We will stop him."

"No . . . Bradford is more dangerous than you know. He's planned this." Rafael glanced at the bound lawyer. Alvin couldn't have overheard their conversation, but he looked suspicious. "It may already be too late."

"We can't talk now. There will be another time." Diego paused. "I've got a plan. Jump me, and I'll fall as if you knocked me out. Release Alvin—go to Tewa." He looked into Rafael's eyes, and his heart filled with love and compassion. "I will save your wife and your children. I swear to you, I won't let you down."

Rafael's dark eyes glittered with tears, and he gripped Diego's arm. "My brother . . . You never have."

"How did he know it was me?" Diego had made his way back to his room at the Chateau, replaced Will in his sickbed, and found Melanie still waiting for him. "And didn't I tell you to return to Victoria's inn?"

Melanie's brow angled. "I chose not to. As for how your brother recognized you, it's obvious. He knows you, just as I do."

"Where is he now?"

Melanie went to the door and listened. "He's in the dining room with Mr. Bradford and Chen. I think Harriet's there, too."

"Bradford will keep him under watch constantly. If only I could speak with him alone, just for a few minutes! There must be some clues as to where Bradford has hidden Evelyn and the children."

"Hush." Melanie leaned forward to listen. "Chen is telling your brother about your injury."

She frowned, then rolled her eyes. "Harriet just said something about how handsome you both are." Melanie's voice became suddenly high-pitched and coy as she mimicked Harriet. " 'Good looks must run in your family. You both must be such awful rakes.' "

Diego shuddered. "Don't do that. You're frightening me."

Melanie closed the door quickly, then hopped back. "They're coming up here. Bradford insisted Rafael visit you. Your brother suggested letting you sleep."

Pride surged in his chest. "He probably thinks I haven't had time to get back." Diego lay back, his arms folded behind his head, smiling. Melanie struck him.

"You're supposed to be grievously wounded. Put your hand on your chest. Maybe hang one at your side."

"That's a little dramatic, Melanie."

"You were in that position when I first visited you."

True enough, but he had wanted her sympathy then. "That was different." Diego assumed a more natural position, but Melanie didn't seem to find it sufficient.

She adjusted his white shirt to reveal a portion of his bruised chest, then stood back. "How do I explain my presence here?"

"I suppose it wouldn't be wise to introduce you

as my woman, not when Bradford suspects you're smitten with the Renegade, too."

Her small face knit in a frown. "You're right, I know. I'll be careful to make it clear that I have no interest in you at all. Still, I wish . . ." She stopped and sighed.

Diego took her hand and kissed it. "When the time is right, I will introduce you not as my woman . . . but as my wife."

Her eyes widened and she caught her breath. "Your wife?"

He wanted to say more, to tell her that because they were one in body and in soul, they should be in life, too, but the door opened. Melanie stepped back from his bedside. Chen held the door open and Rafael entered, followed by Bradford and Harriet.

Diego eyed Rafael casually, then yawned. "You're back. What a relief." He motioned at Melanie, then snapped his fingers. "If you please, señorita . . ."

She hesitated, uncertain what he wanted and probably unwilling to do anything preceded by a snap. "What?"

"Help me up."

Her eyes darkened, but she came to his bedside and assisted him into an upright position. She might have adjusted his position a little too forcefully, then punched his pillow with too much vigor, but otherwise, she obeyed well enough. He caught a dark, warning look that told him if he went too far, he would pay dearly as soon as they were alone.

Rafael glanced between them, and for the first time, his expression softened. "You've hired a nurse?" Rafael assessed Melanie, who glared. "A beautiful nurse."

Melanie faced him. She stiffened her spine in a way that Diego suspected made her feel taller, then looked Rafael straight in the eye. "I am not his nurse, sir, nor did he hire me. In fact, it is your miscreant brother who is in my employ."

Rafael's brow arched in genuine surprise. "Indeed? Doing what?"

"Until his unfortunate accident, which, incidentally, would not have occurred if he'd been paying attention to his current duties rather than a bottle, he served adequately as my guide."

Diego smiled, although she was carrying it a little far, probably for Bradford's benefit. "Allow me to introduce Miss Melanie Ann Muessen. She is a traveling photographer from . . ." He stopped and glanced at Melanie.

She supplied, "Vermont," and Diego nodded.

"Vermont. The señorita has already photographed many of our wonders, including Will and our esteemed grandfather. She hasn't nabbed Chen yet, but I've no doubt he's next on her list of targets."

She frowned. "Subjects, not targets."

Harriet nodded enthusiastically. "Miss Muessen

took an absolutely lovely picture of me. Mr. Bradford thought highly of the work."

Bradford placed his hand on Harriet's shoulder. "The subject is the true work of art, my dear. But a photographer needs no talent to capture your beauty."

Rafael went to Diego's side and seated himself on his bedside. He tucked in the blanket, a gesture carried over from Diego's childhood, but more, brought on by remorse from their fight. Rafael spotted the purple bruise beneath Diego's open shirt, and his eyes widened. Diego knew what his brother was thinking—that he had inflicted the wounds during their fight. "Unsightly, isn't it? And all thanks to the merciless Renegade." Rafael looked confused, but he didn't question the unlikely assertion.

Bradford's mouth curled, somewhere between a smirk and a frown. "Your brother has already encountered the Renegade. But Mr. Alvin tells us that the man who first wore the mask proved the more adept fighter, and incapacitated the villain."

Diego adjusted his blanket, feigning disinterest. "I'm glad to hear it. He deserves whatever blow you delivered for what he did to me. Heaven knows how long I'll be here. Only today I tried to walk just a few steps, and as Miss Muessen can attest, found the act impossible, as well as brutally painful."

Rafael looked into Diego's eyes with a meaningful light. "My brother needs to be more careful."

Diego gazed up at him through heavy lids. He had mastered the look of boredom and carelessness to perfection. "Idleness doesn't suit me, Rafe. Do you know how many pleasant visits to the saloon I've already missed?"

Melanie huffed. "And it's only been one day. Think of the damage you could have inflicted in a week!"

She was quick. He had to give her that. "The señorita doesn't approve of my taste in recreation."

Chen stepped forward. "No one does. He has been worse since you left, Señor de Aguirre. I'm pleased you're back, if only for the sake of my own peace. I trust you will be staying?"

Rafael glanced at Bradford. "I'm afraid not, Chen. I left Evelyn and the children in Spain and will return there shortly. I came back only to set things straight here, to be sure you all understood . . ." He stopped and swallowed.

Diego yawned again. "We know—I have failed dismally as your successor, so you've chosen a more capable leader to walk in your stead. I can't say that I'm flattered, but I never did like the idea of running your school."

Harriet fanned herself idly. "That will be my duty, as Mr. Bradford has suggested."

Rafael's dark eyes flashed and his jaw tensed. Diego's heart moved in sympathy. He glanced at Harriet. "I hope that's a wise decision, Miss Richardson. You know the Renegade has beaded his unsavory attention upon you, for God knows what demonic purpose. It may be that he'll make your life difficult."

Harriet tapped Rafael's shoulder with her fan. "You may find this hard to believe, but at first, I thought Diego was the Renegade."

Rafael didn't hesitate. "Obviously you don't know my brother."

"Oh, I do now! He's much too sweet to terrorize anyone."

Rafael nodded. "I take it the new Renegade has been . . . less than sweet?"

Bradford's jaw hardened. "That outlaw has been a scourge upon this pueblo. With your return, Señor de Aguirre, the people of this pueblo will settle down and accept the changes that have occurred here."

Melanie huffed. "If they can be convinced those changes weren't shoved down their throats."

Diego gulped, then forced a laugh. "Miss Muessen objects to Mr. Bradford's methods more than most of the people here. It's the artistic temperament. High-strung."

Bradford's sharp gaze moved to Melanie. "I suggest she keep her attention on her camera rather than interfering with matters that don't pertain to her."

Diego didn't like Bradford's tone toward Melanie, nor the implied threat, but he forced an idle yawn. "How long will you be in Tewa, Rafe? A few days, at least. I'm somewhat short of cash . . ." This sounded plausible, assuming Bradford didn't know how little Diego spent, and how much sat untouched in Chen's safe. Rafael knew better, but he offered a weary sigh.

Bradford answered for Rafael. "I'm sorry to disappoint all of you, but Señor de Aguirre will stay only this night. Tomorrow morning, he will speak in the plaza to reassure the people of the correctness of his decision. But as you can imagine, he is eager to return to his wife. A remarkably beautiful woman, as I understand. I'm sure he doesn't want to be parted from her for long."

Rafael didn't speak, but Diego saw his pain and his fear. It was all he could do to keep his tone light and unconcerned. "A shame. But tomorrow? Surely my brother can be persuaded to stay with us a few days longer than that?"

Again, it was Bradford who answered. "I'm afraid that's not possible. My coach will deliver him to the train station in Santa Fe, and he will depart before evening. It's scheduled, and I'm sure you'll understand that any disruption would throw off his future plans."

*You'll face more disruption than you know . . .* There was so little time. As Diego looked into Bradford's fathomless blue eyes, another truth dawned on him. This man would never let Rafael go free, never let him return to his wife. He needed Rafael to subdue the Tewa people—and after that task was accomplished, Rafael would remain a threat ever after. Bradford was too thorough and methodical a man to allow for any unchecked factors.

Unless the Renegade acted, and decisively, Rafael would never reach Santa Fe alive.

# Chapter Fourteen

"I've been thinking about the things I saw in Bradford's room." Melanie sat close beside Diego, her chin in her hand.

"What did you see again? Letters from a woman, a map?"

"Yes. A map of the kivas. The letters, I'm sure, were from Harriet."

"As I said, she's playing him."

Chen knocked on the door, and Melanie went to let him in. His face was set and grim. "Bradford had Rafael's room guarded all night—he claimed it was for Rafael's protection, in case a disgruntled Tewa citizen chose to assassinate him."

Diego paced around the room like a caged lion. "It's as we expected. But we can't let them take my brother from here, Chen. You know as well as I do what will happen if they get him away."

"I know. They'll kill him."

Melanie looked between them. "What about his wife and their children?"

Chen sank into a chair, his head bowed. "I don't know."

Melanie chewed the inside of her lip as she considered Bradford's most likely course of action. "Mr. Bradford is a careful man. If he kills them, he'll want the murder disguised as an accident. It would be unwise to kill them separately, so we have time, a little time."

Diego folded his arms over his chest and stood like a strong young king in the midst of war. "If you're right, he'll bring Rafael to wherever he has Evelyn hidden, then try to do away with them. If that's the case, then I can follow the coach and intercept them once they're reunited."

Chen nodded. "It seems the only way. As the Renegade, you must follow Rafael's coach, and you must be sure no one sees you. We'll cover for you here. Bradford intends to have Rafael speak to our people in the plaza this morning. You need to be ready outside the pueblo before that."

Something seemed wrong. They were acting too quickly, before they were sure of Bradford's next move. Melanie wasn't sure why, but it seemed too straightforward, too obvious, when Bradford had always twisted the obvious for his own ends. "Do you believe that Bradford has Rafael's wife hidden near here?"

Chen considered this. "Probably in Santa Fe. Bradford wouldn't risk a long train ride, not when there's a chance of Rafael escaping. I doubt he'd leave his hostages far from a place where he can monitor the situation."

Diego glanced out the window, then stepped away lest he be noticed from below. "They've set up the podium down there again—probably for Rafael's speech. There's a coach already waiting."

Another thought occurred to Melanie. "Bradford will have Rafael visit you again before he leaves. You can't go until then. What if he comes after the speech, rather than before?"

Chen rose and went to the door. "We'll have to prevent that. I'll go down and speak to Bradford now. I'll tell them Diego had a bad night and encourage Rafael to come up here now rather than later."

Diego returned to his bed, but he seemed tense, like a caged animal. "Send Will for my horse and have him ready in the woods outside the pueblo. I don't want to lose sight of that coach."

Chen agreed, then headed off down the stairs. Melanie stood in the doorway with a frown tightening her face. "You're going to have to wait until the coach is away from here—that leaves time . . ."

Diego looked as uncertain as Melanie felt. "Chen is right. Bradford needs to reunite Rafael with his family before he can stage any 'accident.' He won't risk anything, and he'll have Rafael under guard. He won't be worried."

"But Diego, he will expect the Renegade to act."

"He'll think his guards can handle the Renegade."

"Why? They never have before. No, there's something troubling in all this. Why send Rafael off in the light of day, why not secretly? He has to expect the Renegade to follow."

"I don't know what else to do, Melanie. I have to save my brother."

Rafael and Bradford came up the stairs, interrupting their conversation. Melanie adjusted her skirt nervously, and Diego took his place on the bed. He nodded at the door. "Let them in."

Melanie opened the door, then stood back. Rafael glanced at her as he passed. The strain on his face had increased since the previous day, and he looked tired, as if he hadn't slept. She tried to offer a reassuring smile, but her own doubts remained too strong. Bradford entered the room and stood back to watch, like a general observing his troops.

Rafael went to Diego's side and seated himself on the bedside chair. He laid his hand on his brother's shoulder and seemed to be fighting back emotion. "I'm afraid I'll have to leave you again, little brother."

Diego gazed languidly at Rafael. "One of these trips, you might consider taking me with you."

"Not this time. Maybe another."

"I'll be with you in spirit."

Apparently, Rafael caught Diego's hidden meaning, because his dark eyes flashed. "You would be wiser to remain here, where no other misfortune can befall you."

Diego sighed. "I'm sure you're right. France, they say, can be tedious if you don't care for wine."

He said "France" with a certain emphasis, though Melanie wasn't sure what it might mean to Rafael. Rafael bent and kissed Diego's forehead. Melanie hadn't understood, not fully, how much Diego's brother meant to him until she saw them together. There was no jealousy, no envy, as she had first imagined might exist between the brothers. It was, instead, that Diego thought so highly of his older brother than he couldn't imagine any man as his equal, least of all himself.

But now Rafael needed him, and Diego would hold his life in his hands. Melanie knew how much it meant to him, and she knew he was afraid. But when he looked up at Rafael, she saw the bright flicker of determination in his eyes. "Take care, Rafe. It's a long road to Santa Fe, but never so long as it seems."

Melanie glanced at Bradford, but he checked his pocket fob and didn't seem to be listening. "Come, Señor de Aguirre, it's time for you to speak to the citizens, then leave. You don't want to risk missing your train. Your wife would be sorely disappointed if you were late."

Rafael's shoulders tensed, but he offered no argument as he stood. He looked down at Diego, and Melanie saw the glimmer of tears in his eyes. "Take care, Diego. I'm sorry not to have spent more time with you. Many things appear to have changed in your life, and I would have liked to hear more of them." He glanced at Melanie, and a slight smile curved his lips. "Miss Muessen, I hope you will look after my brother. You are, it seems, more than adequate to the task."

He was saying good-bye, truly and forever. Melanie heard it in his voice. Rafael didn't expect to live, but she knew he expected, somehow, to save his wife and children. He would fight, because he would forever have the heart of a Renegade, but alone, cornered, he had little chance. A man like Rafael wouldn't give up, but he also knew when the odds were stacked against him.

Melanie went to his side and touched his arm. "I will take care of him. You have my word. We do whatever is necessary, don't we? But sometimes, when you think you are alone, you might be surprised to learn how many others there are looking out for you. That is true for everyone, not just Diego."

Bradford hadn't caught Diego's intimations, but his eyes narrowed at Melanie's words. She might have said too much, but Rafael needed to hear that there was hope lest he act in haste. Bradford held the door open, then motioned to Melanie. "You might want to join us in the plaza, Miss Muessen. Given your admiration for the Renegade, I'm sure you expect him to make an appearance today. I trust you'll want to be there when he arrives."

"I do not expect him, Mr. Bradford. As you pointed out, Señor de Aguirre already defeated him once."

"Maybe—but I doubt he'll let this event pass without making a stand. Unless, of course, he has something else planned."

"I will be down shortly." Melanie stood back, but she caught Bradford's brief laugh as he led Rafael away. She slammed the door, not meaning to, then went to the window. "He is a distasteful, evil person. Do you think he knows what you're planning?"

Diego rose and looked over her shoulder, careful not to be seen. "I don't know. Maybe. There's nothing I can do about that now. I have to act, and act quickly."

Chen entered the room behind them, his expression grave. "Will has your horse, Diego. I suggest you ride out ahead, then follow them from a safe distance once the coach passes."

Melanie looked out the window. "Bradford is taking your brother to the podium. A crowd has gathered. I'll go down to listen, and pretend to look for the Renegade. I don't think it will matter much if he doesn't believe us already, but it's worth a try."

Diego gathered his cape and mask. "I'll go now. Be sure my door is locked." He turned to Melanie and touched her chin. "Don't worry, love. I know what I'm doing." Despite the assurance of his words, he seemed less confident than she had seen him in the past. He kissed her gently, then donned his cape. Without another word, he slipped from the room and disappeared down the backstairs toward the kitchen.

Chen stood with Melanie, but neither spoke. They left Diego's bedroom and went out into the plaza to hear Rafael's farewell.

Rafael spoke to the people of Tewa without emotion, and they listened stunned, too disappointed to react. Even Miguel offered no outburst. Rafael explained that his desire to live abroad with his wife inspired the sale of Tewa, and that he had faith in Bradford's ability to lead the pueblo. His words sounded hollow. His voice caught at the mention of his school, and he refused to cite Harriet as his successor, though Bradford hurriedly interjected the information.

Rafael fell silent at the podium, and no one in the crowd made a sound. For a moment, all Melanie heard was the far-off wind in the mountains. But the wind carried no hoofbeats this time, and those who looked for the new Renegade were disappointed.

Rafael looked out over his people, and from the far side of the crowd, Melanie could feel how painful the words were for him. "I hope you will remember me, no matter how far I have gone from you. I will remember you."

He said no more, and no one reacted to his final, sorrowful words. He expected to die; Melanie felt sure of it. As soon as he left the podium, Bradford escorted him to the coach, and four guards went with him, again "for protection." No one in the crowd moved. They didn't try to follow their former leader, or call to him, or beg him again to save them. It was as if they all knew, each one of them, that whatever Rafael now faced, he faced alone, and nothing that afflicted them could come close to whatever he suffered.

Before he entered the coach, Rafael glanced up at the Chateau, toward the room where Diego supposedly lay. He was worried about his younger brother; he had to know Diego wouldn't let him face danger alone. A guard edged him forward, and Rafael disappeared into the coach.

"I know where they are!" Melanie came up behind Will in the stables as he replenished the horses's already overstocked hay bins. Will jumped at her sudden voice.

He wiped his brow and shook his head. "Where who is, miss?"

"Rafael's wife and children, of course—who else?"

Will glanced to the side. "Where?"

"Well, I don't know for sure, but I have a pretty good guess. It's worth a look, anyway."

"Shouldn't we tell Diego and Chen?"

"Diego is gone, and Chen is waiting on Bradford at the Chateau. I couldn't get his attention without alerting Bradford. That leaves just you and me, and we have to act now, before it's too late."

"I still think we should tell Chen."

"There's no time for that! If I'm right, Rafael and his family are in greater danger than we realized. I think they're leading the Renegade on a wild-goose chase tonight."

"Why do you think that, miss?"

"Mr. Bradford must suspect that both Chen and Diego know the Renegade—even if he doesn't believe it's Diego. He wanted them to think they were taking Rafael on the coach to Santa Fe. The only reason he'd want them to think that is because he has something else in mind. But he wanted to send them in that direction—why? Because his real destination is much closer." She paused. "But it might just give us enough time to find Rafael's family ourselves."

Will's gaze drifted to the side. "Where do you think they are?"

"In the kiva ruins, Will. I'm sure of it!"

"Why?"

Melanie puffed an impatient breath. "Because of the map I saw in Bradford's room, with a ruin marked in red. That's the same ruin his guards have been digging. But they're not after gold. He's not digging up the most likely spot, he's digging the easiest. I don't think he's looking for something. I think he's hiding it. It's a prison, Will, and if we're not quick, it may end up as a grave."

"And if we're not . . . quick?"

"I drew a picture of the ruins and marked the kiva. If I haven't returned by the time Diego comes back, he'll check my room—that is certain. I couldn't leave a note in case Bradford checks, but I think the map I drew will be enough."

Will looked uneasy, but he shrugged in acquiescence. "I hope you're right. But I'm coming with you."

"Thank you, Will. It will look more plausible for me to leave the pueblo if you're with me. We'll tell them I'm going to take more pictures."

Melanie saddled the mare Diego had given her, and Will fetched his stout pinto. They went out into the plaza, and Bradford spotted them as he left the Chateau.

"Miss Muessen . . . Will . . . where are you headed? Can't you see that a storm is imminent?"

Melanie mounted and eyed him without concern. "My profession requires that I move on, Mr. Bradford, despite any inclement weather. Such weather provides interesting shots." She adjusted her cloak and pulled up the hood. "Since Diego is incapacitated, I've enlisted Will as an assistant. He suggested we photograph Rafael's hacienda, and that's just what I'm going to do. It will be a dramatic focus with storm clouds in the background."

Bradford looked suspicious but offered no further argument. "Take care, Miss Muessen. You never know what pitfalls await you if you stray from the wise path."

A less than subtle warning . . . Melanie urged her mare forward, and Will followed on his pinto. She didn't look back, but she knew Bradford watched them until they passed through the gate. As soon as the gates closed behind them, Melanie turned to Will. "Do you think he'll have us followed?"

"I can't think why he would, miss. But it might be wise to go by way of the hacienda, just in case."

"It's longer, but you're right. I don't want him to know what we're up to."

Will's brow rose. "That won't be hard, miss, because I don't know, either."

They rode casually, even though Melanie felt the urge to gallop. They reached Rafael's hacienda, but no one seemed to have followed. Will led them through a winding path, but the mare labored over the rocks. Both Will and Melanie had to dismount to lead their horses over the rough ground. By the time they reached the kivas, the afternoon had waned and a light rain had begun to fall.

Will looked around, shading his eyes against the slanting rain. "I don't see anything, miss. No guards."

"Why aren't they here?" Melanie dismounted, pondering the issue. "They may have gone to meet Bradford, and to fetch Rafael. That's my guess, anyway. We can investigate the site where they've been digging, but remember, they could return at any moment. We have to be quick."

Will hitched the horses to a shrub, then followed Melanie down over the wet ground to the first kiva. She picked her way through new puddles and earth uprooted by the heavy boots of the guards. She found discarded shovels, but no guards were present. She called to Will. "They've cleared this one out completely, but I don't see . . ." A long ladder lay beside the kiva. "Help me with this!"

Will picked up the ladder and lowered it into the dark pit. Melanie started to climb in, but he caught her arm. "Let me go first, miss."

She hesitated. "If the ladder breaks, I'll need you to throw me a rope and pull me out. I should be the one to go down."

He didn't argue, so Melanie climbed into the hole, then picked her way down. She reached the kiva floor. As soon as she stepped off the ladder, she knew she wasn't alone. "Hello?"

Melanie's heart thudded in fear. Footsteps came closer to her. Small footsteps, followed by a tiny voice. "Mama, it's a girl!"

Before Melanie could respond, something poked her in the back of her knee. It felt like a small stick . . . or a knife. "Don't move!"

Melanie looked over her shoulder. As her eyes grew accustomed to the dim light, a little girl became visible, a girl with black hair wound in long braids. "I won't hurt you. My name is Melanie."

The little girl's eyes narrowed. "You're not a guard."

A woman appeared from farther in the kiva, carrying another child, a small boy. Her hair fell in long, tangled curls around her face, but despite the thinness of her face, her stomach was round. She was pregnant. "Señora de Aguirre?"

"I am." Evelyn called to her small, fierce daughter. "It's all right, Catherine. Come here." Evelyn's voice was soft, and she sounded tired as she faced Melanie. "Who are you? You're not the woman who took the children."

She must have meant Harriet. "No. I'm Melanie Muessen. I'm a photographer. A . . . friend of Diego's."

"Diego?" Evelyn drew a quick breath. "Is he all right? We feared he would . . . do something rash."

"He has done a lot, that's for certain." Melanie's heart raced with excitement. "There's no time to explain. Will is waiting with the ladder. We have to get you out of here before a guard returns."

"They can't be far. They're never far."

"It's raining quite hard, so maybe they went into the woods for shelter. We saw no one."

Evelyn touched Melanie's arm, almost as if to be sure she was real. "Have you seen . . . have you seen my husband?"

"Mr. Bradford brought him to the pueblo, but they've taken him again, supposedly to rejoin you. Diego went after him."

Evelyn brightened. "And you came for us? How did you know we were here?"

"It was a guess on my part. Unfortunately, Will and I are the only ones who know about it because we had to act quickly."

Melanie pulled Evelyn to the ladder. "I'll explain later. We have to get out of here."

Evelyn helped her daughter onto the ladder, and the little girl climbed fast, like a small spider. Evelyn carried her son and climbed out more slowly, and Melanie followed. She emerged from the kiva, greeted by torrential rain, but Will was nowhere in sight. "Will?"

Three guards stepped from behind a clump of boulders. Will lay in a heap near the horses. Melanie's heart quailed, fearing he was dead, but he stirred, then struggled to his feet. One of the guards seized him and dragged him to Melanie. "Looks like you'll be joining the ladies, boy. Aren't you the lucky one?"

Melanie stepped forward, but the guard pulled a gun and aimed it at her head. "You'll be having even more company soon. I'd be patient if I were you."

At gunpoint, the guards forced Melanie, Evelyn, and the children back down into the kiva, then pulled up the ladder, the only means of escape. They shoved Will in after them, and Melanie caught him before he fell. Though bruised and in obvious pain, Will went to Evelyn and hugged her, then knelt before her children. They hugged him, too, and seated themselves beside him as he patiently began telling them stories.

Evelyn and Melanie stood side by side, staring up through the kiva entrance. Melanie glanced at Evelyn. "What did they mean by company?"

"I'm not sure. Nor do I understand why they put us here in the first place."

"Whatever it is, Bradford had it well planned from the beginning. He's been digging this kiva out since he took over. I think he dug it planning to use it . . ." She stopped, but Evelyn nodded.

"As a grave."

Melanie swallowed. "That is my fear, yes."

"Bradford intercepted us in San Francisco and took the schoolchildren from us. He coerced Rafael into giving up the pueblo by abducting the pueblo children—and by holding me as a hostage."

"Diego always knew Rafael wouldn't sell the pueblo, so we knew he was in danger."

"My husband's heart broke to sign those papers. I have never seen him in such pain. He tried in his letter to give signs to Diego that it was coerced."

"Signs Diego recognized. He knew what to do."

Evelyn smiled. "He always did. Only Diego doubted himself."

Melanie smiled, too. "Miguel the baker had a few doubts, as well."

Evelyn winced. "I do recall that Diego tormented Miguel quite badly as a child. As a youth, too. His pranks were always good-natured, but Miguel has no sense of humor."

They sat together while Will entertained the children. Evelyn opened a sack of old bread and they ate, then drank water that seemed no fresher. "I have never felt so helpless in my life. They took him from me, then brought us here—days and days, we've been here." Evelyn leaned back against the kiva wall. "I've always been able to help him before, but he's alone now."

"Not alone."

Evelyn sighed. "You're right. He has Diego."

Melanie gripped Evelyn's arm. "He has the Renegade."

Evelyn's eyes widened and a smile grew on her face. "He took the mask?"

"Reluctantly, but he took it."

"Rafael always believed he would, but sometimes I thought it was a futile hope." Evelyn gazed into Melanie's eyes. "You love him."

"I have loved him from the moment I met him, though he seemed the most unwise choice of any man I'd ever met." Melanie looked around the dark kiva. "He brought me to this place on the day I arrived. I think it holds all his fears, all he feels he can't do. He thinks he failed here."

"I know that." Evelyn sighed. "I was with him, you see. No man was ever more heroic or brave than Diego that day. He was sixteen years old, and he never once thought of himself. He never panicked. He just did what he had to do, and he got everyone out."

"Everyone but himself."

"Yes. His leg was crushed, and he told me to leave him. I didn't, of course, and we got him out. But Rafael was taken, and if not for the Zunis' help, we would all have died. Diego believed he had failed, and nothing we have ever said has alleviated his pain. He thought he could carry the world on his shoulders, as all young men do, but more. He thought he was invincible. He learned, that day, that he was not."

Melanie looked around the dark pit that now served as her prison. It might be that this would, indeed, end as a grave. Her grave, too. But she had seen Diego's heart, and it gave her strength. Strength to believe her future involved much more than a grave.

A lantern appeared above the kiva entrance, and Melanie heard muffled voices. She and Evelyn rose, silent. "That's Mr. Bradford's voice. Have they come for us, do you think?"

Evelyn shook her head. "I don't know. He hasn't been here before."

The guards lowered the ladder back into the kiva, and Melanie seized the opportunity to scurry up. She poked her head out and looked around, then spotted Bradford standing back as four guards shoved a hooded man toward the kiva. Bradford noticed her and laughed.

"Miss Muessen, I hadn't expected to include you in this little party. What a pleasant surprise!"

Melanie extracted herself from the kiva and backed away, but the guards prevented any escape. "I cannot say the same myself."

"Ah, but you've given me just what I need in case our Renegade should show himself again—a weapon against him."

"He's too smart for that."

Bradford laughed. "Is that so? But I fear your Renegade will find his efforts wasted tonight. Once again I have outsmarted him, and when I lure him here, my troubles with all of you will be over."

336

Bradford turned to his captive and yanked off the man's hood. Rafael struggled against his guards, but with his hands tightly bound, he had no chance of victory. He met Melanie's shocked gaze but said nothing. A guard drove the butt of his rifle into Rafael's back, and he stumbled forward, then climbed down into the kiva with his family.

Before the guards reached her, Melanie retreated into the kiva and slid down the ladder to rejoin the others. The guards pulled up the ladder, but Bradford's laugh penetrated the darkness, followed by the sounds of hoofbeats as he rode away.

Melanie untied Rafael's bound hands, then sank back against the kiva wall. Evelyn and Rafael stood looking at each other, not moving. Without a word, they fell into each other's arms. They kissed and held each other, and Evelyn's sobs were muffled against his chest. Melanie heard her broken voice: "You're alive, my love, my love."

Rafael kissed his wife's face, her forehead, then brushed her tangled hair. His children left Will, and he knelt to hug them, too. With their father's presence, all fear left the children, a testimonial to the faith they had in him, no matter what had happened.

The little girl, Catherine, peered up adoringly at her father. "Will says Uncle will fetch us soon. I miss him, you know."

Rafael kissed his daughter, then closed his eyes. "Diego will come, and you can tell him then. Go back with Will, Catherine. Tell him a story or two. He looks afraid."

Catherine nodded. "I made a bandage for his head, and for his arm where those men hit him." Her small face puckered. "Maybe I should bandage his foot, too."

Rafael touched her head. "You do that." Will held up his foot as if it pained him, and Catherine set to work ministering to the perceived injury.

Rafael turned to Melanie. "Miss Muessen, what are you doing here? Did Diego send you?"

She sighed. "Unfortunately, he doesn't know we left the pueblo. Will and I were about to free your wife and children."

Rafael looked surprised. "How did you know where they were?"

"I didn't know for certain. But Mr. Bradford was awfully smug—I felt sure he was sending the Renegade in the wrong direction, after your coach. I knew he'd been digging up one of the kivas, but none of us thought it was for treasure. So I convinced Will to come out here and check."

Rafael nodded. "The treasure, it seems, was my family." He shook his dark head, frustrated. "They pulled me from the coach in the wooded area beyond the pueblo."

"And Diego was waiting for the coach where the road forks to your hacienda. He will have no way of knowing you're not still in the coach until he intercepts it. I left him a message in my room, and I think he will understand what it means."

# The Renegade's Heart

Rafael raked his fingers through his long hair. "It may be a long while before he returns, Miss Muessen. He may reach Santa Fe before he realizes his error. Bradford seems to want to lure the Renegade here, but he can't know it's my brother who pursues him."

"Diego has been a thorn in his side since the first day."

Rafael smiled. "I would have liked to see my brother in action." He paused. "Then again, my own encounter with the Renegade proved somewhat . . . painful."

Evelyn fiddled with his hair; she touched him as if she could never be close enough. Melanie watched them, and she saw herself with Diego, when every portion of him fascinated her, when there was nothing so sweet as to feel his hair beneath her fingertips. "I believe it was painful for him, too."

Evelyn looked confused. "What did you do to each other?"

Rafael sighed and wrapped his arm around his wife. "Something we've never done before, Evie. We fought."

Evelyn kissed his face gently, with infinite tenderness. "Fear, sometimes, obliterates all else. All else but love."

"I didn't think he understood how much was at stake. He couldn't have known you were in danger. When I told him, he gave way. But I hope I never face my brother in combat again—he's a more able

339

fighter than I ever imagined, especially with a sword."

A small smile formed on Melanie's lips and she sighed wistfully. "He was most impressive. Bradford was terrified."

Rafael cast a knowing glance at his wife and smiled, too. "I wasn't surprised to find my brother wearing the Renegade's mask or holding up coaches. What astonished me was to see him starry-eyed in love."

Will nodded, a happy smile on his face despite their dark circumstances. "Except when Miss Muessen hit him, of course. Then he was just in pain." Beside him, Catherine balled her hand into a small fist and tried a punch into the air. "Chen told me the story four times, at least. Little Miss Muessen here caught Diego off guard and laid him out good."

Melanie clapped her hand over her forehead. "Nothing in my life is private."

Rafael seemed impressed. "You punched him?"

Evelyn shook her head. "I'd hate to think what he did to deserve it."

Will adjusted his newly bandaged foot and presented Catherine with the other leg, indicating a sore knee. "He courted her as both himself and the Renegade. Chen warned him, and I don't think he meant to do it."

Melanie huffed. "I knew from the beginning who he was."

Will nodded. "She tested him by a kiss. Diego claims it's 'distinctive.' "

Melanie blushed furiously. "He is distinctive in . . . many ways."

"That's for certain. You should have seen him, sir, that night he caught Miss Muessen snooping in Bradford's room and hauled her out of there. Swinging across the plaza, carrying Miss Muessen, leaping along the pueblo walls. . . . He was something."

Rafael eyed Melanie. "What were you doing in Bradford's room?"

"I wanted to find out who his Californian benefactors were. Do you know?"

"I have no idea. Did you find anything?"

"Only a few letters from a woman. I believe they were Harriet's—the woman who came here with the pueblo children. But I'm not sure what her connection is to all this."

Rafael's brow rose. "From what I observed of her interaction with Bradford at the Chateau, it's a strong connection. And I'd say Harriet is the one holding the leash."

"That's what Diego says, too. She seems so passive to me, as if Bradford is running everything. Why do you two think differently?"

Rafael smiled. "A general, Miss Muessen, leads from behind."

Evelyn watched Melanie with admiration. "You were brave to sneak into Mr. Bradford's room like that. What if he'd caught you?"

Will huffed from the corner. "She never thinks of what might happen. I've noticed that. She just flings herself wherever her notions lead."

Melanie's face twisted in offense. "I might be a little impulsive, it's true."

Rafael's brow arched. "A little? Or was this jaunt into a rainy night Will's idea?"

Will shook his head vigorously. "No, sir. It was Miss Muessen who dragged me out here." He rubbed his head. "I had a bad feeling about it, but she talked me into it."

Melanie frowned. "I was right, wasn't I? Now we just have to get out of here and warn Diego."

Evelyn gestured at the kiva entrance. "Without the ladder, it's impossible, Melanie. These walls are sheer. Believe me, I've tried."

Rafael agreed. "Even if we could get up there, don't forget the guards. We wouldn't get far."

"Diego will come when he gets the message I left him, Rafael. He may come too late, but he'll be here."

Rafael sighed. "If that's true, then it's not only ourselves in danger. It's my brother most of all."

# Chapter Fifteen

A wild bolt of lightning split and crackled not ten feet from the road, striking in unison with a resounding crash of thunder. Diego bent low over his horse's neck, his face sprayed by sheets of rain. The harness horses pulling the coach startled and neighed, but the mustang never flinched. He galloped on, as if his own heart bent itself on their quarry ahead.

The rainfall had slowed the coach, but Diego had let it get farther ahead through a long, open passage, lest he be seen. Something stronger drove him forward now. The closer he got, the more he felt sure he was wrong. Twice now, he had thrown a rock at the coach's window, hoping to get Rafael's attention. He needed a sign that his brother knew he followed, but none came.

Rafael might be bound and unable to react, but Diego's fear grew. It was a risk, but if he stopped the coach and freed Rafael, two brothers known as Renegades might force the truth from the driver.

His choice was made. Diego urged the mustang faster, then caught up with the coach. The rain cloaked his approach, and he reached his target unseen. He leapt from the horse onto the coach, then made his way over the roof to the driver. Before the man could react, Diego caught him by the neck, bound and gagged him, then left him tied.

Without a whip to spur them on or hands guiding their reins, the horses slowed their pace. Diego crept around the coach, drew his sword, then burst the door inward, shattering it. A man was startled from sleep, but even as Diego positioned his sword at the passenger's neck, the man laughed. Bradford's attorney recoiled from Diego's blade, but he radiated victory.

"It seems you've been led astray, Renegade. The treasure you seek this time is long gone."

Diego glared in fury. "I hope the ruse was worth your life."

Alvin arched his brow in mockery of Diego's threat. "Do you intend to kill me? And what? Leave Rafael de Aguirre responsible for my murder? One way or another, you will be accused of his."

Diego's breath caught and held tight in his chest. Was this the plan? That he would be accused of killing his own brother? Was Rafael already dead?

He fought to clear his thoughts, to ward off fear when it threatened to consume him. "What about his wife and children, Alvin? Am I to be accused of their deaths, too?"

Alvin smirked, an expression resembling Bradford's. "How fast can you ride, Renegade? And where would you go to save them? You've guessed well. Not only will Rafael de Aguirre meet his untimely end, but his unfortunate family will be with him."

Then Evelyn had to be closer to the pueblo than they'd guessed. Closer, but where?

Diego gripped the hilt of his sword, and fear flashed in the lawyer's eyes. "Where are they?"

"Gone, Renegade. You're too late. We've outsmarted you this time. Rafael de Aguirre, his family—even his ne'er-do-well brother—you've lost them all."

Obviously, part of Alvin's story was a lie. Diego pressed the point of his sword against the lawyer's throat, and a trickle of blood emerged. "Then I have no reason to keep you alive, do I?"

Alvin tried to swallow, but Diego, furious, edged the blade deeper. "Wait . . . stop. I'll tell you."

Diego relaxed the pressure only a fraction. "Speak, and make it the truth this time. Next time, this sword finds the back of your neck."

"They're not dead, yet. But they will be soon."

"Where are they?"

"Hidden, in the old kivas."

Diego moved the sword aside. "The kivas?" To

be buried alive. Diego's heart quailed. Of all places, to return to the site of his first failure, a place that had defeated him once, and maybe forever.

The lawyer wiped sweat from his lip, then gasped for air. "I've told you where they are. You have to let me go. He'll kill me for this."

Something in the lawyer's manner had the effect of an act, theatrical. "You betrayed your master quickly—but I have no intention of killing you, señor."

A strange object caught Diego's eye, and he stopped. The photograph Melanie had taken of Harriet lay on the seat next to Alvin. And then Diego knew—they were fighting the right war, but against the wrong commander. "You've done well by your master, Señor Alvin. I hope the reward you seek is worth the price."

"You'd best hurry, Renegade. Once Rafael Aguirre has rejoined his wife, Bradford has no reason to keep them alive."

Diego knew what Alvin expected—Bradford would kill Rafael and his family, and Diego would kill Bradford in revenge. Without responding, he struck Alvin hard on the head with his sword hilt. He dragged the driver and stuffed him in the coach with Alvin, then freed the harness horses to roam.

He leapt astride his black mustang, his heart beating with a clear purpose as he turned back toward Tewa. He knew what he had to do and where he had to go. He knew Bradford and his guards would be waiting. Beyond his enemy, it was the dark futility of his past that he would face tonight. But tonight, he felt something deeper, stronger than anything he had known before.

He felt Melanie's faith in him. He felt his own faith in love.

The rain never ceased; it didn't abate even as dawn crept through the sky. By the time Diego reached the ancient kivas, tiny streams overflowed the road where normally no water ran at all. Nature itself seemed to rise up against him, filled with the anguish of the past and the fear of all he couldn't do.

Diego rode to the crest of the last hill overlooking the kivas, then dismounted. He hid his horse behind a boulder, then placed the mask over his face. The last time he had fought in these hills, he had been a boy. This day, he was the Renegade.

Guards were posted around the first kiva, and a coach stood by, also guarded. There was no chance of the Renegade slipping in unseen and nabbing the occupant, most likely Bradford himself.

Diego counted twelve guards, four short of the total Bradford had enlisted for service at Tewa. These weren't trained soldiers, men in service to their country. More likely, these men had been taken from prisons and were willing to do whatever Bradford ordered.

Diego crept silently, moving between the boulders with the stealth of a panther. He moved ever closer, then positioned himself behind the first guard. He caught the man by the neck, pinned him back, and then dragged him behind the rock. He disabled the guard with a quick blow, then gagged him and left him bound. Two guards stood together on watch. Diego leapt up behind them, then smashed their heads together, stunning both. Surprised at his success, he shoved them behind another rock. He tied them together with their own belts and left them gagged.

So far, no one had taken note of the three missing men. The rain fell hard, and men stood huddled beneath coats, an advantage Diego seized. He slipped from rock to rock, waited, then ran silently across the open ground to cover closer to four more guards. He hesitated, considering his next attack. He saw no way to incapacitate four men at once. He looked around. They stood beneath a ledge as minimal shelter from the rain. Above it, a round boulder rocked in the driving rain.

Diego smiled. Maybe his ancestors were with him, after all. He climbed the ledge, keeping low, then came up behind the boulder. He shoved at it, but found it harder to move than he'd hoped. With all his might, he braced his shoulder against the boulder, but though it rocked slightly, it remained far from rolling down on the heads of his enemies.

Diego strained against the immobile rock, and though it seemed impossible, he refused to give up. *I am alone. They have no one but me.* The wind rose behind him, like a charge of warriors down from the western mountains, and with its force, the rain slanted away from his face. The wind swirled around him and through him, and with its power, Diego tried again. The boulder rocked, and he shoved once more. The power of the wind soared in unison with his own, and with a suddenness that caught him off guard, the boulder rolled, then crashed over the ledge.

The guards shouted below and Diego leapt down behind the ledge, out of sight. Seven men could no longer stand against him. That left five, and five he would face alone.

Diego waited until the remaining guards came to investigate the results of the wind's assault. "What the hell happened?"

"Get Bradford! Damned boulder fell on us. We're pinned here! George's leg's busted."

Diego came around the corner of the ledge, and he drew his sword. "For the rock and your leg's unfortunate condition you have my ancestors to thank. For what comes next, you have only yourselves."

The guards fumbled for their guns, but Diego was quicker. He knocked a rifle from one man's hands, then leapt aside, whirled, and tripped the next who bounded toward him. A third guard took aim, but Diego ducked and rolled, then lunged forward, his sword swift as he caught the guard's shoulder. The man howled in pain, then fell backward. The two remaining guards aimed together and fired, too soon.

Diego jumped aside, then used his sword like a staff. He struck one, then the other, knocking both men off their feet. He caught a rifle in midair, spun it, and then aimed it at their heads. "This is too much work for so early in the morning, gentlemen."

A strange sound, haunting amid the downfall of rain, caught Diego's attention. Applause, from a single person's hands, came from behind him. Diego turned, the rifle ready.

Bradford walked along the ledge toward the site of Diego's victory, holding before his body an impenetrable shield: Melanie. His heart held its beat as he stared at her in astonishment. She didn't look frightened. She looked angry as she struggled against Bradford. No matter how small she was, or how vulnerable, she always seemed willing to fight. Diego's breath caught in his throat. Bradford held a knife poised between her shoulders. He must have pierced her flesh with the blade, because she cried out and twisted to escape him.

"Melanie, no . . ."

"Rafael is in the kiva. His family, too. Don't . . ."

Bradford twisted her arm. "Let the Renegade decide, Miss Muessen. Your life, or his own."

Melanie's face blanched. "No!"

Bradford dragged Melanie back toward the kiva. Diego eased forward, keeping a safe distance. With one hand, Bradford seized a wooden lever. Melanie fought with sudden ferocity despite the knife. "He's going to cave in the entrance!"

Diego bounded forward, but too late. Bradford

pulled the lever, and the kiva entrance collapsed, trapping anyone inside beneath an avalanche of rocks and dirt. Shadows of his past crashed in around Diego, trapping him in his own dark memory.

Bradford hauled Melanie toward his coach. "Follow me, Renegade, and your mistress dies."

Melanie screamed and fought like a wild animal, but Bradford struck her hard, then shoved her into the coach. A whip cracked, and the team jumped forward. The coach drove away, and Diego ran to the collapsed kiva's entrance.

Rain and tears stung his face as he grabbed a shovel and dug. He hauled boulders with strength double what he'd ever imagined he possessed. He found a rope, wrapped it around the horse's powerful shoulders, and then hauled a larger boulder from the entrance. A wall of dirt and debris crashed inward, but Diego fought. He fought himself and his fear that life was futile; he fought the past.

As if drawn by the commotion, the herd of mustangs led by Rafael's old horse, Frank, appeared on the shadowy horizon. In the distance they watched as Diego fought against time.

He broke through, and a small section opened to the kiva below. "Rafael! Are you there?" Thunder punctuated his shout, but a voice answered.

"Diego, we're here." It was Evelyn, but she seemed to be crying. "Is there a rope?"

Diego jabbed at the dirt with the shovel. "If I

can get it through . . . My brother. Where is my brother?"

"He's here." She was crying, and Diego's heart quailed. "He got us out of the way, but the roof caved in. He's alive . . ." Her voice broke on a sob. "Will is here, too, but he's hurt."

Anguish tore at Diego. His brother was injured, and Will. Bradford had taken Melanie. "Go after Bradford. I'm all right," Rafael called to him, his voice strong. "We'll get ourselves out of here."

Diego unhitched the rope from his horse, then shoved it in a small hole. He tied the other end to a pole, then put the ladder within reach. "I should be able to get the shovel in . . ." He managed to wedge it between two rocks, and Rafael called up to him.

"We can manage, Diego. Go after Bradford."

*He took Melanie . . .* Diego ran back to his black mustang and leapt astride. The wind and the rain swirled around him, cloaking him in mist as he raced toward the pueblo. His fears held no weight now. The woman he loved needed him, and this time he would not fail.

It wasn't a mile from the kivas to the pueblo, but an eternity dragged before Diego reached the outskirts of Tewa. He dismounted and set the mustang free. Diego climbed the wall behind the stable and, from the roof, looked out across the plaza. The Tewa people had gathered in the plaza, but no one seemed to know what to do. Bradford had Melanie near the podium, a knife at her throat, but she was uninjured, and Diego drew a tight breath of relief.

Chen stood with Victoria outside her inn, but both seemed helpless while Bradford held the knife. Chen caught sight of Diego, but then lowered his head so as not to alert Bradford. Diego drew his sword and crept along the pueblo roof. He leapt from building to building until he came close behind Bradford's position. A guard spotted him and shouted. Bradford whirled, shocked by the Renegade's return. Bradford held his knife at Melanie's throat and again positioned her as a shield.

"So you chose your mistress over Rafael. Does a woman mean that much to you, Renegade?"

Diego looked around. "She means all to me, Señor Bradford. But I think you know that as well as I do. Tell me, where is Harriet in all this destruction? You've done a lot at her bidding."

Diego's accusation inflamed Bradford. "Harriet has nothing to do with this. You risk your mistress's neck by your accusations, Renegade."

Diego took a step closer, then stopped. "Is that so? You've mentioned benefactors before, haven't you? But there are no such investors, are there?"

Harriet came forward from the steps of the Chateau. "As it happens, my family, the Richardsons, purchased this pueblo. Mr. Bradford didn't disclose this information to protect my privacy, but there is nothing untoward about it."

"You said your parents were among the richest in California, but you told us you were a governess in San Francisco. The children of such wealth rarely embark on careers."

"That's a lie, all of it! My parents visited this Tewa in grand style."

"They visited, but my guess is that they were the Richardsons' servants. You heard their stories of this place and, with your lover, came up with a plan to profit from it. No one 'bought' this pueblo because it was coerced from Rafael by force. You just manipulated your aging, conceited lover into doing what you wanted."

Harriet flushed with anger. "How dare you insinuate anything untoward between myself and Mr. Bradford? He has proposed marriage, which I am considering in all good faith."

Diego laughed. "Is that so? And are you also considering Señor Alvin's proposal? But no, you accepted Alvin long ago, didn't you?" Harriet blanched, and he knew his guess was accurate. "I left him last night bound, I'm afraid, rather uncomfortably in his coach."

Bradford looked between them. "What was Alvin doing in that coach? I sent him back two days ago."

Diego saw Bradford's doubt. "It seems your guards and your woman both adhere to the wishes of another man."

Harriet quivered with fury. She drew a small white pistol from her crocheted handbag and pointed it at Diego. "How dare you? None of this is true, none of it!"

Bradford looked between them. Diego saw the doubt on his face, that the younger man was Harriet's more likely suitor despite his own wealth and power. Conceit and arrogance warred against reason, and in the battle there was no room for dreams or faith or the sweet imaginings of love. All was power to Bradford, and to Harriet as well. Diego looked into Melanie's eyes and saw all that the other misguided lovers lacked—he saw her faith, her hope, and her dreams, and in hers, he saw his own.

Melanie stood trapped by Bradford, a knife at her throat. Slowly, as if nothing could truly threaten her or hurt her now, she placed her free hand over her heart. He heard her silent vow. *You are in my heart.*

His gaze on hers, Diego repeated the gesture, placing his hand over his own heart. *As you live in mine.*

Harriet witnessed their exchange, and more fury flared in her eyes than he'd seen when he accused her of betrayal. He knew why, and now he fully understood her jealousy of Melanie. Nothing she could connive, no strength she could derive from manipulation or using the iron locks of desire could come close to the power of Melanie's love.

Harriet turned her bitter gaze to Bradford. "He's using lies to come between us. I barely know Mr. Alvin."

Melanie twisted around in Bradford's grasp. "That's not true. When I was taking your portrait,

Mr. Alvin stopped to see it. He said it was even better than the one your parents' commissioned. The same picture you told me hung in your bedroom!"

Harriet tensed, and her gaze darted to Bradford. "I have no idea how he might have seen that portrait." She gulped, but Diego saw his chance to add a twist to Harriet's scheme.

"You would share with her the profits from this pueblo, señor. But what of the Spanish treasure? Would she share her portion with you . . . or him?"

Bradford looked genuinely shocked. "There is no treasure, Renegade."

"Ah, but there is. Señor Alvin has a large chest filled with Aztec gold, with jewels so bright and so rare . . ." Harriet's harsh cry of outrage interrupted Diego's lavish description. Diego paused, feigning surprise. "Didn't he tell you? While Bradford's guards worked to open a kiva jail for his hostages, your noble Señor Alvin busied himself in the old ruins—and apparently at a fine profit. The chest I saw was twice as big as the one we found ten years ago."

Harriet spit fury like embers of fire. "How dare he? He was looking for treasure all along!"

Diego issued a *tsk* and shook his head, then sighed. "He found it, and left without you, it seems. So much gold, so many jewels—those things do much to compete with your tarnished charms, señorita." Mockery rang in Diego's voice, and it had the desired effect on Harriet.

She pointed at Melanie, her face reddening with anger. "It is your whore who is tarnished!"

Diego hesitated. "Strong words from a woman bedding two men. Alvin must know of your duplicity, but Señor Bradford, sadly, appears to have been in the dark."

Harriet's eyes glowed with her anger. "That is a lie! It is you who have been cuckolded, Renegade. Everyone knows your mistress spent all day in Diego de Aguirre's bed."

Bradford laughed, quick to believe his young mistress. "It is you, Renegade, who has been betrayed, not I."

Diego shook his head. "Ah, Señor Bradford, don't you know? Appearances are, more often than not, deceiving." Smiling, Diego pulled off the Anasazi mask and tossed it aside.

Seeing Diego, their most unlikely hero, the people of Tewa gasped. Miguel the baker dropped a loaf of bread that he'd been holding like a weapon, and his wife fell to her knees as if in prayer. The saloonkeeper's mouth dropped open, but several children laughed, as if they'd suspected Diego at this game all along. Now that they knew he was the Renegade, no one seemed to have any idea what to say.

The man beneath the mask didn't surprise Harriet, but Bradford was astounded. "Diego de Aguirre! It can't be."

Harriet eyed Bradford scornfully. "I told you it was him, but you refused to believe me. Now he makes a mockery of us by revealing his face."

Melanie cranked her head around. "I was not the mistress of two men. Only one. Unlike yourself, Harriet!"

"Like your rogue lover, you lie." Harriet's jaw tightened as she turned to Bradford. "Tie them together, Carlton. If Mr. Alvin has the chest, we can reach him by sundown."

Bradford motioned to the guards who stood by the bonfire, then shoved Melanie forward toward the podium. He tied her to a pole, her hands behind her back. Harriet stood with the gun aimed at Melanie's head, and Diego dared not act.

Bradford bound Melanie's feet, then turned toward Diego. "You, too. Unless you want to see her throat cut right now."

Diego hesitated. Bradford edged the blade under Melanie's chin, but she didn't flinch.

Harriet waved her gun. "Do it. Now! Or I'll shoot her myself." Bradford might hesitate before cutting a woman's throat, but Harriet would not.

Diego came forward, but Bradford hesitated. Diego saw his chance. He relaxed his muscles and leaned back against the pole that held Melanie. Bradford moved cautiously toward him, and Diego didn't move. He kept his gaze pinned on his enemy's eyes and saw the moment when Bradford turned his attention to the bind. Diego drove his elbow into Bradford's gut, and Bradford stumbled back with a thick grunt.

Diego swung, but a shot rang out, and he turned

as Harriet reloaded her gun. "Do you think I won't shoot her, Renegade? Move back against the pole, now!"

Diego obeyed, and this time, Bradford tied him fast to the pole so that he stood back-to-back with Melanie. Bound this way, what could he hope to do for his people? Melanie's fingers found his and entwined with them. He felt the small, curling pinky and his eyes filled with tears.

"I love you so."

Her fingers tightened around his. "I love you, too. We're together, Diego. *Together.* There is nothing we can't do."

She hadn't given up. Though she had been taken captive and, rather than saving her, he was a prisoner, too, she believed in him. Beyond reason, beyond the reach of logic, Diego's confidence returned. *There is nothing we can't do.*

Bradford stepped aside and took Harriet's arm. "Come, my dear. We must leave this place."

Harriet looked furious. "We can't leave with nothing! You gave all the money we acquired to the Renegade. What about all the things you promised me? Where is my treasure?"

"We have each other, Harriet."

Harriet wasn't impressed. "I want more."

Diego saw Bradford's disappointment, but the man bowed his head, unwilling to look true defeat in its cold blue eyes. "Chen must have money in *the Chateau.* We can take what's in his safe."

Harriet stomped her foot like an impatient child. "Get it!"

Bradford turned to Chen, but Chen folded his arms over his chest. "The combination of your safe, Chen. Now!"

Chen met his eyes without wavering. "That is a secret I will hold through death. I have no reason to tell you when you plan to kill all of us, anyway."

Bradford seized Victoria and held the knife at her throat. "Your woman, isn't she? But perhaps you aren't as romantic as our Renegade. Let us test the matter, shall we?"

It required no test. Chen turned and walked into the hotel. Bradford hesitated, confused, but Harriet waved her hand fiercely. "Go after him, Carlton!"

Bradford followed, and Melanie twisted around behind Diego. "What is Chen doing?"

Diego sighed. "Chen's pride is an odd thing. He wouldn't give the combination. But he will give his treasure."

"You love him very much."

Diego's throat felt tight. Love . . . Had he ever called what he felt for his friends love before? But it was love that bonded them, all of them. "I do."

Chen emerged from the hotel in front of Bradford. Bradford carried a large box—the contents of Chen's safe. Chen turned to Victoria, and Diego saw tears glimmer in his friend's eyes. All that he'd hoped to offer his new wife, the life they would live, now faded before their eyes. Diego didn't care

360

about treasure, but he knew what it meant to Chen.

Bradford was wavering. Diego didn't see the light of a killer in his eyes. What he saw was weakness, and that might be just as dangerous. Bradford could be swayed, but it was Harriet who held the most power over him. "Now what, Bradford? You and your precious fiancée have what you want. Leave us in peace and go."

Bradford glanced toward Harriet. For an instant it looked as if Bradford might accept. Harriet had a darker heart. "Don't be a fool, Carlton! We want to live our lives in grandeur after we leave here— not be hunted criminals! We must burn this village! If anyone—do you understand—*anyone* is left alive, it will endanger us. Do you want me to suffer that way?"

Bradford gulped, cowed by his insensitivity toward his beloved, no doubt. Diego sighed and shook his head. *She's good at running him, no question.*

Bradford's hesitation disappeared and he shouted to his guards. "All of them; get these worthless people into the western buildings and lock them in. You, Chen, all of you, or I will kill Victoria now!"

Diego watched in fury and frustration as the guards drove the Tewa people into the western buildings. Those constructions were the oldest part of the pueblo, and the most hastily constructed, with more wood than adobe in places. These buildings would burn quickest, and with the most deadly fire. Eventually, the whole pueblo would be destroyed—but its people were its greatest treasure, and they would be the first to go.

Diego looked around desperately. Two guards barred the gates. There would be no escape should the fire spread. His only hope was Bradford's doubt. The man wasn't a murderer at the core—he was a helpless lover. "Even if you leave here with no witnesses, señor, you will never be safe. What will you do about Señor Alvin?"

It was Harriet who answered. "We will find him and kill him, then take the treasure he stole from me." Bradford glanced at her in surprise, but she didn't flinch. "They will believe he, too, was killed in this fire."

Diego grit his teeth, fighting his binds. "He was her lover, Bradford. She has used both of you for her own gain."

Bradford's jaw set hard. "You lie." Harriet fumed, then aimed her gun to kill. Bradford caught her arm. "There's no need. They'll burn with the rest of this pueblo." He took her gun, and Diego laughed.

"You don't want to see blood on those pure white gloves, do you, Mr. Bradford? But beware, the blood on those hands may still be yours."

Melanie nodded vigorously. "It appears you've lost something of Mr. Bradford's trust, Harriet. He's not willing to leave you armed."

Harriet pulled back her hand as if weighted with anger, then slapped Melanie's face. Her rage surprised even Bradford. He caught her arm. "Come, my dear. We must leave now, for your safety."

Harriet whirled around. She pulled free from his grasp, then yanked the gun from Bradford's hand. "We must see that it is done correctly, leaving no one alive! Order the men to set fire to these buildings!"

Bradford motioned to the guards, who brandished wood from the bonfire. They went first to Victoria's inn, then tossed a lit branch through her window. Victoria broke free from Bradford and raced into her small inn. Chen bounded after her, and the chef, Massimo, followed them. Two guards barred any escape from the inn, but Diego could see Chen with Victoria and Massimo desperately trying to put out the flames.

Bradford laughed, but the sound was hollow. He witnessed true love and courage in the face of his own mistress's icy heart. Diego knew the man was not unmoved by the sacrifice. "It seems we won't have to force Chen into the fire—he has gone willingly."

Diego called to Bradford again. "Haven't you also gone into a fire, señor? A fire hotter and more permanent than any that might engulf Chen?"

Melanie sputtered in agreement. "He means the fires of hell, Mr. Bradford!"

Bradford didn't answer, but Harriet scoffed. "Hell? What do you know of hell, Miss Muessen?

Hell is being born with all the qualities of a lady, yet to stupid, worthless parents, mere servants. Hell is having beauty and grace, yet having no brighter future than playing governess to spoiled children, waiting on others. I know hell—no flames can frighten me."

Bradford took Harriet's hand, as if her story moved him deeply, but Diego just stared. He might reach Bradford's heart, but never Harriet's. She snatched her hand away, and Diego nodded thoughtfully. "Hell is also having to endure the love of a man to get what you want, it seems."

Harriet's face flushed with greater fury. "Hurry them, Carlton! What is taking so long? Why won't these buildings burn?"

"The air is damp from the rain, my darling. But it will burn." His voice had changed—Diego heard the man's doubt. All the fog of Harriet's flattery was beginning to fade. But would it fade in time to save Tewa? Bradford directed the guards in a methodical, orderly destruction of Tewa. The stables caught fire, trapping those within. Diego fought his ties desperately. The nightmare he faced long ago at the kiva was nothing to the agony of watching his people destroyed before his own helpless eyes.

Melanie fought, too. He felt her tugging at the ropes. "They'll die. Diego . . . what do we do?"

Once again, Diego called out to their assailant. "Alvin has your lover's portrait, señor. Ask her. Where is it? You don't want it burning in the flames, do you?"

Amid the methodical destruction of Tewa, Bradford turned slowly to Harriet. "Fetch it, my dear. We don't want to lose such a precious object, one that so perfectly captures your beauty."

Harriet's eyes darted and she licked her lips. "Don't be foolish, Carlton. The pueblo is burning. We have to get out of here."

"It's in the Chateau." Bradford took a step toward her. "The flames are nowhere near Chen's hotel."

Harriet backed away, still clutching her small gun. "It's not there. . . . I did give it to Mr. Alvin, but only for safekeeping."

Diego watched as his words hit their mark at last. Rage flared through Bradford like the fire burning behind him. "What else have you given him, Harriet? How many times did you lie with him? Or did you creep into his bed, too, and torment him with what he couldn't have, as you did to me so many nights until I went mad with desire?"

Harriet's face changed even as Bradford came toward her. He raised his fist, but she laughed as she poised her gun. "Tormented him? Never. What I denied you, he enjoyed many times. You served a purpose, Carlton, but no more."

Bradford ignored the gun in her hand. "Denied me? You lay with me here, Harriet. You reveled in the lust we shared."

He took another step, but the truth of his words was too much for Harriet. She pulled the trigger and the gun fired. Bradford crumpled at her feet, clutching his side in agony. She cast a disparaging glance at her agonized lover, then backed away.

Diego's hope that the guards would falter without their leader failed, but there was still hope. Someone shouted from outside the pueblo, and the guards opened the gate. The lawyer, Alvin, left his coach and raced to Harriet's side. She gasped, astonished to see the man who had supposedly betrayed her, but Diego laughed.

"By the way, Harriet, I lied about the treasure."

Her eyes widened in shock, and Diego laughed. "Two can play at the game of deceit, Harriet. It's not my favorite weapon, but it worked today. You intended Bradford's death all along, didn't you? He would kill my brother and his family—I would kill Bradford."

Bradford lay on the ground, in agony, but not dead. "No . . . Harriet . . ."

"She's made you a fool, Bradford, and she'll leave you here bleeding to death while she runs off with her lover."

Flames leapt from the windows of Victoria's inn, people screamed and wept, but Diego fought to keep reason. "You gave Harriet your only treasure, Señor Bradford. You gave her your love. And this is how she repays you?" Bradford looked up at Diego, who saw a pain deeper than the physical in his eyes. "Don't let her get away with it, because she's carrying your soul along with her."

Bradford struggled to rise, but he was losing

blood fast and his face had gone pale. He picked up the knife in white, shaking fingers, then grasped the pole that held Melanie and Diego bound. He pulled himself up by the strength of some inner will Diego hadn't imagined Bradford possessed. He choked back the pain of death's onslaught and braced himself on the pole. His jaw clenched and words tore from inside him. "For love's sake, forgive me." He cut their ties with one swift slice. The knife slipped from his fingers, and Bradford crumpled lifeless to the ground.

They were free.

# Chapter Sixteen

Diego broke free of their tattered bonds, then cut Melanie loose. They looked at each other amid rising smoke clouds, and the flames reflected in his dark eyes. Diego gripped Melanie's shoulders. "Melanie, I have to get those people out of here. Wait for me outside."

"You know I won't go without you. You need my help."

He accepted her decision, and together they ran from the podium. Flames leapt from the windows of Victoria's inn, already ablaze. Harriet spotted them, and she shouted to the guards, but they didn't hear her above the screams and crackling fire. Melanie heard gunfire, but she didn't look back. Apparently, Harriet's aim lacked accuracy beyond a few feet.

Harriet screeched in fury, but Alvin grabbed her arm. "We've got to get out of here, Harriet!"

"No, no! I won't leave with nothing. Get the box of Chen's treasure! It's there by Carlton's body!"

Confused but obedient, Alvin raced to where Bradford lay dead and picked up the box. Diego ran on toward the captive people, but Melanie stopped. "We can't let them go free!"

Diego called to her, running. " 'Forget them, Melanie. They will never be free now."

With an enraged scream, Harriet scrambled into Alvin's coach and he cracked the whip over the horses's backs. Melanie turned back to the burning building. Diego slammed his shoulder against the door of Victoria's inn and it gave way. Smoke billowed out the door, but no people came. Melanie tore off her cape and held it over her face. Diego did likewise, and they entered the crumbling inn together. Melanie heard shouts from inside the next room. "In there! Diego, they're in the dining room."

Shading their faces from thick clouds of smoke, Diego and Melanie pushed their way through crumbling debris. Chen and Massimo pounded against a small window, but as Melanie entered the room, the chef collapsed into a faint from the smoke. Victoria fought the flames with wild desperation, batting the burgeoning fire with a table-cloth. She wept as her small inn faced insurmountable destruction.

A beam had collapsed between them and the

exit. Diego jumped over the beam as it withered into black embers. Her long skirt made an equal jump impossible, so Melanie cleared a passage for their escape instead. Diego bounded across the burning room, and Chen turned to him. For a strange, timeless moment amid the terror, Chen looked at his friend, and a slow smile grew on his face. Melanie couldn't hear him speak, but she saw him mouth the words, *"I knew you would."*

Diego lifted the hefty Massimo and somehow managed to carry the chef over his shoulder. Melanie remembered when he'd carried her, and how she'd feared she'd been too heavy. She felt strangely dizzy and light-headed, but she managed to shove aside a crumbling door so that they could pass. Chen dragged Victoria from the dining room. She sobbed as he pulled her out into the plaza. "My inn, my inn. I have nothing, all I worked for . . ." Her voice caught on harsh sobs. Chen gathered her in his arms and spoke softly to her, in a language that Melanie guessed was Chinese. Victoria buried her face against his shoulder and cried.

Diego carried Massimo away from the flames, then ran to the stable, where many of the Tewa people were still trapped. Melanie and Chen followed, but Chen was already weakened from breathing smoke, and he stumbled to his knees before they reached the stable doors. Diego waved him back, and though Chen tried to follow, he staggered. Victoria caught his arm to stop him, but Melanie was still strong enough to help.

Diego burst through the wide stable doors and raced inward. Melanie feared the worst, but the people had taken refuge near the stable trough, and together had formed a bucket line to keep down the fire. To Melanie's astonishment, the people stayed calm. They hurried the children out of the building, but several remained behind to free the trapped horses.

Melanie looked around desperately and found Porticus in the last stall, wide-eyed and rearing, his small legs flailing as he fought his tie. The larger horses broke their leads, but Porticus was trapped. Melanie heard Diego shouting, and she knew he told her to stay back, to get out of there, but she couldn't leave the pony this way.

She pulled her skirt above her knees and tied it in a bunch, her hands shaking as she picked her way through piles of burning hay. Porticus saw her and neighed wildly. She bounded over fallen beams to reach him. Her hands shook as she untied his lead, but Porticus calmed unexpectedly and allowed her to lead him from the stable.

Diego met her at the door. His face was smudged with soot and his black cape was burned, but he looked otherwise unharmed. He caught her arm. "Are you all right?"

"I'm fine. Is that everyone?"

"The townspeople have bound the guards already. Well done!" Diego looked around. "I don't see Miguel or anyone in his family. They must be in the bakery." He didn't wait. Diego ran from the stable, his long legs carrying him faster than Melanie could run with her skirt bunched around her. He broke through the bakery door and disappeared into a cloud of smoke and red flames. Melanie tried to follow, but the burning heat and thick smoke were like an impenetrable wall. She tried again, but the flames lapped at her legs.

Time moved like an ice flow, and nothing seemed real. The smoke and heat of the fire had left her dazed, and Melanie's senses reeled. Tewa citizens surrounded guards, and Bradford's confused men threw down their weapons. Again, Melanie tried to enter the ravaged bakery. *Please, come out. Please . . .*

As if in answer to her prayer, Diego emerged carrying Miguel's wife, Miguel close behind. The woman didn't move, but when Diego laid her on the ground, she stirred, her eyes wide with panic. "Our son. He's still in there."

Diego headed back into the bakery, and Melanie's own panic soared as she raced after him. For an instant, he looked into her eyes. "There's nothing we can't do."

She knew, because she knew him, that he had to go, and she didn't try to stop him. But when he vanished again into the black smoke, her heart seemed to leave her body and go with him.

She waited for what seemed an eternity. As the fire engulfed Victoria's inn, then the stable, the people of Tewa joined her, silent. Chen stood with Victoria, but he wept, and Miguel clasped his wife in his arms, stunned by the man who had saved them.

"Up here!" Diego's voice startled everyone, and a loud cry rang out from the crowd as they spotted him on the bakery roof holding Miguel's son.

Diego put the boy down and directed him along the Renegade's former pathway to freedom, and the boy scurried down to his father. Diego started to follow, but the roof crashed inward, followed by a great roar from the fire within. Melanie screamed and tried to enter the building, but Chen grabbed her and held her back.

Riding as if with the wind, a man galloped in on a dark gray horse, a horse Melanie recognized as Rafael's old mount, Frank. To Melanie's shock, Alvin's coach came back through the gate, too, but it was Evelyn, Will, and the children who emerged when it stopped. Evelyn looked proud as she gestured inside the coach to where Harriet and Alvin were bound. Chen marched to the coach, reached in, and grabbed his treasure, then gave it to Victoria, who held it close to her heart.

Melanie shouted wildly to Rafael. "Diego is in the bakery! He fell and we can't get him out!"

Rafael leapt from his horse and ran toward the fire. He grabbed the discarded Anasazi mask as he ran and placed it over his face to shield himself against the smoke. He pulled his cape tight around his body, and then entered the crumbling bakery.

People shouted, and the shout became a chant as one Renegade raced to save another. Evelyn ran to

Melanie's side, and they stood together waiting, both too terrified to breathe.

After a timeless wait, Rafael emerged from the fire carrying Diego. What remained of the bakery caved in, adobe bricks crumbling among burning wood. He carried Diego from the pueblo, and the Tewa people gathered outside the gate as the oldest of their buildings burned beyond restoration.

Rafael placed Diego gently on the damp earth, and the first light of dawn cut without warning through the storm clouds of night. The soft rain stopped as the clouds passed overhead, and the thunder faded into the mountains like a retreating army.

Melanie sank to her knees beside Diego, weeping as she brushed his long hair from his forehead. Black soot covered his face, burns scorched his hands, and his boots were burned through from the fiery clay. He coughed and choked for air, then opened his eyes. He saw Melanie and smiled. "I told you, Melanie. There's nothing we can't do."

Melanie squeezed his shoulder as tears streamed down her cheeks. "It was the other way around—*I* told *you*."

"Stubborn to the end." Diego's gaze shifted to his brother and his smile grew. "I see the Renegade has finally returned."

"Not this time, Diego." Rafael pulled off the mask, and his dark eyes glittered with tears. "I am only the older brother of a great man. The Renegade hasn't returned. He has been here all along."

The pueblo damage was severe, but with the combined help of everyone in Tewa, as well as a large group sent from Diego's grandfather in Tesuque, much of the pueblo was restored to its former condition. The renovations left the western buildings better than they had been before the fire.

Victoria's inn proved impossible to salvage. Surprising everyone, Victoria donated what remained of her inn to be rebuilt as a hospital. She and Chen seemed to have reached an understanding, though both were too private to discuss the matter. Melanie suspected that Chen had talked to Diego. Though she attempted to gain information from him, he had little to say, other than a strange remark about Chen's willingness to spend money in surprising places.

Diego himself had been behaving strangely, and Melanie had no idea why. For the first week or so, she attributed his odd, tense behavior to the aftermath of the fire and the hard work of rebuilding the pueblo. But as the days passed, she realized he was nervous around her, at times shy and at other times simply peculiar.

He had spent the last two days at his brother's hacienda, only returning to Tewa for dinner. The oddest change in his character was a sudden adherence to propriety. He hadn't taken her to his bed once since the fire, nor had he teased her, other than one remark made at dinner when she requested a second helping of dessert. He'd cut himself off before she responded, and apologized several times afterward.

Melanie had no idea what afflicted him this time. Just when she thought she knew him, he changed. He spent a great deal of time consulting with Chen, and even more with his brother. Whenever Melanie overheard his conversation, she gathered he was seeking advice, but as soon as he noticed her, he fell silent and pretended nothing was wrong.

She had made up her mind to talk to him about it, but he was locked away in conference in Chen's office and she didn't dare interrupt. Melanie waited outside the door. Rafael emerged, met her suspicious gaze, and sighed. He patted her shoulder, then sighed again. "My brother is crazy. You have my sympathy, Miss Muessen."

Melanie's eyes narrowed to slits. "What do you mean? What is he doing?" She wasn't sure she wanted to know, but when Chen came out of the office, she caught his arm. "What's going on, Chen?"

Chen gazed heavenward. "Crazy. He's crazy. Good luck, Miss Muessen."

Melanie peeked through the door and found Diego pacing back and forth in front of Chen's desk, talking to himself. "Diego?"

He jumped at her voice and then affected the least plausible expression of casual unconcern she'd ever seen. "Melanie . . . How are you? Fine?"

She shifted her weight from foot to foot, then pinned a fierce, threatening gaze upon him.

"What's the matter with you? Of course I'm fine! Why are you acting . . ." She paused to make a fist. "Crazy?"

"Am I?" He looked genuinely surprised, then took her hand and kissed it. He seemed more nervous than usual and drew a quick breath. "Might we take a walk, my dear?"

"If you wish." Melanie paused. "Where do you want to go?"

"There's a new bench in the plaza, where Will and Victoria planted flowers. We could go there."

"Very well . . . I have something to tell you, too."

To her surprise, Diego's face paled. "You're not . . . leaving, are you?"

"No! Of course not. But this morning I learned what happened at Harriet's trial."

Diego grimaced. "They aren't hanging her, are they?"

"No. It's much better than that. She's been sentenced to prison, where she will spend her time washing dishes and the other prisoners' clothing. As she told us herself, that is her idea of hell. Mr. Alvin's sentence was lighter, because he didn't actually kill anyone, but he has been disbarred."

"That sounds fair. Harriet was the real leader, anyway."

Melanie nodded. "I felt sorry for Mr. Bradford at the end; in his way he really loved her. But I don't feel much sympathy for Harriet."

"I never did."

"You are very wise, Diego."

Again, he surprised her when he blushed. "I am glad you think well of me."

"So what did you want to talk to me about?" And why had he asked if she was leaving? He hadn't approached her romantically since the fire, though he had been gracious and polite. That in itself was unnerving, since it wasn't Diego's usual way. If he started to say something blunt and direct, he stopped himself, and he had even once diverted her by inaccurately reciting a poem Rafael had once taught him. He translated it into Spanish, saying it sounded better in that language, but she suspected he had forgotten the verses and found it easier to skip those lines in a language she didn't understand.

The afternoon sun hung heavy and warm over the plaza, slanting its light across the new garden and filtering through the soft green leaves of a tree Rafael and Diego had uprooted from the woods and placed in the center of the plaza. Diego directed her to the new adobe bench, and she seated herself. Diego didn't seem satisfied with her pose— he adjusted her blue silk skirt to splay over the bench, then fiddled with her hair until it hung like a long river over her right shoulder.

"What are you doing? Are you planning to take my picture, or have you just lost your mind?"

Diego gulped. "I like the way the sun looks on your hair. Like a river of gold."

"My hair is brown. Light brown, but brown."

"Dark gold." It was like him to argue. At least this felt more familiar. Miguel the baker emerged from his new shop, marched to Diego, and presented him with a freshly baked loaf of bread. Diego eyed it doubtfully. "What's this for? You gave me bread this morning, Miguel. The Chateau is overflowing with your wares."

"Well, you're a young man. You need nourishment." Miguel slapped Diego's shoulder awkwardly, then thumped back into his bakery. Diego arched his brow and turned back to Melanie.

"What's gotten into him lately?"

"I was just about to ask the same of you. As for Miguel, it's obvious; he's trying to make up for the way he treated you. You saved his life and his family, Diego. You're more than the Renegade to them now. You're someone they thought they knew but misunderstood completely." She paused. "I know how they feel."

"I don't know why. I haven't changed."

"To them, you have, because they never really knew you in the first place."

Diego shrugged. "It becomes tiresome. They're treating me like a hero now, all of them. They're treating me like Rafael."

Melanie looked up at him. "You are a hero, Diego. Don't you know?"

"I did what I had to do, but Melanie, this isn't the life I want."

Diego's expression changed. He drew a quick breath, then knelt before her. He took her hand in his, then kissed it. One by one, the Tewa people came out of their doors, and some watched through windows. Rafael stood in the door of his schoolhouse beside his small daughter. He motioned to Evelyn, who came out holding their son.

Melanie looked around. "What are they looking at?"

Diego frowned, then sighed in resignation. "Nothing in my life is private. Well, so be it. The time has come, señorita." He bowed his head as if to gather courage. A man who had walked countless times into fire now needed courage to face her.

He looked up, and all his heart shone in his eyes. "I love you, Melanie. I've loved you since you first came here, leading your fat pony and your cart filled with your dreams and your sense of justice, and the sweet beauty of your soul. I love you so much that I can't imagine a day without you."

Melanie's eyes filled with sudden tears. "I love you, too, Diego. You are the best thing in my life. I can't imagine a day without you, either."

He swallowed hard, cleared his throat, and then kissed her hand again. "I know you have dreams, Melanie. I think of it often, of you traveling around the world, turning your camera on people and sites in a way no one has ever seen them before."

It had always been her dream, but she had thought of it very little since meeting Diego. "I would rather be with you."

"I wouldn't take you from your dreams, Melanie."

She hesitated, wondering what this might mean. "Would you . . . share them?"

He squeezed her hand. "If you'll have me, I'd follow you anywhere. I'll carry your gear. I'll carry Porticus, if it means I can be near you."

Melanie smiled. "I don't think that's a very good idea. Your back would suffer from hoisting him about, and then what use would you be to me?"

He liked her intimation, and a grin formed on his lips, familiar and yet not seen in many days. "What use I would be . . ." He stopped and shook his head, as if he hadn't meant to comment on the suggestiveness of her remark. He looked up at her, and his dark eyes shone with love. "Señorita, I have loved you as two men, both myself and as the Renegade. In myself, you found a hero, and in the Renegade, you found a heart where I believed there was none. I ask you now, would you consider becoming the wife of a Renegade and a rogue?"

Melanie's heart filled with happiness. Diego held his breath, and suddenly she realized every person in the pueblo held theirs, too. She looked around and love surrounded her, love for her and the Renegade who had saved every one of them. "I love you, Diego, rogue and Renegade, and I will be happy and honored to become your wife."

He looked surprised, astonished. Then he closed his eyes and issued a silent prayer of thanks while Melanie stared down at him, her heart filled with love. She placed her small hands on either side of his face, then bent to kiss him. He kissed her back, but tears of joy filled his eyes. "Is this why you've been so strange and so nervous? Because you were planning to propose?"

"I had to do it right. I've made so many mistakes in the past. I knew you loved me, but somehow, whenever I started to offer marriage, it seemed inadequate."

"So you asked Chen and your brother for advice?"

He nodded. "Rafael said I should just tell you what I feel for you. That sounded simple, but it wasn't so easy putting it into words. Chen gave me a written speech—I think it's the same one he used on Victoria. It worked for him, because she said yes, but I just couldn't imagine myself calling you 'thee.' "

Melanie laughed. "Victoria did tell me Chen's proposal was very formal. It pleased her, but coming from you, it would just have confused me. I prefer your own words."

Diego smiled and reached into his pocket. "Chen did give me one suggestion I liked, however."

"What was that?"

Diego withdrew a golden ring studded with emeralds. It looked old, even ancient, and Melanie's eyes widened. "Is that for me?"

Diego took her hand and examined each curved finger. "This ring came from my portion of the treasure. I'd forgotten I had it—my treasure was with Chen's when Harriet stole it—but Chen reminded me and suggested it might be a good token of my promise to you. Do you like it?"

"It's beautiful." Diego slipped the ring on her finger, then kissed her hand. Tears filled his eyes as he looked up at her. "You're really mine. I never thought I deserved a woman like you, but now that you're mine, I will treat you like a princess. You are my dearest treasure, Melanie, and there is nothing I wouldn't do to protect you."

Melanie reached for him and pulled him into her arms. She hugged him tight, so filled with happiness that it seemed impossible ever to move from this sacred spot in the sun. "Diego, you have made me feel like a treasure, and I never thought that could happen. I am the luckiest woman to have you."

They looked at each other, and she felt as if she looked into a part of herself she hadn't understood. They were connected, more deeply than anything, and all that they did together would be blessed by love. "Diego, there's one other thing that I must ask of you."

"What, love? Anything."

"I miss your teasing."

"Do you?" He rose to his feet, glowing with happiness. "Good, because over the last week or so, I've had much to say."

"Not about what I had for dinner?"

"I did want to ask if a third dessert would please you."

She groaned. "When we reach Egypt, I may regret this, but for now, tease at will."

"More than your appetite has intrigued me, however. Three times in the past week, you've referenced our day of passion. Subtly, true, but it was there. You have no idea how hard it was not to point that out to you. I tried to restrain myself, but it wasn't easy."

"What stopped you?"

"I wanted you to say 'yes.' "

"Did you really doubt?"

"Melanie, when a man loves, he doubts."

Melanie held his hand against her heart. "A woman, too."

"We have wasted too much time in fear. Let us waste no more."

He took her hand in his and they walked together through the plaza. The people of Tewa made way for their passage as Diego led her from the gate, then followed. Diego noticed their casual pursuit and frowned. With a meaningful glare, he closed the pueblo gates, shutting out the watchful eyes of his people. He turned to Melanie and smiled. "Alone at last."

He took her in his arms and kissed her, first gently and then with the growing passion they'd both resisted since the fire. The real fire was within, and proved an irresistible force as they sank deeper into each other's arms. Melanie wrapped her arms around his neck and kissed him as their bodies molded to each other. She felt his arousal against her body and tingled in response.

Diego stopped and eyed the gate. "I should have

shut them out, not us." He walked back to the gate, but it opened from within. The people of Tewa stood back, each one bearing a knowing look as they made way for Diego's passage back to the Chateau.

Chen stood at the entrance of his hotel, smiling as he held open the door for them. Diego led Melanie past, and they both pretended that no one knew where they were going. He led her upstairs to his room and they closed the door, and all else was forgotten while they loved.

Melanie lay in his arms, home at last; safe where she had always belonged, knowing all her life had found its answer in him. Wherever they went, he would bring that unique joy, the irresistible light of his soul, and she would love him, the Renegade and the rogue, in a place where only love was king.

# *Epilogue*

*Two years later*

"Put it above the reception desk, Diego. Where else?" Chen positioned himself in the center of the Chateau Renegade's newly remodeled foyer, studying the wall for the perfect location for his gift. "A little to the left."

Diego adjusted the framed portrait, but Chen wasn't satisfied. "To the right."

Diego obeyed, then glanced over his shoulder. "How is this?"

Chen tipped his head one way, then the other, then frowned. "Higher."

Grinding his teeth, Diego lifted the portrait. "Well?" He looked back and saw Chen's face twist to the side. "If you should, even in your wildest, most dictatorial dreams, even whisper the word, 'lower,' know that I will come down off this ladder and kill you slowly, inflicting searing pain."

Melanie tapped his knee. "That seems a little strong, my love." She glanced apologetically at Chen. "It was a long train ride, you see. Diego takes it upon himself to wake the baby every few hours, to be sure he's alive." She eyed Diego pointedly, but he refused to respond. "And so it's possible that he's overtired."

Chen eyed her doubtfully. "Who? Diego or your son?"

"Both, though Alejandro weathers traveling much better than his father." That much was certain. They had been all over the world, or at least to Egypt and Greece, and after a few months back in Tewa, they planned to head off to South America to search out ancient Indian ruins. They had together photographed more wonders than Diego knew existed, although Rafael had reminded him that each had been covered in school. Their days had been sweet, filled with delight and as much adventure as Diego ever dreamed possible. But their nights had been magic, and the wonders they shared alone together surpassed all else.

Somehow, that their passion should have created a child had surprised Diego, and each time he looked at the tiny baby, his astonishment grew. Alejandro had Diego's eyes, clearly, but his expression was Melanie's, as well as a certain wistfulness, which often accompanied a weary sigh when Diego woke him.

Diego banged in the nail without Chen's permission, then hung the portrait. "Where's Victoria? This gift was for her, too."

"She's instructing Massimo in the correct production of sweets. He has been using ingredients we both consider too expensive, and he needs to find simpler . . ."

"Cheaper . . ."

Chen frowned. "*Better* ways of fulfilling his recipes."

Diego straightened the portrait, then climbed down the ladder to survey his handiwork. "I assume that as your recipes have become better, your rates have gone up as well?"

Chen never flinched. "Of course. Thanks to your reviving the Renegade legend, demands for my rooms have doubled. Victoria has added a certain homey, warm appeal, and the Chateau Renegade has been cited in traveler's journals all over the world. Only last week, we entertained a group of German tourists. I think they enjoyed themselves, though they didn't actually say so."

Diego picked up a strange object that looked like a jagged dagger. "What's this?"

Chen snatched it out of his hand and replaced it in its stand, which was lit by a small golden light. "Don't touch that! It's priceless."

"What is it?"

Chen glanced furtively around, then lowered his

voice. "It's the Renegade's secret weapon."

Diego frowned, and Melanie clamped her hand over her mouth to keep from laughing. "So secret I don't recall using it. Why do I doubt Rafael had such a tool in his armory either?"

Chen glared. "Never mind that. If you'd had more sense, you *would* have used such a weapon."

"What? To pry my way through your roast quail? Or to hold you at knifepoint for misrepresenting my legacy?"

Chen pretended not to have heard Diego's comment, a trait he must have learned from Victoria. A guest arrived and he bowed, glowing with the joyous welcome of a successful hotelier. The guest caught sight of the new portrait and issued praise, then retreated to the dining room. Victoria emerged from the kitchen and dusted her hands on an unused apron.

"Massimo has seen the error of his ways and will limit the unnecessary spattering of sweets about the serving trays." She removed her apron, revealing a perfect, spotless violet taffeta skirt. "As I told him . . ." Her voice broke and stopped as she saw the portrait hanging over the reception desk.

Diego took Melanie's hand, and together they watched as Victoria moved closer, as her eyes filled with tears. Chen stood beside her and they stared up at the large photograph, made from Melanie's new camera, a plate that measured an unprecedented twenty by sixteen in dimension. "Not only was this made from the best camera in the world, it was taken by the best photographer."

Neither Victoria nor Chen were able to speak, but Victoria brushed away tears and nodded, then whispered, "Thank you."

As Diego gazed up at Melanie's latest work, he saw her own special insight in the faces of her subjects. In the portrait, Chen stood poised and proud behind his wife's chair, his hand on her shoulder. Victoria was seated, their first son perched on her lap. Though his parents were somber, their baby looked both happy and proud. It was the picture of a family who had forged the life they wanted, and more than anything else, they looked fulfilled.

Melanie's photographs now decorated much of the Chateau. Pictures of the Renegade as she had known him dotted the dining room walls, as well as many of Diego in poses he hadn't known he'd assumed. Rafael had agreed to goad his horse, Frank, into several dramatic poses, too, but Diego's favorite pictures of his brother were those where he sat at his desk in his ever-growing school, his spectacles low on his nose, his dark eyes glowing with happiness.

Miguel the baker had requested several photographs for his shop, and seemed particularly pleased with those of Egyptian pyramids. Diego's grandfather had devoted an entire room to Melanie's work, ignoring all European or African landscapes in favor of Tesuque images. The gallery he had created now drew tourists, most of whom he didn't want, but once he realized he could charge a fee for admission, the old fellow grudgingly accepted.

Chen and Victoria stood gazing up at their portrait, both filled with emotion. Diego took Melanie's hand and they returned to their bedroom. Thanks to Diego's newfound prominence as the resurrected Renegade, Chen had given him a larger suite for those times he returned to Tewa. In payment, he was expected to give lengthy accounts of the Renegade's daring rides to Chen's enthralled guests, many of which had already been embellished by Chen.

Diego held open the door to their suite, and Melanie entered. She checked their sleeping son, but when Diego reached to prod him, she caught his hand. "You don't need to wake him every hour, my love."

Diego studied his son's small, sleeping face. "He appears to be sleeping very deeply. I wonder if that's healthy?"

Melanie pulled him from the crib, then led him forcibly into the next room. "It's time I distracted you."

"Distracted me? Why?"

The look in her eyes caught his attention. The soft blue darkened, and her lips curved in a way that never failed to send shivers of desire down his spine. "How would you distract me, my angel?"

She answered by peeling back her snug bodice; then slowly, with tantalizing skill, she slipped each element of clothing, piece by piece, to the floor.

Diego stared, spellbound, a man who had no limit of desire for his wife. He wanted to love her gently, but instead, Melanie seemed to want something more powerful, more overwhelming.

As he moved to take her in his arms, he knew what it was she craved. She wanted the Renegade, and for an hour of love, that's just what he would be.

# STOBIE PIEL BLUE-EYED BANDIT

Darian Woodward had been a hero in the War Between the States, but somewhere he's been blown off course. Unjustly ruined by a superior officer, the handsome soldier turns to crime. His blue eyes and daring deeds earn him a name throughout the old Southwest, but bandits seek gold, and this gunfighter's interests are entirely different. Fate has blown in a sexier bounty.

Though she is swept away by it, Emily Morgan is less awed by the mystic whirlwind that carries her into the past than by the handsome desperado who greets her. Joining the man's close-knit band of outlaws, Emily learns the fun of being bad—but also its dangers. And when the Feds come to capture her Blue-Eyed Bandit, Emily will prove that Western justice has its limits, and that true love can break any laws—even those of time and space.

___52394-9                                    $5.50 US/$6.50 CAN

**Dorchester Publishing Co., Inc.**
**P.O. Box 6640**
**Wayne, PA 19087-8640**

# THE WHITE SUN
## STOBIE PIEL

Sierra of Nirvahda has never known love. But with her long dark tresses and shining eyes she has inspired plenty of it, only to turn away with a tuneless heart. Yet when she finds herself hiding deep within a cavern on the red planet of Tseir, her heart begins to do strange things. For with her in the cave is Arnoth of Valenwood, the sound of his lyre reaching out to her through the dark and winding passageways. His song speaks to her of yearnings, an ache she will come to know when he holds her body close to his, with the rhythm of their hearts beating for the memory and melody of their souls.

\_\_\_52292-6                                      $5.50 US/$6.50 CAN

**Dorchester Publishing Co., Inc.**
**P.O. Box 6640**
**Wayne, PA 19087-8640**

Please add $1.75 for shipping and handling for the first book and $.50 for each book thereafter. NY, NYC, and PA residents, please add appropriate sales tax. No cash, stamps, or C.O.D.s. All orders shipped within 6 weeks via postal service book rate. Canadian orders require $2.00 extra postage and must be paid in U.S. dollars through a U.S. banking facility.

Name_____
Address_____
City_____State_____Zip_____
I have enclosed $_____ in payment for the checked book(s).
Payment <u>must</u> accompany all orders. ☐ Please send a free catalog.
      CHECK OUT OUR WEBSITE! www.dorchesterpub.com

# LYNSAY SANDS
## The Reluctant Reformer

Everyone knows of Lady X. The masked courtesan is reputedly a noblewoman fallen on hard times. What Lord James does not know is that she is Lady Margaret Wentworth—the feisty sister of his best friend, who has forced James into an oath of protection. But when James tracks the girl to a house of ill repute, the only explanation is that Maggie is London's most enigmatic wanton.

Snatching her away will be a ticklish business, and after that James will have to ignore her violent protests that she was never the infamous X. He will have to reform the hoyden, while keeping his hands off the luscious goods that the rest of the ton has reputedly sampled. And, with Maggie, hardest of all will be keeping himself from falling in love.

____4974-0                                  $5.99 US/$7.99 CAN

# Desert Bloom
## Ronda Thompson

For Lilla Traften, the Texas Panhandle is nothing but hot cactus and dirt, its inhabitants worse. Grady Finch, the rugged foreman of the WC Ranch may be devastatingly handsome, but he is tactless. Worse, the heat is getting to her; sunstroke is making her dream of Grady's hands upon her, of the sweaty love they might make in the dust. Hardly normal thoughts for a proper miss and charm-school teacher! Still, she can't help wondering what will win the heart of a man like Grady. She'll have to prove she can survive on her own. He'll have to see that not only the land can undergo transformation, but that Lilla, too, can flower in the desert.

___4943-0                                    $5.99 US/$6.99 CAN

**Dorchester Publishing Co., Inc.**
**P.O. Box 6640**
**Wayne, PA 19087-8640**

Please add $2.50 for shipping and handling for the first book and $0.75 for each additional book. NY and PA residents, add appropriate sales tax. No cash, stamps, or C.O.D.s. All Canadian orders require $5.00 for shipping and handling and must be paid in U.S. dollars. Prices and availability subject to change. **Payment must accompany all orders.**

Name _____

Address_____

City_____ State_____ Zip _____

E-mail_____

I have enclosed $_____in payment for the checked book(s).
❑Please send me a free catalog.

CHECK OUT OUR WEBSITE at www.dorchesterpub.com!

# Belle

## Melanie Jackson

**AVAILABLE MARCH 2002!**

**FROM**

**LEISURE B BOOKS**

# Belle

## Melanie Jackson

With the letter breaking his engagement, Stephan Kirton's hopes for respectability go up in smoke. Inevitably, his "interaction with the lower classes" and the fact that he is a bastard have put him beyond the scope of polite society. He finds consolation at Ormstead Park; a place for dancing, drinking and gambling . . . a place where he can find a woman for the night.

He doesn't recognize her at first; ladies don't come to Lord Duncan's masked balls. This beauty's descent into the netherworld has brought her within reach, yet she is no girl of the day. Annabelle Winston is sublime. And if he has to trick her, bribe her, protect her, whatever—one way or another he will make her an honest woman. And she will make him a happy man.

___4975-9                                   $5.99 US/$7.99 CAN